Praise for **Fern Michaels**

"Fern Michaels provides a variety of lively, sympathetic characters and turns a difficult subject into an intensely crafted and involving story. . . ."

—*Romantic Times*

Praise for **Kat Martin**

"Kat Martin delivers what her readers desire: an exciting, sensual, engrossing romance whose characters use the power of their love to give them strength."

—*Romantic Times*

Praise for **Jo Beverley**

"Arguably today's most skillful writer of intelligent historical romance . . ."

—*Publishers Weekly*

Praise for **Katherine Sutcliffe**

"Katherine Sutcliffe writes romantic, exciting stories filled with memorable characters and delightful surprises."

—Linda Lael Miller

Praise for **Brenda Joyce**

"Joyce's writing is like silk! Powerful, evocative and emotionally charged!"

—*Literary Times*

FIVE
GOLDEN
RINGS

Fern Michaels
Kat Martin
Jo Beverley
Katherine Sutcliffe
Brenda Joyce

ZEBRA BOOKS
KENSINGTON PUBLISHING CORP.
http://www.zebrabooks.com

CONTENTS

A BRIGHT RED RIBBON

Fern Michaels

Dear Readers,

There's something about a bright red ribbon that I've always loved. Everything important in my life from the time I was a child had, in some way, a bright red ribbon attached to it. The first time my hair was long enough to braid, my mother tied a red ribbon around it. When I got my first dog, she had a red ribbon on her collar. On my first date with my husband he brought me a box of candy with a red ribbon. Anytime he ever gave me a present after that, it had a red ribbon. My first car came with one, the real estate people tied the mortgage papers on my first house with a red ribbon. Then of course, there were all those wonderful Christmases and the piles of presents tied with red ribbons. To this day, I still wrap all presents and tie them with bright red ribbons.

So, when it was time to do this Christmas story, I naturally thought of all the good things that came tied in a bright red ribbon, one of which is the title for this story. I wanted to give all my readers a bright red ribbon as a special Christmas present from me to you. I hope you enjoy the unlikely hero in "A Bright Red Ribbon" and his partner, Murphy, as much as I enjoyed writing it.

Here's wishing you a very Merry Christmas with lots and lots of bright red ribbons under your own Christmas tree.

Fern Michaels

Even in her dream, Morgan Ames knew she was dreaming, knew she was going to wake with tears on her pillow and reality slapping her in the face. She cried out, the way she always did, just at the moment Keith was about to slip the ring on her finger. That's how she knew it was a dream. She never got beyond this point. She woke now, and looked at the bedside clock; it was 4:10. She wiped at the tears on her cheeks, but this time she smiled. Today was the day. Today was Christmas Eve, the day Keith was going to slip the ring on her finger and they would finally set the wedding date. The big event, in her mind, was scheduled to take place in front of her parents' Christmas tree. She and Keith would stand in exactly the same position they stood in two years ago today, at the very same hour. Romance was alive and well.

She dropped her legs over the side of the bed, slid into a daffodil-colored robe that was snugly warm, and pulled on thick wool socks. She padded out to the miniature kitchen to make coffee.

Christmas Eve. To her, Christmas Eve was the most wonderful day of the year. Years ago, when she'd turned into a teenager, her parents had switched the big dinner and gift opening to Christmas Eve so they could sleep late on Christmas morning. The dinner was huge; friends dropped by before evening services, and then they opened their presents, sang carols, and drank spiked eggnog afterward.

Mo knew a watched kettle never boiled so she made herself some toast while the kettle hummed on the stove. She was so excited her hands shook as she spread butter and jam on the toast. The kettle whistled. The water sputtered over the counter as she poured it into the cup with the black rum tea bag.

In about sixteen hours, she was going to see Keith. At last. Two years ago he had led her by the hand over to the twelve-foot Christmas tree and said he wanted to talk to her about something. He'd been so nervous, but she'd been more nervous, certain the something he wanted to talk about was the engagement ring he was going to give her. She'd been expecting it, her parents had been expecting it, all her friends had been expecting it. Instead, Keith had taken both her hands in his and said, "Mo, I need to talk to you about something. I need you to understand. This is my problem. You didn't do anything to make me . . . what I'm trying to say is, I need more time. I'm not ready to commit. I think we both need to experience a little more of life's challenges. We both have good jobs, and I just got a promotion that will take effect the first of the year. I'll be working in the New York office. It's a great opportunity, but the hours are long. I'm going to get an apartment in the city. What I would like is for us to . . . to take a hiatus from each other. I think two years will be good. I'll be thirty and you'll be twenty-nine. We'll be more mature, more ready for that momentous step."

The hot tea scalded her tongue. She yelped. She'd yelped that night, too. She'd wanted to be sophisticated, blasé, to say, okay, sure, no big deal. She hadn't said any of those things. Instead she'd cried, hanging on to his arm, begging to know if what he was proposing meant he was going to date others. His answer had crushed her and she'd sobbed then. He'd said things like, "Ssshhh, it's going to be all right. Two years isn't all that long. Maybe we aren't meant to be with each other for the rest of our lives. We'll find out. Yes, it's going to be hard on me, too. Look, I know this is a surprise . . . I didn't want . . . I was going to call . . . This is what I propose. Two years from tonight, I'll meet you right here, in front of the tree. Do we have a date, Mo?" She nodded miserably. Then he'd added, "Look, I have to leave, Mo. My boss is having a party in his townhouse in Princeton. It won't look good if I'm late. Christmas parties are a good way to network. Here, I got you a little something for Christmas." Before she could dry her eyes, blow her nose, or tell him she had a ton of presents for him under the tree, he was gone.

It had been the worst Christmas of her life. The worst New Year's, too. The next Christmas and New Year's had been just as bad because her parents had looked at her with pity and then anger. Just last week they had called and said, "Get on with your life, Morgan. You've already wasted two years. In that whole time, Keith hasn't called you once or even dropped you a post card." She'd been stubborn, though, because she loved Keith. Sharp words had ensued, and she'd broken the connection and cried.

Tonight she had a date.

Life was going to be so wonderful. The strain between her and her parents would ease when they saw how happy she was.

Mo looked at the clock. Five-thirty. Time to shower, dress, pack up the Cherokee for her two-week vacation. Oh, life was good. She had it all planned. They'd go skiing, but first she'd go to Keith's apartment in New York, stay over, make him breakfast. They'd make slow, lazy love and if the mood called for it, they'd make wild, animal love.

Two years was a long time to be celibate—and she'd been celibate. She winced when she thought about Keith in bed with other women. He loved sex more than she did. There was no way he'd been faithful to her. She felt it in her heart. Every chance her mother got, she drove home her point. Her parents didn't like Keith. Her father was fond of saying, "I know his type—he's no good. Get a life, Morgan."

Tonight her new life would begin. Unless . . . unless Keith was a no show. Unless Keith decided the single life was better than a married life and responsibilities. God in heaven, what would she do if that happened? Well, it wasn't going to happen. She'd always been a positive person and she saw no reason to change now.

It wasn't going to happen because when Keith saw her he

was going to go out of his mind. She'd changed in the two years. She'd dropped twelve pounds in all the right places. She was fit and toned because she worked out daily at a gym and ran for five miles every evening after work. She'd gotten a new hair style in New York. And, while she was there she'd gone to a color specialist who helped her with her hair and makeup. She was every bit as professional looking as some of the ad executives she saw walking up and down Madison Avenue. She'd shed her scrubbed girl-next-door image. S.K., which stood for Since Keith, she'd learned to shop in the outlet stores for designer fashions at half the cost. She looked down now at her sporty Calvin Klein outfit, at the Ferragamo boots and the Chanel handbag she'd picked up at a flea market. Inside her French luggage were other outfits by Donna Karan and Carolyn Roehm.

Like Keith, she had gotten a promotion with a hefty salary increase. If things worked out, she was going to think about opening her own architectural office by early summer. She'd hire people, oversee them. Clients she worked with told her she should open her own office, go it alone. One in particular had offered to back her after he'd seen the plans she'd drawn up for his beach house in Cape May. Her father, himself an architect, had offered to help out and had gone so far as to get all the paperwork from the Small Business Administration. She could do it now if she wanted to. But, did she want to make that kind of commitment? What would Keith think?

What she wanted, really wanted, was to get married and have a baby. She could always do consulting work, take on a few private clients to keep her hand in. All she needed was a husband to make it perfect.

Keith.

The phone rang. Mo frowned. No one ever called her this early in the morning. Her heart skipped a beat as she picked up the phone. "Hello," she said warily.

"Morgan?" Her mother. She always made her name sound like a question.

"What's wrong, Mom?"

"When are you leaving, Morgan? I wish you'd left last night like Dad and I asked you to do. You should have listened to us, Morgan."

"Why? What's wrong? I told you why I couldn't leave. I'm about ready to go out the door as we speak."

"Have you looked outside?"

"No. It's still dark, Mom."

"Open your blinds, Morgan, and look at the parking lot lights. It's snowing!"

"Mom, it snows every year. So what? It's only a two-hour drive, maybe three if there's a lot of snow. I have the Cherokee. Four-wheel drive, Mom." She pulled up the blind in the bedroom to stare out at the parking lot. She swallowed hard. So, it would be a challenge. The world was white as far as the eye could see. She raised her eyes to the parking lights. The bright light that usually greeted her early in the morning was dim as the sodium vapor fought with the early light of dawn and the swirling snow. "It's snowing, Mom."

"That's what I'm trying to tell you. It started here around midnight, I guess. It was just flurries when Dad and I went to bed but now we have about four inches. Since this storm seems to be coming from the south where you are, you probably have more. Dad and I have been talking and we won't be upset if you wait till the storm is over. Christmas morning is just as good as Christmas Eve. Just how much snow do you have, Morgan?"

"It looks like a lot, but it's drifting in the parking lot. I can't see the front, Mom. Look, don't worry about me. I have to be home this evening. I've waited two long years for this. Please, Mom, you understand, don't you?"

"What I understand, Morgan, is that you're being foolhardy. I saw Keith's mother the other day and she said he hasn't been home in ten months. He just lives across the river, for heaven's sake. She also said she didn't expect him for Christmas, so what does that tell you? I don't want you risking your life for some foolish promise."

Mo's physical being trembled. The words she dreaded, the words she didn't ever want to hear, had just been uttered:

Keith wasn't coming home for Christmas. She perked up almost immediately. Keith loved surprises. It would be just like him to tell his mother he wasn't coming home and then show up and yell, "Surprise!" If he had no intention of honoring the promise they made to each other, he would have sent a note or called her. Keith wasn't that callous. Or was he? She didn't know anything anymore.

She thought about the awful feelings that attacked her over the past two years, feelings she pushed away. Had she buried her head in the sand? Was it possible that Keith had used the two-year hiatus to soften the blow of parting, thinking that she'd transfer her feelings to someone else and let him off the hook? Instead she'd trenched in and convinced herself that by being faithful to her feelings, tonight would be her reward. Was she a fool? According to her mother she was. Tonight would tell the tale.

What she did know for certain was, nothing was going to stop her from going home. Not her mother's dire words, and certainly not a snowstorm. If she was a fool, she deserved to have her snoot rubbed in it.

Just a few short hours ago she'd stacked up her shopping bags by the front door, colorful Christmas bags loaded with presents for everyone. Five oversize bags for Keith. She wondered what happened to the presents she'd bought two years ago. Did her mother take them over to Keith's mother's house or were they in the downstairs closet? She'd never asked.

She'd spent a sinful amount of money on him this year. She'd even knitted a stocking for him and filled it with all kinds of goodies and gadgets. She'd stitched his name on the cuff of the bright red stocking in bright green thread. Was she a fool?

Mo pulled on her fleece-lined parka. Bundled up, she carried as many of the bags downstairs to the lobby as she could handle. She made three trips before she braved the outdoors. She needed to shovel and heat the car up.

She was exhausted when she tossed the fold-up shovel into the back of the Jeep. The heater and defroster worked furiously, but she still had to scrape the ice from the windshield and driver's side window. She checked the flashlight in the glove compartment. She rummaged inside the small opening, certain she had extra batteries, but couldn't find any. She glanced at the gas gauge. Three-quarters full, enough to get her home. She'd meant to top off last night on her way home from work, but she'd been in a hurry to get home to finish wrapping Keith's presents. God, she'd spent hours making intricate, one-of-a-kind bows and decorations for the gold-wrapped packages. A three-quarter tank would get her home for sure. The Cherokee gave her good mileage. If memory served her right, the trip never took more than a quarter of a tank. Well, she couldn't worry about that now. If road conditions permitted, she could stop on 95 or when she got onto the Jersey Turnpike.

Mo was numb with cold when she shrugged out of her parka and boots. She debated having a cup of tea to warm her up. Maybe she should wait for rush hour traffic to be over. Maybe a lot of things.

Maybe she should call Keith and ask him point blank if he was going to meet her in front of the Christmas tree. If she did that, she might spoil things. Still, why take her life in her hands and drive through what looked like a terrible storm, for nothing. She'd just as soon avoid her parents' pitying gaze and make the trip tomorrow morning and return in the evening to lick her wounds. If he was really going to be a no show, that would be the way to go. Since there were no guarantees, she didn't see any choice but to brave the storm.

She wished she had a dog or a cat to nuzzle, a warm body that loved unconditionally. She'd wanted to get an animal at least a hundred times these past two years, but she couldn't bring herself to admit that she needed someone. What did it matter if that someone had four legs and a furry body?

Her address book was in her hand, but she knew Keith's New York phone number by heart. It was unlisted, but she'd managed to get it from the brokerage house Keith worked for. So she'd used trickery. So what? She hadn't broken the rules and called the number. It was just comforting to know she could call if she absolutely had to. She squared her shoulders as she reached for the portable phone on the kitchen counter. She looked at the range-top clock. Seven forty-five. He should still be home. She punched out the area code and number, her shoulders still stiff. The phone rang five times before the answering machine came on. Maybe he was still in the shower. He always did cut it close to the edge, leaving in the morning with his hair still damp from the shower.

"C'mon, now, you know what to do if I don't answer. I'm either catching some z's or I'm out and about. Leave me a message, but be careful not to give away any secrets. Wait for the beep." Z's? It must be fast track New York talk. The deep, husky chuckle coming over the wire made Mo's face burn with shame. She broke the connection.

A moment later she was zipping up her parka and pulling on thin leather gloves. She turned down the heat in her cozy apartment, stared at her small Christmas tree on the coffee table, and made a silly wish.

The moment she stepped outside, grainy snow assaulted her as the wind tried to drive her backward. She made it to the Cherokee, climbed inside, and slammed the door. She shifted into four-wheel drive, then turned on the front and back wipers. The Cherokee inched forward, its wheels finding the traction to get her to the access road to I-95. It took her all of forty minutes to steer the Jeep to the ramp that led onto the Interstate. At that precise moment she knew she was making a mistake, but it was too late and there was no way now to get off and head back to the apartment. As far as she could see, it was bumper-to-bumper traffic. Visibility was almost zero. She knew there was a huge green directional sign overhead, but she couldn't see it.

"Oh, shit!"

Mo's hands gripped the wheel as the car in front of her slid to the right, going off the road completely. She muttered her favorite expletive again. God, what would she do if the wipers iced up? From the sound they were making on the windshield, she didn't think she'd have to wait long to find out.

The radio crackled with static, making it impossible to hear what was being said. Winter advisory. She already knew that. Not only did she know it, she was participating in it. She turned it off. The dashboard clock said she'd been on the road for well over an hour and she was nowhere near the Jersey Turnpike. At least she didn't think so. It was impossible to read the signs with the snow sticking to everything.

A white Christmas. The most wonderful time of the year. That thought alone had sustained her these past two years. Nothing bad ever happened on Christmas. Liar! Keith dumped you on Christmas Eve, right there in front of the tree. Don't lie to yourself!

"Okay, okay," she muttered. "But this Christmas will be different, this Christmas it will work out." Keith will make it up to you, she thought. Believe. Sure, and Santa is going to slip down the chimney one minute after midnight.

Mo risked a glance at the gas gauge. Half. She turned the heater down. Heaters added to the fuel consumption, didn't they? She thought about the Ferragamo boots she was wearing. Damn, she'd set her rubber boots by the front door so she wouldn't forget to bring them. They were still sitting by the front door. She wished now for her warm ski suit and wool cap, but she'd left them at her mother's last year when she went skiing for the last time.

She tried the radio again. The static was worse than before. So was the snow and ice caking her windshield. She had to stop and clean the blades or she was going to have an accident. With the faint glow of the taillights in front of her, Mo steered the Cherokee to the right. She pressed her flasher button, then waited to see if a car would pass her on the left and how much room she had to exit the car. The parka hood flew backward, exposing her head and face to the snowy onslaught. She fumbled with the wipers and the scraper. The swath they cleared was almost minuscule. God, what was she to do? Get off the damn road at the very next exit and see if she could find shelter? There was always a gas station or truck stop. The problem was, how would she know when she came to an exit?

Panic rivered through her when she got back into the Jeep. Her leather gloves were soaking wet. She peeled them off, then tossed them onto the back seat. She longed for her padded ski gloves and a cup of hot tea.

Mo drove for another forty minutes, stopping again to scrape her wipers and windshield. She was fighting a losing battle and she knew it. The wind was razor-sharp, the snow coming down harder. This wasn't just a winter storm, it was a blizzard. People died in blizzards. Some fool had even made a movie about people eating other people when a plane crashed during a blizzard. She let the panic engulf her again. What was going to happen to her? Would she run out of gas and freeze to death? Who would find her? When would they find her? On Christmas Day? She imagined her parents' tears, their recriminations.

All of a sudden she realized there were no lights in front of her. She'd been so careful to stay a car length and a half behind the car in front. She pressed the accelerator, hoping desperately to keep up. God in heaven, was she off the road? Had she crossed the Delaware Bridge? Was she on the Jersey side? She simply didn't know. She tried the radio again and was rewarded with squawking static. She turned it off quickly. She risked a glance in her rearview mirror. There were no faint lights. There was nothing behind her. She moaned in fear. Time to stop, get out and see what she could see.

Before she climbed from the car, she unzipped her duffel bag sitting on the passenger side. She groped for a T-shirt and wrapped it around her head. Maybe the parka hood would stay on with something besides her silky hair to cling to. Her hands touched a pair of rolled-up sleep sox. She pulled them on. Almost as good as mittens. Did she have two pairs? She found a second pair and pulled them on. She flexed her fingers. No thumb holes. Damn. She remembered the manicure scissors she kept in her purse. A minute later she had thumb holes and was able to hold the steering wheel tightly. Get out, see what you can see. Clean the wipers, use that flashlight. Try your high beams.

Mo did all of the above. Uncharted snow. No one had gone before her. The snow was almost up to her knees. If she walked around, the snow would go down between her boots and stirrup pants. Knee highs. Oh, God! Her feet would freeze in minutes. They might not find her until the spring thaw. Where was she? A field? The only thing she knew for certain was, she wasn't on any kind of a road.

"I hate you, Keith Mitchell. I mean, I really hate you. This is all your fault! No, it isn't," she sobbed. "It's my fault for being so damn stupid. If you loved me, you'd wait for me. Tonight was just a time. My mother would tell you I was delayed because of the storm. You could stay at my mother's or go to your mother's. If you loved me. I'm sitting here now, my life in danger, because . . . I wanted to believe you loved me. The way I love you. Christmas miracles, my ass!"

Mo shifted gears, inching the Cherokee forward.

How was it possible, Mo wondered, to be so cold and yet be sweating? She swiped at the perspiration on her forehead with the sleeve of her parka. In her whole life she'd never been this scared. If only she knew where she was. For all she knew, she could be driving into a pond or a lake. She shivered. Maybe she should get out and walk. Take her chances in the snow. She was in a no-win situation and she knew it. Stupid, stupid, stupid.

Maybe the snow wasn't as deep as she thought it was. Maybe it was just drifting in places. She was saved from further speculation when the Cherokee bucked, sputtered, slugged forward, and then came to a coughing stop. Mo cut the engine, fear choking off her breathing. She waited a second before she turned the ignition key. She still had a gas reserve. The engine refused to catch and turn over. She turned off the heater and the wipers, then tried again with the same results. The decision to get out of the car and walk was made for her.

Mo scrambled over the back seat to the cargo area. With

cold, shaking fingers she worked the zippers on her suitcases. She pulled thin, sequined sweaters—that would probably give her absolutely no warmth—out of the bag. She
shrugged from the parka and pulled on as many of the deco-
rative designer sweaters as she could. Back in her parka, she
pulled knee-hi stockings and her last two pairs of socks over
her hands. It was better than nothing. As if she had choices.
The keys to the jeep went into her pocket. The strap of her
purse was looped around her neck. She was ready. Her sigh
was as mighty as the wind howling about her as she climbed
out of the Cherokee.

The wind was sharper than a butcher knife. Eight steps in
the mid-thigh snow and she was exhausted. The silk scarf
she'd tied around her mouth was frozen to her face in the
time it took to take those eight steps. Her eyelashes were
caked with ice as were her eyebrows. She wanted to close
her eyes, to sleep. How in the hell did Eskimos do it? A
gurgle of hysterical laughter erupted in her throat.

The laughter died in her throat when she found herself
facedown in a deep pile of snow. She crawled forward. It
seemed like the wise thing to do. Getting to her feet was the
equivalent of climbing Mt. Rushmore. She crab-walked until
her arms gave out on her, then she struggled to her feet and
tried to walk again. She repeated the process over and over
until she was so exhausted she simply couldn't move. "Help
me, someone. Please, God, don't let me die out here like this.
I'll be a better person, I promise. I'll go to church more
often. I'll practice my faith more diligently. I'll try to do
more good deeds. I won't be selfish. I swear to You, I will.
I'm not just saying this, either. I mean every word." She
didn't know if she was saying the words or thinking them.

A violent gust of wind rocked her backward. Her back
thumped into a tree, knocking the breath out of her. She
cried then, her tears melting the crystals on her lashes.

"Help!" she bellowed. She shouted until she was hoarse.

Time lost all meaning as she crawled along. There were
longer pauses now between the time she crawled on all fours
and the time she struggled to her feet. She tried shouting

again, her cries feeble at best. The only person who could hear her was God, and He seemed to be otherwise occupied.

Mo stumbled and went down. She struggled to get up, but her legs wouldn't move. In her life she'd never felt the pain that was tearing away at her joints. She lifted her head and for one brief second she thought she saw a feeble light. In the time it took her heart to beat once, the light was gone. She was probably hallucinating. Move! her mind shrieked. Get up! They won't find you till the daffodils come up. They'll bury you when the lilacs bloom. That's how they'll remember you. They might even print that on your tombstone. "Help me. Please, somebody help me!"

She needed to sleep. More than anything in the world she wanted sleep. She was so groggy. And her heart seemed to be beating as fast as a racehorse's at the finish line. How was that possible? Her heart should barely be beating. Get the hell up, Morgan. Now! Move, damn you!

She was up. She was so cold. She knew her body heat was leaving her. Her clothes were frozen to her body. She couldn't see at all. Move, damn you! You can do it. You were never a quitter, Morgan. Well, maybe where Keith was concerned. You always managed, somehow, to see things through to a satisfactory conclusion. She stumbled and fell, picked herself up with all the willpower left in her numb body, fell again. This time she couldn't get up.

A vision of her parents standing over her closed coffin, the room filled with lilacs, appeared behind her closed lids. Her stomach rumbled fiercely and then she was on her feet, her lungs about to burst with her effort.

The snow and wind lashed at her like a tidal wave. It slammed her backward and beat at her face and body. Move! Don't stop now! Go, go, go, go.

"Help!" she cried. She was down again, on all fours. She shook her head to clear it.

She sensed movement. "Please," she whimpered, "help me." She felt warm breath, something touched her cheek. God. He was getting ready to take her. She cried.

"Woof!"

A dog! Man's best friend. *Her* best friend now. "You aren't better than God, but you'll damn well do," Mo gasped. "Do you understand? I need help. Can you fetch help?" Mo's hands reached out to the dog, but he backed away, woofing softly. Maybe he was barking louder and she couldn't hear it over the sound of the storm. "I'll try and follow you, but I don't think I'll make it." The dog barked again and as suddenly as he appeared, he was gone.

Mo howled her despair. She knew she had to move. The dog must live close by. Maybe the light she'd seen earlier was a house and this dog lived there. Again, she lost track of time as she crawled forward.

"Woof, woof, woof."

"You came back!" She felt her face being licked, nudged. There was something in the dog's mouth. Maybe something he killed. He'd licked her. He put something down, picked it up and was trying to give it to her. "What?"

The dog barked, louder, backing up, then lunging at her, thrusting whatever he had in his mouth at her. She reached for it. A ribbon. And then she understood. She did her best to loop it around her wrist, crawling on her hands and knees after the huge dog.

Time passed—she didn't know how much. Once, twice, three times, the dog had to get down on all fours and nudge her, the frozen ribbon tickling her face. At one point when she was down and didn't think she would ever get up, the dog nipped her nose, barking in her ear. She obeyed and moved.

And then she saw the windows full of bright yellow light. She thought she saw a Christmas tree through the window. The dog was barking, urging her to follow him. She snaked after him on her belly, praying, thanking God, as she went along.

A doggie door. A large doggie door. The dog went through it, barking on the other side. Maybe no one was home to open the door to her. Obviously, the dog intended her to follow. When in Rome . . . She pushed her way through.

The heat from the huge, blazing fire in the kitchen

slammed into her. Nothing in the world ever felt this good. Her entire body started to tingle. She rolled over, closer to the fire. It smelled of pine and something else, maybe cinnamon. The dog barked furiously as he circled the rolling girl. He wanted something, but she didn't know what. She saw it out of the corner of her eye—a large, yellow towel. But she couldn't reach it. "Push it here," she said hoarsely. The dog obliged.

"Well, Merry Christmas," a voice said behind her. "I'm sorry I wasn't here to welcome you, but I was showering and dressing at the back end of the house. I just assumed Murphy was barking at some wild animal. Do you always make this kind of entrance? Mind you, I'm not complaining. Actually, I'm delighted that I'll have someone to share Christmas Eve with. I'm sorry I can't help you, but I think you should get up. Murphy will show you the way to the bedroom and bath. You'll find a warm robe. Just rummage for whatever you want. I'll have some warm food for you when you get back. You are okay, aren't you? You need to move, get your circulation going again. Frostbite can be serious."

"I got lost and your dog found me," Mo whispered.

"I pretty much figured that out," the voice chuckled.

"You have a nice voice," Mo said sleepily. "I really need to sleep. Can't I just sleep here in front of this fire?"

"No, you cannot." The voice was sharp, authoritative. Mo's eyes snapped open. "You need to get out of those wet clothes. Now!"

"Yes, sir!" Mo said smartly. "I don't think much of your hospitality. You could help me, you know. I'm almost half-dead. I might still die. Right here on your kitchen floor. How's that going to look?" She rolled over, struggling to a sitting position. Murphy got behind her so she wouldn't topple over.

She saw her host, saw the wheelchair, then the anger and frustration in his face. "I've never been known for my tact. I apologize. I appreciate your help and you're right, I need to get out of these wet clothes. I can make it. I got this far.

I would appreciate some food though if it isn't too much trouble . . . Or, I can make it myself if you . . ."

"I'm very self-sufficient. I think I can rustle up something that doesn't come in a bag. You know, real food. It's time for Murphy's supper, too."

His voice was cool and impersonal. He was handsome, probably well over six feet if he'd been standing. Muscular. "It can't be suppertime already. What time is it?"

"A little after three. Murphy eats early. I don't know why that is, he just does."

She was standing—a feat in itself. She did her best to marshal her dignity as Murphy started out of the kitchen. "I'm sorry I didn't bring a present. It was rude of me to show up like this with nothing in hand. My mother taught me better, but circumstances . . ."

"Go!"

Murphy bounded down the hall. Mo lurched against the wall again and again, until she made it to the bathroom. It was a pretty room for a bathroom, all powdery blue and white with matching towels and carpet. And it was toasty warm. The shower was obviously for the handicapped with a special seat and grab bars. She shed her clothes, layer by layer, until she was naked. She turned on the shower and was rewarded with instant steaming water. Nothing in the world had ever looked this good. Or felt this good, she thought as she stepped into the spray. She let the water pelt her and made a mental note to ask her host where he got the shower head that massaged her aching body. The soap was Ivory, clean and sweet-smelling. The shampoo was something in a black bottle, something manly. She didn't care. She lathered up her dark, wet curls and then rinsed off. She decided she liked the smell and made another mental note to look closely at the bottle for the name.

When the water cooled, she stepped out and would have laughed if she hadn't been so tired. Murphy was holding a towel. A large one, the mate to the yellow one in the kitchen. He trotted over to the linen closet, inched it open. She watched him as he made his selection, a smaller towel obviously for her hair. "You're one smart dog, I can say that for you. I owe you my life, big guy. Let's see, I'd wager you're a golden retriever. My hair should be half as silky as yours. I'm going to send you a dozen porterhouse steaks when I get home. Now, let's see, he said there was a robe in here. Ah, here it is. Now, why did I know it was going to be dark green?" She slipped into it, the smaller towel still wrapped around her head. The robe smelled like the shampoo. Maybe the stuff came in a set.

He said to rummage for what she wanted. She did, for socks and a pair of long underwear. She pulled on both, the waistband going all the way up to her underarms. As if she cared. All she wanted was the welcome warmth.

She looked around his bedroom. His. Him. God, she didn't even know his name, but she knew his dog's name. How strange. She wanted to do something. The thought had come to her in the shower, but now it eluded her. She saw the phone and the fireplace at the same time. She knew there would be no dial tone, and she was right. She sat down by the fire in the nest of cushions, motioning wearily for the dog to come closer. "I wish you were mine, I really do. Thank you for saving me. Now, one last favor—find that Christmas ribbon and save it for me. I want to have something to remember you by. Not now, the next time you go outside. Will you do that for . . . ?" A moment later she was asleep in the mound of pillows.

Murphy sat back on his haunches to stare at the sleeping girl in his master's room. He walked around her several times, sniffing as he did so. When he was satisfied that all was well, he trotted over to the bed and tugged at the comforter until he had it on the floor. Then he dragged it over to the sleeping girl. He pulled, dragged, and tugged until he had it snugly up around her chin. The moment he was finished, he beelined down the hall, through the living room, past his master, out to the kitchen where he slowed just enough to go through his door. He was back in ten minutes with the red ribbon.

"So that's where it is. Hand it over, Murphy. It's supposed

to go on the tree." The golden dog stopped in his tracks, woofed, backed up several steps, but he didn't drop the ribbon. Instead, he raced down the hall to the bedroom, his master behind him, his chair whirring softly. He watched as the dog placed the ribbon on the coverlet next to Mo's face. He continued to watch as the huge dog gently tugged the small yellow towel from her wet head. With his snout, he nudged the dark ringlets, then he gently pawed at them.

"I see," Marcus Bishop said sadly. "She does look a little like Marcey with that dark hair. Now that you have the situation under control, I guess it's time for your dinner. She wanted the ribbon, is that it? That's how you got her here? Good boy, Murphy. Let's let our guest sleep. Maybe she'll wake up in time to sing some carols with us. You did good, Murph. Real good. Marcey would be so proud of you. Hell, I'm proud of you and if we don't watch it, I have a feeling this girl is going to try and snatch you away from me."

Marcus could feel his eyes start to burn when Murphy bent over the sleeping girl to lick her cheek. He swore then that the big dog cried, but he couldn't be certain because his own eyes were full of tears.

Back in the kitchen, Marcus threw Mo's clothes in the dryer. He spooned out wet dog food and kibble into Murphy's bowl. The dog looked at it and walked away. "Yeah, I know. So, it's a little setback. We'll recover and get on with it. If we can just get through this first Christmas, we'll be on the road to recovery, but you gotta help me out here. I can't do it alone." The dog buried his head in his paws, but made no sign that he either cared or understood what his master was saying. Marcus felt his shoulders slump.

It was exactly one year ago to the day that the fatal accident had happened. Marsha, his twin sister, had been driving when the head-on collision occurred. He'd been wearing his seat belt; she wasn't wearing hers. It took the wrecking crew four hours to get him out of the car. He'd had six operations and one more loomed on the horizon. This one, the orthopedic specialists said, was almost guaranteed to make him walk again.

This little cottage had been Marcey's. She'd moved down here after her husband died of leukemia, just five short years after her marriage. Murphy had been her only companion during those tragic years. He'd done all he could for her, but she'd kept him at a distance. She painted, wrote an art column for the *Philadelphia Democrat*, took long walks, and watched a lot of television. To say she withdrew from life was putting it mildly. After the accident, it was simpler to convert this space to his needs than the main house. A ramp and an oversized bathroom were all he needed. Murphy was happier here, too.

Murphy belonged to both of them, but he'd been partial to Marcey because she always kept licorice squares in her pocket for him.

He and Murphy had grieved together, going to Marcey's gravesite weekly with fresh flowers. At those times, he always made sure he had licorice in his pocket. More often than not, though, Murphy wouldn't touch the little black squares. It was something to do, a memory he tried to keep intact.

It was going to be nice to have someone to share Christmas with. A time of miracles, the Good Book said. Murphy finding this girl in all that snow had to constitute a miracle of some kind. He didn't even know her name. He felt cheated. Time enough for that later. Time. That was all he had of late.

Marcus checked the turkey in the oven. Maybe he should just make a sandwich and save the turkey until tomorrow when the girl would be up to a full sit-down dinner.

He stared at the Christmas tree in the center of the room and wondered if anyone else ever put their tree there. It was the only way he could string the lights. He knew he could have asked one of the servants from the main house to come down and do it just the way he could have asked them to cook him a holiday dinner. He needed to do these things, needed the responsibility of taking care of himself. In case this next operation didn't work.

He prided himself on being a realist. If he didn't, he'd be

sitting in this chair sucking his thumb and watching the boob tube. Life was just too goddamn precious to waste even one minute. He finished decorating the tree, plugged in the lights, and whistled at his marvelous creation. He felt his eyes mist up when he looked at the one-of-a-kind ornaments that had belonged to Marcey and John. He wished for children, a houseful. More puppies. He wished for love, for sound, for music, for sunshine and laughter. Someday.

Damn, he wished he was married with little ones calling him Daddy. Daddy, fix this; Daddy, help me. And some pretty woman standing in the kitchen smiling, the smile just for him. Marcey said he was a fusspot and that's why no girl would marry him. She said he needed to be more outgoing, needed to smile more. Stop taking yourself so seriously, she would say. Who said you have to be a better engineer than Dad? And then she'd said, *If you can't whistle when you work you don't belong in that job.* He'd become a whistling fool after that little talk because he loved what he did, loved managing the family firm, the largest engineering outfit in the state of New Jersey. Hell, he'd been called to Kuwait after the Gulf War. That had to mean something in terms of prestige. As if he cared about that.

His chair whirred to life. Within seconds he was sitting in the doorway, watching the sleeping girl. He felt drawn to her for some reason. He snapped his fingers for Murphy. The dog nuzzled his leg. "Check on her, Murph—make sure she's breathing. She should be okay, but do it anyway. Good thing that fireplace is gas—she'll stay warm if she sleeps through the night. Guess I get the couch." He watched as the retriever circled the sleeping girl, nudging the quilt that had slipped from her shoulders. As before, he sniffed her dark hair, stopping long enough to lick her cheek and check on the red ribbon. Marcus motioned for him. Together, they made their way down the hall to the living room and the festive Christmas tree.

It was only six o'clock. The evening loomed ahead of him. He fixed two large, ham sandwiches, one cut into four neat squares, then arranged them on two plates along with pickles and potato chips. A beer for him and grape soda for Murphy. He placed them on the fold-up tray attached to his chair. He whirred into the room, then lifted himself out of the chair and onto the couch. He pressed a button and the wide screen television in the corner came to life. He flipped channels until he came to the Weather Channel. "Pay attention, Murph, this is what you saved our guest from. They're calling it The Blizzard. Hell, I could have told them that at ten o'clock this morning. You know what I never figured out, Murph? How Santa is supposed to come down the chimney on Christmas Eve with a fire going. Everyone lights their fireplaces on Christmas Eve. Do you think I'm the only one who's ever asked this question?" He continued to talk to the dog at his feet, feeding him potato chips. For a year now, Murphy was the only one he talked to, with the exception of his doctors and the household help. The business ran itself with capable people standing in for him. He was more than fortunate in that respect. "Did you hear that, Murph? Fourteen inches of snow. We're marooned. They won't even be able to get down here from the big house to check on us. We might have our guest for a few days. Company." He grinned from ear to ear and wasn't sure why. Eventually he dozed, as did Murphy.

Mo opened one eye, instantly aware of where she was and what had happened to her. She tried to stretch her arms and legs. She bit down on her lower lip so she wouldn't cry out in pain. A hot shower, four or five aspirin, and some liniment might make things bearable. She closed her eyes, wondering what time it was. She offered up a prayer, thanking God that she was alive and as well as could be expected under the circumstances.

Where was her host? Her savior? She supposed she would have to get up to find out. She tried again to boost herself to a sitting position. With the quilt wrapped around her, she stared at the furnishings. It seemed feminine to her with the priscilla curtains, the pretty pale blue carpet, and satin-striped chaise longue. There was also a faint powdery scent to the room. A leftover scent as though the occupant no longer lived here. She stared at the large louvered closet that took up one entire wall. Maybe that's where the powdery smell was coming from. Closets tended to hold scents. She looked down at the purple and white flowers adorning the quilt. It matched the drapes. Did men use fluffy yellow towels? If they were leftovers, they did. Her host seemed like the green, brown, and beige type to her.

She saw the clock, directly in her line of vision, sitting next to the phone that was dead.

The time was 3:15. Good Lord, she'd slept the clock around. It was Christmas Day. Her parents must be worried sick. Where was Keith? She played with the fantasy that he was out with the state troopers looking for her, but only for a minute. Keith didn't like the cold. He only pretended to like skiing because it was the trendy thing to do.

She got up, tightened the belt on the oversize robe, and hobbled around the room, searching for the scent that was so familiar. One side of the closet held women's clothes, the other side, men's. So, there was a Mrs. Host. On the dresser, next to the chaise longue, was a picture of a pretty, dark-haired woman and her host. Both were smiling, the man's arm around the woman's shoulders. They were staring directly at the camera. A beautiful couple. A friend must have taken the picture. She didn't have any pictures like this of her and Keith. She felt cheated.

Mo parted the curtains and gasped. In her life she'd never seen this much snow. She knew in her gut the Jeep was buried. How would she ever find it? Maybe the dog would know where it was.

Mo shed her clothes in the bathroom and showered again. She turned the nozzle a little at a time, trying to get the water as hot as she could stand it. She moved, jiggled, and danced under the spray as it pelted her sore, aching muscles. She put the same long underwear and socks back on and rolled up the sleeves of the robe four times. She was warm, that was all that mattered. Her skin was chafed and wind-burned. She needed cream of some kind, lanolin. Did her host keep things like that here in the bathroom? She looked under the sink. In two shoeboxes she found everything she needed. Expensive cosmetics, pricey perfume. Mrs. Host must have left in a hurry or a huff. Women simply didn't leave a fortune in cosmetics behind.

She was ready now to introduce herself to her host and sit down to food. She realized she was ravenous.

He was in the kitchen mashing potatoes. The table was set for two and one more plate was on the floor. A large turkey sat in the middle of the table.

"Can I do anything?" Her voice was raspy, throaty.

The chair moved and he was facing her.

"You can sit down. I waited to mash the potatoes until I heard the shower going. I'm Marcus Bishop. Merry Christmas."

"I'm Morgan Ames. Merry Christmas to you and Murphy. I can't thank you enough for taking me in. I looked outside and there's a lot of snow out there. I don't think I've ever seen this much snow. Even in Colorado. Everything looks wonderful. It smells wonderful, and I know it's going to taste wonderful, too." She was babbling like a schoolgirl. She clamped her lips shut and folded her hands in her lap.

He seemed amused. "I try. Most of the time I just grill something out on the deck. This was my first try at a big meal. I don't guarantee anything. Would you like to say grace?"

Would she? Absolutely she would. She had much to be thankful for. She said so, in great detail, head bowed. A smile tugged at the corners of Bishop's mouth. Murphy panted, shifting position twice, as much as to say, let's get on with it.

Mo flushed. "I'm sorry, I did go on there a bit, didn't I? You see, I promised . . . I said . . ."

"You made a bargain with God," Marcus said.

"How did you know?" God, he was handsome. The picture in the bedroom didn't do him justice at all.

"When it's down to the wire and there's no one else, we all depend on that Supreme Being to help us out. Most times we forget about Him. The hard part is going to be living up to all those promises."

"I never did that before. Even when things were bad, I didn't ask. This was different. I stared at my mortality. Are you saying you think I was wrong?"

"Not at all. It's as natural as breathing. Life is precious. No one wants to lose it." His voice faltered, then grew stronger.

Mo stared across the table at her host. She'd caught a glimpse of the pain in his eyes before he lowered his head. Maybe Mrs. Bishop was . . . not of this earth. She felt flustered, sought to change the subject. "Where is this place, Mr. Bishop? Am I in a town or is this the country? I only saw one house up on the hill when I looked out the window."

"The outskirts of Cherry Hill."

She was gobbling her food, then stopped chewing long enough to say, "This is absolutely delicious. I didn't realize I had driven this far. There was absolutely no visibility. I didn't know if I'd gone over the Delaware Bridge or not. I followed the car's lights in front of me and then suddenly the lights were gone and I was on my own. The car just gave out even though I still had some gas left."

"Where were you going? Where did you leave from?"

"I live in Delaware. My parents live in Woodbridge, New Jersey. I was going home for Christmas like thousands of other people. My mother called and told me how bad the snow was. Because I have a four-wheel drive Cherokee, I felt confident I could make it. There was one moment there before I started out when I almost went back. I wish now I had listened to my instincts. It's probably the second most stupid thing I've ever done. Again, I'm very grateful. I could have died out there and all because I had to get home. I just had to get home. I tried the telephone in the bedroom but the line was dead. How long do you think it will take before it comes back on?" How anxious her voice sounded. She cleared her throat.

"A day or so. It stopped snowing about an hour ago. I heard a bulletin that said all the work crews are out. Power is the first thing that has to be restored. I'm fortunate in the sense that I have gas heat and a backup generator in case power goes out. When you live in the country these things are mandatory."

"Do you think the phone is out in the big house on the hill?"

"If mine is out, so is theirs," Marcus said quietly. "This is Christmas, you know."

"I know," Mo said, her eyes misting over.

"Eat!" Marcus said in the same authoritative tone he'd used the day before.

"My mother always puts marshmallow in her sweet potatoes. You might want to try that sometime. She sprinkles sesame seeds in her chopped broccoli. It gives it a whole different taste." She held out her plate for a second helping of turkey.

"I like the taste as it is, but I'll keep it in mind and give it a try someday."

"No, you won't. You shouldn't say things unless you mean them. You strike me as a person who does things one way and is not open to anything but your own way. That's okay, too, but you shouldn't humor me. I happen to like marshmallows in my sweet potatoes and sesame seeds in my broccoli."

"You don't know me at all so why would you make such an assumption?"

"I know that you're bossy. You're used to getting things done your way. You ordered me to take a shower and get out of my wet clothes. You just now, a minute ago, ordered me to eat."

"That was for your own good. You are opinionated, aren't you?"

"Yep. I feel this need to tell you your long underwear

scratches. You should use fabric softener in the final rinse water."

Marcus banged his fist on the table. "Aha!" he roared. "That just goes to show how much you really know. Fabric softener does something to the fibers and when you sweat the material won't absorb it. So there!"

"Makes sense. I merely said it would help the scratching. If you plan on climbing a mountain . . . I'm sorry. I talk too much sometimes. What do you have for dessert? Are we having coffee? Can I get it or would you rather I just sit here and eat?"

"You're my guest. You sit and eat. We're having plum pudding, and of course we're having coffee. What kind of Christmas dinner do you think this is?" His voice was so huffy that Murphy got up, meandered over to Mo, and sat down by her chair.

"The kind of dinner where the vegetables come in frozen boil bags, the sweet potatoes in boxes, and the turkey stuffing in cellophane bags. I know for a fact that plum pudding can be bought frozen. I'm sure dessert will be just as delicious as the main course. Actually, I don't know when anything tasted half as good. Most men can't cook at all. At least the men I know." She was babbling again. "You can call me Mo. Everyone else does, even my dad."

"Don't get sweet on my dog, either," Marcus said, slopping the plum pudding onto a plate.

"I think your dog is sweet on me, Mr. Bishop. You should put that pudding in a little dessert dish. See, it spilled on the floor. I'll clean it up for you." She was half out of her chair when the iron command knifed through the air.

"Sit!" Mo lowered herself into her chair. Her eyes started to burn.

"I'm not a dog, Mr. Bishop. I only wanted to help. I'm sorry if my offer offended you. I don't think I care for dessert or coffee." Her voice was stiff, her shoulders stiff, too. She had to leave the table or she was going to burst into tears. What was wrong with her?

"I'm the one who should be apologizing. I've had to learn

to do for myself. Spills were a problem for a while. I have it down pat now. I just wet a cloth and use the broom handle to move it around. It took me a while to figure it out. You're right about the frozen stuff. I haven't had many guests lately to impress. And you can call me Marcus."

"Were you trying to impress me? How sweet, Marcus. I accept your apology and please accept mine. Let's pretend I stopped by to wish you a Merry Christmas and got caught in the snowstorm. Because you're a nice man you offered me your hospitality. See, we've established that you're a nice man and I want you to take my word for it that I'm a nice person. Your dog likes me. That has to count."

Marcus chuckled. "Well said."

Mo cupped her chin in her hands. "This is a charming little house. I bet you get the sun all day long. Sun's important. When the sun's out you just naturally feel better, don't you think? Do you have flowers in the spring and summer?"

"You name it, I've got it. Murphy digs up the bulbs sometimes. You should see the tulips in the spring. I spent a lot of time outdoors last spring after my accident. I didn't want to come in the house because that meant I was cooped up. I'm an engineer by profession so I came up with some long-handled tools that allowed me to garden. We pretty much look like a rainbow around April and May. If you're driving this way around that time, stop and see for yourself."

"I'd like that. I'm almost afraid to ask this, but I'm going to ask anyway. Will it offend you if I clean up and do the dishes?"

"Hell, no! I hate doing dishes. I use paper plates whenever possible. Murphy eats off paper plates, too."

Mo burst out laughing. Murphy's tail thumped on the floor.

Mo filled the sink with hot, soapy water. Marcus handed her the plates. They were finished in twenty minutes.

"How about a Christmas drink? I have some really good wine. Christmas will be over before you know it."

"This is good wine," Mo said.

"I don't believe it. You mean you can't find anything

wrong with it?" There was a chuckle in Marcus's voice so Mo didn't take offense. "What do you do for a living, Morgan Ames?"

"I'm an architect. I design shopping malls—big ones, small ones, strip malls. My biggest ambition is to have someone hire me to design a bridge. I don't know what it is, but I have this . . . this thing about bridges. I work for a firm, but I'm thinking about going out on my own next year. It's a scary thought, but if I'm going to do it, now is the time. I don't know why I feel that way, I just do. Do you work here at home or at an office?"

"Ninety percent at home, ten percent at the office. I have a specially equipped van. I can't get up on girders, obviously. I have several employees who are my legs. It's another way of saying I manage very well."

"It occurs to me to wonder, Marcus, where you slept last night. I didn't realize until a short while ago that there's only one bedroom."

"Here on the couch. It wasn't a problem. As you can see, it's quite wide and deep—the cushions are extra thick.

"So, what do you think of my tree?" he asked proudly.

"I love the bottom half. I even like the top half. The scent is so heady. I've always loved Christmas. It must be the kid in me. My mother said I used to make myself sick on Christmas Eve because I couldn't wait for Santa." She wanted to stand by the tree and pretend she was home waiting for Keith to show up and put the ring on her finger, wanted it so bad she could feel the prick of tears. It wasn't going to happen. Still, she felt driven to stand in front of the tree and . . . pretend. She fought the burning behind her eyelids by rubbing them and pretending it was the wood smoke from the fireplace that was causing the stinging. Then she remembered the fireplace held gas logs.

"Me, too. I was always so sure he was going to miss our chimney or his sleigh would break down. I was so damn good during the month of December my dad called me a saint. I have some very nice childhood memories. Are you okay? Is something wrong? You look like you lost your last friend suddenly. I'm a good listener if you want to talk."

Did she? She looked around at the peaceful cottage, the man in the wheelchair, and the dog sitting at his feet. She belonged in a scene like this one. The only problem was, the occupants were all wrong. She was never going to see this man again, so why not talk to him? Maybe he'd give her some male input where Keith was concerned. If he offered advice, she could take it or ignore it. She nodded, and held out her wineglass for a refill.

It wasn't until she was finished with her sad tale that she realized she was still standing in front of the Christmas tree. She sat down with a thump, knowing full well she'd had too much wine. She wanted to cry again when she saw the helpless look on Marcus's face. "So, everyone is entitled to make a fool of themselves at least once in their life. This is . . . was my time." She held out her glass again, but had to wait while Marcus uncorked a fresh bottle of wine. She thought his movements sluggish. Maybe he wasn't used to so much wine. "I don't think I'd make a very good drunk. I never had this much wine in my whole life."

"Me either." The wine sloshed over the side of the glass. Murphy licked it up.

"I don't want to get sick. Keith used to drink too much and get sick. It made me sick just watching him. That's sad, isn't it?"

"I never could stand a man who couldn't hold his liquor," Marcus said.

"You sound funny," Mo said as she realized her voice was taking on a sing-song quality.

"You sound like you're getting ready to sing. Are you? I hope you aren't one of those off-key singers." He leered down at her from the chair.

"So what if I am? Isn't singing good for the soul or something? It's the feeling, the thought. You said we were going to sing carols for Murphy. Why aren't we doing that?"

"Because you aren't ready," Marcus said smartly. He lowered the footrests and slid out of the chair. "We need to sit together in front of the tree. Sitting is as good as standing . . . I think. C'mere, Murphy, you belong to this group."

"Sitting is good." Mo hiccupped. Marcus thumped her on the back and then kept his arm around her shoulder. Murphy wiggled around until he was on both their laps.

"Just what exactly is wrong with you? Or is that impolite of me to . . . ask?" She swigged from the bottle Marcus handed her. "This is good—who needs a glass?"

"I hate doing dishes. The bottle is good. What was the question?"

"Huh?"

"What was the question?"

"The question is . . . was . . . do all your parts . . . work?"

"That wasn't the question. I'd remember if that was the question. Why do you want to know if my . . . parts work? Do you find yourself attracted to me? Or is this a sneaky way to try and get my dog? Get your own damn dog. And my parts work just fine."

"You sound defensive. When was the last time you tried them out . . . what I mean is . . . how do you know?" Mo asked craftily.

"I know! Are you planning on taking advantage of me? I might allow it. Then again, I might not."

"You're drunk," Mo said.

"Yep, and it's all your fault. You're drunk, too."

"What'd you expect? You keep filling my glass. You know what, I don't care. Do you care, Marcus?"

"Nope. So, what are you going to do about that jerk who's waiting by your Christmas tree? Christmas is almost over. D'ya think he's still waiting?"

Mo started to cry. Murphy wiggled around and licked at her tears. She shook her head.

"Don't cry. That jerk isn't worth your little finger. Murphy wouldn't like him. Dogs are keen judges of character."

"Keith doesn't like dogs."

Marcus threw his hands in the air. "There you go! I rest

my case." His voice sounded so dramatic, Mo started to giggle.

It wasn't much in the way of a kiss because she was giggling, Murphy was in the way, and Marcus's position and clumsy hands couldn't seem to coordinate with her. "That was sweet," Mo said.

"Sweet! Sweet!" Marcus bellowed in mock outrage.

"Nice?"

"*Nice* is better than *sweet*. No one ever said that to me before."

"How many were there . . . before?"

"None of your business."

"That's true, it isn't any of my business. Let's sing. 'Jingle Bells.' We're both too snookered to know the words to anything else. How many hours till Christmas is over?"

Marcus peered at his watch. "A few." He kissed her again, his hands less clumsy. Murphy cooperated by wiggling off both their laps.

"I liked that!"

"And well you should. You're very pretty, Mo. That's an awful name for a girl. I like Morgan, though. I'll call you Morgan."

"My father wanted a boy. He got me. It's sad. Do you know how many times I used that phrase in the past few hours? A lot." Her head bobbed up and down for no good reason. "Jingle Bells . . ." Marcus joined in, his voice as off-key as hers. They collapsed against each other, laughing like lunatics.

"Tell me about you. Do you have any more wine?"

Marcus pointed to the wine rack in the kitchen. Mo struggled to her feet, tottered to the kitchen, uncorked the bottle, and carried it back to the living room "I didn't see any munchies in the kitchen so I brought us each a turkey leg."

"I like a woman who thinks ahead." He gnawed on the leg, his eyes assessing the girl next to him. He wasn't the least bit drunk, but he was pretending he was. Why? She was pretty, and she was nice. So what if she had a few hangups. She liked him, too, he could tell. The chair didn't intimidate

her the way it did other women. She was feisty, with a mind
of her own. She'd been willing to share her private agonies
with him, a stranger. Murphy liked her. He liked her, too.
Hell, he'd given up his room to her. Now, she was staring at
him expectantly, waiting for him to talk about himself. What
to tell her? What to gloss over? Why couldn't he be as open
as she was?

"I'm thirty-five. I own and manage the family engineering firm. I have good job security and a great pension plan.
I own this little house outright. No mortgages. I love dogs
and horses. I even like cats. I've almost grown accustomed
to this chair. I am self-sufficient. I treat my elders with respect. I was a hell of a Boy Scout, got lots of medals to prove
it. I used to ski. I go to church, not a lot, but I do go. I believe
in God. I don't have any . . . sisters or brothers. I try not to
think too far ahead and I do my best not to look back. That's
not to say I don't think and plan for the future, but in my
position, I take it one day at a time. That pretty much sums
it up as far as my life goes."

"It sounds like a good life. I think you'll manage just fine.
We all have to make concessions . . . the chair . . . it's not
the end of the world. I can tell you don't like talking about
it, so, let's talk about something else."

"How would you feel if you went home this Christmas
Eve and there in your living room was Keith in a wheelchair? What if he told you the reason he hadn't been in touch
was because he didn't want to see pity in your eyes? How
would you feel if he told you he wasn't going to walk again?
What if he said you might eventually be the sole support?"
He waited for her to digest the questions, aware that her
intoxicated state might interfere with her answers.

"You shouldn't ask me something like that in my . . . condition. I'm not thinking real clear. I want to sing some more.
I didn't sing last year because I was too sad. Are you asking
about this year or last year?"

"What difference does it make?" Marcus asked coolly.

"It makes a difference. Last year I would have . . . would

have . . . said it didn't matter because I loved him . . . Do all his parts . . . work?"

"I don't know. This is hypothetical." Marcus turned to hide his smile.

"I wouldn't pity him. Maybe I would at first. Keith is very active. I could handle it, but Keith couldn't. He'd get depressed and give up. What was that other part?"

"Supporting him."

"Oh, yeah. I could do that. I have a profession, good health insurance. I might start up my own business. I'll probably make more money than he ever did. Knowing Keith, I think he would resent me after awhile. Maybe he wouldn't. I'd try harder and harder to make it all work because that's the way I am. I'm not a quitter. I never was. Why do you want to know all this?"

Marcus shrugged. "Insight, maybe. In case I ever find myself attracted to a woman, it would be good to know how she'd react. You surprised me—you didn't react to the chair."

"I'm not in love with you," Mo said sourly.

"What's wrong with me?"

"There's nothing wrong with you. I'm not that drunk that I don't know what you're saying. I'm in love with someone else. I don't care about that chair. That chair wouldn't bother me at all if I loved you. You said your parts work. Or, was that a lie? I like sex. Sex is wonderful when two people . . . you know . . . I like it!"

"Guess what? I do, too."

"You see, it's not a problem at all," Mo said happily. "Maybe I should just lie down on the couch and go to sleep."

"You didn't answer the second part of my question."

"Which was?"

"What if you had made it home this Christmas and the same scenario happened? After two long years. What would be your feeling?"

"I don't know. Keith whines. Did I tell you that? It's not manly at all."

"Really."

"Yep. I have to go to the bathroom. Do you want me to get you anything on my way back? I'll be on my feet. I take these feet for granted. They get me places. I love shoes. Well, what's your answer? Remember, you don't have any munchies. Why is that?"

"I have Orville Redenbacher popcorn. The colored kind. Very festive."

"No! You're turning into a barrel of fun, Marcus Bishop. You were a bossy, domineering person when I arrived through your doggie door. Look at you now! You're skunked, you ate a turkey leg, and now you tell me you have colored popcorn. I'll be right back unless I get sick. Maybe we should have coffee with our popcorn. God, I can't wait for this day to be over."

"Follow her, Murph. If she gets sick, come and get me," Marcus said. "You know," he said, making a gagging sound. The retriever sprinted down the hall.

A few minutes later, Mo was back in the living room. She dusted her hands together as she swayed back and forth. "Let's do the popcorn in the fireplace! I'll bring your coffeepot in here and plug it in. That way we won't have to get up and down."

"Commendable idea. It's ten-thirty."

"An hour and a half to go. I'm going to kiss you at twelve o'clock. Well, maybe one minute afterward. Your socks will come right off when I get done kissing you! So there!"

"I don't like to be used."

"Me either. I'll be kissing you because I want to kiss you. So there yourself!"

"What will Keith think?"

"Keith who?" Mo laughed so hard she slapped her thighs before she toppled over onto the couch. Murphy howled. Marcus laughed outright.

On her feet again, Mo said, "I like you, you're nice. You have a nice laugh. I haven't had this much fun in a long time. Life is such a serious business. Sometimes you need to stand back and get . . . what's that word . . . perspective? I like amusement parks. I like acting like a kid sometimes. There's this water park I like to go to and I love Great Adventure. Keith would never go so I went with my friends. It wasn't the same as sharing it with your lover. Would you like to go and . . . and . . . watch the other people? I'd take you if you would."

"Maybe."

"I hate that word. Keith always said that. That's just another way of saying no. You men are all alike."

"You're wrong, Morgan. No two people are alike. If you judge other men by Keith you're going to miss out on a lot. I told you, he's a jerk."

"Okayyyy. Popcorn and coffee, right?"

"Right."

Marcus fondled Murphy's ears as he listened to his guest bang pots and pans in his neat kitchen. Cabinet doors opened and shut, then opened and shut again. More pots and pans rattled. He smelled coffee and wondered if she'd spilled it. He looked at his watch. In a few short hours she'd be leaving him. How was it possible to feel so close to someone he'd just met? He didn't want her to leave. He hated, with a passion, the faceless Keith.

"I think you need to swing around so we can watch the popcorn pop. I thought everyone in the world had a popcorn popper. I'm improvising with this pot. It's going to turn black, but I'll clean it in the morning. You might have to throw it out. I like strong black coffee. How about you?"

"Bootblack for me."

"Oh, me, too. Really gives you a kick in the morning."

"I don't think that's the right lid for that pot," Marcus said.

"It'll do—I told you I had to improvise."

"Tell me how you're going to improvise this!" Marcus said as the popping corn blew the lid off the pot. Popcorn flew in every direction. Murphy leaped up to catch the kernels, nailing the fallen ones with his paws. Marcus rolled on the floor as Mo wailed her dismay. The corn continued to pop and sail about the room. "I'm not cleaning this up."

"Don't worry, Murphy will eat it all. He loves popcorn.

How much did you put in the pot?" Marcus gasped. "Coffee's done."

"A cup full. Too much, huh? I thought it would pop colored. I'm disappointed. There were a lot of fluffies—you know, the ones that pop first."

"I can't tell you how disappointed I am," Marcus said, his expression solemn.

Mo poured the coffee into two mugs.

"It looks kind of . . . syrupy."

"It does, doesn't it? Drink up! What'ya think?"

"I can truthfully say I've never had coffee like this," Marcus responded.

Mo settled herself next to Marcus. "What time is it?"

"It's late. I'm sure by tomorrow the roads will be cleared. The phones will be working and you can call home. I'll try and find someone to drive you. I have a good mechanic I'll call to work on your Jeep. How long were you planning on staying with your parents?"

"It was . . . vague . . . depending . . . I don't know. What will you do?"

"Work. The office has a lot of projects going on. I'm going to be pretty busy."

"Me, too. I like the way you smell," Mo blurted. "Where'd you get that shampoo in the black bottle?"

"Someone gave it to me in a set for my birthday."

"When's your birthday?" Mo asked.

"April tenth. When's yours?"

"April ninth. How about that? We're both Aries."

"Imagine that," Marcus said as he wrapped his arm around her shoulder.

"This is nice," Mo sighed. "I'm a home and hearth person. I like things cozy and warm with lots and lots of green plants. I have little treasures I've picked up over the years that I try to put in just the right place. It tells anyone who comes into my apartment who I am. I guess that's why I like this cottage. It's cozy, warm, and comfortable. A big house can be like that, too, but a big house needs kids, dogs, gerbils, rabbits, and lots of junk."

He should tell her now about the big house on the hill being his. He should tell her about Marcey and about his upcoming operation. He bit down on his lip. Not now—he didn't want to spoil the moment. He liked what they were doing. He liked sitting here with her, liked the feel of her. He risked a glance at his watch. A quarter to twelve. He felt like his eyeballs were standing at attention from the coffee he'd just finished. He announced the time in a quiet voice.

"Do you think he showed up, Marcus?"

He didn't think any such thing, but he couldn't say that. "He's a fool if he didn't."

"His mother told my mother he wasn't coming home for the holidays."

"Ah. Well, maybe he was going to surprise her. Maybe his plans changed. Anything is possible, Morgan."

"No, it isn't. You're playing devil's advocate. It's all right. Really it is. I'll just switch to Plan B and get on with my life."

He wanted that life to include him. He almost said so, but she interrupted him by poking his arm and pointing to his watch.

"Get ready. Remember, I said I was going to kiss you and blow your socks off."

"You did say that. I'm ready."

"That's it, you're ready. It would be nice if you showed some enthusiasm."

"I don't want my blood pressure to go up," Marcus grinned. "What if . . ."

"There is no *what if.* It's a kiss."

"There are kisses and then there are kisses. Sometimes . . ."

"Not this time. I know all about kisses. Jackie Bristol told me about kissing when I was six years old. He was ten and he knew *everything.* He liked to play doctor. He learned all that stuff by watching his older sister and her boyfriend."

She was *that* close to him. She could see a faint freckle on the bridge of his nose. She just knew he thought she was all talk and no action. Well, she'd show him and Keith, too. A kiss was . . . it was . . . what it was was . . .

It wasn't one of those warm, fuzzy kisses and it wasn't one of those feathery light kind, either. This kiss was reckless and passionate. Her senses reeled and her body tingled from head to toe. Maybe it was all the wine she'd consumed. She decided she didn't care what the reason was as she pressed not only her lips, but her body, against his. He responded, his tongue spearing into her mouth. She tasted the wine on his tongue and lips, wondered if she tasted the same way to him. A slow moan began in her belly and rose up to her throat. It escaped the moment she pulled away. His name was on her lips, her eyes sleepy and yet restless. She wanted more. So much more.

This was where she was supposed to say, *Okay, I kept my promise, I kissed you like I said.* Now, she should get up and go to bed. But she didn't want to go to bed. Ever. She wanted . . . needed . . .

"I'm still wearing my socks," Marcus said. "Maybe you need to try again. Or, how about I try blowing *your* socks off?"

"Go for it," Mo said as she ran her tongue over her bruised and swollen lips.

He did all the things she'd done, and more. She felt his hands all over her body—soft, searching. Finding. Her own hands started a search of their own. She felt as warm and damp as he felt to her probing fingers. She continued to tingle with anticipation. The heavy robe was suddenly open, the band of the underwear down around her waist, exposing her breasts. He was stroking one with the tip of his tongue. When the hard pink bud was in his mouth she thought she'd never felt such exquisite pleasure.

One minute she had clothes on and the next she was as naked as he was. She had a vague sense of ripping at his clothes as he did the same with hers. They were by the fire now, warm and sweaty.

She was on top of him with no memory of getting there. She slid over him, gasped at his hardness. Her dark hair fanned out like a waterfall. She bent her head and kissed him again. A sound of exquisite pleasure escaped her lips when he cupped both her breasts in his hands.

"Ride me," he said hoarsely. He bucked against her as she rode him, this wild stallion inside her. She milked his body, gave a mighty heave, and fell against him. It was a long time before either of them moved, and when they did, it was together. She wanted to look at him, wanted to say something. Instead, she nuzzled into the crook of his arm. The oversized robe covered them in a steamy warmth. Her hair felt as damp as his. She waited for him to say something, but he lay quietly, his hand caressing her shoulder beneath the robe. Why wasn't he saying something?

Her active imagination took over. One night stand. Girl lost in snowstorm. Man gives her shelter and food. Was this her payback? Would he respect her in the morning? Damn, it was already morning. What in the world possessed her to make love to this man? She was in love with Keith. *Was. Was* in love. At this precise moment she couldn't remember what Keith looked like. She'd cheated on Keith. But, had she really? *No,* her mind shrieked. She felt like crying, felt her shoulders start to shake. They calmed immediately as Marcus drew her closer.

"I . . . I never had a one night stand. I would hate . . . I don't want you to think . . . I don't hop in and out of bed . . . this was the first time in two years . . . I . . ."

"Shhh, it's okay. It was what it was—warm, wonderful, and meaningful. Neither one of us owes anything to the other. Sleep, Morgan," he whispered.

"You'll stay here, won't you?" she said sleepily. "I think I'd like to wake up next to you."

"I won't move. I'm going to sleep, too."

"Okay."

It was a lie, albeit a little one. As if he could sleep. Always the last one out of the gate, Bishop. She belongs to someone else, so don't get carried away. How right it all felt. How right it still felt. What had he just said to her? Oh yeah—*it was what it was.* Oh yeah, well, fuck you, Keith whatever-

your-name-is. You don't deserve this girl. I hope your damn
dick falls off. You weren't faithful to this girl. I know that as
sure as I know the sun is going to rise in the morning. She
knows it, too—she just won't admit it.

Marcus stared at the fire, his eyes full of pain and sadness.
Tomorrow she'd be gone. He'd never see her again. He'd go
on with his life, with his therapy, his job, his next operation.
It would be just him and Murphy.

It was four o'clock when Marcus motioned for the retriever to take his place under the robe. The dog would keep
her warm while he showered and got ready for the day. He
rolled over, grabbed the arm of the sofa and struggled to his
feet. Pain ripped up and down his legs as he made his way
to the bathroom with the aid of the two canes he kept under
the seat cushions. This was his daily walk, the walk the
therapists said was mandatory. Tears rolled down his cheeks
as he gritted his teeth. Inside the shower, he lowered himself
to the tile seat, turned on the water and let it beat at his legs
and body. He stayed there until the water turned cool.

It took him twenty minutes to dress. He was stepping into
his loafers when he heard the snowplow. He struggled, with
his canes, out to the living room and his chair. His lips were
white with the effort. It took every bit of fifteen minutes for
the pain to subside. He bent over, picked up the coffeepot,
and carried it to the kitchen where he rinsed it and made
fresh coffee. While he waited for it to perk he stared out the
window. Mr. Drizzoli and his two sons were maneuvering
the plows so he could get his van out of the driveway. The
younger boy was shoveling out his van. He turned on the
outside lights, opened the door, and motioned to the young-
ster to come closer. He asked about road conditions, the road
leading to the main house, and the weather in general. He
explained about the Cherokee. The boy promised to speak
with his father. They'd search it out and if it was driveable,
they'd bring it to the cottage. "There's a five gallon tank of
gas in the garage," Marcus said. From the leather pouch
attached to his chair, he withdrew a square white envelope:
Mr. Drizzoli's Christmas present. Cash.

"The phones are back on, Mr. Bishop," the boy volunteered.

Marcus felt his heart thump in his chest. He could unplug it. If he did that, he'd be no better than Keith what's-his-name. Then he thought about Morgan's anxious parents. Two cups of coffee on his little pull-out tray, Marcus maneuvered the chair into the living room. "Morgan, wake up. Wake her up, Murphy."

She looked so pretty, her hair tousled and curling about her face. He watched as she stretched luxuriously beneath his robe, watched the realization strike her that she was naked. He watched as she stared around her.

"Good morning. It will be daylight in a few minutes. My road is being plowed as we speak and I'm told the phone is working. You might want to get up and call your parents. Your clothes are in the dryer. My maintenance man is checking on your Jeep. If it's driveable, he'll bring it here. If not, they'll tow it to a garage."

Mo wrapped the robe around her and got to her feet. Talk about the bum's rush. She swallowed hard. Well, what had she expected? One night stands usually ended like this. Why had she expected anything different? She needed to say something. "If you don't mind, I'll take a shower and get dressed. Is it all right if I use the phone in the bedroom?"

"Of course." He'd hoped against hope that she'd call from the living room so he could hear the conversation. He watched as she made her way to the laundry room, coffee cup in hand. Watched as she juggled cup, clothing, and the robe. Murphy sat back on his haunches and howled. Marcus felt the fine hairs on the back of his neck stand on end. Murphy hadn't howled like this since the day of Marcey's funeral. He had to know Morgan was going away. He felt like howling himself.

Marcus watched the clock, watched the progress of the men outside the window. Thirty minutes passed and then thirty-five and forty.

Murphy barked wildly when he saw Drizzoli come to what he thought was too close to his master's property.

Inside the bedroom, with the door closed, Morgan sat down, fully dressed, on the bed. She dialed her parents' number, nibbling on her thumbnail as she waited for the phone to be picked up. "Mom, it's me."

"Thank God. We were worried sick about you, honey. Good Lord, where are you?"

"Someplace in Cherry Hill. The Jeep gave out and I had to walk. You won't believe this, but a dog found me. I'll tell you all about it when I get home. My host tells me the roads are cleared and they're checking my car now. I should be ready to leave momentarily. Did you have a nice Christmas?" She wasn't going to ask about Keith. She wasn't going to ask because suddenly she no longer cared if he showed up in front of the tree or not.

"Yes and no. It wasn't the same without you. Dad and I had our eggnog. We sang 'Silent Night,' off-key of course, and then we just sat and stared at the tree and worried about you. It was a terrible storm. I don't think I ever saw so much snow. Dad is whispering to me that he'll come and get you if the Jeep isn't working. How was your first Christmas away from home?"

"Actually, Mom, it was kind of nice. My host is a very nice man. He has this wonderful dog who found me. We had a turkey dinner that was pretty good. We even sang 'Jingle Bells.' "

"Well, honey, we aren't going anywhere so call us either way. I'm so relieved that you're okay. We called the state troopers, the police, everyone we could think of."

"I'm sorry, Mom. I should have listened to you and stayed put until the snow let up. I was just so anxious to get home." Now, *now* she'll say if Keith was there.

"Keith was here. He came by around eleven. He said it took him seven hours to drive from Manhattan to his mother's. He was terribly upset that you weren't here. This is just my opinion, but I don't think he was upset that you were stuck in the snow—it was more that he was here and where were you? I'm sorry, Morgan, I am just never going to like that young man. That's all I'm going to say on the matter. Dad feels the same way. Drive carefully, honey. Call us, okay?"

"Okay, Mom."

Morgan had to use her left hand to pry her right hand off the phone. She felt sick to her stomach suddenly. She dropped her head into her hands. What she had wanted for two long years, what she'd hoped and prayed for, had happened. She thought about the old adage: Be careful what you wish for because you might just get it. Now, she didn't want what she had wished for.

It was light out now, the young sun creeping into the room. The silver-framed photograph twinkled as the sun hit it full force. Who was she? She should have asked Marcus. Did he still love the dark-haired woman? He must have loved her a lot to keep her things out in the open, a constant reminder.

She'd felt such strange things last night. Sex with Keith had never been like it was with Marcus. Still, there were other things that went into making a relationship work. Then there was Marcus in his wheelchair. It surprised her that the wheelchair didn't bother her. What did surprise her was what she was feeling. And now it was time to leave. How was she supposed to handle that?

Her heart thumped again when she saw a flash of red go by the bedroom window. Her Jeep. It was running. She stood up, saluted the room, turned, and left.

Good-byes are hard, she thought. Especially this one. She felt shy, schoolgirlish, when she said, "Thanks for everything. I mean to keep my promise and send Murphy some steaks. Would you mind giving me your address? If you're ever in Wilmington, stop . . . you know, stop and . . . we can have a . . . reunion . . . I'm not good at this."

"I'm not, either. Here's my card. My phone number is on it. Call me anytime if you . . . if you want to talk. I listen real good."

Mo handed over her own card. "Same goes for me."

"You just needed some antifreeze. We put five gallons of gas in the tank. Drive carefully. I'm going to worry so call me when you get home."

"I'll do that. Thanks again, Marcus. If you ever want a building or a bridge designed, I'm yours for free. I mean that."

"I know you do. I'll remember."

Mo cringed. How polite they were, how stiff and formal. She couldn't walk away like this. She leaned over, her eyes meeting his, and kissed him lightly on the lips. "I don't think I'll ever forget my visit." *Tell me now, before I leave, about the dark-haired, smiling woman in the picture. Tell me you want me to come back for a visit. Tell me not to go. I'll stay. I swear to God, I'll stay. I'll never think about Keith, never mention his name. Say something.*

"It was a nice Christmas. I enjoyed spending it with you. I know Murphy enjoyed having you here with us. Drive carefully, and remember to call when you get home."

His voice was flat, cool. Last night was just what he said; *it was what it was.* Nothing more. She felt like wailing her despair, but she damn well wasn't going to give him the satisfaction. "I will," Mo said cheerfully. She frolicked with Murphy for a few minutes, whispering in his ear. "You take care of him, you hear? I think he tends to be a little stubborn. I have my ribbon and I'll keep it safe, always. I'll send those steaks Fed Ex." Because her tears were blinding her, Mo turned and didn't look at Marcus again. A second later she was outside in the cold, bracing air.

The Cherokee was warm, purring like a kitten. She tapped the horn, two light taps, before she slipped the gear into four-wheel drive. She didn't look back.

It was an interlude.

One of those rare happenings that occur once in a lifetime.

A moment in time.

In a little more than twenty-four hours, she'd managed to fall in love with a man in a wheelchair—and his dog.

She cried because she didn't know what else to do.

Mo's homecoming was everything she had imagined it would be. Her parents hugged her. Her mother wiped at her tears with the hem of an apron that smelled of cinnamon and vanilla. Her father acted gruff, but she could see the moistness in his eyes.

"How about some breakfast, honey?"

"Bacon and eggs sounds real good. Make sure the . . ."

"The yolk is soft and the white has brown lace around the edges. Snap-in-two bacon, three pieces of toast for dunking, and a small glass of juice. I know, Morgan. Lord, I'm just so glad you're home safe and sound. Dad's going to carry in your bags. Why don't you run upstairs and take a nice hot bath and put on some clothes that don't look like they belong in a thrift store."

"Good idea, Mom."

In the privacy of her room, she looked at the phone that had, as a teenager, been her lifeline to the outside world. All she had to do was pick it up, and she'd hear Marcus's voice. Should she do it now or wait till after her bath when she was decked out in clean clothes and makeup? She decided to wait. Marcus didn't seem the type to sit by the phone and wait for a call from a woman.

The only word she could think of to describe her bath was *delicious*. The silky feel of the water was full of Wild Jasmine bath oil, her favorite scent in the whole world. As she relaxed in the steamy wetness, she forced herself to think about Keith. She knew without asking that her mother had called Keith's mother after the phone call. Right now, she was so happy to be safe, she would force herself to tolerate Keith. All those presents she'd wrapped so lovingly. All that money she'd spent. Well, she was taking it all back when she returned to Delaware.

Mo heard her father open the bedroom door, heard the sound of her suitcases being set down, heard the rustle of the shopping bags. The tenseness left her shoulders when the door closed softly. She was alone with her thoughts. She wished for a portable phone so she could call Marcus. The thought of talking to him while she was in the bathtub sent shivers up and down her spine.

A long time later, Mo climbed from the tub. She dressed,

blow-dried her hair, and applied makeup, ever so sparingly, remembering that less is better. She pulled on a pair of Levis and a sweater that showed off her slim figure. She spritzed herself lightly with perfume, added pearl studs to her ears. She had to rummage in the drawer for thick wool socks. The closet yielded a pair of Nike Air sneakers she'd left behind on one of her visits.

In the kitchen her mother looked at her with dismay. "Is that what you're wearing?"

"Is something wrong with my sweater?"

"Well, no. I just thought . . . I assumed . . . you'd want to spiff up for . . . Keith. I imagine he'll be here pretty soon."

"Well, it better be pretty quick because I have an errand to do when I finish this scrumptious breakfast. I guess you can tell him to wait or tell him to come back some other time. Let's open our presents after supper tonight. Can we pretend it's Christmas Eve?"

"That's what Dad said we should do."

"Then we'll do it. Listen, don't tell Keith. I want it to be just us."

"If that's what you want, honey. You be careful when you're out. Just because the roads are plowed, it doesn't mean there won't be accidents. The weatherman said the highways were still treacherous."

"I'll be careful. Can I get anything for you when I'm out?"

"We stocked up on everything before the snow came. We're okay. Bundle up—it's real cold."

Mo's first stop was the butcher on Main Street. She ordered twelve porterhouse steaks and asked to have them sent Federal Express. She paid with her credit card. Her next stop was the mall in Menlo Park where she went directly to Gloria Jean's Coffee Shop. She ordered twelve pounds of flavored coffees and a mug with a painted picture of a golden retriever on the side, asking to have her order shipped Federal Express and paying again with her credit card.

She spent the balance of the afternoon browsing through

Nordstrom's department store—it was so full of people she felt claustrophobic. Still, she didn't leave.

At four o'clock she retraced her steps, stopped by Gloria Jean's for a takeout coffee, and drank it sitting on a bench. She didn't want to go home. Didn't want to face Keith. What she wanted to do was call Marcus. *And that's exactly what I'm going to do. I'm tired of doing what other people want me to do. I want to call him and I'm going to call him.* She went in search of a phone the minute she finished her coffee.

Credit card in one hand, Marcus's business card in the other, Mo placed her call. A wave of dizziness washed over her the minute she heard his voice. "It's Morgan Ames, Marcus. I said I'd call you when I got home. Well, I'm home. Actually, I'm in a shopping mall. Ah . . . my mother sent me out to . . . to return some things . . . my dad was on the phone, I couldn't call earlier."

"I was worried when I didn't hear from you. It only takes a minute to make a phone call."

He was worried and he was chastising her. Well, she deserved it. She liked the part that he was worried. "What are you doing?" she blurted.

"I'm thinking about dinner. Leftovers or Spam. Something simple. I'm sort of watching a football game. I think Murphy misses you. I had to go looking for him twice. He was back in my room lying in the pillows where you slept."

"Ah, that's nice. I Federal Expressed his steaks. They should get there tomorrow. I tied the red ribbon on the post of my bed. I'm taking it back to Wilmington with me. Will you tell him that?" Damn, how stupid could one person be?

"I'll tell him. How were the roads?"

"Bad, but driveable. My dad taught me to drive defensively. It paid off." This had to be the most inane conversation she'd ever had in her life. Why was her heart beating so fast? "Marcus, this is none of my business. I meant to ask you yesterday, but I forgot. Who is that lovely woman in the photograph in your room? If it's something you don't care to talk about, it's okay with me. It was just that she sort of looked like me a little. I was curious." She was babbling again.

"Her name was Marcey. She died in the accident I was in. I was wearing my seatbelt, she wasn't. I'd rather not talk about it. You're right, though—you do resemble her a little. Murph picked up on that right away. He pulled the towel off your head and kind of sniffed your hair. He wanted me to . . . to see the resemblance, I guess. He took her death real hard."

She was sorry she'd asked. "I'm sorry. I didn't mean to . . . I'm so sorry." She was going to cry now, any second. "I have to go now. Thank you again. Take care of yourself." The tears fell then, and she made no move to stop them. She was like a robot as she walked to the exit and the parking lot. Don't think about the phone call. Don't think about Marcus and his dog. Think about tomorrow when you're going to leave here. Shift into neutral.

She saw his car and winced. Only a teenager would drive a canary yellow Camaro. She swerved into the driveway. Here it was, the day she'd dreamed of for two long years.

"I'm home!"

"Look who's here, Mo," her mother said. That said, she tactfully withdrew, her father following close behind.

"Keith, it's nice to see you," Mo said stiffly. Who was this person standing in front of her, wearing sunglasses and a houndstooth cap? He reeked of Polo.

"I was here—where were you? I thought we had a date in front of your Christmas tree on Christmas Eve. Your parents were so worried. You look different, Mo," he said, trying to take her into his arms. She deftly sidestepped him and sat down.

"I didn't think you'd show," she said flatly.

"Why would you think a thing like that?" He seemed genuinely puzzled at her question.

"Better yet," Mo said, ignoring his question, "what have

you been doing these past two years? I need to know, Keith?"

His face took on a wary expression. "A little of this, a little of that. Work, eat, sleep, play a little. Probably the same things you did. I thought about you a lot. Often. Every day."

"But you never called. You never wrote."

"That was part of the deal. Marriage is a big commitment. People need to be sure before they take that step. I don't believe in divorce."

How virtuous his voice sounded. She watched, fascinated, as he fished around in his pockets until he found what he was looking for. He held the small box with a tiny red bow on it in the palm of his hand. "I'm sure now. I know you wanted to get engaged two years ago. I wasn't ready. I'm ready now." He held the box toward her, smiling broadly.

He got his teeth capped, Mo thought in amazement. She made no move to reach for the silver box.

"Aren't you excited? Don't you want to open it?"

"No."

"No *what?*"

"No, I'm not excited; no, I don't want the box. No, I don't want to get engaged and no, I don't want to get married. To you."

"Huh?" He seemed genuinely perplexed.

"What part of *no* didn't you understand?"

"But . . ."

"But *what*, Keith?"

"I thought . . . we agreed . . . it was a break for both of us. Why are you spoiling things like this? You always have such a negative attitude, Mo. What are you saying here?"

"I'm saying I had two long years to think about us. You and me. Until just a few days ago I thought . . . it would work out. Now, I know it won't. I'm not the same person and you certainly aren't the same person. Another thing, I wouldn't ride in that pimpmobile parked out front if you paid me. You smell like a pimp, too. I'm sorry. I'm grateful to you for this . . . whatever it was . . . hiatus. It was your idea, Keith. I want you to know, I was faithful to you." And she had been. She didn't make love with Marcus until Christmas Day, at which point she already knew it wasn't going to work out between her and Keith. "Look me in the eye, Keith, and tell me you were faithful to me. I knew it! You have a good life. Send me a Christmas card and I'll do the same."

"You're dumping me!" There was such outrage in Keith's voice, Mo burst out laughing.

"That's exactly what you did to me two years ago, but I was too dumb to see it. All those women you had, they wouldn't put up with your bullshit. That's why you're here now. No one else wanted you. I know you, Keith, better than I thought I did. I don't like the word *dump*. I'm breaking off our relationship because I don't love you anymore. Right now, for whatever it's worth, I wouldn't have time to work at a relationship anyway. I've decided to go into business for myself. Can we shake hands and promise to be friends?"

"Like hell! It took me seven goddamn hours to drive here from New York just so I could keep my promise. You weren't even here. At least I tried. I could have gone to Vail with my friends. You can take the responsibility for the termination of this relationship." He stomped from the room, the silver box secure in his pocket.

Mo sat down on the sofa. She felt lighter, buoyant somehow. "I feel, Mom, like someone just took fifty pounds off my shoulders. I wish I'd listened to you and Dad. You'd think at my age I'd have more sense. Did you see him? Is it me or was he always like that?"

"He was always like that, honey. I wasn't going to tell you, but under the circumstances, I think I will. I really don't think he would have come home this Christmas except for one thing. His mother always gives him a handsome check early in the month. This year she wanted him home for the holidays so she said she wasn't giving it to him until Christmas morning. If he'd gotten it ahead of time I think he would have gone to Vail. We weren't eavesdropping—he said it loud enough so his voice carried to the kitchen. Don't feel bad, Mo."

"Mom, I don't. That dinner you're making smells soooo good. Let's eat, open our presents, thank God for our wonderful family, and go to bed."

"Sounds good to me."

"I'm leaving in the morning, Mom. I have some things I need to . . . take care of."

"I understand."

"Merry Christmas, Mom."

Mo set out the following morning with a full gas tank, an extra set of warm clothes on the front seat, a brand new flashlight with six new batteries, a real shovel, foot warmers, a basket lunch that would feed her for a week, two pairs of mittens, a pair of fleece-lined boots, and the firm resolve never to take a trip without preparing for it. In the cargo area there were five shopping bags of presents that she would be returning to Wanamaker's over the weekend.

She kissed and hugged her parents, accepted change from her father for the tolls, honked her horn, and was off. Her plan was to stop in Cherry Hill. Why, she didn't know. Probably to make a fool out of herself again. Just the thought of seeing Marcus and Murphy made her blood sing.

She had a speech all worked out in her head, words she'd probably never say. She'd say, *Hi, I was on my way home and thought I'd stop for coffee.* After all, she'd just sent a dozen different kinds. She could help cook a steak for Murphy. Maybe Marcus would kiss her hello. Maybe he'd ask her to stay.

It wasn't until she was almost to the Cherry Hill exit that she realized Marcus hadn't asked if Keith showed up. That had to mean he wasn't interested in her. *It was what it was.* She passed the exit sign with tears in her eyes.

She tormented herself all of January and February. She picked up the phone a thousand times, and always put it back down. Phones worked two ways. He could call her. All she'd gotten from him was a scrawled note thanking her for the coffee and steaks. He did say Murphy was burying the bones under the pillows and that he'd become a coffee addict. The last sentence was personal. *I hope your delayed Christmas was everything you wanted it to be.* A large scrawled "M." finished off the note.

She must have written five hundred letters in response to that little note. None of which she mailed.

She was in love. Really in love. For the first time in her life.

And there wasn't a damn thing she could do about it. Unless she wanted to make a fool of herself again, which she had no intention of doing.

She threw herself into all the details it took to open a new business. She had the storefront, she'd ordered the vertical blinds, helped her father lay the carpet and tile. Her father had made three easels and three desks, in case she wanted to expand and hire help. Her mother wallpapered the kitchen, scrubbed the ancient appliances, and decorated the bathroom while she went out on foot and solicited business. Her grand opening was scheduled for April first.

She had two new clients and the promise of two more. If she was lucky, she might be able to repay her father's loan in three years instead of five.

On the other side of the bridge, Marcus Bishop wheeled his chair out onto his patio, Murphy alongside him. On the pull-out tray were two beers and the portable phone. He was restless, irritable. In just two weeks he was heading back to the hospital. The do-or-die operation he'd been living for, yet dreading. There were no guarantees, but the surgeon had said he was confident he'd be walking in six months. With extensive, intensive therapy. Well, he could handle that. Pain was his middle name. Maybe then . . . maybe then, he'd get up the nerve to call Morgan Ames and . . . and chat. He wondered if he dared intrude on her life with Keith. Still, there was nothing wrong with calling her, chatting about

Murphy. He'd be careful not to mention Christmas night and their love-making. "The best sex I ever had, Murph. You know me—too much too little too late or whatever that saying is. What's she see in that jerk? He is a jerk, she as much as said so. You're a good listener, Murph. Hell, let's call her and say . . . we'll say . . . what we'll do is . . . *hello* is good. Her birthday is coming up—so is mine. Maybe I should wait till then and send a card. Or, I could send flowers or a present. The thing is, I want to talk to her now. Here comes the mailman, Murph. Get the bag!"

Murphy ran to the doggie door and was back in a minute with a small burlap sack the mailman put the mail in. Murphy then dragged it to Marcus on the deck. He loved racing to the mailman, who always had dog biscuits as well as Mace in his pockets.

"Whoaoooo, would you look at this, Murph? It's a letter or a card from you know who. Jesus, here I am thinking about her and suddenly I get mail from her. That must mean something. Here goes. Ah, she opened her own business. The big opening day is April first. No April Fool's joke, she says. She hopes I'm fine, hopes you're fine, and isn't this spring weather gorgeous? She has five clients now, but had to borrow money from her father. She's not holding her breath waiting for someone to ask her to design a bridge. If we're ever in Wilmington we should stop and see her new office. That's it, Murph. What I could do is send her a tree. Everyone has a tree when they open a new office. Maybe some yellow roses. It's ten o'clock in the morning. They can have the stuff there by eleven. I can call at twelve and talk to her. That's it, that's what we'll do." Murphy's tail swished back and forth in agreement.

Marcus ordered the ficus tree and a dozen yellow roses. He was assured delivery would be made by twelve-thirty. He passed the time by speaking with his office help, sipping coffee, and throwing a cut-off broom handle for Murphy to fetch. At precisely 12:30, his heart started to hammer in his chest.

"Morgan Ames. Can I help you?"

"Morgan, it's Marcus Bishop. I called to congratulate you. I got your card today."

"Oh, Marcus, how nice of you to call. The tree is just what this office needed and the flowers are beautiful. That was so kind of you. How are you? How's Murphy?"

"We're fine. You must be delirious with all that's happening. How did Keith react to you opening your own business? For some reason I thought . . . assumed . . . that opening the business wasn't something you were planning on doing right away. Summer . . . or did I misunderstand?"

"No, you didn't misunderstand. I talked it over with my father and he couldn't find any reason why I shouldn't go for it now. I couldn't have done it without my parents' help. As for Keith . . . it didn't work out. He did show up. It was my decision. He just . . . wasn't the person I thought he was. I don't know if you'll believe or even understand this, but all I felt was an overwhelming sense of relief."

"Really? If it's what you want, then I'm happy for you. You know what they say, if it's meant to be, it will be." He felt dizzy with her news.

"So, when do you think you can take a spin down here to see my new digs?"

"Soon. Do you serve refreshments?"

"I can and will. We have birthdays coming up. I'd be more than happy to take you out to dinner by way of celebration. If you have the time."

"I'll make the time. Let me clear my decks and get back to you. The only thing that will hinder me is my scheduled operation. There's every possibility it will be later this week."

"I'm not going anywhere, Marcus. Whenever is good for you will be good for me. I wish you the best. If there's anything I can do . . . now, that's foolish, isn't it? Like I can really do something. Sometimes I get carried away. I meant . . ."

"I know what you meant, Morgan, and I appreciate it. Murphy is . . . he misses you."

"I miss both of you. Thanks again for the tree and the flowers."

"Enjoy them. We'll talk again, Morgan."

The moment Marcus broke the connection his clenched fist shot in the air. "Yessss!" Murphy reacted to this strange display by leaping onto Marcus's lap. "She loves the tree and the flowers. She blew off what's-his-name. What that means to you and me, Murph, is maybe we still have a shot. If only this damn operation wasn't looming. I need to think, to plan. I'm gonna work this out. Maybe, just maybe we can turn things around. She invited me to dinner. Hell, she offered to pay for it. That has to mean something. I take it to mean she's interested. In *us,* because we're a package deal." The retriever squirmed and wiggled, his long tail lolling happily.

"I feel good, Murph. Real good."

Mo hung up the phone, her eyes starry. Sending the office announcement had been a good idea after all. She stared at the flowers and at the huge ficus tree sitting in the corner. They made all the difference in the world. He'd asked about Keith and she'd responded by telling him the truth. It had come out just right. She wished now that she had asked about the operation, asked why he was having it. Probably to alleviate the pain he always seemed to be in. At what point would referring to his condition, or his operation, be stepping over the line? She didn't know, didn't know anyone she could ask. Also, it was none of her business, just like Marcey wasn't any of her business. If he wanted her to know, if he wanted to talk about it, he would have said something, opened up the subject.

It didn't matter. He'd called and they sort of had a date planned. She was going to have to get a new outfit, get her hair and nails done. Ohhhhh, she was going to sleep so good tonight. Maybe she'd even dream about Marcus Bishop.

Her thoughts sustained her for the rest of the day and into the evening.

* * *

Two days later, Marcus Bishop grabbed the phone on the third ring. He announced himself in a sleepy voice, then waited. He jerked upright a second later. "Jesus, Stewart, what time is it? Five o'clock! You want me there at eleven? Yeah, yeah, sure. I just have to make arrangements for Murphy. No, no, I won't eat or drink anything. Don't tell me not to worry, Stewart. I'm already sweating. I guess I'll see you later."

"C'mon, Murph, we're going to see your girlfriend. Morgan. We're going to see Morgan and ask her if she'll take care of you until I get on my feet or . . . we aren't going to think about . . . we're going to think positive. Get your leash, your brush, and all that other junk you take with you. Put it by the front door in the basket. Go on."

He whistled. He sang. He would have danced a jig if it was possible. He didn't bother with a shower—they did that for him at the hospital. He did shave, though. After all, he was going to see Morgan. She might even give him a good luck kiss. One of those blow-your-socks-off kisses.

At the front door he stared at the array Murphy had stacked up. The plastic laundry basket was filled to overflowing. Curiously, Marcus leaned over and poked among the contents. His leash, his brush, his bag of vitamins, his three favorite toys, his blanket, his pillow, one of his old slippers and one of Marcey's that he liked to sleep with, the mesh bag that contained his shampoo and flea powder.

"She's probably going to give us the boot when she sees all of this. You sure you want to take all this stuff?" Murphy backed up, barking the three short sounds that Marcus took for affirmation. He barked again and again, backing up, running forward, a sign that Marcus was supposed to follow him. In the laundry room, Murphy pawed the dryer door. Marcus opened it and watched as the dog dragged out the large yellow towel and took it to the front door.

"I'll be damned. Okay, just add it to the pile. I'm sure it will clinch the deal."

Ten minutes later they were barreling down I-95. Forty minutes after that, with barely any traffic on the highway, Marcus located the apartment complex where Morgan lived. He used up another ten minutes finding the entrance to her building. Thank God for the handicapped ramp and door. Inside the lobby, his eyes scanned the row of mailboxes and buzzers. He pressed down on the button and held his finger steady. When he heard her voice through the speaker he grinned.

"I'm in your lobby and I need you to come down. Now! Don't worry about fixing up. Remember, I've seen you at your worst."

"What's wrong?" she said, stepping from the elevator.

"Nothing. Everything. Can you keep Murphy for me? My surgeon called me an hour ago and he wants to do the operation this afternoon. The man scheduled for today came down with the flu. I have all Murphy's gear. I don't know what else to do. Can you do it?"

"Of course. Is this his stuff?"

"Believe it or not, he packed himself. He couldn't wait to get here. I can't thank you enough. The guy that usually keeps him is off in Peru on a job. I wouldn't dream of putting him in a kennel. I'd cancel my operation first."

"It's not a problem. Good luck. Is there anything else I can do?"

"Say a prayer. Well, thanks again. He likes real food. When you go through his stuff you'll see he didn't pack any."

"Okay."

"What do you call that thing you're wearing?" Marcus asked curiously.

"It's my bathrobe. It used to be my grandfather's. It's old, soft as silk. It's like an old friend. But better yet, it's warm. These are slippers on my feet even though they look like fur muffs. Again, they keep my feet warm. These things in my hair are curlers. It's who I am," Mo said huffily.

"I wasn't complaining. I was just curious. I bet you're a

knockout when you're wearing makeup. Do you wear makeup?"

Mo's insecurities took over. She must look like she just got off the boat. She could feel a flush working its way up to her neck and face. She didn't mean to say it, didn't think she'd said it until she saw the look on Marcus's face. "Why, did Marcey wear lots of makeup? Well, I'm sorry to disappoint you, but I wear very little. I can't afford the pricey stuff she used. What you see is what you get. In other words, take it or leave it and don't ever again compare me to your wife or your girlfriend." She turned on her heel, the laundry basket in her arms, Murphy behind her.

"Hold on! What wife? What girlfriend? What pricey makeup are you talking about? Marcey was my twin sister. I thought I told you that."

"No, you didn't tell me that," Mo called over her shoulder. Her back to him, she grinned from ear to ear. Ahhh, life was lookin' good. "Good luck," she said, as the elevator door swished shut.

In her apartment with the door closed and bolted, Mo sat down on the living room floor with the big, silky dog. "Let's see what we have here," she said, checking the laundry basket. "Hmmm, I see your grooming is going to take a lot of time. I need to tell you that we have a slight problem. Actually, it's a large, as in *very large,* problem. No pets are allowed in this apartment complex. Oh, you brought the yellow towel. That was sweet, Murphy," she said, hugging the retriever. "I hung the red ribbon on my bed." She was talking to this dog like he was a person and was going to respond any minute. "It's not just a little problem, it's a big problem. I guess we sleep at the office. I can buy a sleeping bag and bring your gear there. There's a kitchen and a bathroom. Maybe my dad can come down and rig up a shower. Then again, maybe not. I can always come back to the apartment and shower. We can cook in the office or we can eat out. I missed you. I think about you and Marcus a lot. I thought I would never hear from him again. I thought he was married. Can you beat that?

"Okay, I'm going to take my shower, make some coffee, and then we'll head to my new office. I'm sure it's nothing like Marcus's office and I know he takes you there with him. It's a me office, if you know what I mean. It's so good to have someone to talk to. I wish you could talk back."

Mo marched into the kitchen to look in the refrigerator. Leftover Chinese that should have been thrown out a week ago, leftover Italian that should have been thrown out two weeks ago, and last night's pepper steak that she'd cooked herself. She warmed it in the microwave and set it down for Murphy, who lapped it up within seconds. "Guess that will hold you till this evening."

Dressed in a professional, spring-like suit, Mo gathered her briefcase and all the stuff she carried home each evening into a plastic shopping bag. Murphy's leash and his toys went into a second bag. At the last moment she rummaged in the cabinet for a water bowl. "Guess we need to take your bed and blanket, too." Two trips later, the only thing left to do was call her mother.

"Mo, what's wrong? Why are you calling this early in the morning?"

"Mom, I need your help. If Dad isn't swamped, do you think you guys could come down here?" She related the events of the past hours. "I can't live in the office—health codes and all that. I need you to find me an apartment that will take a dog. I know this sounds stupid, but is it possible, do you think, to find a house that will double as an office? If I have to suck up the money I put into the storefront, I will. I might be able to sublease it, but I don't have the time to look around. I have so much work, Mom. All of a sudden it happened. It almost seems like the day the sign went up, everybody who's ever thought about hiring an architect chose me. I'm not complaining. Can you help me?"

"Of course. Dad's at loose ends this week. It's that retirement thing. He doesn't want to travel, he doesn't want to garden, he doesn't know what he wants. Just last night he was talking about taking a Julia Child cooking course. We'll get ready and leave within the hour." Her voice dropped to a whisper. "You should see the sparkle in his eyes—he's ready now. We'll see you in a bit."

Once they reached the office, Murphy settled in within seconds. A square patch of sun under the front window became his. His red ball, a rubber cat with a hoarse squeak, and his latex candy cane were next to him. He nibbled on a soup bone that was almost as big as his head.

Mo worked steadily without a break until her parents walked through the door at ten minutes past noon. Murphy eyed them warily until he saw Mo's enthusiastic greeting, at which point he joined in, licking her mother's outstretched hand and offering his paw to her father.

"Now, that's what I call a real gentleman. I feel a lot better about you being here alone now that you have this dog," her father said.

"It's just temporary, Dad. Marcus will take him back as soon as . . . well, I don't know exactly. Dad, I am so swamped. I'm also having a problem with this . . . take a look, give me your honest opinion. The client is coming in at four and I'm befuddled. The heating system doesn't work the way he wants it installed. I have to cut out walls, move windows—and he won't want to pay for the changes."

"In a minute. Your mother and I decided that I will stay here and help you. She's going out with a realtor at twelve-thirty. We called from the car phone and set it all up. We were specific with your requirements so she won't be taking your mother around to things that aren't appropriate. Knowing your mother, I'm confident she'll have the perfect location by five o'clock this evening. Why don't you and your mother visit for a few minutes while I take a look at these blueprints?"

"I think you should hire him, Mo," her mother stage-whispered. "He'd probably work for nothing. A couple of days a week would be great. I could stay down here with him and cook for you, walk your dog. We'd be more than glad to do it, Mo, if you think it would work and we wouldn't be infringing on your privacy."

"I'd love it, Mom. Murphy isn't my dog. I wish he was. He saved my life. What can I say?"

"You can tell me about Marcus Bishop. The real skinny, and don't tell me there isn't a skinny to tell. I see that sparkle in your eyes and it isn't coming from this dog."

"Later, okay? I think your real estate person is here. Go get 'em, Mom. Remember, I need a place as soon as possible. Otherwise I sleep here in the office in a sleeping bag. If I break my lease by having a pet, I don't get my security deposit back and it was a hefty one. If you can find something for me it will work out perfectly since my current lease is up the first of May. I'm all paid up. I appreciate it, Mom."

"That's what parents are for, sweetie. See you. John . . . did you hear me?"

"Hmmmnn."

Mo winked at her mother.

Father and daughter worked steadily, stopping just long enough to walk Murphy and eat a small pizza they had delivered. When Mo's client walked through the door at four o'clock, Mo introduced her father as her associate, John Ames.

"Now, Mr. Caruthers, this is what Morgan and I came up with. You get everything you want with the heating system. See this wall? What we did was . . ."

Knowing her client was in good hands, Mo retired to the kitchen to make coffee. She added some cookies to a colorful tray at the last moment. When she entered the office, tray in hand, her father was shaking hands and smiling. "Mr. Caruthers liked your idea. He gets what he wants plus the atrium. He's willing to absorb the extra three hundred."

"I'm going to be relocating sometime in the next few weeks, Mr. Caruthers. Since I've taken on an associate, I need more room. I'll notify you of my new address and phone number. If you happen to know anyone who would be interested in a sublease, call me."

Caruthers was gone less than five minutes when Helen Ames bustled through the door, the realtor in tow. "I found it! The perfect place! An insurance agent who had his office in his home is renting it. It's empty. You can move in tonight or tomorrow. The utilities are on, and he pays for them. It was part of the deal. It's wonderful, Mo—there's even a fenced yard for Murphy. I took the liberty of okaying your move. Miss Oliver has a client who does odd jobs and has his own truck. He's moving your furniture as we speak. All we have to do is pack up your personal belongings and Dad and I can do that with your help. You can be settled by tonight. The house is in move-in condition. That's a term real estate people use," she said knowledgeably. "Miss Oliver has agreed to see if she can sublease this place. Tomorrow, her man will move the office. At the most, Mo, you'll lose half a day's work. With Dad helping you, you'll get caught up in no time. There's a really nice garden on the side of the house and a magnificent wisteria bush you're going to love. Plus twelve tomato plants. The insurance man who owns the house is just glad that someone like us is renting. It's a three-year lease with an option to buy. His wife's mother lives in Florida and she wants to be near her since she's in failing health. I just love it when things work out for all parties involved. He didn't have one bit of a problem with the dog after I told him Murphy's story."

Everything worked out just the way her mother said it would.

The April showers gave way to May flowers. June sailed in with warm temperatures and bright sunshine. The only flaw in Mo's life was the lack of communication where Marcus was concerned.

Shortly after the Fourth of July, Mo piled Murphy into the Cherokee on a bright sunshiny Sunday and headed for Cherry Hill. "Something's wrong—I just feel it," she muttered to the dog all the way up the New Jersey Turnpike.

Murphy was ecstatic when the Jeep came to a stop outside his old home. He raced around the side of the house, barking and growling, before he slithered through his doggie door. On the other side, he continued to bark and then he howled.

With all the doors locked, Mo had no choice but to go in the same way she'd gone through on Christmas Eve.

Inside, things were neat and tidy, but there was a thick layer of dust over everything. Obviously Marcus had not been here for a very long time.

"I don't even know what hospital he went to. Where is he, Murphy? He wouldn't give you up, even to me. I know he wouldn't." She wondered if she had the right to go through Marcus's desk. Out of concern. She sat down and thought about her birthday. She'd been so certain that he'd send a card, one of those silly cards that left the real meaning up in the air, but her birthday had gone by without any kind of acknowledgment from him.

"Maybe he did give you up, Murphy. I guess he isn't interested in me." She choked back a sob as she buried her head in the retriever's silky fur. "Okay, come on, time to leave. I know you want to stay and wait, but we can't. We'll come back again. We'll come back as often as we have to. That's a promise, Murphy."

On the way back to her house, Mo passed her old office and was surprised to see that it had been turned into a Korean vegetable stand. She'd known Miss Oliver had subleased it with the rent going directly to the management company, but that was all she knew.

"Life goes on, Murphy. What's that old saying, time waits for no man? Something like that anyway."

Summer moved into autumn and before Mo knew it, her parents had sold their house and rented a condo on the outskirts of Wilmington. Her father worked full-time in her office while her mother joined every woman's group in the state of Delaware. It was the best of all solutions.

Thanksgiving was spent in her parents' condo with her mother doing all the cooking. The day was uneventful, with both Mo and her father falling asleep in the living room after dinner. Later, when she was attaching Murphy's leash, her mother said, quite forcefully, "You two need to get some help in that office. I'm appointing myself your new secretary and first thing Monday morning you're going to start accepting applications for associates. It's almost Christmas and none of us has done any shopping. It's the most wonderful time of the year and last year convinced us that . . . time is precious. We all need to enjoy life more. Dad and I are going to take a trip the day after Christmas. We're going to drive to Florida. I don't want to hear a word, John. And you, Mo, when was the last time you had a vacation? You can't even remember. Well, we're closing your office on the twentieth of December and we aren't reopening until January second. That's the final word. If your clients object, let them go somewhere else."

"Okay, Mom," Mo said meekly.

"As usual, you're right, Helen," John said just as meekly.

"I knew you two would see it my way. We're going to take up golf when we get to Florida."

"Helen, for God's sake. I hate golf. I refuse to hit a silly little ball with a stick and there's no way I'm going to wear plaid pants and one of those damn hats with a pom-pom on it."

"We'll see," Helen sniffed.

"On that thought, I'll leave you."

At home, curled up in bed with Murphy alongside her, Mo turned on the television that would eventually lull her to sleep. She felt wired up, antsy for some reason. Here it was, almost Christmas, and Marcus Bishop was still absent from her life. She thought about the many times she'd called Bishop Engineering, only to be told Mr. Bishop was out of town and couldn't be reached. "The hell with you, Mr. Marcus Bishop. You gotta be a real low-life to stick me with your dog and then forget about him. What kind of man does that make you? What was all that talk about loving him? He misses you." Damn, she was losing it. She had to stop talking to herself or she was going to go over the edge.

Sensing her mood, Murphy snuggled closer. He licked at her cheeks, pawed her chest. "Forget what I just said, Murphy. Marcus loves you—I know he does. He didn't forget you, either. I think, and this is just my own opinion, but I think something went wrong with his operation and he's recovering somewhere. I think he was just saying words when he said he was used to the chair and it didn't bother him. It does. What if they ended up cutting off his legs? Oh, God," she wailed. Murphy growled, the hair on the back of his head standing on end. "Ignore that, too, Murphy. No such thing happened. I'd feel something like that."

She slept because she was weary and because when she cried she found it difficult to keep her eyes open.

"What are you going to do, honey?" Helen Ames asked as Mo closed the door to the office.

"I'm going upstairs to the kitchen and make a chocolate cake. Mom, it's December twentieth. Five days till Christmas. Listen, I think you and Dad made the right decision to leave for Florida tomorrow. You both deserve sunshine for the holidays. Murphy and I will be fine. I might even take him to Cherry Hill so he can be home for Christmas. I feel like I should do that for him. Who knows, you guys might love Florida and want to retire there. There are worse things, Mom. Whatever you do, don't make Dad wear those plaid pants. Promise me?"

"I promise. Tell me again, Mo, that you don't mind spending Christmas alone with the dog."

"Mom, I really and truly don't mind. We've all been like accidents waiting to happen. This is a good chance for me to laze around and do nothing. You know I was never big on New Year's. Go, Mom. Call me when you get there and if I'm not home, leave a message. Drive carefully, stop often."

"Good night, Mo."

"Have a good trip, Mom."

On the morning of the twenty-third of December, Mo woke early, let Murphy out, made herself some bacon and eggs, and wolfed it all down. During the night she'd had a dream that she'd gone to Cherry Hill, bought a Christmas tree, decorated it, cooked a big dinner for her and Murphy, and . . . then she'd awakened. Well, she was going to live the dream.

"Wanna go home, big guy? Get your stuff together. We're gonna get a tree, and do the whole nine yards. Tomorrow it will be a full year since I met you. We need to celebrate."

A little after the noon hour, Mo found herself dragging a Douglas fir onto Marcus's back patio. As before, she crawled through the doggie door after the dog and walked through the kitchen to the patio door. It took her another hour to locate the box of Christmas decorations. With the fireplaces going, the cottage warmed almost immediately.

The wreath with the giant red bow went on the front door. Back inside, she added the lights to the tree and put all the colorful decorations on the branches. On her hands and knees, she pushed the tree stand gently until she had it perfectly arranged in the corner. It was heavenly, she thought sadly as she placed the colorful poinsettias around the hearth. The only thing missing was Marcus.

Mo spent the rest of the day cleaning and polishing. When she finished her chores, she baked a cake and prepared a quick poor man's stew with hamburger meat.

Mo slept on the couch because she couldn't bring herself to sleep in Marcus's bed.

Christmas Eve dawned, gray and overcast. It felt like snow, but the weatherman said there would be no white Christmas this year.

Dressed in blue jeans, sneakers, and a warm flannel shirt, Mo started the preparations for Christmas Eve dinner. The house was redolent with the smell of frying onions, the scent of the tree, and the gingerbread cookies baking in the oven. She felt almost light-headed when she looked at the tree with the pile of presents underneath, presents her mother had warned her not to open, presents for Murphy, and a present for Marcus. She would leave it behind when they left after New Year's.

At one o'clock, Mo slid the turkey into the oven. Her

plum pudding, made from scratch, was cooling on the counter. The sweet potatoes and marshmallows sat alongside the pudding. A shaker of sesame seeds and the broccoli were ready to be cooked when the turkey came out of the oven. She took one last look around the kitchen, and at the table she'd set for one, before she retired to the living room to watch television.

Murphy leaped from the couch, the hair on his back stiff. He growled and started to pace the room, racing back and forth. Alarmed, Mo got off the couch to look out the window. There was nothing to see but the barren trees around the house. She switched on more lights, even those on the tree. As a precaution against what, she didn't know. She locked all the doors and windows. Murphy continued to growl and pace. Then the low, deep growls were replaced with high-pitched whines, but he made no move to go out his doggie door. Mo closed the drapes and turned the floodlights on outside. She could feel herself start to tense up. Should she call the police? What would she say? My dog's acting strange? Damn.

Murphy's cries and whines were so eerie she started to come unglued. Perhaps he wasn't one of those dogs that were trained to protect owner, hearth, and home. Since she'd had him he'd never been put to the test. To her, he was just a big animal who loved unconditionally.

In a moment of blind panic she rushed around the small cottage checking the inside dead bolts. The doors were stout, solid. She didn't feel one bit better.

The racket outside was worse and it all seemed to be coming from the kitchen area. She armed herself with a carving knife in one hand and a cast iron skillet in the other. Murphy continued to pace and whine. She eyed the doggie door warily, knowing the retriever was itching to use it, but he'd understood her iron command of *No*.

She waited.

When she saw the doorknob turn, she wondered if she would have time to run out the front door and into her

Cherokee. She was afraid to chance it, afraid Murphy would bolt once he was outside.

She froze when she saw the thick vinyl strips move on the doggie door. Murphy saw it, too, and let out an ear-piercing howl. Mo sidestepped to the left of the opening, skillet held at shoulder height, the carving knife in much the same position.

She saw his head and part of one shoulder. "Marcus! What are you doing coming in Murphy's door?" Her shoulders sagged with relief.

"All the goddamn doors are locked and bolted. I'm stuck. What the hell are you doing here in my house? With my dog yet."

"I brought him home for Christmas. He missed you. I thought . . . you could have called, Marcus, or sent a card. I swear to God, I thought you died on the operating table and no one at your company wanted to tell me. One lousy card, Marcus. I had to move out of my apartment because they don't allow animals. I gave up my office. For your dog. Well, here he is. I'm leaving and guess what—I don't give one little shit if you're stuck in that door or not. You damn well took almost a year out of my life. That's not fair and it's not right. You have no excuse and even if you do, I don't want to hear it."

"Open the goddamn door! Now!"

"Up yours, Marcus Bishop!"

"Listen, we're two reasonably intelligent adults. Let's discuss this rationally. There's an answer for everything."

"Have a Merry Christmas. Dinner is in the oven. Your tree is in the living room, all decorated, and there's a wreath on the front door. Your dog is right here. I guess that about covers it."

"You can't leave me stuck like this."

"You wanna bet? Toy with *my* affections, will you? Not likely. Stick *me* with your dog! You're a bigger jerk than Keith ever was. And I fell for your line of bullshit! I guess I'm the stupid one."

"Morgannnn!"

Mo slammed her way through the house to the front door. Murphy howled. She stooped down. "I'm sorry. You belong with him. I do love you—you're a wonderful companion and friend. I won't ever forget how you saved my life. From time to time I'll send you some steaks. You take care of that . . . that big boob, you hear?" She hugged the dog so hard he barked.

She was struggling with the garage door when she felt herself being pulled backward. To her left she heard Murphy bark ominously.

"You're going to listen to me whether you like it or not. Look at me when I talk to you," Marcus Bishop said as he whirled her around.

Her anger and hostility dropped away. "Marcus, you're on your feet! You can walk! That's wonderful!" The anger came back as swiftly as it had disappeared. "It still doesn't excuse your silence for nine whole months."

"Look, I sent cards and flowers. I wrote you letters. How in the damn hell was I supposed to know you moved?"

"You didn't even tell me what hospital you were going to. I tried calling till I was blue in the face. Your office wouldn't tell me anything. Furthermore, the post office, for a dollar, will tell you what my new address is. Did you ever think of that?"

"No. I thought you . . . well, what I thought was . . . you absconded with my dog. I lost the card you gave me. I got discouraged when I heard you moved. I'm sorry. I'm willing to take all the blame. I had this grand dream that I was going to walk into your parents' house on Christmas Eve and stand by your tree with you. My operation wasn't the walk in the park the surgeon more or less promised. I had to have a second one. The therapy was so intensive it blew my mind. I'm not whining here, I'm trying to explain. That's all I have to say. If you want to keep Murphy, it's okay. I had no idea . . . he loves you. Hell, *I* love you."

"You do?"

"Damn straight I do. You're all I thought about during my recovery. It was what kept me going. I even went by that

Korean grocery store today and guess what? Take a look at this!" he held out a stack of cards and envelopes. "It seems they can't read English. They were waiting for you to come and pick up the mail. They said they liked the flowers I sent from time to time."

"Really, Marcus!" She reached out to accept the stack of mail. "How'd you get out of that doggie door?" she asked suspiciously.

Marcus snorted. "Murphy pushed me out. Can we go into the house now and talk like two civilized people who love each other?"

"I didn't say I loved you."

"Say it!" he roared.

"Okay, okay, I love you."

"What else?"

"I believe you and I love your dog, too."

"Are we going to live happily ever after even if I'm rich and handsome?"

"Oh, yes, but that doesn't matter. I loved you when you were in the wheelchair. How are all your . . . parts?"

"Let's find out."

Murphy nudged both of them as he herded them toward the front door.

"I'm going to carry you over the threshold."

"Oh, Marcus, really!"

"Sometimes you simply talk too much." He kissed her as he'd never kissed her before.

"I like that. Do it again, and again, and again."

He did.

Dear Readers,

Josh and Angel's story really began when my husband and I took a trip to Savannah. Being history buffs, we visited one of the Civil War forts in the area, and I became fascinated by the discovery that General Sherman and his men had arrived in a conquered Savannah on Christmas Eve. What must it have been like for the beleaguered, near-starving population to be occupied by Sherman and his Union forces? What sort of Christmas could they have had?

And what would it have been like for Angel Summers when the only man she ever loved returned to his homeland a traitor—a doctor in the Union Army?

I hope you enjoy Josh and Angel's story and have as much fun reading it as I did writing it.

All best wishes,

Kat Martin

CHRISTMAS ANGEL

Kat Martin

One

Yankees. More damn blue-belly Yanks. Angel Summers's lips went thin just to look at them. She swept back her skirts to let one of them pass, then glared at his blue-coated back with all the venom that had built inside her these four long years.

Just thinking of the Federal troops who had occupied Savannah for almost twelve months made a bad taste surface in her mouth. She swallowed to chase it away, but the bitter taste of defeat remained. She wondered if it would ever completely fade.

Lifting her chin, determined to ignore the soldiers making their way along the boardwalk, a new batch that had arrived three days ago on the military train from Atlanta, Angel stepped into the open door of Whistler's Dry Goods store.

"Mornin', Miz Summers." The balding merchant stood behind the counter, a green leather apron tied around his ample girth.

"Good mornin', Mr. Whistler." She asked about his wife and daughter's health, and he asked about her little brother, the only member of her family left since the war. "Willie's just fine. Growin' like a weed. He's gonna be even taller than our daddy."

She didn't like to think of their father, killed in the fighting at Shiloh, or her mother, who had taken to her bed not long after and died of a broken heart. Instead she thanked God for sparing little Willie. William Summers, Jr., blond and blue-eyed, just as she was. Seven-year-old Willie, who was now her whole world.

"The boy is surely full of mischief," she said with a smile, "but he's smart as a whip. He loves to read, and already he can cipher faster than I can." She didn't say he was also desperately lonely, that he ached for his parents, for the loving home they'd all shared before the war.

She didn't say that she ached for them, too. That she missed the days of grandeur when she was the belle of Summers End, her family's cotton plantation, and every young man in Savannah was out to capture her hand.

She tried not to think of those days anymore. It hurt too much when she looked down at her threadbare clothes, at the white pique cuffs on her blue wool dress that were frayed but finely mended, at the worn, pill-sized balls in the palms of her white cotton gloves, the mended holes in her stockings.

Four years ago, wearing such clothing would have been unheard of. She had dressed in silks and satins then, worn hoops so large they barely fit through the huge, carved front door. Now her hoops were discarded for more practical clothes, like the ones she had on.

And she was lucky to have those.

"What can I get you, Miz Summers?" The merchant scratched his balding head. "Whatever it is, it's likely we'll be out of it." The shelves of the store were nearly stripped bare. Only remnants remained, mostly bags of dried fruit, a few kegs of salt pork, some salted cod, a crate of sugar cones, and a few meager sacks of flour. A half-empty barrel of pickles sat in the corner. The cracker barrel was empty and covered with dust.

Supplies were a luxury, the shortages even worse since the Yankees had occupied the city.

"I just need a can of baking powder, Mr. Whistler. Christmas is coming. I was hoping to do some special cooking for the holidays, but it looks like it won't be much. I'm afraid the cow's gone dry."

The merchant simply nodded. Nothing was easy these days.

She paid for the baking powder and Mr. Whistler put it into her basket.

"There was one new shipment that come in," he said. "Yard goods from down to the mill near Charleston. Some of it's real purty." His glance ran over her mended dress. "You might want to have a look."

Ignoring the wash of color that rose into her cheeks, Angel headed toward the wall where he pointed, then stood staring at the beautiful lengths of cloth. A green plaid tartan wool, a calico cotton, some plain black bombazine for mourning. She hadn't dressed in mourning for over a year. She vowed that in the streets of Savannah, she had seen so much black she would never wear the hideous color again.

She ran a finger lovingly over a length of rich plum velvet. The cloth was so fine it made her ache inside just to touch it. It had been years since she'd worn anything so lovely—not since her girlhood, not since the days before the war when the future had stretched so shiny bright in front of her. When her life had been filled with joy and she had been so very much in love.

She eyed the fabrics a little while longer, enjoying the starchy smells and luxurious feel, escaping from thoughts that only brought pain. Then heavy footfalls caught her attention, swinging her mind in a different direction. She felt his presence even before he spoke and for an instant she wondered if her thoughts had somehow conjured him.

"Good morning . . . Angel . . ."

The words whispered past her ear and her breath caught inside her. She didn't need to turn to recognize the man who stood so near. The man she hadn't seen in over four years.

She pivoted slowly to face him, her heart thumping a maddening tattoo. He was taller than she remembered, his skin a burnished, suntanned hue nearly as dark as his thick chestnut hair. His shoulders were wider, layered with muscle, his eyes a darker brown than she recalled.

"Joshua . . ." With his winsome smile, dark eyes, and

finely arched brows, he'd been the handsomest boy in Chatham County. Now Josh Coltrane was a man, and the creases beside his eyes and the hard line of his jaw only made him more attractive.

"I saw you walk in," he said. "It's good to see you, Angel."

Dear God, Josh was here. A flesh-and-blood man standing right in front of her. Memories rushed in. The first time they had danced, the first time he had kissed her beneath the mistletoe at Christmas just this time of year. The ache returned, stronger than before, a pain she had dealt with, she thought. Josh was alive. She hadn't known for sure, hadn't allowed herself to care one way or the other. She took a deep breath, forcing a stiffness into her spine and courage into her suddenly weakened limbs.

"My name is Angela. I wish I could say it was good to see you, Josh, but it isn't. I can't believe you would have the nerve to come back here."

The smile on his beautiful mouth slid away. "The war's over—in case you haven't noticed. I'm still in the army, which means I go wherever they send me. I'm assigned to the hospital at Fort James Jackson."

His dark blue uniform fit him perfectly, stretching across his broad shoulders, tapering to a narrow waist, the color a glaring reminder of why they had parted. A stripe ran the length of his long, lean legs, and high black boots rose to his knees. She pulled her gaze back to his face, tried to ignore the shivery feeling inside her.

"That's right," she said. "How could I have forgotten? It's Dr. Coltrane now." She studied the gold bars on his shoulders—he was a captain, but also a Union doctor.

"Funny . . ." His eyes ran over her from head to foot, unreadable as they assessed her. "I haven't forgotten a single thing about you, Angel."

Her pulse went faster. She forced her chin up a notch. "I told you my name is—"

"Sorry, sweeting, I don't take orders from you. I never

did, if you recall." A corner of his mouth curved faintly. "There was a time that was something you liked about me."

"There was a time you weren't a traitor—a dirty, blue-belly Yank."

His jaw went tight. "My mother was born in Pennsylvania. I went to medical school there. I was as much a Northerner as I was from the South. I had to follow my conscience. I told you that the day I left."

"Yes, you did. And I told you that if you joined the Union, as far as I was concerned you were dead. I meant what I said. Now if you'll excuse me, Captain Coltrane, I have better things to do than waste my time talking to a good for nothin' Yank."

She started toward the door, her heart still thudding in a way she wished it wouldn't, when the bell above the church at the end of the street began to clang. This time of day, the frantic ringing of iron could only mean trouble, and an unwelcome shiver ran down her spine.

"What's going on?" Josh asked, coming up beside her just as she opened the door.

"I—I don't know. Everybody's running toward the train station."

He glanced off toward the tracks that had been repaired and put back into service since the end of the war. They disappeared into the forest—and so did a goodly portion of Savannah's townspeople.

Angel stopped Eliza Barkley, her closest neighbor, as the heavyset woman ran out the door of the feed store next to the mercantile. "Mrs. Barkley—what in the name of heaven is going on?"

"Yankee supply train comin' in from Atlanta's been derailed. Union goods is strewn all over the forest." The laugh she loosed was so shrill it sounded more like a cackle. "You best get a move on. Stuff's just lyin' there—free for the pickin's." Lifting her skirt up out of the way, she waddled off toward the disappearing tracks.

"Sonofabitch," Josh said, "that train was carrying medical supplies for the hospital out at Fort Jackson. We've run

out of nearly everything." He started walking with the rest
of the people, his long-legged strides eating up the distance.
Although she wasn't short, Angel had to hurry to keep up.

After all these years, it felt odd to be walking at Josh
Coltrane's side, though once she thought she'd be facing life
beside him every day. Just as they neared the forest, she
stumbled. Josh caught her arm, and a strong hand wrapped
around her waist to steady her.

"All right?" he asked.

Her cheeks flamed and her mouth went dry. She'd forgotten what it had felt like when he touched her, the way her
stomach went all buttery and soft. "I'm fine," she snapped,
jerking away, undone and embarrassed by her reaction. "I
don't need any help from you."

He looked at her hard. "Sorry. Yankee or not, I guess I'm
still too much of a gentleman to stand by and let a lady take
a fall." He stepped away from her then, touched the brim of
his cockaded hat in farewell. "Have a good day, Miss Summers." He didn't look back as he headed toward a group of
approaching soldiers.

He hadn't seemed surprised to see her. She wondered if
he knew that her parents were dead and that she and Willie
were barely subsisting at Summers End, once one of Savannah's most successful plantations. She glanced down at her
threadbare clothes and it galled her that he should see her
brought so low.

A group of giggling matrons walked past, but Angel's
eyes remained locked on Josh Coltrane's tall, broad-shouldered form as he walked away. Warm, sweet memories of the
happy times they'd shared mixed with the anger she felt at
his betrayal, the hatred of the Yankees who'd destroyed her
world, and the ache she felt at seeing him again.

How long would he stay? she wondered. How many times
would she run into him? How would she be able to avoid
him?

Feeling the hard knot of misery unraveling in her stomach, she only knew that somehow she would have to make
certain she did.

* * *

"Cap'n Coltrane?"

"Yes, Lieutenant?"

"We've formed a perimeter around the wrecked train, just like you said, but, sir, by the time we got there, most of the goods were already gone."

"That's right, sir," a gangly corporal named Baker put in. "This wasn't no accident. They were waiting when the train ran off the tracks. They must've done something to cause it."

"Just because the war is over, Corporal Baker, doesn't mean people forget. Unfortunately, that takes time." Josh knew that firsthand—after the way Angel had greeted him today. Then again, he wasn't surprised by her reaction. He had known, the day he headed north, that it was over between them. He had sacrificed his love for Angela Summers for the cause that he believed in.

Seeing her today he wondered, as he had a thousand times these past four years, if the sacrifice had been worth it.

"Damn—we really need those supplies," the bearded lieutenant was saying.

Josh's face went hard. "I know." God, did they. The men at Fort Jackson were some of the last casualties of the war— men injured in one of the final battles, too sick to make the long journey home, or never would.

They needed morphine to ease their pain and quinine to fight the malaria. Gauze and bandages were aboard that train, along with laudanum, chloroform, blue pill, Spirit of Nitre, calomel, and a dozen other medicines—and he needed all of them badly. "I'll speak to Colonel Wilson. He's probably already got men out there searching. Maybe he'll be able to find the people who took it and bring the stuff back."

"Odds aren't good, sir. Half the folks in Savannah went away with an armload of goods. They'll be eatin' and drinkin' high off the hog tonight."

"If they do, it'll be the first time in a very long time. At any rate, most of the foodstuffs were headed for the officers' tables. The men can get along without them. It's the medical supplies we need, and the townfolks don't need them the way we do. If we're lucky, they'll give them back."

The bearded man snorted. "Not likely, sir. Damned Johnny Rebs got the notion they're entitled."

Josh said nothing. Lieutenant Ainsley was right. Hatred against the Union forces ran high in Savannah, especially with Christmas approaching. It had been almost a year—December 20, 1864—since Sherman had stormed into Savannah on his march to the sea. Fort Jackson had fallen, along with the city, leaving a devastated populace in its wake.

They wouldn't give up the supplies unless they were forced to, and no one even knew who had them.

"It's gonna be a helluva rotten Christmas for those men," the lieutenant said.

Josh simply nodded. And an equally bad one for him, he added silently as he walked back toward town, his thoughts returning to Angel, remembering how he'd felt the moment he'd seen her.

He had told himself it was over between them, that he could come to Savannah as he had been ordered, that he could see her and not feel a thing. He was in love with Sarah Wingate, a woman he had met in Pennsylvania. Well, maybe not in love, but they had a lot in common and they were good together. There were no scars between them, no past to haunt them. He cared about Sarah and though he hadn't asked her to marry him, he planned to as soon as he returned.

Now all he could think of was Angel. How much she had changed in the last four years, that she had grown from a girl into a woman. A beautiful, sensuous woman. She was just seventeen when he had left. Now she would be twenty-one.

Though she was older, her face looked much the same, the smooth, wide forehead with its widow's peak in front, the high cheekbones, the small cleft in her chin. He knew she hadn't married. He'd checked on her when he'd first arrived in Savannah—just as a friend, of course. She had never had a husband or children, yet her figure was riper, her breasts fuller, even more seductive than he remembered. Four years ago, every time they'd been together, he had ached to touch them, counted the days till they'd be married and she would be his.

He had told himself he was over her, but the moment he had seen her, he'd been nearly overcome with the same hot lust he had felt so long ago. It was followed by a powerful urge to pull her into his arms.

Damnation! Angel Summers was a ghost from his past, nothing more. He wanted her, yes. Now he knew he probably always would. But any chance for happiness they'd ever had had been lost with the war.

Angel would never forgive him for fighting for the Union, and with her parents both dead, her hatred was even greater.

It was hopeless even to think of her.

Yet Josh Coltrane discovered in the days to come that as hard as he tried, he could not stop.

A great big, juicy Virginia ham. Angel hadn't seen the likes of it in years. At least not on the Summerses' usually very sparse table.

"Boy, that ham sure looks good." Slender seven-year-old Willie knelt on the seat of a high-backed chair in the dining room, staring at the bounty in front of him.

"Yes, suh, Master William," said Serge, once the Summerses' Negro butler, "it shorely do. We gots ham an' corn cakes an' yo' Aunt Ida done made some o' dat redeye gravy."

Angel smiled at the gray-haired black man who was now a member of the odd little foursome that had made up her family since the war. "I guess we can finally thank the Yankees for somethin'," she said with a glance at the ham.

"Oughts to be thankin' 'ol Pete Thompson an' his boys," Serge countered. "Way I hear it, him an' Harley Lewis is the ones what took out dat train."

Angel frowned at the stoop-shouldered old man. "Well, for heaven's sake, if they are, they had better keep quiet about it. Those Yanks have been runnin' all over the countryside tryin' to catch whoever did it and looking for the stolen supplies."

"Liberated," corrected Angel's aunt, Ida Summers-Dixon, a beefy woman with coarse, iron-gray hair. "That's what our neighbor, Mrs. Barkley, says." Ida had come to Summers End just after the war, her husband dead, her house burned to the ground, another lost soul looking for solace in a world gone mad.

"Dat's right," Serge said. "Miz Barkley says all them goods was bein' held prisoner by the Yanks an' them boys just come along an' set it free." He grinned, exposing a flash of white against his shiny black skin. He had turned sixty-seven just last week, had been with the family for as long as Angel could remember. When the war ended and the slaves on the plantation were freed, Serge remained. Summers End was his home, he'd said. As long as he was welcome, he would stay.

Angel thought that perhaps that was another thing they could thank the Yankees for. Until the war, it had never occurred to her there was anything wrong with slavery. She had been raised to believe it was just part of living in the South. Now, after working side by side with Serge, Miles, Betty, and others of her father's former slaves, she couldn't imagine treating them as anything but equals.

"Liber . . . liber . . ." Willie struggled with the word as they finished saying grace and began to pass around the steaming bowls of food.

"Liberated," Angel supplied. She smiled as she handed her plate to Serge, who filled it with a thick slab of the luscious sugar-cured ham. "Mrs. Barkley can be very convincing. When she sent over the ham, she reminded me of all the foodstuffs the Yankees plundered when they came through here last year."

"Mrs. Barkley had quite a bit to say, as a matter of fact," Ida said, passing the platter of corncakes to Serge. "She told me Josh Coltrane was back in Savannah. She said she saw you talking to him the day of the train wreck. Is Josh back, Angel?"

The gravy ladle she held tilted precariously, nearly spilling the rich, dark liquid onto the frayed but spotless white tablecloth. "Yes . . . yes, he is."

"Why didn't you tell me?"

Angel took extra care as she poured the gravy over the ham and set the ladle back in the chipped china gravyboat, the last of a broken set that was once her family's pride and joy. "Because it doesn't matter whether he's here or not. Josh Coltrane is a Yankee traitor. Whatever was between us is over and done."

Ida's round face looked skeptical. "What did the two of you talk about? Did you ask him if he was married?"

"M—married?" The thought had never occurred to her. She couldn't imagine Josh Coltrane married to anyone but her. It was insane to feel that way, yet the notion of Josh with a wife and children made her suddenly sick to her stomach.

"That's what I asked," her aunt repeated as if Angel were a little slow-witted. "Did you find out if Josh has a wife?"

"I don't know if he's got a wife—I didn't ask him. Why would I? I don't give a damn if he's married or not!"

The table fell silent. Even little Willie stopped wolfing down his food.

"Wh—what I mean is, it's none of my business what Josh Coltrane is or isn't. What he does is none of my concern." She frowned at her aunt. "And I'm surprised at you, Aunt Ida. The Yanks killed your husband and your brother. I'd think you'd hate Josh Coltrane and everything he stands for."

Ida lifted her china cup and took a sip of the chicory they pretended was coffee. "A lot of good men believed in the Union. My husband's cousin was a Yank. So was Josh Coltrane's mama. She and I were best friends once. I know the way you felt about Josh. I just thought that maybe . . . now that the war is over . . ."

Angel tried to swallow a bite of ham, but the meat stuck in her throat. She tossed her napkin down on the table and stood up. "The Yanks destroyed my family. They destroyed Summers End and left Willie and me all by ourselves. You may be able to forgive Josh Coltrane, but the war will never be over for me!"

Angel left the table and fled the dining room, her eyes suddenly wet with tears. It hadn't happened since her mother died. Josh Coltrane had done what no amount of hardship had done for the past two years. It was just one more strike against him.

Fort James Jackson overlooked the Savannah River just a few miles east of the city. It was started in the early 1800's, a huge brick fortress built much like a castle that even had a moat and a drawbridge. In December a year ago, William T. "Cump" Sherman had captured the fort when his troops overran the city on his infamous march to the sea.

The fort was used as a hospital now, the place Josh had recently been stationed. It was hardly a spot he would have chosen, since the structure was in such bad repair. With the Confederacy gone broke, there hadn't been money to spend on the neglected buildings, and the Union had done little better. Water dripped through holes in the barracks' ceilings, bricks crumbled at the rear of the magazine, and the cisterns clogged up and often wouldn't run.

Josh had set men to work making the needed repairs, but the government had no long-range plans for the fort, and money for construction was sparse. With the war so recently ended, materials were sparse as well.

As he stood at the entrance to the makeshift hospital in one of the drafty converted barracks, Josh stared down the long row of wooden cots. Forty-five sick and injured men huddled beneath their threadbare blankets, some of them sweating with fever, others shaking with cold. A moan rose from somewhere down the line, and off in the distance he could hear a soldier weeping.

As he started through the line of injured men, Josh thought of the military train that had been derailed and the valuable supplies they had lost. The government was still chaotic. The requisition for supplies had taken weeks and now those supplies were lost. How many more weeks could these men hang on?

Cursing beneath his breath, he strode along the row of cots, stopping to check on a patient here and there or offer a moment of comfort, then finally reached the young blond soldier who was crying.

"Pain that bad, Bennie?" he asked, squatting at the young man's bedside.

The boy sniffed a little, then wiped his eyes with the cuff of his nightshirt. Bennie was only sixteen. "Sorry, Doc. I don't know what got into me . . ." He tried to smile, but it came out crooked and forlorn. "Pain's no worse than it has been. Guess maybe it's just that . . . well, it's almost Christmas. I was hopin' I'd be home."

Josh squeezed the young soldier's hand. "You'll get home, Ben. Maybe not in time for Christmas, but you'll get there. You've got to believe that." The boy had taken a lead ball in the leg at Citronelle in Alabama last May, a battle fought after the war was officially ended. Complications set in. Benjamin Weatherby lost a leg, and he still wasn't healed enough to make the long journey back to South Carolina. Only time would tell if he ever would be.

"Can I get you anything?" Josh asked.

"You already did, Doc. Thanks for the encouragement. I'm gonna get home, Doc, just like you said."

Josh squeezed the young man's shoulder. "Good boy." They talked for a little while longer, then Josh moved up the aisle once more.

He paused at the door to the barracks, turning to speak to his assistant. "Dr. Medford?"

The tall, gaunt man looked up from the patient he worked over. "Yes, Doctor?" He was two years younger than Josh but the war had made him look older, his sandy brown hair already thinning, his eyes sunken into a weathered face.

"I'm going into town to see Colonel Wilson. I want to find out if he has any leads on who might have taken those medical supplies. I've got to convince him how badly we need them. He's got to do whatever it takes to get them back."

"The men are suffering terribly," Silas Medford said.

Josh nodded. "It may take me a while. Can you handle things here while I'm gone?"

"Of course."

"If you need me, you know where to find me. If I'm not there, I'll leave word where I've gone."

Si Medford smiled. "Yes, sir."

Josh knew they were counting on him. He had seen it in each man's eyes as he'd walked down the aisle. He wouldn't let them down, he vowed. They'd been let down too many times already.

Two

Josh leaned over the wide mahogany desk in the study of the Davenport house on State Street across from Columbia Square. Colonel Wilson was using the beautiful old home as his headquarters until more permanent quarters could be built.

"We need those medical supplies, Colonel Wilson," Josh said. "The men are in terrible shape. Surely there is something you can do."

The stout, barrel-chested colonel leaned back in his brown leather chair. "We know the stuff wasn't destroyed in the wreck. The car containing the medical supplies was one of the few that came through the derailment undamaged. Unfortunately, by the time our men got there, it was totally cleaned out. Somebody's got your supplies, but any tracks they might have left were erased by the hordes of people who came to pick through the wreckage."

"What about a reward?" Josh suggested. "Most of these people need money pretty badly."

"We've already done that. Posters will be up all over town by the end of the day." The colonel riffled through a stack of paperwork in front of him. "A reward might work, but I doubt it. In their own way, these people are still fighting the war. Giving back supplies is tantamount to aiding the enemy. They simply won't help us."

Josh ran a hand through his thick, dark-brown hair. "Surely there's some way to convince them."

"Perhaps there is."

Josh leaned closer. "Sir?"

"The best hope we have, Captain Coltrane, is you."

"Me!"

"That's right. You grew up here in Savannah. You know these people better than anyone else in the regiment. I'd suggest you talk to them, convince them to give back those supplies you need so badly."

Josh scoffed. "If I may say so, sir, I'm the last person they'd be willing to listen to."

"That may be so. But it appears to me it's the only option you have. In the meantime, I've already sent in another requisition order. Eventually the stuff you need will get here."

Eventually, Josh thought. In the meantime, his patients were dying . . . or lying there in pain.

The colonel shoved back his chair and came to his feet. "Good luck, Captain Coltrane."

Josh quietly saluted. He'd need a lot more than luck if he was going to get back those badly needed medicines.

Closing the study door behind him, he walked through the lovely old home beneath molded plaster ceilings, past the beautiful elliptical stairway, and made his way out the front door. Calling on his former friends, people who felt he'd betrayed them by joining the North, wasn't something he looked forward to doing, but with every step he took, he thought of young Ben Weatherby and his determination strengthened.

Perhaps he could convince them. He had to give it a try.

It was warm this December, even for the South. Clouds floated overhead and late afternoon rays dampened his back beneath his blue wool coat as another door slammed behind him. The day had passed in a nightmare of disappointment and rejection. It didn't take long to discover most of the young men he had known had been killed in the war; others were still scattered across the country, trying to make their way home.

Kirby Fields, once his neighbor to the east, met him on

the porch with a shotgun. Red Donnelley stood on crutches, one arm gone above the elbow, his surly manner speaking more eloquently than his brief, pointed "Go to hell" words.

By late afternoon, he'd exhausted most of his list of former acquaintances and found himself just below the road leading into what had once been Coltrane Farms. He'd been there only once since his return. His parents were no longer living and the place was so rundown and overgrown it made his chest hurt just to look at it. He'd walked through the cold, empty house, overwhelmed with bitter memories. He'd locked the door, hung a "For Sale" sign on the gate, and ridden away.

As a boy, he'd loved the farm, couldn't wait till he grew up and could help his father run it. But the South was no longer his home. Once his enlistment was up, he'd be returning to Philadelphia to set up his medical practice. His mother's family owned a number of northern factories. During the war, their profits had soared. His mother's share had gone to him. He was a rich man now, one of few men from the South who had come out of the war ahead.

Philadelphia and Sarah Wingate—that was his destiny now. With luck, he would make a home there and finally settle down.

Josh glanced ahead, a feeling of familiarity running through him as he passed over the old bridge and continued up the lane. He was riding toward the farm again today, on his way to Summers End. The huge plantation bordered Coltrane Farms to the south, just a quarter-mile off the road leading to Fort Jackson.

Angel Summers was his last chance to make people listen. He had to convince her to help him.

Or maybe he just wanted an excuse to see her again.

Whatever the truth, a few minutes later he had crossed the bridge, turned off the road, and ridden up behind the big white house. Dismounting, he led his bay horse beneath the branches of a huge magnolia tree, then stood watching the slender blond woman working on her hands and knees in the vegetable garden.

It was a sight almost hard to believe. The lovely Miss Summers, once the belle of Savannah, up to her elbows in dirt. And yet she looked as beautiful as she had in peach moire silk. Maybe even more so. The sun had tinted her cheeks a rosy pink and freckled her nose. Strands of her golden hair nestled against her throat, loose from the simple snood that rested on her shoulders.

Her breasts heaved with exertion, ripe and straining against her dress. Unhindered by stays or hoops, her simple brown skirt clung to her hips, outlining the rounded curves. Desire slid through him. He wanted to reach out and touch her, to cup the fullness of her breasts, to stroke them until they hardened against his hand. Even after four long years, he could still recall the berry taste of her lips, the span of her narrow waist.

His body hardened, his blood going thick and heavy, pounding as if he were still twenty-three and she just seventeen.

As though he had never been with a woman.

Josh Coltrane had been with a number of women in the past four years. At first he had done it to forget her, to wash Angel from his mind and heart. Then, as the war progressed, because he needed the solace, the few short hours to forget the blood and gore of the battlefield.

Now, looking at Angel, he realized he felt more just watching her work in the garden than he'd felt with the most practiced whore.

Angel gripped the trowel and jammed it into the dirt, unseating another stubborn weed. She was working along a row planted with cabbage and kale, hoping the winter wouldn't be too hard on them. They needed fresh vegetables desperately, and they couldn't afford to reseed. And Christmas was coming. She tried to make the holidays special for Willie, to keep their family traditions alive, even though their parents were gone. A big Christmas dinner was one of them.

The trowel slammed down and she dug out a weed, then winced as something thorny bit into her hand. "Ouch!" A soft curse escaped, followed by the rumble of a man's deep voice.

"You all right, Angel?"

Her head snapped up, whipped toward the sound. Her body went as stiff as the hoe on the ground beside her. She took a deep breath and released it slowly, collecting herself, forcing away the pain, burying the hurt beneath her anger. "Well, if it isn't the infamous Captain Coltrane."

"Dr. Coltrane at present, since it appears you're in need of one." His voice still carried a trace of the South, she noticed, a soft drawl that whispered over her like the gentlest wind.

"I—I'm fine," she said, wiping away the dirt as he knelt beside her, then sucking at a single drop of blood. When she looked up, Josh was staring at her mouth.

"I'd be happy to do that for you," he said softly.

Her stomach contracted; moist heat unfurled. He was kneeling so close she could feel the warmth of his body, hear the rustle of fabric when the muscles moved beneath his sky blue shirt.

"I told you I was fine." She came to her feet, dusting off her hands, brushing the dirt off her brown woolen skirt, trying to ignore the too-rapid patter of her heart. She looked up and Josh was smiling, his brown eyes full of mirth. "What's so funny?"

"Hold still." His hand came up to her cheek. "You've got a smudge of dirt on your nose." He cradled her face as he brushed it off and his gentle touch made her tremble.

Angel quickly stepped away. "Wh—what do you want? Why did you come here?"

He assessed her a moment, as if he sized her up. "I need your help, Angel. I hate to ask you. If there was anyone else I could turn to, I would. I was hoping . . . for old times' sake . . . you might agree."

Angel eyed him warily, trying not to notice the way his shirt stretched over his powerful shoulders, the way his breeches hugged his hard-muscled thighs. His face was tanned and lean, his features harder than she remembered. She wanted to reach out and touch him, assure herself he was really there. "You want me to help you do what?"

"That train your friends derailed was loaded with medical supplies. The hospital's been waiting for them for weeks. Without them, the men are suffering badly. I was hoping you would help me get them back."

Angel said nothing for the longest time, her mind clouding with thoughts of betrayal. "I can't believe it. You actually came here to ask me for help? You must be out of your mind."

Josh's mouth went thin. "Maybe I am. Maybe I was fool enough to remember the compassionate young woman I once fell in love with. A woman who couldn't stand to see anyone suffer, not even an animal. Remember the fawn you found with the broken leg? You cried for hours when your daddy had to shoot it. You remember that, Angel?"

She sniffed and glanced away. "I remember."

"There are forty-five men in that hospital. Some of them are young, some are old, some are dying, some are fighting desperately to live. All of them need comfort, Angel. You can help me give it to them."

Her chest squeezed, tightened a hard knot inside her. He was painting a terrible picture. She didn't like to think of Union soldiers as men. They were simply blue-belly Yanks. The enemy. She only shook her head. "I can't help you."

Josh gripped her arms. "You could if you wanted to. The townspeople have always respected the Summers family. They respect you, Angel. They've got no real use for that much medicine and we'll pay them to give it back. They'll do it if you ask them to."

Angel jerked away. "Well, I won't ask them. Not for a bunch of blue-belly Yanks." She whirled, pointing toward the house with its peeling paint and broken shutters, to the withered fields, empty ramshackle barn, and beyond.

"Take a look around, Josh. Summers End is gone. Mama and Daddy are dead. Everything I once loved is gone. The

North did that. Your precious Union. If you think I'm going to help even one Union soldier, you are sorely mistaken."

"The war is over, Angel."

"Not around here, it isn't."

"For God's sake, Angel, it's Christmas. Doesn't that count for something?"

"It didn't count for much last year when Sherman rolled over us like so much flour under a millstone. Savannah was a Christmas gift for Lincoln—that's what he said."

He looked at her and his eyes grew dark with disappointment. It made her heart twist inside her. Dear God, how could she still care what Josh Coltrane thought of her?

"You've changed, Angel," he said softly.

Hurt rippled through her, yet she knew it was the truth. "And you haven't?"

His mouth thinned faintly. "You're right. Both of us have changed. I wish I could say it was for the better." He backed up a few paces, his eyes still on her face. Then he touched the brim of his hat in farewell. "Good-bye, Miss Summers. I hope you have a very merry Christmas."

He turned away from her then and set off toward his horse. Just watching him walk away made her stomach tighten inside her. Her heart was pounding, hammering against her ribs. Dear God, she didn't want him to leave. She damned him to hell for making her feel that way, damned him for the power to still make her care when she'd believed that power was gone.

Anger rose like a tidal wave inside her. Josh Coltrane had betrayed her. He had chosen his precious cause over a lifetime together. He hadn't loved her enough to stay.

Now he needed her help and he actually expected her to give it. Well, Josh Coltrane could just go straight to hell!

Josh and his assistant, Silas Medford, worked through most of the night. Without the drugs he needed, his patients weren't sleeping, either. Still, by nine o'clock that morning, he was mounted and on the road, riding beneath a wintry blue sky. He had thought of a couple more people who might help him, then he was headed back to Summers End for another talk with Angel.

Strangely, considering how badly his first attempt to convince her had gone, he'd decided to try again.

He had thought about it all of last night, running the minutes they'd shared, the words she had spoken, back through his mind. There was something he had seen in her eyes, something that didn't match the harsh words she had spoken, something of pain and regret.

The war had done that to her. It had taken her mama and daddy, destroyed her home, her way of life. And he had done it when he'd left her. He knew he had hurt her. Until he had seen her, he hadn't known how much.

The war had forced her to grow up, had taught her to be tough to survive, to protect her little brother.

But strength did not preclude compassion. It was buried, perhaps, but Josh believed that it was still there. Compassion had been a deeply rooted part of the woman he had loved. Though she had done her best to convince him it was gone, he believed he had seen it; behind the pain, behind the anger, it flickered in those clear blue eyes.

And there was something else that might work in his favor. Ida Dixon lived with Angel. He'd discovered that when he'd arrived in Savannah, and Ida was once his mother's friend.

Riding to the front of the house this time, he reined up, tied the horse to the hitching post out in front, and climbed the wide porch stairs. The house was built in the Federal style with huge white Doric columns. Once it was a showplace. Now broken green shutters hung at the windows and the ornate front door needed a fresh coat of paint. He stood in front of it, thinking of the last time he had come here before the war, the time he'd said good-bye to Angel, the pain that had lashed through them both as he'd ridden away. Steeling himself, he knocked on the door, then waited with his plumed hat in his hand.

The door creaked open. "Yes, suh?" The Summerses' aging butler stood framed in the opening. Only his clothing had changed. Worn canvas breeches and a faded gingham shirt replaced the immaculate white linen jacket and tailored black trousers he had always worn.

"Hello . . . Serge." He had to stretch for the name, then he smiled as he recalled it.

Serge smiled, too. "Mista Josh. I hardly recognized you."

"Four years of war can do that to a man."

Serge nodded, knowing the words were true.

Josh noticed the old man's hair had turned completely gray. "I came to see Mrs. Dixon and Miss Summers. Do you know if they happen to be in?"

"Who is it, Serge?" a woman's husky voice called out. He could hear her heavy footsteps as she walked into the entry.

"It's Mista Josh, ma'am. He come to see you an' Miz Angel."

The older woman swept past the butler, stopped to give Josh an assessing glance, then surprised him with a wide, welcoming smile, the first he'd received since his return to Savannah.

"Good Lord, Josh Coltrane, you surely are a sight for sore eyes. Come in, come in."

The hug the big woman delivered felt good. Damn good. It made him feel like he was home. He wasn't, of course. Savannah would never be his home again.

"I brought this for you." He held out a small brown paper sack and Ida took it, opened the sack, and stared at the contents.

"Coffee! Real fresh-ground coffee!" She took a long, lingering sniff. "Landsakes, it's been ages since we had any of that 'round here." She smiled. "All I got is chicory on the stove. I can make some of this if you—"

"What you've got is fine, Mrs. Dixon."

"Aunt Ida," she corrected. "I was always Aunt Ida to you before. The war hasn't changed that, has it?"

Josh smiled. "Not for me. It's good to see you, Aunt Ida."

"It's good to see you, too, Josh. Angel's gone across the

way to fetch Willie home for supper, but she'll be back shortly. You can wait for her in the parlor."

"Actually, I came to see you, too." He passed the door to the parlor and followed the beefy woman into the steamy kitchen. There was a separate kitchen outside, he recalled, for use in the summer and to help prevent fires, but the household was so small now, apparently they cooked inside. And the old black cookstove would help to heat the house.

"Angel told me you came by," Ida said, pouring him a cup of the chicory they used for coffee, then one for herself. "I guess she wasn't much pleased to see you."

"I don't suppose she was."

"What about you?" Ida asked, as direct as he remembered. "Were you glad to see her?"

Too glad, he thought. Too damned glad. "She's still as pretty as ever. Maybe even prettier."

"That's not what I asked you, Josh."

"The war ended whatever we might have had, Aunt Ida. Surely you know that."

"You married?" she asked and he smiled.

"No."

"Got a girl somewheres?"

His mouth curved. "Kind of."

"Where?"

"Philadelphia."

"You goin' back there when you get out?"

"I plan to set up my medical practice there."

"Gonna marry the girl?"

"I'm not sure." Where had that come from? He'd been pretty damned sure two weeks ago. But two weeks ago he hadn't seen Angel Summers again. "I imagine, sooner or later, we'll marry. I haven't asked her yet."

Ida took a sip of her coffee, set the blue enamel cup back down on the kitchen table. "Angel told me why you came by."

"I need her help, Aunt Ida. I need both of you to help me." He told the buxom woman about the men in the hospital at the fort. About the medicines that had been stolen and how badly he needed them back.

"If you're set on convincing Angel, you've set yourself a sizable task, Josh Coltrane."

A movement sounded in the doorway. "Too sizable, I'm afraid—even for you, Josh."

He came up from his chair and turned to face her, felt his breath lodge just to see her standing so close after all these years. How many times had he seen her like that in his dreams, her cheeks rosy, her golden hair beginning to come undone? How many times had he imagined kissing her, making love to her?

He shook his head, forcing the images away, trying to make the blood stop thundering in his ears.

"I'm not going to help you, Josh." There was turbulence in her eyes, and the pain was there. He recognized it now for what it was. He had done that to her. Hurt her far more deeply than he had imagined. It made a knot of regret ball in his stomach.

The screen door slammed. A little boy rushed past her, hurling himself into the room. He stopped dead still when he saw Josh, took a step backward into Angel's skirts. She wrapped an arm protectively around his shoulders.

"You're a Yank," the boy said. "What are you doin' here?"

Josh smiled. "I'm a friend of your sister's. You were pretty small when I left. I guess you don't remember."

"Angel doesn't have no Billy Yanks for friends."

"This is Josh Coltrane, Willie," Angel said gently. "He used to live at Coltrane Farms." All the love and compassion he remembered in the past surfaced as Angel hugged the boy. "He isn't going to hurt us."

Willie's small body trembled, and for the first time Josh realized the boy was afraid. "The war is over, Willie. No one's going to hurt anyone now."

Willie said nothing, just eased farther back against Angel. "Josh is a doctor, not a soldier," she said.

The boy said nothing.

"Why don't you go outside and play for a little while longer," Angel said. "Rusty's still out there, isn't he?"

Willie nodded, his golden hair, lighter than Angel's, shimmering in the light coming in through the window. "I still need more pine branches if we're going to finish decorating for Christmas. Maybe you and Rusty could gather some more and bring them in."

"Can we string holly berries tonight?" the child asked.

"If you two will go pick some." Willie's face lit up. "Go on then. Supper isn't far off. I'll call you when it's ready."

Willie surveyed Josh for a final moment more, turned, and raced back out the door.

"He's a good-looking boy," Josh said.

"He's the spitting image of our father." Angel's spine went stiff. "But he'll never know that because our father is dead. I'm not going to help you, Josh."

His gaze swung away from the tight lines of Angel's face. "Then perhaps Ida will." He turned to the older woman, praying that in Ida he had finally found someone who could see beyond the past.

Ida's glance traveled from Josh to Angel and back again. "I'm from Macon, Josh, not Savannah. I've only been here since the end of the war. But I'll speak to the folks I know, tell them about the sick men in the fort. Maybe I can get them to listen."

"Aunt Ida!" Angel's face went pale. "You can't mean to help the Yankees!"

"They're men, Angel, and they're sick. I got to do what I think is right."

Angel said nothing, just stood there staring at her aunt. Then she turned and walked back through the screen door she had come in.

"Thank you, Ida," Josh said, dragging his attention back to the woman on the opposite side of the table. "You can't know how much I appreciate what you're doing."

"Don't count on it doin' much good, Josh. The rest of these folks are even more stubborn than Angel."

Josh just nodded. Angel was stubborn, all right. She always had been. But it was anger and pain she was fighting. It was hurt and betrayal that was keeping her from doing what was right.

For the ten thousandth time, he wished he could change the past, that the war had never come.

Unfortunately, it had—and nothing could ever change that.

Three

Standing at the side of the house, Angel watched Josh Coltrane ride away. In the past, Coltrane Farms had raised beautiful blooded horses. Angel had never seen a man who could sit a horse as gracefully as Josh.

She watched him until his tall frame crested the rise and disappeared over the hill, but she couldn't stop thinking about him. He was a harder man now, rugged in a way he wasn't before, yet the tenderness inside him remained, the warmth in his expression. Where had that tenderness gone in her? When had she lost it?

It hadn't happened all at once, she was sure. It had begun to slip away the day Josh rode off to join the Union Army. More of it died with the news that her father had been killed at Shiloh, the final bits and pieces destroyed when her mother took to her bed and slowly ebbed away, joining Daniel Summers in an early grave.

Now Josh was back but he wouldn't be here long. She'd been standing at the kitchen door far longer than he knew. She had heard him say he was returning to Pennsylvania, marrying a girl who lived there. Just thinking about it made Angel's insides tighten into a hard knot of pain. Why did he have to come back? Why couldn't he have left her alone?

She thought of the way Josh had looked sitting there in the kitchen, his mouth curved into a smile, his dark eyes glowing with warmth. He looked like he belonged there, as if he had finally come home. It had taken every ounce of her will not to cross the room and throw her arms around him.

Dear God, how could she hate him so much when part of her still loved him? How could she ache for him when part of her wanted him to ride away and never return?

It was that part she had to hang on to. That was the part that would protect her from being hurt again.

Angel brushed at a tear, weary deep down in her bones. Lifting her skirts to avoid the muddy earth, she made her way to the rear of the house, climbed the stairs, and stepped inside the steamy kitchen. She needed to start making supper. Willie would be hungry and when he came in there was no doubt he'd be full of questions about the Yank who had come to Summers End.

Questions about Josh. Questions she didn't know how to answer.

Dragging a big iron frying pan out from under the dry sink, she set to work beside Aunt Ida, trying to drive thoughts of Josh Coltrane out of her head.

Willie Summers ducked beneath the branches of an overhanging willow and watched the uniformed soldier ride away. Blue-belly Yank. What was he doing at Summers End? Why was he talking to Angel? And why was she so upset?

He would probably never know, he figured. Grown-ups never told him anything. They always said he was too young, or that he'd figure it out when he got older.

Willie motioned to his friend as the soldier rode away, and Rusty Lewis raced from his own hiding place into the umbrella of darkness under the willow.

"What'd *he* want?" Rusty asked.

Willie shrugged his thin shoulders. "I don' know. Whatever it was, you can bet my sis didn't give it to 'im."

Rusty laughed. He was a year older than Willie, taller and more filled out. Willie was small for his age, his chest narrow and bony, his short legs rooster-thin.

"I bet she didn't," Rusty said. "Your sis don't like them bluecoats much."

"Me neither," Willie said.

"Me neither," said Rusty, "and that makes three."

Willie laughed and the two of them raced out from under the tree. By the time they got to the top of the hill at the end of the pasture on their way to pick holly berries, they were running flat out, not looking where they were going, paying not the least bit of attention. Neither boy noticed the half-buried barrel of a cannon. They had seen it there some months back, but there was so much abandoned army equipment around that they didn't give it much notice anymore.

As Willie whizzed up the hill and leaped into the air at the top, it was too late to avoid the heavy, rusted-out length of iron. He landed hard on the barrel and his foot gave way beneath him, the bone crunching as it splintered, then gouging him with pain as it knifed its way through the thin skin on his calf.

"Aieee!" he screamed as another wave of pain seared through him, then another and another, until all he felt was a single burning spasm. It sucked his will and his eyes rolled back, dragging him into the darkened tunnel of unconsciousness.

"Miss Summers! Miss Summers, come quick! It's Willie! It's Willie, Miss Summers—he's hurt real bad!"

"Oh, dear God!" Angel ran toward the commotion out back—the patter of small running feet and the shout of her brother's name. The child was nearly hysterical and talons of fear cut into her.

"Willie!" Racing out on the porch, she nearly collided with Rusty, whose face was red, his breath coming out in a series of wheezes.

"Where's Willie? Rusty, please, you have to tell me where he is."

Serge ran up before he could answer. "What's happened, Miz Angel?"

"Willie's been hurt," Rusty said. "We was racin' across the old cow pasture to the top of the hill. Willie got there first, only he didn't stop. He jumped off that little ledge up there—you know the one, Miss Summers?"

"Yes . . . I—I know the one." She started hurrying in that direction, forcing herself to stay calm, but her knees were shaking beneath her skirt.

"There's an old cannon up there, buried in the dirt. Willie didn't see it when he jumped and he landed right on the barrel. He broke his leg real bad and he was yellin'. Then he stopped movin'. We gotta hurry, Miss Summers."

But Angel was already running, old Serge right beside her. The ancient man was breathing hard trying to keep up, but Angel didn't dare slow.

When she topped the rise and saw Willie's crumpled figure lying at the bottom, she nearly blacked out herself. "Oh, God." Avoiding the ledge, she rounded the hill and ran straight to her brother's unconscious figure.

"Willie! Willie, can you hear me?" He moaned a little and his eyes fluttered open as she shifted his head onto her lap. Serge knelt beside her, surveying the bone that protruded through his pantleg.

"It's broke real bad, Miz Angel, gone clean through the skin." He jerked off the scarf around his neck and tied it around the leg above the break to stop the bleeding. "I'll go get the wagon so's we can get him back to the house, then I'll go fetch Dr. Gordon."

Angel nodded weakly. She couldn't seem to think. "Oh, Willie." She stroked the small blond head, then Serge's words began to penetrate her cold haze of fear. Dr. Gordon was the only doctor left in Savannah, a drunk who was usually nowhere to be found. Their neighbor, Mrs. Barkley, was good at doctoring, but she couldn't set a bone as badly broken as Willie's.

Her mind veered to tall, capable Josh Coltrane. Josh would know what to do but there was no way she could ask him for help—not when she'd just refused to help *him*.

She would find Doc Gordon and make sure he was sober. He had set plenty of broken bones in his day, but the thought of the drunken doctor working over her little brother made her stomach knot with worry. She would figure out something, she vowed. She couldn't stand to see Willie suffer.

By the time Serge arrived with the wagon, she had fashioned a splint from an old piece of wood and secured the leg to it with strips of her petticoat, making the limb immobile. Willie had regained consciousness, which eased her fear, but pain contorted his small features, making her feel even worse. He was trying not to cry as she held him in her lap for the short ride back to the house, but tears kept rolling down his cheeks.

"It's all right, honey," she said, but her own eyes glistened with tears. "Everything's going to be fine."

When they reached the house, Aunt Ida waited on the porch. "Get him upstairs and out of those clothes," she commanded. "Serge, you go after Josh Coltrane. He was headed back to the fort."

Angel bristled. "I'm not asking Josh for help." She glanced down at the child's bloody pantleg. "Doc Gordon can set the leg."

Ida frowned. "He can, long as he's sober. Guess we'll just have to wait and see."

Angel chewed her bottom lip. She ought to go to Josh, ask him to help Willie. She would, she vowed, but only if she had to.

"I'll be back quick as a wink," Serge said, creaking his way back up to the seat of the wagon. "Willie's gonna be jes' fine. Old Serge says so." With a flick of his long, wrinkled fingers, the reins slapped hard on the bony horse's rump and the wagon rolled away.

Doc Gordon was sober, thank God. The leg was set with what appeared to be competence and efficiency, and Angel breathed a sigh of relief as she followed the doctor back down the stairs from Willie's room.

"The laudanum will help him sleep. Give him a drop or two in a glass of warm milk whenever he needs it." She thought of the drugs she had seen in his bag—each of them marked with Union Army labels—and knew they had come from the train wreck. She didn't feel one bit guilty, since Willie had need of them, but she couldn't help wondering if Doc Gordon had the rest of the medical supplies.

"Keep him warm," Doc said. "Make certain there are no drafts in the room. There is always the possibility of putrefaction with an injury like this, but William is young and healthy. He should heal just fine as long as he stays off the leg."

He pulled his stethoscope from around his fleshy neck and stuffed it into his black leather bag. He was a man in his late fifties, ruddy complected with a round, veined, drinker's nose. "I'll be back tomorrow to see how he's doing."

"Thank you, Dr. Gordon." She walked him to the door determined not to ask, but the words seemed to come of their own volition. "I was wondering . . . I noticed the laudanum you left upstairs has a Union label on it."

He nodded. "The train wreck, you know. Can't say as I'm sorry."

"D-did you wind up with all the medicine out of the supply car?"

"Good heavens, no. I couldn't use that much stuff in the next three years. There was a box of medicine and bandages and blankets on my door when I came into the office. I have no idea where it came from, but it was surely appreciated."

Angel's glance strayed upstairs. "It surely is, Dr. Gordon." She bit down on her lip. "About your fee . . . I'll pay you the rest of what we owe just as soon as the laundry money comes in." She had given him all of her egg money. She prayed the hens kept laying.

The doctor left and Angel went back upstairs. Willie was sleeping, his small form huddled beneath the quilt Aunt Ida had made for him on his seventh birthday. She gently brushed the blond hair out of his face, then ran her fingers over his name where it was embroidered with loving care on the edge of the quilt.

She bent and kissed his forehead. "Sleep tight, sweetheart," she said into the stillness of the room. Tomorrow he would feel better. In the meantime, he would need hot, nourishing food, and to see that he got it, there was a mountain of work to do.

Angel bent over the steaming tub of laundry that boiled next to the outside kitchen. It galled her to wash the Union officers' dirty clothes, but they needed the money and there wasn't much else she could do. Except maybe sell Summers End, and she wasn't yet ready to do that. Just the thought of leaving her beloved home made an aching knot ball inside her chest. Besides, with money so tight, there probably wouldn't be any buyers.

Angel blotted her forehead with an elbow, stirred the huge iron cauldron, and glanced up at the sun. It was growing late in the afternoon and the doctor still hadn't returned. Willie was restless and only the laudanum helped ease his pain. He looked pale and sunken, and she was worried about him.

Evening came but the doctor didn't. Angel spent a restless night beside Willie, who fretted and tossed and fought the covers, complaining he was too warm. By morning, she was exhausted.

She sent Serge back into town for the doctor, but no one knew where he was. Someone said he had gone out in the country to deliver a baby. Perhaps he had. Perhaps he'd gone off on another of his benders.

By the morning of the third day, Angel was flat-out scared.

"He isn't any better, Aunt Ida," she said, as she walked into the kitchen. "His leg is all swollen and red and now he has a fever."

"Did he drink all of Mrs. Barkley's fever medicine?"

Remembering the face her brother had made, Angel almost smiled. "He said it tasted like pig slop, but he got the last of it down."

Ida shook her head. "I don't know . . . maybe by tomorrow . . ."

But Angel kept on walking. "I'm not waiting until tomorrow. I'm not going to let Willie suffer because of my pride. I'm going after Josh."

Ida's broad face lit up. "Now you're talkin'. Josh will know what to do."

"I should have gone to him in the first place. I should have—"

"There's not a darn thing wrong with Doc Gordon—leastwise not when he's off the bottle—and he was good and sober the day he worked on Willie. You don't worry none about what you did or didn't do. You just go get Josh and everything will be all right."

"I hope so, Aunt Ida. I'd never forgive myself if something happened to Willie." The back door slammed behind her as she hurried out to the stable. The old sorrel gelding, the only horse they had left, usually pulled the wagon. She could go faster riding across the fields, taking the shortcut through Coltrane Farms, so she dragged out a worn old saddle and lifted it up on the horse's bony back.

Jamming her sturdy brown shoe into the stirrup, she pulled herself up on the hard leather seat and tried not to think of the picture she made with her skirts rucked up and her stockings exposed nearly to her knees. She tried not to remember her lovely padded sidesaddle or her royal blue velvet riding habit with the jaunty little hat cocked over her forehead.

Instead, she dug her heels into the old horse's ribs and set off toward Fort Jackson.

Half an hour later, she was riding up in front, staring up at the imposing brick fortress, shading her eyes against the sun so she could see.

"Hold it there, miss," one of the soldiers called out as she rode across the moat, which these days looked more like a giant mud sump. "I'm afraid you'll have to state your business before I can let you in."

Her chin went up. "I—I'm a friend of Dr. Coltrane's. I'm here on a matter of urgency. Please . . . you must let me see him."

"Of course, miss," the soldier said. "If you'll just follow me, I'll see if I can find out where he is."

She rode the horse behind the lanky soldier, then dismounted and waited while he went into the barracks that served as a hospital, but apparently Josh wasn't there. They found him in the back of the quartermaster's office, rummaging through boxes, rounding up supplies. At the sound of her voice, he came up from where he knelt and his hard features softened when he realized who it was.

"I—I'm sorry to bother you, Captain Coltrane, but I was hoping I might speak to you for a moment."

"Of course." Long strides carried him to her side. He caught her arm and led her into a small, barren office, where he seated her on a rickety wooden chair and closed the door.

"What's wrong, Angel? You're as pale as a sheet."

"It's Willie." Tears burned her eyes. She tried to blink them away, but several spilled down her cheek. "He's sick, Josh. He broke his leg clear through the skin. The doctor set it, but he isn't any better. If anything, he's worse. I—I know I have no right to ask, but could you—"

"Of course I'll come." He reached for her hand and gave it a squeeze, and her body went weak with relief. "And you have every right to ask me. Whether you believe it or not, I'm still your friend."

Angel glanced away, unable to look into those warm brown eyes a moment more. He wasn't her friend. He was the enemy. She had to remember that. But in moments like these, it was hard to convince herself.

"When did this happen?" Josh asked.

"Three days ago. Dr. Gordon was supposed to come back and see him, but he never showed up."

Josh frowned. "Yes, I remember Doc Gordon. He's the best you've got left in Savannah?"

"He's the only doctor we have, Josh."

"As I recall, he's good when he's sober."

"He was sober when he worked on Willie. Otherwise, I never would have let him."

A corner of his mouth kicked up. "No, I don't imagine

you would have." He took her arm again, urging her toward the door, and as worried as she was, she noticed the heat of his hand through her clothes. There was strength there, too, and some of it began seeping into her.

"Let me get my bag and we'll go," he said.

Angel merely nodded. Josh was coming. She had told herself he would, but she hadn't really been certain. Josh would help Willie. That was all that mattered now.

Four

Josh rose from the little boy's bedside. Willie was sleeping again, his face flushed with fever.

"Doc Gordon did a fine job setting the leg. It's properly aligned. The bone should mend without a problem. Unfortunately, the tear in the skin where the bone protruded doesn't look good. I'm afraid there may be some infection."

"You—you mean it's putrefied?" Angel asked, her big blue eyes wide with horror.

His jaw clamped. He had seen so much of that during the war, and too many cases of amputation. "Not yet. There's a lot of inflammation, though. That's what's causing his fever." He looked down at the boy's thin leg where it sat propped on a pillow. He had changed the dressing, but beneath the splint the flesh was red and swollen, warm to the touch. Willie's fever was rising and his pulse was too fast.

"I've cleaned the wound again and given him some more of the laudanum." His gaze flicked to the bottle stamped "Union Army" that sat on the dresser, and he had to clamp hard on his jaw not to ask her where it had come from. "I have to go back to the fort for a while. I'll return as soon as I can."

"Tomorrow?" she asked, hope mixed with fear in her voice.

He thought how much she had suffered these past four years. In her own way as much as the men on the battlefield. He smiled. "Tonight—if you can manage a place for me to sleep."

Angel's smile held relief, a soft smile that made her look like the young girl she had been. "We've got plenty of room. Nothing so grand as the old days, but at least your bed will be clean and warm." She walked with him out the bedroom door and down the stairs, then paused a moment in the entry.

"About the laudanum," she said, as he opened the door, "I asked Doc Gordon about it. He said he found a box of supplies on his doorstep. That's all he has from the wreck and he doesn't know where those came from."

His gaze ran over her, came back to her face. Lines of fatigue marred her forehead. Worry darkened her bright blue eyes. "Thanks for asking, Angel." He wanted to hold her, to take her in his arms and comfort her, to erase the past and every bitter word that had ever passed between them. He wanted things to be like they were, but he knew they never could be.

"As I said, I'll be back as soon as I can. In the meantime, Willie's going to need a number of different medicines, supplies that were lost in the train wreck. If you can't find Doc Gordon or he doesn't have them, maybe you can find a way to get them."

Her jaw firmed up. "I'll get them. I'll do whatever it takes to see that they're here."

He smiled. If she had been a handful before—and she surely had—he could only imagine the man it would take to deal with her stubborn will now. "Try to get some Dover's powder. I'll need blue pill, quinine, some ipecacuanha powder, barley water, Spirit of Nitre, and some cream of tartar. Can you remember all that?"

She repeated the items aloud. "I'll write them down as soon as you're gone."

"Then I'll see you tonight."

"Yes . . ." she said. "Tonight," and the word and her smile washed over him.

Forcing his gaze from her face, he crossed the porch, still seeing her features, her pretty blue eyes, and the cleft in her chin. Untying his horse, he swung up on its back, then reined off toward the shortcut through Coltrane Farms. Knowing how worried she was, he hated to leave her, but there were patients who needed him more. He hated to make the trip across land that had once been his home—the memories were always too painful. He hated to come back to Summers End, knowing he still wanted Angel, knowing he couldn't have her, knowing that each moment he spent with her would make his need for her even more fierce.

So much hate. No wonder there wasn't the slightest chance that things could be mended between them.

The moon was up, nearly full tonight, but the wind had shifted and blown a cloud cover in. Angel waited anxiously by the window watching for Josh to ride up, then hurried out on the porch to greet him.

"Are you still planning to stay?" she asked with a glance toward the saddlebags slung over the back of his horse.

"I told you I would. How's the boy?"

Walking toward him, she watched his easy movements as he swung down from the saddle. "Unfortunately, he looks about the same. You go on in. I'll take care of your horse."

He started to protest, snapped his mouth closed and nodded. It wasn't like Josh to let a woman do a man's work and undoubtedly he remembered the pampered young lady she had been. But Willie came first. There really was no choice.

"Go on," she urged with a smile that came close to amusement. "Believe me, I've done this before. I won't be gone long."

He went inside and she led his horse out to the stable for water and a forkful of hay. When she returned to the house, she found Josh with Ida, upstairs in Willie's bedroom.

He glanced from her brother to her as she walked in, and the tension in his jaw sent a spiral of fear shooting through her. "It's not good, Angel. I need those medicines badly."

She had gone to her neighbor, Mrs. Barkley, as soon as Josh had left the house. Rumor had it that one of the Barkley boys had been involved in the train wreck. If anyone could get what they needed, it was Eliza Barkley.

"We should have them first thing in the morning," Angel said. "I still don't know who has your supplies, but I have friends who know. They said they could get what we need."

"Good enough," Josh said, turning back to the boy.

"He's been real fitful," Ida said, rocking in a chair across from where Willie was sleeping. He lay tossing and turning on the bed, his hair damp with perspiration and sticking to his temples. Josh sat beside him, pressing cold, wet cloths against his forehead.

"He took some broth a little earlier," Ida said, "but he seems awful weak to me."

"We'll keep an eye on him tonight. If those medicines arrive in the morning, there's a chance they'll do the trick."

They took turns sitting with Willie. At two in the morning, Ida walked in to relieve her, but Angel was too worried to sleep.

"I'm all right, Ida. I'll stay with him. You go on back to bed."

But her aunt simply pulled her to her feet. "Go on now. At least go out and stretch your legs for a while. Fix yourself a glass of warm milk or somethin'."

Her muscles did need stretching. Her back ached from sitting in one place for so long, and a slight headache banged at her temple. Making her way out the door, she went downstairs, but she didn't head for the kitchen. Instead, she pulled her blue woolen wrapper more closely around her and made her way outside, onto the wide covered porch.

The wind was still blowing, whistling through the trees, ruffling the pale hair that hung down her back and fluttering the hem of her robe. Leaning against a tall white column, she stared out into the darkness, thinking of Willie, worrying about him, thinking of the dark-haired man upstairs.

At least she thought he was in the house till his tall figure stepped out of the shadows on the porch.

"You should be sleeping, Angel. Worrying about Willie won't make him get well any faster."

She turned in his direction, watched his long graceful strides as he approached her, tried to control the gnawing ache that rose in her chest just to look at him. "You aren't sleeping, either."

He stopped next to her, smiled down into her face. "What I do doesn't matter. I'm bigger, I'm older, and I'm a doctor. That means you're supposed to do what I say."

The breeze mussed his hair. A strand tipped forward above his dark eyes, and she fought an urge to brush it into place. "I never did what you said before. I don't suppose I'm going to start now."

His smile grew broader, a gleam of white in a strong, hard jaw. "No, you didn't, and no, I don't suppose you will." His hand came up to her cheek, lifted a windblown curl away, and tucked it behind an ear. "What would you have done if we had gotten married? The vows say a wife is supposed to love, honor, and obey."

Her heart clenched, tightening painfully inside her. She stared into those compelling brown eyes and memories threatened to overwhelm her. "I'd have done my best to be a good wife to you, Josh. I would have done everything I could to make you happy."

His gaze slid down to her mouth. She could feel it as if he touched her, and her bottom lip began to tremble. Josh reached out and stilled it with the pad of his thumb. His eyes grew more intense and she thought she heard him groan. Then he was tilting her head back, bending forward, settling his mouth over hers.

Dear God, it was the sweetest, most devastating kiss she had ever known. The softest caress, a moment of aching tenderness, then his lips crushed down, and heat swept through her.

She was in his arms before she realized what was happening. By then she didn't care. She only knew it was Josh, that in an instant, four long, agonizing years had been washed away, that for these few bittersweet moments the past did not exist. She was the girl who loved Josh Coltrane and he was the man who loved her.

She gave in to the sweetness, the yearning, kissing him back, parting her lips as he urged her to do, allowing his tongue to sweep in. He smelled faintly of leather and horses, and a man's scent that was Josh's alone. Warmth slid through her; sweet, damp heat seeped into her core. She wound her fingers in his hair, let the strands slip through, felt the muscles bunch in his neck and shoulders.

His chest pressed into her breasts and her nipples tightened beneath her cotton night rail. His hands roamed her back and everywhere he touched her she burned. He cupped her face and deepened the kiss, drinking in more of her, allowing her to take more of him. He had kissed her before, but never like this. This was a man's kiss. And now she was a woman.

A lonely woman who had loved this man and never thought to feel his touch again. His mouth moved to her ear. He pressed kisses there, then trailed a line of kisses along the column of her throat. Warmth spiraled through her, waves of building heat that crested and peaked and scorched even hotter.

"Joshua . . ."

"Angel . . . God, how I've missed you." The robe fell open. His fingers tugged at the tie on her nightgown, allowing it to fall off one shoulder. His lips pressed there, firm and warm, softer than she would have expected, hotter, more determined. She gripped his shoulders as he bared a breast, stared at it with reverence, then took her nipple into his mouth.

Scorching pleasure. Hot ripples of flame. Dear God, she had never imagined . . .

"Angel . . ." His hand cupped her breast as he kissed her again, urging her back against the big white pillar. His arousal pressed against her, a rock-hard ridge she finally recognized for what it was, a man's rampant desire for her. Little by little, it burned through her haze of pleasure and began to shout a warning. Josh had been gone four years. Men changed in four years. The war changed them. Josh was a Yank. Yankees took what they wanted. They had raped women all over the South—she had heard the terrible stories.

She broke free of the kiss, breathing hard, her senses spinning, the warning growing louder, a buzzing that filled her ears. "Josh, please . . . we can't . . . we can't do this." She thought of the woman Josh would marry, a Northerner, someone more like him. He was in love with the woman, not with her. She wondered if he simply meant to use her, if he had become that kind of man since the war.

He kissed her again, pulled her back into his arms, found her mouth, and captured her lips. Heat roared, made her dizzy, but still she pushed him away. "Josh! Y—you have to stop. We—we can't do this!"

His breathing came fast and rough, his eyes were as dark as the night around them. She had never seen him look that way. Hard. Ruthless. Determined. A man used to command, used to getting what he wanted.

A shiver of fear slid through her.

Josh must have felt it, for his head fell back and he sucked in a great breath of air. "I'm sorry, Angel. I never meant for that to happen. You don't have to be afraid."

"I—I'm not afraid." But she was. And not just of Josh. Thinking of what she'd let happen, Angel was afraid of herself. She took a step backward, pulling the robe closed around her with a shaky hand.

"I'm sorry," Josh repeated. "I promise it won't happen again." His fists were clenched, she saw, and his jaw looked tight. He worked to force himself under control.

"It was my fault as well," she admitted softly, hoping he couldn't see the rose in her cheeks as she thought of the way he had touched her. "We loved each other once. Your coming back just made us remember."

He raked a hand through his thick chestnut hair. "I suppose that's it." He glanced up and fixed his eyes on her face. "I won't lie about it, Angel. I wanted you then. I want you now. I know it wouldn't work, that there's too much grief between us, but it doesn't make me want you any less."

Angel said nothing. Her breast still ached from the way he had touched her. Her mouth still tingled from his kiss.

"I won't hurt you, Angel. Not again. I give you my word."

No, she thought. He wouldn't hurt her again. She wasn't going to let him. "We had better go back in."

Josh simply nodded. Willie was all that mattered. At least they both felt the same about that.

Josh tossed and turned, but he couldn't fall asleep. He wasn't even certain he wanted to. Every time he closed his eyes, he saw Angel. Angel with her golden hair sliding through his hands like silk, Angel with her head thrown back, her pale skin flushed with passion. Angel with her breasts bare, more sensuous than he had imagined. He could still taste her mouth on his lips. Her scent still clung to his clothes.

He fisted his hands, recalling the softness of her skin, the tightness of her nipples. He was hard as he lay on the bed, his body throbbing with a bittersweet fire. He had known it would be like this, the wanting. Known it, but it was far worse.

Now as he lay beneath a quilt she had fashioned, trying to ignore the soft ache in his groin, he told himself again that he wanted her but he didn't love her.

Part of him believed it. Just as he had abandoned her, Angel had abandoned him. If she had loved him, she would have understood why he'd had to leave. If she had cared enough, she would have accepted his decision, hoped and prayed he would return.

Get out, Josh Coltrane! she had shouted instead. *You're dead to me—do you hear? Dead to me and everyone here who ever loved you. Don't come back, Josh. If you do—if Confederate soldiers don't kill you first—I swear to you I will!*

She couldn't have loved him, not the way he thought she did. At least that's what he had believed. But the years had eased the pain and he'd had time to think. Eventually, he had come to understand how young she was. How young they both were. Young and naive.

Now she was a woman. Different from the one he remembered. Different and far more attractive than she had ever been as a flighty, pampered young girl.

Josh rolled over on the bed, wishing the morning would come, wishing he could stop thinking of Angel, hoping the boy in the room next door wouldn't be another casualty in a war that never seemed to end.

Eventually, he gave up, dragged his shirt and breeches on, and hauled himself downstairs for a cup of coffee. By the time the first gray light of dawn broke over the horizon, the supplies he needed sat on the porch. Old Serge found them and came creaking up the stairs, carrying them in his arms, hauling them into the room where Josh sat next to Willie.

"They here, Mista Josh. Dat medicine you needed—it's done showed up on the porch!"

"Thank God." He took the box from Serge's wrinkled hands and immediately began to take inventory. Everything he'd asked for and more, along with cotton pads and bandages. He'd been using home remedies so far, a concoction of whatever medicinals he could conjure: chamomile out of the garden, root of sweet weed Serge had dug from a swampy spot in the river, milkweed from the thicket. They all had their value and he wasn't completely convinced that their use, on occasion, wasn't more successful that the latest modern drugs.

Still, he was relieved the supplies had come. He only wished he had more for his patients at the fort.

"Is dey anythin' I can do?" Serge asked, still standing in the doorway.

"You can get me some more hot water. I'd like to change the dressing on Willie's leg before I leave."

The little boy stirred. He blinked when he saw Josh's uniform, and sat up in the bed. "What—what're *you* doin' here? You get away from me! I don't want no dirty Yank touchin' me." It was the first time the child had been awake enough to realize he was there. Josh might have smiled if that had been a good sign, but the fever dulling the boy's light blue eyes was hardly good news.

"It's all right, Willie, I'm a doctor. Doctors aren't the

same as regular soldiers. It doesn't really matter what color their uniform is."

A rustle of skirts drew his attention. Angel stood not two feet away, one eyebrow cocked as if neither she nor Willie believed what he said.

"Make him go away, Angel," the boy said. "I don't want no Billy Yank—"

"Hush, sweetheart." Angel knelt beside him, reached out and took his hand. Watching her, Josh ignored the tightness binding his chest. "Dr. Coltrane is a very old friend. He used to be our neighbor. He's come to help you get better."

"It hurts," Willie said, his eyes tearing up. "It hurts so bad."

"I know, sweetheart. Pretty soon you'll feel better."

Willie just looked at her. When? his blue gaze silently asked. Then his eyelids slowly closed and he drifted back to sleep. Josh applied the salves he had made, gave Angel instructions on what medicines Josh should have, when, and how much. Then the dressings were changed and he was finally ready to leave.

"When—when will you be back?" she asked and there was that look of fear again.

"Tonight. Let's hope there's some change for the better." But he wasn't sure there would be and he wasn't sure what he would do if there wasn't.

Five

Angel paced in front of the hearth in the downstairs parlor. The room had once been grand—Persian carpets on the inlaid parquet floors, expensive Chinese vases, heavy brocade silk draperies. Now the carpets and vases had been sold, the floors were scuffed, and the draperies were faded.

Funny how much the loss had mattered before. Now, with Willie so terribly sick upstairs, it didn't seem to matter anymore.

For the tenth time that afternoon she walked to the window. Long pine boughs had been linked together to form evergreen garlands that hung from the top of the windows. They'd cut snowflakes from white paper squares and pasted them on the glass, and a wreath of holly decorated the wall above the mantel. They had started getting ready for Christmas, but Willie's accident had put an end to what little holiday spirit they had been able to muster.

The only present she wanted now was for her little brother's leg to get well.

Angel stared out the window as she had done before, but it was too early for Josh's return. She should be taking the soldiers' clean laundry back to town, or collecting eggs from the hen house, since Willie wasn't able. Instead, she stood there staring, worrying about her brother, waiting for Josh and hoping he would come early.

But none of the four mounted men she spotted riding up the lane to Summers End was Joshua Coltrane. Since the end of the war, it was common for Confederate soldiers to stop by on their journey back home, and the butternut color of the men's jackets, ragged and dirty as they were, said that's what these men were.

Angel pushed open the door as the soldiers drew near, then suddenly wished that she hadn't. The war had taken the cream of Southern men. Those still living had returned to their families as swiftly as they could. Those who hadn't yet gone home were often wanderers, outcasts with no family to return to.

Still, it was the Yankees she feared, not war-torn Confederate troops, no matter how hardened they might appear.

"Afternoon, gentlemen." Angel smiled up at their beefy leader, a sergeant according to the yellow stripes on his jacket sleeve. "Welcome to Summers End."

"Thank you, ma'am." He tipped his hat. "Your man around?"

"My father died at Shiloh. What can I do for you, sergeant?"

"Sorry to bother you, ma'am, but me and the boys is headin' home. We've traveled a goodly distance. Thought maybe you might find us a bite of food or at least let us water our horses."

She pointed toward the rear of the house. "The watering trough is out back. We haven't got much to eat around here, but I imagine I can rustle up something."

"That'd be mighty obligin'," a bearded soldier said.

"You go on and tend your horses," Angel said. "I'll bring the food out as soon as it's ready."

The sergeant touched the brim of his wide-brimmed gray hat. "Thank you, ma'am."

As the men rode away, Angel returned inside the house. Ida was already at work in the kitchen. Apparently, she had seen the men from upstairs.

"Those poor boys sure look the worse for wear, don't they?"

"They're going home," Angel said. "I feel sorry for them." She walked to the dry sink. "How's Willie?"

" 'Bout the same, I'm afraid. Serge is with him. I'll be glad when Josh gets back."

So would she, Angel thought. At least part of her would be. The other part tried not to remember the way she had felt when he had kissed her. Instead, she set to work beside Ida, heating a kettle of beans, carving thick chunks of bread and several slabs of cheese.

"I'll take it out to them," Ida said, but Angel shook her head.

"I'll do it. You've been working all day. You've got to be dead on your feet. Why don't you go back up and sit with Willie? Let Serge catch a nap if he can."

Ida smiled with a hint of relief. She was a heavy woman. Since morning, she'd been making mincemeat from the last of the dried fruit and a haunch of venison. Standing as she had for so many hours made her thick legs ache unbearably.

"I won't be long."

"Take your time," Ida said. "Those boys look like they could use a little friendly conversation."

Slinging a towel over one shoulder, Angel picked up the tray and started for the door. The youngest soldier saw her and came to help her carry it. He couldn't have been more than eighteen. On a second trip, she brought out the beans, setting the kettle on a tree stump near the watering trough.

It was brisk but not cold. A milky sun kept the temperature from falling. Still, something about the men made her uneasy and she decided not to stay, turning instead back toward the house.

"Where you goin', pretty girl?" the sergeant asked, setting his tin plate of food on the ground and coming quickly to his feet. "Why don't you stay and keep us company for awhile?"

Unconsciously, she backed up as he drew near, caught herself and stood her ground. "I—I have to go in."

His hand came out, his skin rough, the fingernails long and dirty as he caught her chin. "Not yet, you don't. Right, boys?"

Two of them laughed. "That's right, Sarge." In minutes, the four of them stood around her.

"We don't mean to hurt ya, ma'am," the bearded soldier said, "but me and the boys, we ain't been with a woman in more'n two years. We done talked it over, and well, we just gotta have ya."

"What—what are you talking about?" She started backing away, praying she had misunderstood his words.

"I'll take her first," the sergeant said, blocking her retreat, "seein' as it was my idea to come here." Before she could run, he caught her arm, clamped a hand over her mouth, and jerked her against him. Fear shot through her, pinpricks of alarm that sent shivers along her spine. She tried to twist free, tried to pry his hand away, but his hold was relentless and he dragged her down on the ground.

"It won't do ya no good to fight, ma'am. Just be easy and ya won't get hurt."

"I'm next," the bearded man said, and Angel began to fight in earnest. Already he was unbuttoning his breeches and so was the sergeant. She felt the bigger man's hands on her leg, shoving up her skirt. Her struggles increased and so did her fear. Oh, dear God! She glanced toward the house. Willie's room faced the front, not the rear, and Serge was probably sleeping. She kicked out with her foot, but her shoe slammed into the soldier's thick leather boot. Sinking her teeth into the fleshy hand that covered her mouth, she heard him curse, then felt the burning sting of a slap across her face.

"Dammit, I said to lay still."

"Hurry up!" the bearded soldier hissed. "We ain't got all day." Then the sharp click of a gun being cocked echoed just a few feet away. The rustle of clothing ceased. The sergeant seemed frozen in place, one hand still clutching a button on his trousers.

"Very slowly," a familiar voice said, "let the lady go and back away." The sergeant's hand crept down toward his weapon but Josh's hard voice stopped him. "I wouldn't do that if I were you." He motioned to the others. "You men—

keep your hands out in front of you, well away from those guns, and back away."

Cold air seeped through her thin pantalets as the sergeant lifted his heavy bulk off her. Angel's hands were trembling so badly she could barely pull her skirt back into place.

"You all right, Angel?"

"Y—yes." Josh was here! He had come just like he said. But her teeth were chattering and it wasn't from the cold.

"You men throw down your weapons. Take it nice and easy. Angel, you get over here behind me."

For once, she did as he told her, moving to stand so close to Josh's back she could feel the heat pouring off his hard-muscled body.

"Get me some rope," he told her, his Spencer rifle pointing straight at the sergeant's heart. "You men weren't happy just getting through this war alive. Now you'll be spending the next few years in a Federal prison."

Angel started shaking even harder. Oh, dear God, she knew about those places. Kirby Fields had been in one. He still couldn't talk about it without crying. A grown man like Kirby. He wasn't afraid of anything, but he cried when he talked about Elmira.

"Go on, Angel," Josh said firmly. "Go get the rope."

She still didn't move. They deserved to be in prison for what they'd tried to do, and yet . . . "Let them go, Josh."

He turned a little, till he could see her from the corner of his eye. "Are you insane? These men may be Confederates, but they would have raped you just the same."

"I—I know what they meant to do. I don't think they've done it before. The war did it—it's made them half crazy. It did things to all of us. Let them go, Josh, please. Do it for me."

He cursed long and fluently, words a younger Josh Coltrane wouldn't have said. "You men hear that? Miss Summers wants me to let you go. Unfortunately, the lady is a helluva lot more forgiving than I am." The smile he flashed was wolfish and cold. "I'll make you a deal. I'll give you a head start. You get on those horses and ride out of here. By the time I get back to Fort Jackson and turn you in, you can be a good ways down the road."

The men glanced from one to another. There wasn't one that didn't look a little bit ashamed. "You got a deal, Yank." The sergeant motioned toward Angel. "We didn't come here to hurt her. She was just so damned pretty . . ."

"Get out," Josh said coldly.

Angel didn't realize she was gripping his arm until the men rode out of sight and she felt his fingers curl over her hand. He turned and eased her into his arms, holding tightly against his chest.

"I would have killed them," he said. "I'm a doctor and I swear I would have murdered every last one."

Angel slid her arms around his neck and clung to him, her body still trembling with the remnants of fear. Confederate soldiers would have raped her. A Yankee soldier had saved her. The world had turned upside down, had gone completely insane. Dear God, she was so confused!

"Angel . . ." Josh whispered, stroking a hand through her hair. "Sweeting, are you all right?"

She eased herself away, wanting to escape him. Wanting to stay right where she was. "I'm all right . . . now."

He turned her face to study the red mark on her cheek. "Bastards."

Ignoring the warmth of his hand, she eased herself farther away, smoothing the front of her skirt. She didn't want to think about Josh, the way he had come to her defense. She didn't want to hear her heart thrum the way it was, just being near him.

"We'd better get back to the house," she said. "Willie isn't getting any better. In fact, I think he's worse."

Josh went tense. "Come on." Taking her hand, he led her toward the back door.

Angel paused as he pulled it open. "I'm frightened, Josh. I can't stand to see him hurting. What are we going to do?"

Josh didn't answer. Not until he reached the little boy's bedside. One look at Willie and the lines of his face went grim.

"We've got to take him back to the fort. I need to watch him around the clock. If you want to come with him, I can arrange a place for you to sleep."

"You can't take a little boy to an army post! For heaven's sake, the place is full of Yankee soldiers!"

"Fort Jackson is a hospital, Angel. Willie's fever's got to be stopped. If it isn't, he'll go into convulsions. Since I can't stay here all the time, Willie's got to go there."

Angel bit her lip. Yankees. Would there ever be an end to them? "Are you sure there's no other way?"

"Willie needs constant medical attention. This is his best chance to get it."

Angel looked at little Willie, saw the way his thin chest rose and fell, the way he tossed on the bed. Her brother needed Josh just as she had needed him today. What did it matter where the child was as long as she was with him? "All right, we'll take him to the fort."

"I'll tell Ida to get his things," Josh said. "Tell Serge to hook up the wagon, then pack what you need."

Angel nodded. One look at Willie and her chest went tight. He had to be all right—he had to be!

Twenty minutes later they were packed and ready and loaded aboard the wagon. Before night had fallen they had passed through the heavy stone porticos of Fort Jackson.

"We'll get Willie settled in the hospital," Josh said. "Then I'll find a room for you."

"All right."

He led her toward a wooden barracks, Willie cradled against his broad chest. Pulling open the heavy wooden door, Josh led her into the dimly lit interior. The smell hit her first, as sharp and painful as a blow to the head, sending the bile up in her throat.

"I should have warned you," he said, catching a glimpse of her pale face. "You aren't going to be sick?"

Her chin hiked up but she had to wet her lips. "I'm fine."

"You get used to it after awhile. I should have said something. We're not used to civilians out here."

She fought down another wave of nausea. "It's all right. I

told you, I'm fine." But of course she wasn't. Neither was she prepared for the rows of suffering men she found inside the barracks. Two long lines of white-draped bodies, the bed linens clean but some of the wounds weeping blood, forming dark red patches on the sheets.

The place was clean and neat, meticulously so. Which wasn't surprising. Josh's own home had always been spotlessly cared for. But the stench of ammonia, putrefied wounds, sweat-soaked male bodies, and vomit made drawing a breath nearly impossible.

The building itself contributed to the gloominess. The white-painted walls were yellowed and peeling. The damp smell of mildew rose up from the floors. Whale oil lanterns cast an eerie glow into the open rafters, and the hazy, flickering shadows of the men moved ominously over the walls.

"We'll put Willie on a cot up in the front. Dr. Medford and I will take turns watching him."

"Dr. Medford?"

The sandy-haired man walked up just then. "Did I hear someone mention my name?"

Josh smiled. "Silas, this is Miss Summers. Her brother has a compound fracture. Fever's set in. We'll be keeping an eye on him for a while."

The thin doctor glanced toward the boy on the cot. A sandy brow arched up. "I doubt Colonel Wilson would approve your treating a civilian in an army hospital."

"Colonel Wilson doesn't need to know everything that goes on out here. Miss Summers and I are old friends. Her brother needs help and we're going to help him. Do you have a problem with that, Doctor?"

Silas Medford's thin lips curved upward. "Not in the least." He turned to Angel. "A pleasure meeting you, Miss Summers. I'll do my best for your brother."

Angel simply nodded. It was difficult to concentrate with the unfamiliar sounds in the room. Several men were snoring, others were whispering, one played a soulful harmonica tune. She found herself turning toward the poignant notes and realized a number of the soldiers were staring, their sunken, hollow gazes focused on her.

"They don't mean to be disrespectful," Josh said. "Most of them aren't much more than boys. The others are family men. They miss their wives and daughters. All of them just want to go home."

She studied the men's disheartened faces. "They all look so sad."

Josh's dark gaze moved to her eyes. "They are. Low morale is part of the reason these men haven't gotten well as fast as they should have. It's not an easy thing for the army to treat."

Angel said nothing, just kept staring at the sea of lonely faces staring back at her. Wearing hospital gowns instead of their blue uniforms, they didn't look like Yankee soldiers. They just looked like lonely, suffering men.

"Come on," Josh said. "Silas will watch after Willie while I get you settled in."

Angel let him lead her away, but in her mind's eye, all she could see was the dismal hospital room with its endless rows of beds, and the faces of those poor sick men.

Josh arranged quarters for Angel in a room that had once been occupied by the fort commander's wife. All that remained was an old iron bed, a scarred wooden dresser, a table, and two chairs, but there was a fireplace in one corner to keep the place warm, and it wasn't far from his own quarters, so he could keep an eye on her.

It probably wasn't necessary, he thought as he returned to his own room and readied himself for bed. There weren't that many men at the fort. The officers were all first rate and discipline had never been a problem. Still, since he'd stumbled onto the Confederates who had tried to rape her, he couldn't stand the thought of her being too far away.

He had always been protective of women. As a man raised in the South, it was simply his way. Still, his concern for Angel went beyond Southern manners. He hadn't realized how possessive—how wildly protective—he felt toward Angel until he had seen her with those men.

He hadn't lied to her. He could have strangled every manjack sonofabitch with his own bare hands.

He understood their wanting her. He wanted her that same way, had since the moment he had seen her in Whistler's Dry Goods. But now he realized his feelings went way beyond that. He didn't want another man touching her. He would kill to keep anyone from hurting her.

The thought was unsettling, particularly since his plans for the future did not include Angel Summers. Sarah Wingate was the woman he would marry. He had abandoned the South, given up his birthright when he had joined the Union Army. He was no longer welcome here. He had no choice but to make the North his home. Josh sighed as he pulled back the covers and climbed naked into bed. Just thinking of Angel made him hard, and he only had a few hours to sleep before he had to spell Silas Medford in the ward. He tried to fall asleep, but tossed and turned instead. Finally he got up, dressed, and went back to the hospital. What he didn't expect to find in the barracks this time of the night was Angel Summers.

Angel pressed the tin cup to the young soldier's trembling lips. With his thin frame propped against her shoulder, she helped him steady himself enough to drink.

"Thank you, ma'am," said the dark-haired youth who was sick with a bowel disorder. "That was mighty kind of you." There was such a smile of gratitude on the young corporal's face, Angel's throat went tight.

"Get some sleep," she said to him. "You need your rest if you're going to get well."

"Yes, ma'am. And thank you again." He settled back on the cot and his eyes slid closed. Instead of the restless tossing that had drawn her reluctantly to his bedside, he drifted into a peaceful slumber.

She hadn't meant to get involved with the soldiers. They

were Yankees, after all—she wasn't about to help them. But they were also men, and sitting for so long in the darkness beside Willie's bed, her attention had reluctantly been drawn to the groans of pain, the sleepless thrashing, the sounds of weeping in the darkness. She couldn't just sit there, knowing the men were hurting.

Footsteps coming down the aisle distracted her. Josh appeared like a specter out of the darkness. "You're supposed to be in bed, Angel."

"I couldn't sleep. I thought I might as well be here." She glanced back at the soldier on the bed. "Corporal Miller was thirsty. I brought him some water."

His eyes touched hers and there was so much tenderness in his expression, Angel felt a tightness in her chest.

"Thank you," Josh said. "With the war over and most of the men gone home, we're short-handed here. I'm sure the men appreciate any help you can give them." He didn't say more, just walked her back to the chair beside Willie's bed, then went off to check on his patients.

Angel leaned over, ran her fingers through her brother's tousled blond hair. His breathing was shallow and his face looked flushed, but at least the medicine Josh had given him kept the pain at bay. The men on the cots had little to keep them from hurting.

Her gaze locked with a dark-eyed soldier just a few feet away. He had lost the use of his legs, one of the men had told her, and with them, his dull gaze said, he had also lost the will to live. Her feet moved toward him of their own accord. Try as she might, she couldn't seem to stop them.

"Can I get you something . . . ?" She glanced at the name penned on the paper above the cot. ". . . Lieutenant Langley?"

The man said nothing, but the anguish in his expression seemed to grow worse.

"My name is Angel Summers. Dr. Coltrane is taking care of my little brother."

He was younger than he'd looked from a distance. No

more than twenty-four or -five, yet his face was lined and his skin rough, scarred in several places.

"Are you sure there is nothing I can get you?" He shook his head, but his eyes welled with tears. Angel's stomach knotted. "Are you in pain?"

Another shake of his head. He turned his face away from her into the pillow, but a tear rolled down his cheek.

"Lieutenant Langley, please . . . won't you let me help you?"

The dark eyes were back, and a spark of anger flashed there. "I don't want your help. I don't want to be treated like a helpless cripple . . . even if that's what I am." Absently, he rubbed his lifeless legs. "I want to be the man I was before."

She smoothed the hair back from his forehead. "You are the man you were before. Nothing can change that. You've just lost the use of your limbs."

He only shook his head. "You don't understand."

"Then why don't you explain it to me?"

He turned away, then dragged in a slow, shaky breath. "Seeing you tonight, watching the way you moved, listening to the sound of your voice . . . it reminded me of Laura. She was blond like you . . . beautiful like you. We were going to be married. I've lost her now. I can't ask her to marry me. I couldn't take care of her. I can hardly take care of myself."

Angel's heart turned over. She knew the pain of losing someone you loved. "Does she know you've been injured?"

"You mean does she know I'm a cripple? No, and I'm not going to tell her."

"But you must, Lieutenant. If she loves you, she won't care what's happened to you. She'll just be grateful to God that you're still alive."

But the soldier shook his head. He turned away from her again and the light she had sparked seemed to fade. She left him staring into space, his jaw tight, his features grim, and made her way back to Willie. But she couldn't help thinking about the soldier, wondering if the girl he loved would still want him. She knew if the man had been Josh, if he had been

crippled as he fought for the Southern cause, she would still
have wanted him.

  She glanced toward his tall frame, watched him working
over one of his patients. Josh hadn't been crippled in the war,
he had simply been a traitor. Still the words she had spoken
to the soldier rang in her head. *If she loves you, she won't
care what has happened to you.* True love meant accepting
a man the way he was, without strings, without reservation.
She couldn't help wondering if, in a way, she hadn't failed
Josh just as much as he had failed her.

Six

Josh reined his saddle horse toward the knoll overlooking Coltrane Farms. He'd had to get away from the hospital, from the suffering in his patients' eyes that he could do nothing about. Mostly he had to get away from Angel—and the turmoil just looking at her was doing to his insides.

Josh lifted his hat, letting the cold wind ruffle his dark hair, then settled the brim low across his forehead. Urging the bay to a faster pace, he dropped off the hill toward the house that had once been his home. It wasn't as fancy as the white-columned mansion at Summers End, but it had a sturdy, two-story wood frame, a porch all around, and a well-furnished parlor. There were five bedrooms upstairs—plenty of room for children, his mother had said. But there'd only been him and his sister, and Janie hadn't lived to be ten years old.

It was one of the reasons he had wanted to be a doctor. Perhaps he could have saved her, he used to think.

Josh reined up in front of the empty yellow house. He had always loved the old place. After he'd met Angel, he had dreamed of building one just like it for the two of them and the children they would raise on a piece of this good Coltrane land.

He eyed the "For Sale" sign he had placed in the window. Just looking at the bold black letters made the inside of his mouth feel dry. He didn't want to sell it, not really. Not deep down in his gut. Since his return to Savannah, he had come to realize just how much he had missed the

South. How much he longed for the warm spring evenings, the sweet smell of summer grasses, the taste of Southern home cooking.

Josh swung down from the bay, looped the reins over the hitching post out in front of the house, and stepped up on the porch. It felt so right being here, so good deep down inside. In the past few days, even memories of the parents he had lost weren't enough to dull that sense of belonging.

Gazing off toward the fallow fields, for the first time since his return, Josh admitted how much he wanted to come back home.

A rooster crowed somewhere in the distance, gone wild, he supposed, since the place had been abandoned. He glanced around the yard, pulled open the door that was never locked, and stepped inside the parlor. Much of the furniture was gone, but an amazing amount still remained: petit point pictures his grandmother had stitched, a pair of cut crystal whale oil lamps, a portrait of his parents above the cloth-draped horsehair sofa. In the old days, this time of year the house would have been decorated for Christmas, candles glowing, holly wreaths above the hearth.

The place seemed oddly empty without the holiday cheer, and strangely silent now. He wanted to see it sparkling with light again, filled with the love and laughter he had known in the house as a boy.

Standing in front of the empty hearth, he ran his hand along the mantel, stirring up a small cloud of dust, but his thoughts remained on the farmhouse and the land he had loved. They needed a doctor in Savannah. True, they resented him now, but with time and hard work that resentment could eventually be overcome. He wanted to come home, to rebuild his life here at Coltrane Farms.

As he walked back out on the porch, he admitted something else.

He wanted Angel Summers to be part of that life.

An image of her sitting beside Lieutenant Langley came to mind. She had tried to resist the soldiers she thought of as her enemy, but her compassionate nature just wouldn't let her. He recalled the way she treated old Serge, the tender care she gave her little brother. She was more of a woman than she ever had been before, and the truth was he still loved her.

Time hadn't changed that, as he had once believed. The war hadn't done it. He loved her, and deep down he believed she might still love him.

For the first time in days, Josh really smiled. He had won Angel's hand against half the men in Chatham County. She'd be just as big a challenge now—more so, as much as she hated Yankees—yet if the way she had kissed him was any indication, he believed he had a chance.

Still, with the war and all that had happened, it wouldn't be easy to mend the rift between them and make a life together. And it wasn't just Angel—the whole damned town was against him. It was a perilous undertaking, definitely fraught with risk. It was even more risky to gamble his heart again.

Josh flashed another smile, this one determined. Angel Summers was worth the risk.

Angel paced the floor of Mrs. Barkley's parlor. She hated leaving Willie, but she couldn't stand to sit in the barracks a moment more.

"Please, Mrs. Barkley, you've got to tell me how you got that medicine. I have to speak to the men who took it and convince them to give it back. I heard Harley Lewis was involved and maybe Pete Thompson. I thought perhaps your sons—"

"I'd like to help ya, child, I truly would, but my boys ain't budgin' an inch on this. As far as Harley and Pete is concerned, they ain't got the stuff no more, leastwise not all of it."

"Then where is it?"

"Way I heard tell, it's sorta scattered hereabouts. Some went to Doc Gordon, you got some, other folks took what they wanted. Ain't no one person's got the lot of it."

Angel sank down on the small settee in front of the fire. "Josh needs that medicine. If you could see those men, Mrs. Barkley, I know you'd want to help them. Tell me what I can do."

The older woman sighed. Setting aside her knitting, she came heavily to her feet and walked over to Angel. "You're that bound and determined, there is one thing you might do."

"What's that?"

"There's a big town meetin' in the mornin'. Business is off real bad this year. Everybody's worried about it. 'Course, money's real tight, and they ain't much in the stores for sale, but it's more than that. Streets don't have no decorations this year. Stores ain't done up like they usually are for the holidays. Nobody round here seems to have the spirit of Christmas."

"It's the Yankees," Angel said. "They came bustin' in here last year—Sherman and his soldiers. Everybody still remembers how bad it was."

"I suppose that's it. Whatever it is, Mayor Donaldson is gonna do some speechifyin', try to brighten everybody's mood."

"I heard about the meeting. You're suggesting I talk to folks there?"

"Probably won't do no good, but if I was set on tryin', that's what I'd do."

Angel smiled. She stood up from the sofa, then leaned over and hugged her neighbor. "You're a jewel, Mrs. Barkley, you truly are."

The older woman waived her words away. "I don't like to see men hurtin' any more than you do, not if there's somethin' I can do to stop it."

Angel smiled again. "Thank you, Mrs. Barkley."

"And give that little brother of yours a hug for me. Tell him I'll whip him up a batch of them molasses cookies he likes just as soon as he gets home."

"I'll tell him," she said, seeing Willie's image, one of the prized cookies clutched in each of his small hands. A hard ache rose in Angel's throat. Eliza Barkley was a good friend.

The best. Eliza would stand by her, she knew. Now if she could only manage to convince the rest of the people in Savannah.

Josh strode into the barracks, heading straight for little Willie's bed. An orderly sat beside him while Silas Medford tended one of the patients on the ward. He gave the child a dose of calomel and rhubarb, checked the medicinal plaster he had placed on the boy's narrow chest, but saw that his fever still hovered well above normal.

With a sigh of regret, he turned to the orderly. "Have you seen Angel . . . Miss Summers, that is?" He had already tried her quarters as soon as he'd returned from the farm, but she wasn't in.

The bone-thin orderly, a former patient now recovered but still twenty pounds underweight, moved to the foot of the bed. "She was here all mornin', Doc. Then she said she had an errand to run. Said she'd be back just as quick as she could."

Josh nodded, but his gaze remained on Willie. The boy's appetite had waned, leaving him weak and emaciated. Even the icy water they kept him bathed in hadn't been able to break the fever's raging grip. Josh worked over the child for a little while longer, checking the leg and changing the dressing. As he had said, the bone was well-set and on the mend, but the skin around the tear was purple and swollen, puffy and warm to the touch. If they couldn't stop the infection, the injury would putrefy. Gangrene would mean the boy would lose the leg—or worse.

"We'll have to change those cold compresses more often. Bathe his neck and shoulders as well as his stomach and legs. We've got to get that fever down."

"Yes, sir," the orderly said.

Satisfied he had done all he could, Josh turned away, his thoughts shifting once more to Angel. Where had she gone? he wondered. Whatever she was doing had to be important or she wouldn't have left her brother. More worried than he should have been, it took him several more seconds to realize there was something different about the barracks.

Partly it was the smell. The scent of evergreen drifted up from branches heaped in piles beside the soldiers' beds, helping to mask the nauseous hospital fumes, and mounds of red berry holly were scattered across the rough wooden floors.

"What's all this?" Josh asked the orderly.

"It's Miss Angel. She said the place was depressing. She said it was Christmas and we ought to do somethin' about it. She got some of the off-duty soldiers to go out and scavenge up what they could. Now the patients that are well enough are makin' Christmas garlands and stringin' holly berries. Lieutenant Ainsley volunteered to cut us a big pine tree. Miss Angel says she's gonna help us decorate the tree for Christmas."

Josh glanced around the room. At least half of his patients were involved some way or other in making Christmas decorations. The sight raised an ache in his chest.

Damn, why hadn't he thought of this? Healing was mental as well as physical. He didn't have the medicines his patients needed, but something like this could have helped to lift their spirits.

He looked over at young Ben Weatherly. He hadn't seen the boy smile like that in weeks. He was working a needle and thread—the kind of supplies they had plenty of—pushing it through long green pine stems, sewing the branches together to form a garland for the walls. Other men were making holly wreaths, using pine cones for decoration. Several wreaths were finished and sitting on tables along the walls, a few white candles blazing in the center.

Josh started forward, his smile nearly as big as the men's. Angel had done this. She'd been able to put her prejudice aside and help these men so desperately in need. The hope he had felt at the farm rose up, stronger now than it was before.

Angel, he thought. *You're mine, dammit. You always have*

been. Now all he had to do was find some way to convince her.

It was dark when Angel returned to the fort. Leaving her horse with one of the men, she hurried into the barracks, making her way straight to her brother. His eyes were open, as dull and glazed as they were the last time he'd been awake, but he smiled when he saw her and that gave her hope.

"Willie, sweetheart. How are you feeling?" She reached out and captured his hand. Feeling how hot it was, her hope turned to despair.

"The soldiers are making Christmas stuff. They're gonna put it up on the walls as soon as they get finished."

Tears burned Angel's eyes. This wasn't the Christmas she had wanted for Willie. "That's right, honey. Pretty soon this place will look just like home." Of course, even home wasn't decorated this year. Not with Willie so sick.

"You know what I want for Christmas?" Willie said.

"What, sweetheart?"

"I want to get well so I can go home."

Her heart hurt. "That's what I want, too." It was the truth. It was the only gift she cared about, and she prayed for it every day.

Willie's lackluster gaze moved over the room, watching the soldiers work. "Can I make some decorations, too?" he asked weakly.

Angel forced a smile. "Of course you can. Why don't we string some berries?"

He nodded, but by the time she returned with a bowl of the tiny red berries, he had already drifted back to sleep.

"Where the hell have you been?" Josh's voice slammed into her with the force of a blow, arriving well before the sound of his heavy boots. "It's getting dark out there. After what happened with those Confederates, I thought you'd know better than to—"

"I had something important to do." Her chin came up.

"Besides, it's none of your business where I go—not any more."

"You're wrong, Angel. As long as you're here at the fort, you're my responsibility. That makes it my business."

Angel set her jaw. Josh might have changed in some ways, but he was still the domineering, overprotective male he had always been. "I went to see Mrs. Barkley. You were right— these men need those supplies. I was hoping I could get them."

His anger drained away. Josh sighed wearily. "I'm sorry. I was worried, is all." He raked a hand through his heavy chestnut hair, lifting the dark strands that hung just below his collar. "I shouldn't have yelled at you."

Something warm unfurled inside her. Josh was worried about her. Never mind that it shouldn't matter, that she shouldn't care one whit that a Yankee captain had been concerned. "How's Willie?" she asked, trying not to notice the fatigue in Josh's dark eyes. "He was awake when I got back. I thought maybe his fever had broken, but I don't . . . I don't think it has."

"I wish I could tell you he was better. He's holding his own. That's about it. We're doing the best we can."

Angel glanced away. "I know that, Josh."

"He'll sleep now. The orderly will stay with him. Why don't we go for a walk?"

She glanced at her brother, saw that Josh was right and Willie was deeply asleep. As tired as she was, looking at Josh's handsome features, her fatigue seemed to fade. "I'd like that."

They left the barracks and prowled the mostly empty fort, strolling across the yard, ending up beneath the ramparts where a few battered cannon still protruded from the walls above them.

"I want to thank you, Angel, for what you're doing for the men. I haven't seen that much life in them since I came to the fort."

Angel shook her head. "I never meant to help them. As

far as I was concerned, they were Yankees. I never meant to
lift a finger."

They stopped in the shadows behind an empty barracks.
"Then why did you?" Darkness threw his face into harsh
relief, outlining the hard planes and valleys. Lines of fatigue
dug creases beside his deep brown eyes. He looked older,
more rugged. He was still the handsomest man she had ever
seen.

"You were right about that, too," she said. "They're men,
just like any others. No one should have to suffer that way."

"You spoke to Mrs. Barkley. You tried to help them. You'll
never know how much I appreciate that."

"I haven't given up, Josh. I'm going to try again." She
told him about the town meeting she planned to attend in the
morning, and the pride in his eyes made the breath catch in
her throat.

His hand came up to her cheek. "Angel . . ." Then he was
bending his head, slanting his mouth over hers and capturing
her lips.

Pleasure speared through her, blocking the deepening
chill. Josh pulled her closer, wrapped her in his arms, and
Angel gave in to the incredible sensation, savoring the close-
ness, feeling the old familiar rush of love. Josh deepened the
kiss, probing with his tongue, teasing the corners of her
mouth till she parted her lips, making her tremble. She
clutched his shoulders and he drew her closer, kissing her
more thoroughly, sending little shivers along her spine.

Oh, dear God, it felt so good to kiss him. A tiny voice
whispered that it was wrong, that what she and Josh had was
over, that he belonged to someone else. She tried to ignore
the voice, but the voice would not be still.

"Josh," she whispered, ending the kiss, pulling herself
away. "Please don't do this."

"You wanted me to kiss you, Angel. Don't try to deny it."

She only shook her head. "It's over, Josh. You know it and
so do I."

"Are you sure?"

"You're a Yankee, Josh. This is Georgia. What else is there to say?"

Josh didn't answer. Instead his eyes searched her face—dark eyes, knowing eyes, trying to read her thoughts, assessing her, it seemed.

"It's getting cold out here," he said. "We had better be getting back in."

She nodded, but didn't say more. She almost wished he had argued, tried to convince her it might still work. She should have felt relieved that he hadn't; instead, she felt suddenly sad.

"I ordered a fire made in your quarters," Josh said. "I figured you'd be chilled when you got back."

She gave him a half-hearted smile. He had always been thoughtful that way. "Thank you."

"I suppose you'd think it was scandalous if I came in for a cup of tea." He flashed her a disarming smile and her dismal mood lifted a bit.

"What about Willie?"

"I've given him some laudanum. He won't wake up before morning."

"All right then, Captain Coltrane, you may come in. There's no one around. Besides, I've suffered things far worse than a bit of scandal."

Far worse, Josh thought, recalling the war, the loss, and grief she had known in the last four years. Taking Angel's arm, he led her through the shadows back to her room, guided her inside, and closed the door. All the way there, he was thinking of the way she had kissed him, that he could feel her hunger, nearly as strong as his own.

What he was about to do was rash, and dangerous for both of them. But his time with Angel was limited. Either the boy's fever would break—which he fervently hoped—and Angel would return to Summers End, or the colonel would arrive and demand the child be removed to the care of civilians. Once she was gone, the odds would be against him.

Angel was his—he knew that now. What he needed was a way to make her see. Words wouldn't work—not with Angel. But there was something he could do that might just convince her.

Josh meant to seduce her.

Seven

Josh watched Angel's movements as she hung the tea kettle from the long iron arm suspended above the fire. As she bent toward the hearth, her simple brown wool skirt draped over her rounded hips. Her breasts strained forward, pressing against the front of her white cotton blouse.

Seated in a chair beside the table, his body grew hard just looking at her, his blood heating up, pulsing thickly into his groin. God, he had wanted her for so long.

"Almost ready," Angel said, but her eyes didn't quite meet his. There was something intimate about being in such close quarters, about the simple act of her serving him tea.

Her glance caught his and her cheeks went pink. A stray glance touched the old iron bed in the corner, then slid back to the hearth. She was thinking of their kiss, he knew, perhaps recalling the way he had touched her that night at Summers End. He was thinking of it, too, and he ached to touch her that way again.

"Come here, Angel." She looked up at the tone of his voice, softly commanding yet gently persuasive, and another warm flush lit her cheeks. She turned away from the fire and started toward him, and Josh rose to his feet, blowing out the lamp as he stood up, leaving the glow of the fire to light the room, painting the small space in shades of orange and gold.

"What—what do you want?"

"I want to kiss you, Angel. It's what you want, too. It's why I'm here and both of us know it."

She swallowed and slowly shook her head, but she didn't

back away. Josh cupped her face with his hands, leaned forward and brushed her lips with a kiss. They were as soft as petals, sweet as sugar, and so very warm. He deepened the kiss, molding his mouth over hers, parting her lips with his tongue and stroking deeply inside. He drew her closer, into the circle of his arms, and his fingers found the pins in her long golden hair. He pulled them one by one, setting the heavy mass free, letting it fall past her shoulders, then sifting his fingers through it. It felt like silk against his hand.

"Angel," he whispered, kissing her again—soft, slow kisses, drugging kisses that made her pulse speed up, made it throb, he saw, at the base of her throat. He tasted her there, trailing his mouth along her neck, his hands massaging her back, drifting lower, cupping her bottom and drawing her against his arousal. She sucked in a breath when she felt it and began to pull away. Josh eased his hold and simply kissed her again.

In moments, he felt her relax, trusting him once more—wrongly so, for he meant to take advantage. He had to. He wanted to. It was the right thing for both of them.

Angel returned Josh's kiss, letting the fierce heat roll over her, giving in to the terrible hunger she felt each time she saw him. It's only a kiss, she told herself as his tongue swept in, delving deeply, as his hands roamed down her back, then moved lower, cradling her once more against his sex.

He was hard there, thick and heavy, bigger than she would have imagined. Yet this time she wasn't frightened. She wanted him to kiss her, to touch her. For these few moments, she wanted to forget the past, forget the fear she felt for her brother. She ached to lose herself in the sweetness of his lips, the warmth of his hands moving over her body. She barely noticed when her blouse fell open, the buttons parting as if by magic, the fabric easing from the waistband of her skirt then sliding off her shoulders.

Instead she closed her eyes and slid her fingers into the hair at the nape of his neck, felt his hand at her waist, felt his palm moving upward, gliding over her thin chemise. He eased one of the straps away, lowering the fabric and baring one of her breasts. As the heat of his hand cupped the full-ness, it occurred to her that she should stop him, end this growing madness before it went any further. Then the unwel-come thought slid away.

She didn't want to stop him, not now. She loved Josh Coltrane, had ached for him for the last four years. And the last of her will had entirely slipped away. No matter what the future held, for these few precious moments, Josh belonged to her as he had before, and nothing was going to take those moments away.

"You're so beautiful," Josh whispered, his eyes on her breasts, his long dark fingers caressing them, making the nipples peak. "I want you, Angel. I want you so damned much."

He kissed her again, rained kisses along her bare shoul-ders, bent his head and took a nipple into his mouth. Angel sucked in a breath at the white-hot fire racing through her, the scorching waves of heat that made it impossible to think. Arching her back, she gave herself up to his touch, reveled in it, unconsciously pleaded for more.

"That's right, sweeting, let yourself go. Let me taste you, Angel."

She gave in to his coaxing, her head falling back as he laved her nipple, then gently bit the end. Waves of pleasure washed through her, ripples of heat and wanting, and sud-denly she was desperate to touch him, to caress his hard male flesh as he was caressing her. Frantic fingers worked the buttons on his sky blue shirt, pulled it open, then slid into the softly curling hair across his chest. It was ridged with muscle, thick slabs that tightened wherever she touched. She ringed a flat male nipple and heard Josh groan.

"Angel . . ." Then he was lifting her up, carrying her the few short paces to the old iron bed. She should stop him, she knew. One day he would leave her as he had done before, return to the North and the woman he would marry. He couldn't stay in the South, not anymore. Instead she let him strip away her clothes and settle her in the middle of the old iron bed, then watched as he stripped away his breeches and boots.

Standing naked beside the bed, he looked hard and male, his shaft thrusting forward, firelight playing over the thick bands of muscles on his shoulders, the sinews across his chest.

"I want you," he said, leaning over her, every inch of him sleekly male, dark and masculine and aroused. "I need you, Angel."

She touched his face, felt the firmness of his jaw and the roughness of his day's growth of beard. "I need you, too, Josh." He was a Yankee. It would never work between them, but tonight that didn't matter. She loved him, she needed him, and for now that was enough.

Settling himself beside her on the bed, Josh took her in his arms and captured her lips, fitting them perfectly together. His big hands kneaded her breasts, teasing her nipples, making them ache and distend, then he took the stiff tip into his mouth. Tasting her with his tongue, he laved and suckled until her whole body tingled with pleasure, and fire scorched through her blood.

Damp heat slid through her; an aching warmth settled into her core. He must have sensed it, for his hand moved lower, laced through the soft curls above her sex, and a finger eased inside her. She was hot and wet, throbbing with need, aching for him to touch her, wanting even more.

"You're ready for me, love. Don't be frightened."

"I'm not frightened."

His finger dipped deeply, stretching the soft, plump folds, preparing her. He kissed her as he came up over her, a hot, deep, scorching kiss that had her moaning, her body writhing beneath him.

"You're mine," he whispered as he parted her legs with his knee and eased himself inside. "You've always been mine. Say it, Angel. Tell me you know it's the truth."

"I'm yours, Josh."

His hard body shuddered at her words. When he reached the wall of her innocence, he paused and a soft look stole over his features. Then he took her mouth in another fiery kiss, thrusting deeply with his tongue the same instant he thrust with his body.

Her sharp cry of pain was muffled by his lips. He held himself still, propped on his forearms, the muscles in his shoulders stiff with tension. "I'm sorry, love. I tried not to hurt you."

She reached a shaky hand up to his cheek, rested her palm against it. "It's all right. The pain is fading already." Josh smiled with such tenderness it made her heart turn over. Then he started to move, sliding even deeper, filling her with his hardness and a piercing pleasure that seemed to have no end. When his thick length could go no further, he began to ease himself out, then slowly he sank back in. With each of his movements, the pleasure increased, multiplied tenfold, and in minutes, his slow, deep strokes had her arching beneath him.

Heat roared through her, a lush, glittering fire that beckoned her to far-off places. Out and then in, the rhythm increasing, the flames and the fever, the heavy thrust and drag of his shaft and his slick, hot, burning kisses. A trembling began in her stomach and an odd sort of tightening gripped her muscles lower down.

"Josh . . . ?" she whispered, barely aware she had spoken, feeling the deep, pounding thrusts, lost in passion.

"Let it come, Angel, let it happen. Do it for me."

She relaxed then, letting her uncertainty slide away, and the moment she did, a sweeping wave of pleasure washed over her. Pinpricks of light and pulsing heat mingled with a sweetness she could taste on her tongue. Her body arched upward, taking him deeper, and above her Josh's hard frame went tense. His head fell back as he reached his release, his body tightening, shuddering, and finally going still.

For a moment he seemed frozen, then he sagged against her, his long, lean frame covered with a sheen of perspiration.

She wasn't certain of the words he whispered as he pulled her into his arms. She wanted to believe he had said that he loved her, but she wasn't sure. Her eyelids felt heavy, her body languid as fatigue settled in. They were both so very tired.

They made love once more in the middle of the night, and he held her with aching tenderness.

She didn't awaken till just before dawn.

Angel blinked then blinked again, trying to remember where she was. She noticed a heavy, musky-sweet smell, then felt the warm presence of the man still sleeping beside her. She sat up with a start as images of their hot night of passion came rushing in. Color flooded her cheeks to think that Josh had seduced her.

Or perhaps, she thought, it was she who had seduced him.

Dear God, she had slept with a Yankee! But another part of her remembered the beautiful night they had shared, said that the Yankee was Josh, and that it didn't matter.

Angel leaned closer, hearing the sound of his breathing, knowing she should wake him before dawn lightened the sky. Seeing how deeply he slept, she didn't have the heart.

For most of the three days before, he'd been up around the clock with Willie and he still looked exhausted. Her cheeks grew warm to think their hours of lovemaking had only added to his fatigue, and in truth she wasn't yet ready to face him. She wasn't sure what he would say to her, or what she might say to him. Better to simply avoid him.

She would check on Willie, sit with him for a while, then be on her way to town before Josh ever awakened.

As she dressed in her simple navy blue dress with the white pique cuffs, she couldn't resist a glance to where he lay sleeping. He had tossed off the covers, leaving him bare to the navel and exposing a long, masculine leg. She could still recall the power of his hard-muscled body moving above her, the way it had felt to be joined with him. The love she had felt in his arms.

An ache rose in her throat to think of losing him, yet she had known from the start that he could not stay. He had left the South for good when he had joined the Union Army. There was no place here for him now.

And he had a woman in the North.

A sharp pain knifed through her. Perhaps last night should never have happened. Perhaps she had been a fool.

She didn't care, she thought as she pulled her woolen cloak from the hook beside the door, slipped outside, and closed it behind her. No matter what happened, she would never regret the night they had shared.

It was a memory she would cherish through the long, lonely, bitter years without him.

"Mornin', Miss Angel." The men all called her that now, ever since she had organized the Christmas decorations. "I was just comin' to fetch you." The orderly, Private Vogel, met her at the barracks' door.

"Oh, dear God—Willie!" She started into the barracks, then turned back. "What's happened? He hasn't gotten worse? He's not . . . ?" Her chest constricted with terror. She would never forgive herself if Willie had needed her and she had been making love to Josh instead of being with him.

The red-haired orderly grinned, exposing the gap between his two front teeth. "You got your Christmas wish, ma'am. Your brother's fever broke 'bout an hour ago. The swellin's gone down in his leg. It looks like he's gonna be fine."

Tears rushed into her eyes. "Oh, thank God." Hurrying past him, she raced into the barracks and found Dr. Medford standing beside Willie's cot.

"Good news, Miss Summers. Your brother's fever has gone down. He's definitely on the mend."

She nodded, brushing a tear from her cheek. "Private Vogel told me. I can't thank you enough, Dr. Medford."

"Mostly it was Josh. I think he willed that boy to get well. I've never seen him more determined. Of course, he feels that way about all of his patients."

She sat down next to Willie and took his small hand. "I

know he does. Willie had the medicine he needed to help him get well. If your other patients had it, their chances would be far greater." She smiled down at her brother.

"Hello, sweetheart."

Willie fidgeted and she plumped his pillow. "The doctor says I'm better. Can we go home?"

Angel squeezed his hand. "We'll have to see what Dr. Coltrane says. He might want you to stay another day." Willie's mouth curled down in disappointment. He still looked sunken and thin, but his light blue eyes were alert and a hint of color brightened his pale cheeks.

She pulled the covers up to his chin. "That wouldn't be so bad, would it? If you stayed you could help the men decorate their Christmas tree."

A spark lit his eyes. "Did they get one?"

"Lieutenant Ainsley brought in a great big one. It's sitting just outside."

"I guess it'd be all right if we stayed till the tree was done."

Angel smiled. "In the meantime, would you like me to read to you for a while?"

He surprised her with a shake of his head. "Private Vogel was telling me stories about the war."

She flashed the orderly an uncertain glance and he looked a little sheepish. She wasn't sure war stories were a good idea, but it was obvious Willie was feeling better. She pulled the watch fob from the pocket of her skirt and flipped open the lid to her daddy's gold watch.

"Well, then, if Private Vogel has time for a few more stories and you don't need me for a while, there's something important I need to do in town. I'll be back just as soon as I'm finished, all right?"

Willie nodded. He was looking at the red-haired orderly with undisguised hero worship. She bent over and kissed him on the forehead. "I won't be long, I promise."

Only long enough to attend the town meeting in Savannah. One of her Christmas prayers had been answered. With any luck at all, perhaps the second one would be as well.

* * *

Josh Awoke with a start. He had kicked off the covers and the cold in the room had finally seeped into his sleep-deadened senses. He reached for Angel, felt nothing but the empty bed, glanced around the small room, and realized she had gone.

Sonofabitch! He had planned to talk to her last night after they had made love, while her body was still soft and pliant from his touch. He meant to tell her how much he loved her, explain that he meant to stay in Savannah, to make a place for himself here again. He'd meant to convince her to marry him.

Damnation! What the hell must she be thinking? That he meant to seduce her, then leave her? That all he wanted was to bed her?

Sonofabitch!

The sun was well up when he got to the hospital. He hadn't slept that late in as long as he could remember. He paused at Willie's bedside, his eyes going wide to see the boy propped up on his pillow.

A big grin broke over Josh's lips. "Morning, Willie. How are you feeling?"

"Pretty good, Doc. Private Vogel says you helped me get better. I guess you're not too bad for a Yankee."

Josh smoothed a hand over the boy's rumpled blond hair. "And you're not too bad for a Reb." They talked as Josh checked the leg. "Your sister been in?" he asked with careful nonchalance, certain she had been there as soon as she had awakened.

"She was here first thing," Willie said with a yawn. "She went into town, I think. She said she'd be back as quick as she could."

The town meeting. How the devil could he have forgotten? Then he thought of the night he had spent in her bed and knew exactly how he could forget. Josh smiled. "Get some rest, Willie. Tomorrow's Christmas Eve. Looks like you'll be home in time for Christmas, after all."

The boy beamed at his words. Josh left him with the orderly who seemed to have become his friend, made a quick round of his patients, then headed out to the stable.

The most important thing he could do for the men was get back those medical supplies. If Angel was willing to try, he wanted to be there to help her.

Eight

The meeting at city hall was nearly over by the time Angel dragged open the heavy wooden door. Merchants sat next to housewives on roughhewn benches, men just back from the war sat next to widows whose husbands had been killed. Angel recognized most of the faces, and, of course, Mayor Donaldson, the short, balding man at the podium.

At present, he was speaking to the merchants on their final piece of business—that they should all be friendlier to the Blue Coats—since the town was in need of Yankee dollars.

"It's a sad thing to say, friends and neighbors, but the Yanks are responsible for the hardships we're all suffering. The best revenge we can have is to get our hands on some of that Northern coin."

"Here, here!" Mr. Whistler of the dry goods store put in, followed by a mumble of agreement from the crowd. It wasn't exactly the note she would have chosen to present her case, but a glance at the clock said time was running out.

"Excuse me, Mayor Donaldson. Would it be possible for me to speak to the group for a moment? There's a topic I'd like to discuss."

He tipped his head back and stared at her through his pince-nez spectacles. "Is that you, Miss Summers?"

"Yes, Mr. Mayor." She started up the aisle. Before he could deny her the chance to speak, she'd reached the podium.

"What is it, Miss Summers?" he said with a tone of impatience.

Angel took a deep, calming breath and turned to the people on the benches. "I'd like to talk to you all about the train wreck." She went on to recount the day of the derailment and the goods that were taken. "The Yankees haven't pressed us to give back the food we've all been enjoying, but they need those medical supplies. They were intended for the wounded men at Fort Jackson. I didn't realize how badly they were needed until I went to the hospital and saw the injured soldiers for myself."

"What the devil was you doin' out there, girl?" Kirby Fields' look was accusing. "An army post ain't no place for a decent Southern girl." The others nodded mutely.

Ignoring the disapproval stamped across the sea of faces, Angel explained about Willie and how Josh Coltrane had taken him to the fort to tend his badly broken leg. "Before I went there, I felt just the way you do. I lost my mother and father. Union forces left Summers End in ruins. I hated the Yankees for everything they'd done. But watching those soldiers . . . seeing how much they were suffering, I realized they were men just the same as any others, just like those of you here. They're lonely and they're hurting. All they want to do is get well so they can go home."

"You're just sweet on Coltrane!" someone shouted. "You always were."

"I loved Josh once," she said. *I still do.* "But that's not what this is about. It's about letting go of the past. About seeing things the way they really are. The truth is there are good men and bad men on both sides of a war." She told them about the Confederate soldiers who had come to Summers End, about what they had tried to do. "People were hurt and killed in the North as well as the South. Terrible things were done by men in both armies. The important thing is, the war is over. It's time to forget the past and try to build ourselves a decent future."

A few men mumbled, then a big man shouted from the

crowd, "You can forget the past if you want to. I lost both my brothers at Manassas. I ain't about to forget!"

The air squeezed tight in Angel's chest. She knew what it felt like to lose the people you loved. Still, it was the suffering men who were important now. Surely there was something she could say that would make them see.

"You're right, Hank Larkin. I can't forget what happened, either. I doubt anyone in this room ever will. But it's Christmas. Above the pulpit in the church down the street there's a banner. It reads Peace on Earth, Good Will Toward Men. In the last four years, most of us have forgotten what that means. Now is our chance to remember."

She studied the faces in the crowd. "Those men at Fort Jackson . . . I've come to know a number of them. They're good men. They're sick men who need your help. This meeting today was supposed to be about Christmas, about finding the Christmas spirit Savannah seems to have lost.

"I'm asking you to search your hearts. If you do, you'll see the joy of Christmas is still there. It's always been there, deep down inside you. You've just forgotten how to reach it. If you want to find that joy, if you want to get back the spirit of Christmas, you can do it very simply. You can help those men at the fort."

For long, weighty moments, no one spoke. The crowd just stared at her and didn't say a word. Her heart sank like a stone inside her. She hadn't reached them. They were as stubborn and unbending as she had been. Nothing she had said had done an ounce of good. Fighting the sting of tears, Angel walked back up the aisle, her head held high, glancing neither right nor left. She shoved open the door to the foyer, closed it behind her, and sagged against it.

For a moment she closed her eyes, swamped by feelings of failure. When she opened them again, she saw Josh Coltrane push away from the wall, and her heart starting pounding against her ribs.

"What—what are you doing here?"

He smiled at her softly. "I heard what you said in there. No matter what happens, I'm proud of you for having the courage to say it." His expression was unreadable, yet his dark brown eyes were full of warmth.

Thinking of the night they had shared, Angel glanced away, hoping to hide the color that washed her cheeks. "It didn't do a lick of good."

"You tried. That's all one person can ask of another. It's more than anyone else did." He held open the door and she walked past him out onto the street.

"Willie's better," she said, still unwilling to meet that penetrating gaze. Was he thinking of the night they'd spent together? Was he remembering, as she was trying so very hard not to.

"Your brother's going to be fine. I sent a message to your aunt telling her you and Willie would be home in the morning." His eyes were fastened on her mouth. He looked like he wanted to kiss her.

Her color heightened again as a sliver of heat shimmered through her. Dear God, what the man could do with a single glance. She tried to smile, but all she could think of was Josh. Josh kissing her, Josh touching her.

"Th-thank you for helping Willie . . . and everything else you've done."

"Everything else I've done?" he repeated, taking her arm, urging her forward, pulling her off the boardwalk around a corner out of sight. "Are you thanking me for taking your innocence last night?"

Her face went even hotter. "I—I was thinking about those Confederate soldiers. Last night, I was—"

"What you were last night, my love, was wonderful. We were wonderful, Angel—together. Just the way we were always meant to be."

"What—what are you talking about?"

"I'm telling you that what happened between us proves that we're meant to be together. I love you, Angel. I always have. I'm asking you to marry me."

"M-marry you?"

"That's right. I asked you once before, remember?"

A tight ache rose in her throat. She loved Josh Coltrane.

After last night, she realized just how much. "Savannah is my home, Josh. Your home is in the North. I could never be happy there."

He tipped her chin with a long dark finger. "Coltrane Farms is my home. I'm not letting the war drive me away."

"You can't possibly mean to stay—you know the way you'd be treated!"

"In the meeting you said it was time to forget the past, to start thinking about the future. That's what I'm going to do, Angel. I want that future to be with you. I want you to marry me."

Oh, dear God, was it possible? Her heart thrummed crazily to think of it. "You have a fiancée, Josh. What would she have to say about that?"

Amusement crinkled the corners of his dark eyes. "If you mean Sarah Wingate, she isn't my fiancée."

"You told Aunt Ida you were going to marry her."

"I told your aunt I was thinking about marrying her. And what were you doing eavesdropping? I figured you'd finally outgrown that."

"I wasn't eavesdropping. I just happened to overhear what you said."

He grinned. "The truth is I hadn't made up my mind about Sarah, not until I saw you. Then I knew that as much as I cared for her, I didn't love her. I was in love with a fiery-tempered little baggage with long blond hair and freckles on her nose. I've loved her for as long as I can remember."

"Oh, Josh!" Angel went into his arms and he held her tightly against him. Tears burned her eyes and clogged her throat. She loved him so very much.

"Marry me, Angel." A corner of his mouth tipped up. "Let me make you an honest woman."

Angel pulled away, one blond brow arching up. "That's why you made love to me, isn't it? You seduced me on purpose. You thought that once we made love, I—"

"I figured that once we made love, once you knew how good we were together, you wouldn't be able to refuse me."

"Josh Coltrane, you are—" He pulled her back into his arms and kissed her until she was breathless.

"What am I, Angel?"

A warm smile curved her lips. "You're the most wonderful man I've ever known."

"And?" he prodded.

"And I'd be proud to marry you—even if you are a good for nothin' Yankee."

Josh laughed out loud, a richly male, incredibly happy sound. Then he kissed her, long and deep. "We've waited four years," he said. "Let's get married as soon as we can."

A bright smile curved her lips. "How does tomorrow sound?"

Josh hugged her tight against him. "Perfect." As they walked down the street toward the wagon she had driven into town, only thoughts of the men at the fort, the sick men they had failed to help, kept both of them from grinning.

Tonight was her last night at the fort. Angel couldn't say she was sorry to be leaving, but she couldn't deny there was something poignant in spending Christmas Eve at the hospital with the wounded men.

As soon as she and Josh had returned to Fort Jackson, they had helped the patients finish decorating their towering Christmas tree. Before they'd left town, Josh had stopped at the dry goods store. He had bought her the beautiful length of plum velvet she had been admiring the first day he had seen her and a dozen miniature carved wooden soldiers as a Christmas gift for Willie. He had also purchased every candle Mr. Whistler had in stock.

The huge pine tree glowed with them now, and so did the wreaths on the tables. He'd also bought yards of red ribbon and the men had made big red bows, which hung on the walls and brightened the mantel. Small red bows were tied to the branches of the tree.

"Isn't it beautiful?" Willie said, staring at the imposing tree with his big, bright blue eyes.

"It's wonderful," Angel said.

Josh smiled. "For the first time, it really feels like Christmas."

There was a lighter atmosphere on the ward tonight, yet it didn't stop the dull moans of pain that occasionally rose from the beds, or the fever and chills that tortured a patient in the grips of malaria.

It didn't ease the hurting, but it soothed the men's weary spirits. Angel guessed it would have to be enough.

"Miss Angel?" Private Vogel approached her as she sat by Willie's bed. "Ben Weatherby asked if he could speak to you a moment."

"Of course." The red-haired orderly led her to Corporal Weatherby's cot and she sat down beside him.

"Hello, Benjamin."

"Hello, Miss Angel." He smiled at her shyly. "Me and the boys . . . well, we just wanted to wish you a Merry Christmas. Dr. Coltrane told us what you done, standin' up for us and all."

"It wasn't anything, Ben. I didn't get the medicine you need."

"It might not be anythin' to you, ma'am, but it was somethin' special to us. We wanted you to have this . . . somethin' for you to remember us by." He handed her a small, carved, wooden angel. The face looked remarkably similar to her own. "You're our Christmas Angel, ma'am. Ain't none of us ever gonna forget you."

She blinked to hold back tears, but they burned her eyes just the same, and a hard lump clogged her throat. She glanced around the room and saw that the soldiers were watching. "Thank you, Ben." She smiled at the men and brushed a tear from her cheek. "Thank you all. I hope next year you'll all be home for Christmas."

No one said a word, but there were tears in more than one man's eyes.

"Dr. Coltrane!" someone shouted. "Hey, Doc, you gotta come see this!"

Wondering what the commotion could be, Angel joined

Josh at the door. They went outside and across the yard, then stopped dead still at the gate leading into the fort.

Dozens of candles lit the night. Men and women in wagons rolled down the road and men carried boxes tied to the backs of their horses. It seemed half the people in Savannah had come to the fort this night.

Kirby Fields rode at the front. As the wagons drew near, he left the rest of the group and rode ahead, stopping his horse just a few feet away from where they stood. He tossed down the box he carried, which landed in the dirt at Josh's feet.

"We brought the stuff you wanted. Angel was right in what she said. It's Christmas. God meant for men to share their blessings with those in need of them. There's peace again in this land and we should be grateful." He pointed toward the box he had thrown on the ground. "Those medicines you needed . . . we brung 'em all back, leastwise all we still had. Use 'em to help your sick men."

Josh looked up at the man who had once been his friend. The muscles contracted in his throat; he had to swallow before he could speak. "Thank you, Kirby. You'll never know how much this means." He turned as the others approached, watched in silence as each man rode up and dropped off his load of supplies. "Thank you for what you're doing. God bless you. God bless all of you."

When all the supplies were unloaded, Kirby tipped his hat to Angel and extended a hand to Josh. "Merry Christmas," he said.

Angel smiled, feeling an ache in her throat. "Merry Christmas, Kirby."

By the end of the hour, the supplies had all been carried inside and put away—or put to use where they were needed. Only one mysterious box remained.

"What's in that?" Angel asked.

Josh just smiled. "Come on, I'll show you." Carrying the box over to Lieutenant Langley's bedside, Josh bent down next to the man with the paralyzed legs and lifted the lid.

"This is for you, Lieutenant Langley. It still has to be

assembled but once it is, you can get up out of that bed. I didn't want to mention it until it actually got here, just in case it never made it."

The brooding, dark-eyed soldier looked up. "What the devil is it?"

"A chair on wheels. A wheelchair," Josh said. "You can get around on your own, once we get it put together."

Lieutenant Langley stared at the pieces in the box, then looked up at Angel. "I got a letter from my girl. Someone wrote to her, told her I'd been shot. She knows I can't walk. She says she doesn't care, says she wants me just the same." His eyes held hers, hope and fear mingled in his expression. "Doc says I can probably still have children. Do you think, ma'am . . . do you think a woman could still love a man who had to sit in one of these?"

Oh, dear Lord. Angel imagined how she would feel if the man were Josh. "I'd love him," she said. "I wouldn't baby him, mind you. I'd make him carry his own weight, but I'd love him. I'd marry him and I'd give him dozens of babies."

Lieutenant Langley gave her a smile, the first she had seen. It was amazing how handsome he was. "Thank you, ma'am. Thank you, Doc, and . . . Merry Christmas."

"Merry Christmas, Lieutenant," Josh said softly, leading Angel away before the lieutenant could see the tears shimmering in her eyes. He guided her to the door, pointed to the mistletoe hanging above it, took her in his arms, and kissed her so thoroughly her knees went weak.

"Merry Christmas, Angel," he said.

Angel grinned. "Merry Christmas, Yank," she said, and a cheer went up from the men.

Dear Readers,

Christmas celebrations in Regency England were varied. Some people still held to old traditions such as wassail, yule logs, and Twelfth Night Cakes, while others saw these as peasant activities and not suited to a holy festival. The latter spent Christmas very quietly. When I was asked to do my first Christmas novella, I wanted a rip-roaring festivity and so I invented a family tradition for it, and had great fun with all the ancient English practices.

Of course I had great fun with the main characters, too, both still tangled in the events of years past, where naiveté and interference created disaster. Both think they're the wounded party, but what really happened that Twelfth Night in the past, and who betrayed whom? It all plays out over twelve festive days of Christmas.

I love to hear from readers. You can e-mail me at jobev@poboxes.com, or send a note by mail c/o Meg Ruley, the Jane Rotrosen Agency, 318 East 51st Street, New York, NY 10022. For information about my books, check out www.sff.net/people/jobeverley

Jo Beverley

TWELFTH NIGHT
Jo Beverley

"Ah, there you are at last."

Lady Alice Conyngham looked up from her papers and grinned at her brother. "Yes, Roland, here I am in my study. The last place you would look, of course."

"Well," he said, as he came to perch on the edge of her desk. "It's going to be the last place I look today. Why would I keep looking when I've found you?"

Alice chuckled and rolled her eyes at him.

No one would ever doubt that they were brother and sister. It would not be hard to suppose them twins, though Lord Masham was four years his sister's senior. Both had fine-boned features, wide, humorous mouths, and sparkling hazel eyes. The difference lay in their hair. Lord Masham had dark blond unruly waves; Alice was blessed with a thick, heavy mass of chestnut which fell die straight past her hips.

When newly emerged from the schoolroom she had suffered hours of curling and crimping to achieve a fashionable look, but these days she was wiser and let it be. When she was informal, as now, she simply tied it back with a ribbon.

She looked at her brother severely. "Now that you've found me, Roland, state your business and go away. We've thirty-three guests arriving on Christmas Eve and I have work to do."

"Thirty-six," he said.

"Thirty-three," she repeated firmly. "I should know, since I have the task of allocating bedrooms to them all."

"Thirty-six," he said again. "Forgot to tell you. Invited three fellows before I left Town."

"Roland!"

"Come on," he said beguilingly. "We can't actually have run out of space. Bumped into Lord Ivanridge and Thornton Ewing at White's. Clear they'd nothing particular laid on for Christmas, so I invited them here. After all," he added coaxingly, "they're both war heroes, Al. Bad show if they were left to spend their first Christmas after victory by a lonely fireside."

"I believe I have seen both names mentioned in reports of battle," admitted Alice. "But they're total strangers, Roland, and they must have family."

"Not total strangers," he pointed out. "I was at school with 'em. They were both on the Town before they joined up—you must have met them somewhere. In fact, I rather thought Ivanridge came to a Twelve Days once."

"I don't remember him . . ."

"And I'm not sure they do have family," Roland continued. "Close family, that is. Ivanridge's parents died when he was young. He inherited his uncle's title a few years back and the old man was a bachelor. Anyway, the people invited here aren't exactly orphans, Al. They come because Conyngham Christmases are famous."

Alice sighed but gave in, as she usually did with her brother. And it was true that the twelve-day Christmas festival held each year at Conyngham Castle was a renowned festivity. Invitations to it were prized. The fact that it had not taken place last year because of the death of Alice's mother, the Countess of Raneleigh, made this year's celebration even more anticipated.

It also meant that Alice had the running of it for the first time. The earl and Roland loved the event and could be depended on to organize activities once the guests arrived, but they had no patience with the tedious preliminary work of allocating bedrooms and stabling, ordering supplies, and making sure those guests arriving by stage or mail would be collected. Even with an excellent and experienced staff, Alice had her hands full.

"Very well," she said and frowned at her lists. "But I truly am not sure where to put them. All the good bedrooms are taken."

"Double 'em up," said Roland blithely. "The younger men won't mind. I'll take someone in my room. Bed's big enough for five."

"Invite any more impromptu guests," warned Alice, "and you'll be testing out that theory." She scribbled changes to her room list. "You said three?"

"Ah yes," said Roland, suddenly developing an interest in the winter scene beyond the window. "Well, he was with us, Al. Could hardly leave him out, could I?" At her questioning look he said, "Standon."

Alice stared at him. "Roland. Tell me you're teasing. Please."

He did color up a little. "Devil a bit. Come on, Al. It's six years. Surely you two can meet on good terms."

"Of course we can," she snapped. "We've been meeting on good terms ever since. It must have been the most civilized jilting ever!" Alice pressed her hands together and forced the shrill tone out of her voice. "That does not mean I want Lord Standon here for Christmas."

"Not like you to hold a grudge," Roland reproved. "Fellow's all alone. Parents dead, sister in Canada with her husband . . ."

"But *Christmas,* Roland," Alice pointed out, experiencing familiar exasperation with her brother's insouciant disregard for details. "It was during Christmas at Conyngham six years ago that I jilted the man!"

"Oh," he said with mild surprise. "That must be why he hesitated about accepting. But I made a big thing about how welcome he'd be, Al. Can't fob him off now."

Alice shook her head. "I suppose not," she said bleakly. "But if he does something cakish like offer for me again I shall make you deal with it, Roland."

"You could do worse," he pointed out. "Than take up with him again, I mean."

"Doubtless," she replied tartly. "However, my sentiments have not altered."

"Nor have his, I suppose. Why else hasn't he married? He's turned thirty and has a duty to his name. Don't like to make a point of it, Al, but you're twenty-three yourself. If you're not careful, you'll end up an old maid."

Alice looked him in the eye. "Roland, one thing I promise you. I will not end up an old maid. Now go away and check guns or billiard balls or something."

Recognizing her irritation, he went. Alice rested her head on one hand. Damnable, damnable situation.

She'd made her curtsy at seventeen, highborn, well dowered, and passably good-looking despite the impossibility of holding her hair in any fashionable style. She had been a mild success in the Season of 1809 and, in her mother's opinion at least, it would have been vulgar to be anything more. Let the impoverished and the parvenus seek to be a Toast; a Conyngham had no need of such extremes to marry well: that is, within the inner circle of the *haut monde*.

It had been made quite clear to Alice which were the gentlemen most suitable for her consideration—suitable in terms of politics, wealth, and bloodlines. Most of them were familiar, having been houseguests at Conyngham.

During that Season Alice had enjoyed herself with all of them and waited for love to strike. When that mythic emotion had failed to appear she had happily settled for fondness and accepted Charlie Dearham, Lord Standon, whom she had known from the cradle. He had been, still was, an easygoing man with a gentle wit and a kind heart. She had always enjoyed his company though she had not, in fact, been in a great hurry to wed. The ceremony had been set for May, 1810.

Of course Charlie had been invited to Conyngham for Christmas that year. And that was where it had all fallen apart. All because of a rogue called Tyr Norman. Captain Tyr Norman, newly commissioned to the 10th Light Dragoons, a Hussar regiment, magnificent in his blue dress uniform with silver braid, the dashing fur-trimmed pelisse swinging from one shoulder.

During the Twelve Days at Conyngham the guests were

required to wear medieval garb, but Lord Raneleigh made an exception for serving officers. Perhaps that was what had made Tyr Norman so dazzling to her eyes, the fact that he was in a real uniform and soon to be posted to the Peninsula, whereas most of the other men had been playacting.

He'd been growing the necessary Hussar moustache, she remembered, and had laughed disarmingly about the fact that he couldn't yet twirl the ends like an old hand . . .

It had taken just twelve days of Tyr Norman to turn Alice's life upside down.

Charlie had never understood why she suddenly broke their engagement. She knew he and others had waited for her to show the new attachment which must surely be the cause. She had not been able to explain to him except to say that she found she did not love him as she should.

The truth was that Alice had found that love was not a myth but a painful, maddening reality. But how could she tell anyone that she had given her heart to a rogue and then her virginity, too, and that the rogue had taken both and decamped, leaving her without honor or heart to offer to another?

In the end, unable to bear the burden of guilt, she had confessed all to her mother. Lady Raneleigh had been deeply shocked but surprisingly gentle. She had explained the possible consequences, but when Alice's courses had shown that she was not, at least, pregnant, her mother had recommended that she get on with her life. She had strongly urged a reconciliation with Charlie, using a whole battery of logical arguments.

It had been no good. Tyr Norman had proved a rogue of the first order, but there had been something between them, something extraordinary. Alice had found she could not bear to wed without it. Her mother, she knew, thought that her experience had been distressing and had turned her against marital intimacy. Honesty told Alice that it was quite otherwise. She could not now bear the impersonal couplings her mother earnestly promised her.

Alice was shocked to feel the dampness of tears on her

fingers and angrily brushed them away. It was over. It was ancient history. Tyr Norman was probably dead.

She had guiltily searched out the few mentions of his name in military dispatches—he had distinguished himself at Talavera, she remembered—but all mention had ceased two years before. She must have missed his name in the casualty lists. She had had after all, moments of sanity when she refused to look. She hoped he was dead. He deserved to die in a muddy field somewhere . . .

More tears were squeezing past her lids. Oh damn!

Alice grappled for composure.

Tyr Norman, dead or not, would never show his face at Conyngham again. Charlie Dearham, she reminded herself, was a civilized man and wouldn't create any embarrassment. It would all be all right.

And now, she thought, pulling another sheet of paper closer, she had Twelve Days of celebration to organize.

Christmas Eve was the usual merry chaos, but Alice was relieved to have it come. The hard work of organization was over and now it should be fun. Even the minor calamities, like the stranding of the Duke and Duchess of Portsmouth ten miles away due to a broken axle, could easily be taken care of.

Conyngham Castle—a twelfth-century castle to which pieces of each succeeding style of architecture seemed to have stuck—was lit, from cellar to attic. Inside it was festooned with greenery and ribbons and made cozy by roaring fires. Cheerful servants dashed around, for they loved the celebration as much as anyone, and plenty of extra hands were always hired so the workload was as light as possible.

Besides, the vails were always extraordinary.

Guests arrived all day, breath steaming, laughing and chattering. There was a buffet of hot and cold food set up in the Yellow Saloon, and familiar guests knew to make themselves at home. Alice, her father, and her brother were on hand to look after the less experienced and make them welcome.

Alice had just befriended shy Lady Podbourne, whose new husband had abandoned her when he became caught up in a discussion about fowling pieces, when the doors swung open again to admit a gust of crisp air and new batch of guests.

She introduced Lydia Podbourne to the Beasleys then went to welcome Mr. and Mrs. Digby-Rowles. Behind them she saw Charlie.

The Digby-Rowleses were regular guests and merely waved a greeting before putting themselves into the hands of the bevy of waiting servants. Alice turned to the man she had jilted.

She knew there was nothing he would hate more than any mention of it. "Hello, Charlie," she said and accepted a cool kiss on the cheek. "Lovely to see you here again. I'm afraid you'll have to share a room, though. I've put you in with Lord Ivanridge. I hope that's all right."

"Of course," said Charlie with no hint of awkwardness. He was pleasant by nature and pleasant by looks. He had soft brown hair and a smooth face, fine, kind eyes, and a shapely mouth made for smiling. "We traveled down together. Found we'd both been here once before as well, so we're old hands. No need to fuss over us." He indicated the man behind him and Alice turned with a smile.

Which froze.

"What the devil are you doing here?" she said.

It was, thank God, said softly.

The dark-haired man's courteous smile cooled. "Delighted to meet you too, Lady Alice."

Charlie said, "Is something the matter, Alice?" but his voice seemed faint and far away.

He looked the same and yet different—leaner, with shorter hair, and no trace of the moustache of which he had been so proud.

It was impossible to do as she wished and have him thrown from the house. She'd kept her secret for six years.

She could surely keep it for twelve days more. "No," she
said with a shaky laugh. "I'm sorry. Things are at sixes and
sevens and I'm losing my wits. It's just that I thought this
gentleman was dead." Remaining coherent by force of will,
Alice swallowed, extended a hand, and said, "It is Mr. Norman, isn't it?"

He acknowledged her hand with the briefest of touches,
his mouth smiling, his eyes cool and watchful. "Lord Ivanridge now, Lady Alice. That is doubtless why you were taken
by surprise."

"Indeed," she said. "Congratulations, my lord. As you
will have heard, I have had to put you to share a room with
Standon. I hope you do not mind." At last she could turn
away to summon a maid. "Hattie will show you up. I'm sure
you will remember that we leave our guests to suit themselves until dinner." She turned an impersonal smile on the
group. "I will see you later, gentlemen."

It was only as she walked away that she registered that
there was another man in the group, doubtless Major Ewing,
and she had ignored him. She could do nothing about it now.
She had to escape.

With a smile fixed painfully on her face, Alice walked
composedly across the hall, mounted the stairs, and progressed along corridors to her bedchamber. Once there she
turned the key in the lock with unsteady fingers and collapsed on her bed.

Tyr Norman was here, sans moustache, sans uniform, but
still able to drive wits to wildness in a second. How could
he have done this to her?

Would he have the decency to make an excuse and leave?

Why should he? she thought with a bitter laugh. He, at
least, must have expected this confrontation.

What could his purpose be?

Had he come to gloat over his long-ago conquest?

Had he come to try to repeat it? She'd see him dead first.

Devastating thought. Had that riotous tumble in his bed
been so long ago that it seemed of small importance to him?
Perhaps so. After all, he'd surely spent the past six years

engaged in warfare, killing and wenching his way across
Europe. Why should he remember one silly seventeen-year-
old?

Alice bit on her knuckle. Perhaps he didn't even remember. She found that insupportable. She'd lived with the memory, bittersweet though it was, every day and night since.

How hard he had looked. Where was the young man with
the laughing dark eyes? Latin eyes, her mother had said
dismissively. Where was the smile which had melted her
bones? Swallowed up by war?

She rolled over and buried her head in her hands as the
memories flooded back as if it had all been yesterday. The
way those dark eyes had become even darker, and yet
brighter, when she had shyly slipped off the top of her gown
to expose her breasts.

Where had she gotten the boldness to do such a thing? she
wondered. From twelve days of festivities and an excess of
mulled cider. It was as if she'd been another person that
night.

She remembered the soft music of his voice as he had told
her how beautiful she was and calmed her anxieties; the
sight of his magnificent torso, bronzed by the firelight except where it was darkened by his hair; the feel of that body
beneath her hands. That had been the hardest to forget, the
feel of leashed power beneath her hesitant fingers.

When he'd gone, abandoned her, and she'd realized that
she could never marry, that had been the hardest part—to
know that she would not experience that again, the feel of a
man's body beneath her hands . . .

There was a scratch at the door.

Alice leapt up and quickly washed her face, trying to
wash away her wicked thoughts along with the tear stains.
Had she learned nothing in six years? She went to the door
to open it. A maid was there.

"Sorry to disturb you, milady, but Mr. Kindsy says there's
a problem with the Countess of Jerrold's room. She says the
chimney smokes." This was reported with a resigned tone.
Every year, Alice's godmother, the Dowager Countess of

Jerrold, found something about which to complain. Once
soothed, she settled to be an acceptable guest.

Alice put her moment of wildness behind her and went off
to deal with her godmother.

This event would not be the disaster she feared unless she
allowed her wanton heart to make it so. In the hectic,
crowded days to come it should be easy enough to avoid Tyr
Norman, Lord Ivanridge.

It might be possible to avoid Ivanridge, but it seemed
impossible to keep him out of her thoughts. As she dressed
for dinner that evening, Alice found herself wondering what
he would think of her gown and was instantly annoyed that
she would care.

Six years ago, however, she had been just out of the
schoolroom and her clothes had been chosen by her mother.
They had all been of the highest quality and the finest cut
but demure. For day there had been the universal light mus-
lins, for evening plain pastel silks.

These days, having resigned herself to spinsterdom, Alice
dressed to please herself. She had discovered a taste for
strong colors and unique designs and wore them for her own
pleasure. Her mother had not approved.

Christmas Eve at Conyngham was the last night of modern dress, and Alice's gown for this evening had been chosen
weeks ago—a bright royal blue of simple cut, trimmed with
silver braiding on the bodice and braided leaves around the
hem and down the long sleeves. The plain style might not be
the current vogue, but she thought it suited her, for she was
tall for a woman and had a shapely figure.

Her maid swept her hair up into a coil on her head and
surrounded it with a silver bandeau. Silver and sapphire jewelry completed the outfit.

When she checked the final effect in the mirror, however,
Alice was shocked to realize how much her outfit resembled
a Hussar uniform. It was the blue with the silver braid which
created the effect and was a poignant reminder of Tyr Nor-

man all those years ago. Surely she had never intended this when she'd designed it. Had she?

Would anyone else notice?

She forced herself to be sensible. Even if anyone did, there was only one person who would think it of any significance and he could go to hell.

Alice draped eight feet of silver shawl over her arms and swept out to her first evening as hostess of the Conyngham Twelve Day Festival.

Conyngham Castle was a genuine medieval home. Though it had been extensively added to during the last six hundred years, it retained the original castle at one end—or at least, the bottom two floors.

The lower floor was still used for storage as it had been when first constructed in the twelfth century, though now the cool wine cellars were floored and plastered. The medieval top floor had been greatly altered to make the family chapel. The middle floor was the old Great Hall. This had been preserved in its original form except for the addition of glazing in the windows and more efficient fireplaces, and it would be the center of the medieval Twelve Day Festival.

Tonight, however, was the last night of modern living, and family and guests were gathered in the Blue Saloon which was one of the finest examples of the work of the Adams brothers. Alice reminded herself that she'd designed her gown with this room in mind, not with any thought of a dashing Hussar.

Alice's father came over to her—a tall, hearty man with the same heavy brown hair as his daughter, but muted now by gray. "Everything's as it should be," he said with a wide smile. "Your mother would be proud of you, Alice."

"Thank you, Father, but it is mostly the staff, you know. I think they could run this on their own. They doubtless only consider my instructions unnecessary interference."

"Don't downplay your hard work, my dear. Capital job. Fine company." He beamed around. "All the old favorites and enough new blood to keep us on our toes, eh? Glad to see Standon here." With a slight frown he added, "Bad business, that." Alice wondered if after all these years her father was going to choose this moment to upbraid her for her conduct, though he did not know the whole of it.

She should have known better. He and Roland were very alike. "Seems to have kept him away for some reason," the earl said vaguely. "Shame. Always liked Standon."

He wandered off to have a word with Lord Standon. His place was soon taken by Roland. "What the devil have you got against Ivanridge?" he asked. "Fine fellow."

"What do you mean?" responded Alice coolly.

"You've put Ewing in my room—I'd rather have had Tyr, by the way—and he says you tried to throw him out. Tyr, I mean."

"Nonsense," said Alice with deliberate lack of interest, though she'd just had a paralyzing thought. "I was a little surprised, that's all. I wasn't aware that he'd inherited a title and so I didn't expect him."

"No reason to swear at him. Quite shocked poor old Ewing."

Alice could cheerfully have wrung poor old Ewing's neck, and tension had seized the back of her neck. "He must have misunderstood," she said shortly. "Go and mix, Roland. There must be some quiet souls who need bringing out. And," she added, "don't think of changing your place this year. I've put you by Miss Travis, who's very shy. Look after her."

"Shy girls are a terrible bore," he complained with a twinkle.

"She's tolerable enough when she relaxes. Relax her."

He gave a snort of lewd laughter, and Alice felt her color rise. She remembered a man holding her close and saying, "Relax, *puella miranda*. Relax," as his hand and voice had brought relaxation of the sweetest kind. As if drawn and caught, she found her gaze fixed on Tyr Norman across the room. He returned her gaze pensively.

Alice dragged her eyes away. The thought that was torturing her was that she had carelessly put her seducer and her jilted betrothed to share a room and a bed. She wouldn't put it past Ivanridge to use the occasion to make trouble.

She became aware that she was standing among the company like a wax dummy. She couldn't do anything about the situation at the moment, but tomorrow she'd either find a way to throw Ivanridge out or find him another room, even if it had to be the coal cellar.

Dinner was announced at that moment, and everyone progressed, chattering, into the magnificent dining room with its walls and ceiling painted by Laguerre. A string trio played softly in an anteroom, invisible but audible through the open door.

Despite this grandeur, the tone of the Twelve Days was informal, and so there was no head or foot to the long table and the family was scattered among the guests.

As she took her place, Alice checked and was relieved to see Roland assisting Miss Davis to her seat. Their mother had indulged his yearly game of rearranging places so he was seated by some racy young matron. Alice would have no part of it.

She was seated between the Reverend Herbert, the Conyngham chaplain, and Sir George Young, the local squire. They were the two most boring guests and so she had taken them for herself. As she took her place her attention was all on last-minute checks that everything was in order and everyone was comfortable.

It was only as she settled with relief into her place and pulled off her long white gloves that she realized she was seated opposite Tyr Norman. She'd given no thought when she arranged the table to putting Lord Ivanridge opposite her own seat. Now she cursed the mischance.

He raised a brow, as if implying she had arranged this seating deliberately. She gave him a frigid glare and turned to engage the chaplain in a lengthy discussion of the actual date of Christ's birth.

". . . So you see," he was saying some time later, "that it

was unlikely to be the year zero, Lady Alice, even if there had been a year zero . . ."

Alice saw nothing, for she had only been pretending to listen as she kept a watching brief on Ivanridge. It had occurred to her that he was a very dangerous man, and she had carelessly placed him between two susceptible young women.

On his right was her friend, Rebecca, Lady Frederick Stane. Rebecca was a widow and should know what she was about, but Rebecca had been granted only two months of marriage before her husband had sailed off to the Peninsula and death. That had been two years ago, but she had taken the loss hard and was only just resuming a social life. Also, Alice knew Rebecca was lonely and possibly susceptible to a handsome rogue.

On Ivanridge's left was Miss Bella Carstairs, a local beauty who considered herself up to every trick. Alice was not convinced, and she mistrusted the glittering excitement in the girl's eyes. Had she once looked at Tyr Norman like that? She prayed not.

Surely not, or no one would have been mystified when she threw over Charlie.

Bella was ignoring both the food and the gentleman on her other side. She was not only hanging on Ivanridge's every word but leaning all over him as well. Her bodice was shockingly low. If the table were less wide, Alice would have kicked the chit on the shin.

As best she could tell, Ivanridge was not encouraging either lady but then, Alice remembered, he hadn't appeared to encourage her either. Though he had changed, he was still the sort of man who could draw women to him without any effort at all. Perhaps more so. The sheer anticipation of life which had shone so brightly six years before was muted, but in its place was an aura of achievement, experience, and power.

Alice caught herself up. It was merely a rather showy kind of virility.

"Lady Alice? Lady Alice?"

Alice snapped back her attention to Reverend Herbert. "I'm so sorry, Reverend. I thought there was trouble with the wine." She dredged her mind for the last thing she had heard. "You were referring to the reign of Herod . . ."

"Ah, yes," said the gentleman with a twinkle in his eye.

Alice grinned back at him. That had doubtless been ages ago. "I'm sorry," she said. "I feel I have to keep my eye on so many things."

She resolved to ignore Ivanridge and all his doings. After all, there was nothing she could do about him short of telling her father the truth and having him thrown out on his ear. In that case, however, Roland might feel obliged to call Ivanridge out. She shivered at the thought of that unequal contest.

By the time the meal drew to a close, the situation had given Alice a headache. The music, the chattering voices, the smell of food and candles were all making it worse. If she had not been hostess, she would have slipped away.

At last the meal was over and her father took over the managing of the affair. "My friends," said the earl, "we are set to enjoy twelve right merry days here at Conyngham, but let us not forget the cause of the celebrations. We are here to celebrate the birth of our Saviour."

The candles in the huge chandeliers were extinguished and people put out the table candles nearest to them. Ivanridge reached forward to pinch the one between Alice and him. The room was left dim except for the lamp stands in the corners of the room and the burnishing light of the leaping fire. All was quiet.

Led by the earl and the musicians the company sang the old carols, the holy ones—"O, Come all ye Faithful" "While Shepherds Watched" and "Unto Us is Born a Son." Then began the solos. Lord Raneleigh started with his own setting of Robert Herrick's "What Sweeter Music Can We Sing than a Carol?" Roland obliged with "The Burning Babe," a somewhat startling Puritan hymn which appealed to his sense of humor. He particularly relished the line, "So will I melt into a bath to wash them in my blood!"

There was a pause and then the Duchess of Portsmouth

sang, soon followed by others. Now there was no set program
and the singers were unaccompanied. All went well, however,
for everyone knew the musical standard was high at Conyngham and those who chose to perform were gifted amateurs.

Then Ivanridge rose to his feet. Alice caught her breath.
She had never heard him sing—had no idea whether he could.
What was he up to? Mixed in with suspicion was an absurd
protectiveness. Was he about to make a fool of himself?

His voice was not remarkable, but it was a pleasant bari-
tone. The song was one she had not heard before but clearly
very old. "There is no rose of such virtue as is the rose that
bore Jesu. Alleluia. For in this rose contained was, Heaven
and Earth in little space. Res Miranda . . ."

Miranda! Alice felt her face flame at his use of that name,
the one he had murmured in the dimness of his bedroom.
Puella miranda, deliciae miranda . . . Wonderful girl, wonderful darling. She looked down at her hands and fought to
keep her face blank and at least deprive him of the satisfaction of knowing his weapon had found its mark.

For it must have been planned, this song. He had been
given plenty of time to prepare for this evening while she
was still trying to cope with the shock.

There were three more songs and then Alice saw her father's sign and rose. It must be close to midnight and for the
last ten years she had been the last performer, singing the
haunting old carol, "I Sing of a Maiden."

Her contralto voice was naturally excellent and had been
trained by masters. It filled the beautiful room:

> I sing of a maiden that is makeless.
> The king of all Kings to her son she chese.
> He came all so stille to his mother's bower,
> As dew in Aprille that falleth on the flower.
>
> He came all so stille where his mother lay,
> As dew in Aprille that falleth on the may,
> He came all so stille where his mother was,
> As dew in Aprille that falleth on the grass . . .

Despite her intentions she found herself looking at the man opposite, permitted the foolishness by the fact that he was now looking down. His face was mysterious in the half-light—dark hair, dark eyes, dark shadows like blades across cheek and jaw. She remembered singing this carol six years ago. He had looked up at her then, over half a room, bright-eyed and moved. That was when her heart had first trembled for him.

As the resonance of her last notes faded there was a hushed pause suddenly filled with the sound of distant bells. The servants threw wide the windows and the pealing bells of the village church rippled in on the frosty air.

The candles were lit again, the lamps turned up. "Merry Christmas!" called Lord Raneleigh. "Merry Christmas all!"

It was picked up by the whole company and everyone embraced their neighbors. Bella Carstairs will like that, thought Alice sourly, grateful she had not by mischance put Ivanridge beside herself.

Then the earl led them all in "Christians Awake" as they made a procession into the old part of the house and up the worn stone stairs to the chapel. It was soon packed with the guests and most of the servants, but all found a place to kneel as Reverend Herbert led them in the Christmas service.

Alice loved Christmas. She felt the familiar peace and joy settle in her heart and swell out to encompass her family, the guests, and even Lord Ivanridge. It had all been so long ago. If she had been a naive seventeen, he had only been twenty-one. Mistakes had been made but should be put behind them, and that choice of song had doubtless just been an unhappy accident.

When the service was over the company surged down to the Chinese Room for a nightcap among the scarlet and black lacquer and bamboo-style furnishings. Alice whirled around in high spirits, making sure everyone had their choice of caudle or posset or hot spiced wine.

She was standing and surveying the company with satisfaction when Roland came over, the center of a merry group of bachelors. "Aha!" he declared. "Look where she is, my good men!"

Alice looked at him, then up and sighed. She'd taken a spot under one of the many bunches of mistletoe. "Fair catch," she admitted.

Roland moved forward, but someone else was before him. "We can hardly start Lady Alice's Christmas with a kiss from a mere brother," said Ivanridge. "Allow me."

Alice took one step back but realized in time it would be unpardonable to retreat. But how dare he do this to her? She sent that message full force with her eyes.

As his head came down to hers he murmured, "I've charged an enemy battery, Miranda. Your flaming eyes won't stop me."

It was an appropriate Christmas kiss, just his lips soft and warm against hers, his hands resting light on her shoulders. Alice stood rigid, turned to stone by his brutal use of that name. The song had not, after all, been an accident.

He let her go. "Merry Christmas," he said coolly as he reached up to pluck a berry from the bunch. His eyes were shielded, but she sensed he was not as cool as he wished to be. Could Tyr Norman at long last be experiencing guilt? She prayed for it.

"Now can a mere brother get a peck in?" asked Roland and swung her close for a merry buss.

Major Ewing took his turn next, stiffly but thoroughly, then it was Charlie. His lips were butterfly soft against hers, but his eyes were kind. "Merry Christmas, Alice."

"Merry Christmas, Charlie." If she had any sense she'd marry him, smirched honor or not. She shrugged off the thought. She accepted three more kisses then looked humorously up at the bush. "We certainly made inroads into that one, didn't we? I think you should all go off and assault some other lady." She looked around and then at Ivanridge. "I see Bella Carstairs posted hopefully beneath a kissing bunch, my lord."

"So she is," he said with a smile. "And Christmas kisses don't mean a *lasting* commitment, do they?"

With that he walked away and Alice, by dint of great will power, did not glare after him. As she wandered around checking on her guests, however, the thought rang through her head like the Christmas bells. How dare he taunt her with his own callousness? How dare he?

She'd been wrong. Christmas peace or no, she couldn't have Ivanridge here for twelve long days. She would have to get rid of him, and now was a good time to tell him to go. As the guests began to disperse she longed for her bed too but lingered, hoping for an opportunity to speak to him in private.

It looked for a while as if the younger men were going to make a night of it, but then Roland reminded them they'd be expected to be out early the next morning in medieval garb to find and cut a yule log.

As they began to disperse, Roland said, "You don't have to stay up, Alice. I'll make sure all's right here."

She gave in. It had been sheer desperation which had made her think of confronting Ivanridge at this hour, and it was clearly impractical. As she headed for her room she tried to think of a reasonable way to throw him out without raising anyone's suspicions. The more she thought about it, the less likely it became.

Then, as she walked along the upper gallery, she saw him going down the opposite stairs, which certainly did not lead to his, or any other, bedroom.

She slipped down a different set of stairs and followed.

For a moment she wondered if he was up to no good, thievery even—nothing was too low for this man—but then he turned to a candle in a wall sconce and lit a thin cigarillo. Trailing wisps of aromatic smoke he turned into the conservatory.

Alice followed as if drawn by magnets but hesitated at the doorway. Now that she had come this far, she wasn't at all sure what she was going to say or that this encounter was wise.

She took a step of retreat. He sensed her and turned with alert speed, then relaxed but only slightly. "It's unwise to creep up on a man not long away from war. What do you want?"

The terse rudeness of it brought heat to her cheeks. "I might be here to tell you we do not permit the cigarillo habit in the house."

"Are you?"

Alice felt a fool. "No."

"Didn't think so. Your brother smokes 'em." He blew out a stream of silver-gray. "So?"

He had the manners of an undergroom. Alice grasped her courage. "I want you to leave."

"The conservatory?" he asked mildly.

"Conyngham."

"No."

She hadn't expected such a blunt refusal. "Why not? The situation is damnable. You cannot have thought before you came here."

There was only the moon through the steamy glass to light them, and he seemed shadowed in spirit as well as flesh.

"I thought a great deal before I came here."

"Then why did you come at all? A moment's thought must have shown you how . . . how *improper* it is!"

She saw his teeth glint white in a cruel smile. "It won't be improper unless you start tearing your clothes off again, Miranda."

Alice took three steps forward and hit him with all the rage and pain of six years. He allowed it. She knew that as if everything had slowed down. She watched the angry mark flare on his cheek. She noticed that except for the jerk of his head under the force of her blow he did not move. After a breathless moment he raised the cigarillo to his lips and drew on it. He said nothing.

Alice had no idea what to do or say. Anything would be feeble. "So you refuse to go," she said at last.

He blew out smoke. "I have ghosts to exorcise," he said. "Judging from your performance to date, it should be easy."

"You cannot judge me," she cried. "You took my innocence. You *abandoned* me!"

"Did I? Even so, I would have thought you'd had your pound of flesh."

Alice stepped back, away from his coldness. "I? I have had nothing."

His lips curled up in a smile that didn't reach his eyes. "You've had a good swing at me at least. You can't deny that." He crushed out the cigarillo in a potted fern. "Good night, Lady Alice." With that, he walked by her and was gone.

Alice awoke the next day with a feeling of dread, and this was Christmas Day, which she'd always loved. Had she slept at all? It didn't feel like it, and she remembered countless restless hours tussling with rage, loss, fear, and a twisted, bitter kind of excitement.

Things were better once her maid, Hobly, brought her coffee—the day was now underway and she could pretend, at least, to be in control. It was better still when Rebecca popped her head around the door. "May I come and drink coffee with you, Alice? We'll never have time for a coze otherwise."

Rebecca was a slender blonde whose sweet disposition was written all over her face. It wasn't right, thought Alice with a spurt of anger, that Rebecca had been robbed of her loving husband by a war which had left Tyr Norman untouched.

"Oh, yes, do! You can go, Hobly. I'll ring when I'm ready to dress." Alice leapt out of bed and led Rebecca into her small sitting room.

"This is so comfortable," said Rebecca as they sat in the chairs in front of a new fire. "Perhaps I should demand something like this now I am back at home."

"Why not? I decided, since I will not marry, I might as well have my comforts."

"Will not marry? Alice, of course you will!"

Alice tempered her words. "Let us say, it's beginning to

seem unlikely, and I'm well content. There's space enough for me here even when Roland marries."

"What about Standon?" Rebecca asked tentatively. "He's such a lovely man, and I'm sure he still cares. I never did understand—"

"Oh please!" Alice interrupted as cheerfully as she could. "It's such old history. I'm still fond of Charlie, but I assure you I will not change my mind about marrying him. Surely you," she added gently, "who knew real love, can appreciate that fondness is not enough."

Rebecca looked into the fire, her delicate face unwontedly sober. "I don't know, Alice. Frederick seems so long ago. I'm lonely, and love . . . love exposes us to such terrible pain."

Alice closed her eyes, but she could not shut out the knowledge that she too had loved and been deeply hurt.

"Oh Alice, I'm so sorry!" Alice opened her eyes to see Rebecca's concerned face. "I swore I wouldn't be a shroud at the feast, and here I am giving you a case of the dismals."

Alice gathered her friend in for a hug. "Don't act for me. Don't ever act for me." They smiled at each other somewhat tearfully, then Alice leapt to her feet. "But we must be up and about if we're to inspect the men at their work."

"Cutting the yule log? But Alice, it's supposed to be the fair maidens who go out to tease. I'm no maiden."

"I prefer to interpret it as the available young ladies. After all," she added with a wicked look, "who's to say all the unmarried wenches hereabouts have kept their maidenheads?"

Rebecca gave a startled giggle and hurried off to dress.

Alice rang her bell for Hobly, reflecting that she was going to have to bridle her tongue or she would end up spilling the truth. Having Tyr Norman here had not only brought old feelings to the surface but was prompting her to speak of matters best left unaddressed.

With Hobly's help she was soon dressed in medieval style, ready for the first of the Twelve Days.

It was the custom at Conyngham for all to wear twelfth-century dress during the festival though some guests were loose in their interpretation. Houpelands and even far-thingales had been seen, but generally the loose, comfortable lines of the early middle ages were the norm. The family, of course, had extensive, authentic wardrobes, and there were ample spare costumes for the unprepared guest or one who ran out of appropriate garments.

Alice was soon dressed in a long linen shift, a gunna of finer linen in a rich buttery cream embroidered in brown and red, and a knee-length tunic of warm red wool. The tunic was trimmed at neck, sleeves, and hem with braid. Alice knotted a silken rope around her hips and Hobly braided her hair into two long plaits interwoven with ribbons. This was one time when her hair came into its own. Alice pulled on stockings and then the long loose braies necessary for riding astride. Low red leather boots completed her outfit.

She glanced in the mirror and was satisfied. She loved these clothes. She sometimes thought she would have been happier in medieval times, but then she remembered the cold, harsh castles, the chancy supply of food, and the almost incessant warfare, and was pleased to live in a civilized age.

She picked up her brown cloak lined with vair and went off to collect Rebecca and gather up the other young available ladies.

Rebecca was ready in shades of blue. Miss Carstairs was found to be in a form-fitting outfit more of the fourteenth century than the twelfth, and Alice doubted that even then they had cut the neckline quite so low. The girl was going to freeze for though she had a warm woolen cloak she was leaving it open to display her attributes.

Susan Travis was anxious in a nondescript garment of brown wool tied around the middle. It was, thought Alice, quite authentic if she wished to play the part of a downtrod-den serf. She resolved to take the shy girl on a foray through the Conyngham wardrobes later. For now, she merely sup-plied a warm cloak, which Susan lacked.

Before leaving the house, however, Alice had a word with a maid to check the state of the clothes of Miss Travis's

parents and to offer additions if required. Then she guided
her company to the stables.

It was a beautiful morning, clear and crisp with the
frosted grass crunching under their feet. It was a miracle,
thought Alice, but it seemed that Christmas Day was always
beautiful.

Bella Carstairs shivered. "It's so cold. Where are we going?"

"To find the eligible men," said Alice and pinned the
girl's cloak close around her. "They are off finding and cutting the yule log. We will go and tease them."

Bella cheered up. "Will Lord Ivanridge be there?"

"I suppose so," said Alice.

When they arrived at the stables she said, "In the twelfth
century ladies rode astride, but you may choose sidesaddle
if you wish." Bella and Susan earnestly assured her they did,
and Susan asked for a quiet mount.

Rebecca said to them, "I relish this one chance to ride
astride. You should try it, and your modesty is safe." She
raised her skirt to show the linen leggings she already wore.

Susan gasped. "Heavens! What are they?"

Alice replied. "Leggings, braies, hose. Call them what
you wish." She produced another two pairs from under her
cloak and waved them temptingly. "Are you sure you don't
want to try?"

Bella and Susan were very clear that they did not.

Soon they were mounted. Alice had come to love her
annual experience of riding astride, though she always paid
for it with complaints from muscles unaccustomed to the
work. Now she wanted to race off at full tilt, but she could
see Susan was a nervous rider and Bella was in no mood to
hare around, being more concerned with draping her yellow
silk skirts and white cloak to greatest effect. Silk, thought
Alice, shaking her head. The girl wouldn't wear silk in the
morning ordinarily, so why now?

"Where will we find the men?" Bella asked.

"In the Home Wood somewhere," said Alice. "It's not far.

A few trees have come down there in the last year which will be suitable for burning."

She eventually got her party up to a canter and began to enjoy herself.

They entered the wood and stopped to listen. There were voices over to the right but no sound of work. With a sign to her companions to be as quiet as possible, Alice led the way. Bella opened her cloak again. Susan giggled.

"Good morning, gentlemen," Alice said. "Having difficulty?"

Six men looked up at the four ladies. As well as Roland, Standon, Ewing, and Ivanridge, there were Lord Garstang and Mr. Noonan. The latter was a little old for this, but he was unmarried and so entitled to take part. It was a shame, however, that he'd chosen to wear the fitting hose and short jacket of the fourteenth century, for he was short and plump. He'd have been much better off in the braies and knee-length tunic worn by the other men, and more comfortable as well.

"Not at all," said Roland, pretending offense, though the scene was played out much the same way every year. "We are just resting the saw."

The two-handed saw was propped against the huge tree trunk into which they were cutting. They appeared to have gotten halfway through before stopping to refresh themselves from tankards of ale.

"Don't let it rest too long," said Rebecca with a grin. "We need the yule log today, you know."

Roland scowled at her. "Saucy wench. All right, men, whose turn is it?"

"Mine and Standon's," said Ivanridge, shrugging out of his cloak and going to take one end of the saw.

Alice remembered him taking part in this tradition six years ago, but he'd been in uniform. He'd taken off his jacket and worked in shirtsleeves. He'd been dashing no matter what he wore and still was. His medieval clothes were simple homespun browns, but with his forged hardness and his dark hair slightly long, he suited them perfectly. He could have stepped out of a previous century.

He and Standon began to operate the saw, pushing and pulling smoothly. She dimly heard Rebecca leading the other two maidens in humorous taunts about the men's performance. Even Susan was beginning to get into the spirit of things. Alice was dumb.

She told herself she couldn't actually see the muscles under that loose clothing, so why could she sense the power of them, imagine them beneath her fingers?

She broke the spell he was casting on her. "Really, Lord Ivanridge," she called out. "Is that the best you can do? You're hardly making any impression at all."

He turned with a challenging smile. "Come and assist us then."

Alice felt as if she'd stepped into a trap. This wasn't part of the script at all, but everyone was greeting this with huge merriment.

"You too, Lady Frederick," called Standon. "Come and lend your strength at this end!"

Rebecca complied instantly, so Alice had little choice. She slid off her horse and walked stiffly towards her tormentor. "What do you think you're doing?" she asked, but quietly.

"Cutting a yule log," he said.

He was startlingly unsafe in his loose, homespun garments. As if he sensed her disquiet, he stripped off his tunic to reveal a thin linen shirt. It was slit down the front and showed dark hair curling over hard muscles. Alice's mouth dried.

"Hot work," he said, as he tossed his tunic aside.

Alice found herself within his arms, back pressed to his hard body. She swallowed and grasped the handle of the saw.

"Put your hands on top of mine," he said softly against her ear. "We wouldn't want you to get a blister."

"What of your hands?" she asked.

He spread them momentarily and she saw the hard skin and callouses. "Sabers and other instruments of death," he remarked.

He gripped the wooden handle, and Alice put her hands on top of his, seeing how delicate her white hands looked over his. She wasn't going to do much good in this position, but then that wasn't the point. This situation had been devised to torture her. Or seduce her.

She looked up and saw Rebecca and Charlie on the other end of the saw, laughing. The look Rebecca flashed up at her partner was surprisingly flirtatious.

Right, thought Alice. Tyr Norman isn't going to have it all his own way. She relaxed against his body and let her hands flex against his. "What now?" she asked, deliberately using a husky tone.

"Push and then pull, Lady Alice." He leaned against her so that the saw slid toward Standon. Then the saw was pushed back, forcing her against his body. Push and then pull. Push and then pull. Alice allowed her body to fall hard against his at the end of every pull . . .

He suddenly let go of the saw and stepped back, releasing her. "Whew," he said, wiping his arm against his damp brow. "I think an armful of such beauty saps my strength instead of adding to it."

He said it jokingly, but he was serious. Alice felt a triumphant smile tug at her lips but controlled it. Ivanridge caught it, however. Alice saw the flash of anger in his eyes, followed by a reluctant gleam of admiration.

Ewing and Garstang demanded to try the same system and Bella and Susan were persuaded to assist. Alice strolled back towards the horses.

"You always were full of surprises," Ivanridge said behind her.

She turned and met his eyes. "Best you remember that, Lord Ivanridge."

"Oh, I remember it well, Miranda."

"Stop calling me that!"

"Why? You are certainly a creature of amazing surprises."

Alice closed her eyes briefly. "Why won't you just go away?"

"I told you why."

She glared at him. "I can make your life extremely difficult, Lord Ivanridge."

He laughed shortly. "That's an old weapon and worn very blunt." He turned away dismissively. "They're almost through. Amazing what the presence of a few suitably appreciative damsels will do to a man's strength."

Alice watched him stroll away knowing she was perilously close to tears. She fought them away and pinned on a smile. But what did he mean about an old weapon? She'd never made his life difficult . . .

A triumphant shout told that the task was accomplished. The men mounted their own horses and everyone rode back to the house together. Egged on by Roland, Alice at last indulged in a flat-out gallop, but she noticed that Ivanridge lagged behind with Susan Travis. Now, what was he about?

In the stables she lingered until he arrived and sought another moment alone with him. "You will please leave the young and innocent alone, Lord Ivanridge," she told him.

He led his and Susan's mounts over to a groom. "Am I not allowed simple converse with the female sex?"

"Not with the likes of Susan, no. If you are feeling amorous I can recommend a couple of the matrons who are not averse to variety."

His look was slightly disgusted. "You've added pandering to your hostess duties, have you?"

Alice winced, knowing she deserved that. "You make me behave like this," she said despairingly. "Please, won't you leave?"

"No. And Lady Alice," he said with precision, "I have never *made* you do anything in your life."

He walked away, and Rebecca took his place. "What's the matter? Lord Ivanridge looked . . ."

"Looked what?"

Rebecca thought about it. "Like a soldier, I suppose. One about to kill."

Alice shuddered slightly. That was what she sensed in him. A leashed killing anger. Why?

As Christmas Day progressed, Alice found she had little time to herself, and the little she did steal was spent trying to think of a way to force Ivanridge out or at least change his room. She could come up with neither. There were available rooms, but they were all inferior or very out of the way and she could think of no excuse for the change.

Instead, over tea, she sought out Charlie and probed for details as to his interaction with Ivanridge.

Charlie considered her. "What's up? Anyone would think you suspected the man of being a murderer. Or a madman."

"Of course not," Alice said gaily. "I just feel a little guilty for asking you to share with a stranger."

"It's no problem, except that he's a restless sleeper."

"Then he is making it difficult," she said, thinking she saw an excuse presenting itself.

"Not particularly. Once asleep, I sleep soundly." He apparently felt obliged to reassure her. "We discussed it this morning and he's agreed to wait until I'm asleep before going to sleep himself."

"What was the problem?" Alice asked, knowing she would be wiser to hold on to ignorance.

"War dreams, I suppose," said Standon. "Don't say anything, Alice. I'm sure he wouldn't want it spoken of."

So Tyr Norman had nightmares about the war, did he? Served him right. But Alice was bitterly aware of a desire to hold him in her arms and bring him to a sound sleep.

That night was the Christmas feast, held in the Great Hall. The lofty stone chamber was hung with banners and ancient weapons, and the tables were set down the two long walls. At one end of the large room sat a high table on a dais and at the other stood an enormous fireplace.

The first order of business was for the unmarried men to drag the yule log to the fireplace while being urged on and tormented by the maidens. Alice deliberately let Rebecca lead the ladies and kept well in the background herself. She was giving Ivanridge no further opportunity to harass her.

Once the kindling was lit beneath the log, there was a great cheer and everyone took their places. Alice, Roland, and Lord Raneleigh sat at the high table, but the two central seats there were left vacant for the king and queen of the feast. Alice saw Ivanridge take a place down one side. She had arranged for him to be out of her direct line of sight and between Mrs. Digby-Rowles and Lady Jerrold. Extremely safe.

As soon as everyone was seated, the earl rose, magnificent in a full-length tunic of plum velvet trimmed with fur. "Our first duty this night," he explained, "is to choose our rulers. Here in these chairs we will enthrone a king and queen for our festivities, and within this hall their word shall be law for twelve full days. Behold, here come buxom wenches and bonny lads bearing gifts—gifts for everyone! But one gentleman and one lady will find a bean along with their trinket. They will be our monarchs of mischief!"

To the accompaniment of foot-stamping music, laughing maids and footmen in period costumes entered and passed around the tables, handing out beautifully wrapped boxes, and kisses for those who asked. Most did.

Though the family did not receive these gifts, Alice had had her eye for some time on a particularly fine specimen among the staff, and as he crossed the hall in front of the high table, she called out, "Ho, sirrah! I may not receive a gift, but should I be deprived of a Christmas kiss?"

The handsome fellow grinned cockily. Alice had no doubt he was a devil among the maids. " 'Twouldn't be fair, would it?" he replied. Instead of leaning across the table, he came round and swept her up for a hearty kiss. The hall erupted in cheers, though some of the ladies looked a little shocked.

Alice laughed. "And a merry Christmas to you too, Peter." As she resumed her seat, however, she told herself she should have learned she was no hand at managing men.

Then she realized that the king and queen had been discovered, and Rebecca and Tyr Norman were approaching the table.

Her father leapt to his feet as trumpeters blew a fanfare. "Behold our monarchs! Welcome, Your Majesties!"

Roland was already on his feet, waiting to drape the rich crimson cloak edged with ermine around Rebecca's shoulders. Alice forced herself to her feet to perform the same task for her nemesis. She couldn't believe it. Why was this happening to her?

He was tall and had to bend slightly to allow her to put the cloak on his broad shoulders. As he sat she saw how poorly the mustard color of his outfit went with the cloak, and she took spiteful satisfaction from that. As she'd said earlier, he seemed to be driving her to a mean pettiness of thought and deed.

He examined the enameled card case which had been his gift. "Your family gives handsome gifts, Lady Alice," he said pleasantly. "What a shame you receive none yourselves."

"We exchange gifts privately," she said, thinking that at least in this seating arrangement she didn't have to look at him.

"And perhaps gifts find their way to you later? Let me see. Last time I was here I believe I received a jade pin."

He'd given it to her at some point during the night. She'd thrown it in the lake.

Alice ignored his taunting, determined to be a perfect lady. "Do you have any commands, sire?"

The silence from her right stretched so that in the end she had to look at him. "Come to my room later," he said.

Alice met his cold eyes. "Your commands only hold in the hall, sire . . ."

He smiled. "Intriguing."

". . . and you share a room."

"Beginning to regret that, are you? I'm sure you'll find a way around the problem."

Alice turned to the front and fixed a polite smile on her face. "If you think," she said between her teeth, "I have the slightest intention or desire to visit your room, Lord Ivanridge, you are sorely mistaken."

"Have other game in your sights this year, do you?"

Alice found she had the sharp eating knife tight in her hand and that she was full of desire; the desire to plunge it into him. "Talk to your queen," she said tightly. "Invent some mischief. I am sure you are very good at that."

He proved to be. As the platters of food—fowl, suckling pig, boar's head, peacock, and all the sundry accompaniments came around, he and Rebecca conferred and commanded.

Various guests were ordered to join the musicians and play or sing. Others were ordered to perform a trick or offer a puzzle. Alice noted, however, that no one was asked to do something they could not, and the shy were left in peace. Rebecca's doing, she was sure.

Then Ivanridge turned to her. "Lady Alice, we would have you do Salome's dance for us."

Alice had no cause for complaint. This, like the somersaults Roland had just performed, was part of the tradition. She had been doing her version of the dance since she was fifteen, but for the first time she felt uncomfortable about it.

She went out of the hall briefly and put on her veils—one around her head to cover the lower part of her face and one over her hair. She settled her jeweled girdle lower on her hips. At her signal, the professional musicians began an Eastern melody, and she swayed into the hall.

When she'd first had this idea at fifteen, her version of the dance had been more like a solo country dance, but since then she had researched it and even taken advice of the Persian Ambassador's wife. She knew the moves, though a mild version of the real thing, were suggestive, but that had never bothered her before.

As she swayed her hips and played with her veil she tried to remember dancing like this six years ago. But on Christmas night six years ago Tyr Norman had just been a handsome young Hussar and Charlie had been more on her mind than he. Alice couldn't remember feeling embarrassed to be doing the dance before Charlie.

She tried her hardest not to look at Ivanridge, but it was impossible if for no other reason than that she was supposed to be persuading him to give her the head of St. John. Once she looked, she was captured by those dark eyes. Forbidden passions began to fuel her dance. She danced closer to him, moving her shoulders and swaying her hips, wanting to break through his hard coldness and see desire in his eyes.

So she could laugh in his face.

Though she watched like a hawk, no flicker of emotion showed to reward her. Was he made of stone?

The music stopped and she sank into a curtsy as thunderous applause broke out.

"We will grant you anything in our power," said Ivanridge huskily.

Alice rose. "I would have a rogue's head, sire." With her eyes she told him whose she wished it could be.

A brow twitched, but he said, "Point out the rogue, you luscious wench, and I will call the headsman."

Alice looked around, drawing out the suspense. She'd fully intended to get petty revenge by picking Ivanridge. Now she thought of choosing Charlie, but people would read all kinds of things into that. In the end she pointed to Major Ewing.

Four footmen leapt on the startled major, and a fearsome giant—a local laborer who enjoyed his part in the festivities—stalked in bearing a huge, authentic-looking ax. It was, in fact, authentic, and Alice was always a little nervous the man would handle it carelessly and lop off something or other. Ewing was dragged forward and guests new to Conyngham began to look ill at ease. The rest chanted, "The head! The head!"

At the last moment Rebecca leapt to her feet. "Stop! I am queen as much as this man is king and I will not let an honest man die at a strumpet's whim!"

Alice covered her face in exaggerated shame.

"Release him!" commanded Rebecca. "Good man," she said to Ewing, "resume your seat and enjoy the feast without fear. And you," she said to Alice sternly, "go strip off your veils and act the proper maid."

Shrieking with mock tears, Alice fled the hall. She heard Ivanridge say, "Isn't that just like a woman to spoil a little harmless fun?"

She took a moment to compose herself and to let the hall settle. The scene had gone better than ever. Of course, both Rebecca and Ivanridge had seen it before; sometimes a new-comer was chosen monarch and had to be prompted by her father and brother. Both Rebecca and Ivanridge had showed real dramatic talent.

But then, she knew him to be a facile deceiver.

She slipped back into the hail and to her place.

"Your dancing's improved," he said casually.

"Your acting's as good as ever," she said in the same manner.

"I believe the queen commanded you to act the *proper maid,* Lady Alice."

It sounded like a calculated insult.

There was the dancing to get through. Roland and she demonstrated some simple steps, which were not so very different from the familiar country dances, then they were joined by three couples well used to the business for a more complicated demonstration.

Soon all were on the floor stamping and clapping to the merry, earthy dances.

Alice was glad to lose herself in the dancing. It was true that she had to partner Ivanridge now and then—everyone partnered everyone else at some point—but these were not dances to encourage intimacy but to express the joy of living and moving.

There was an endless supply of wine, punch, and more benign thirst quenchers. There was a buffet of food, and nonstop dancing.

Some of the older people began to drift off to bed, but most of the company stayed on. Chess and backgammon games started up, and some people took breaks for conversation. The kissing bows were stripped of their berries; to-morrow men wanting to steal a kiss would have to seek out the more cunningly hidden ones, which were also the ones well situated for more lingering embraces.

Alice would be sure to avoid them.

Tiredness was beginning to fog Alice's mind when she

realized she was *waltzing* with Lord Standon. "This dance is very anachronistic, Charlie."

"But a lot less exhausting. If the king and queen don't object, what are we poor lesser folk to do?"

Alice saw Rebecca waltzing with Roland, while Ivanridge partnered Bella. There were a dozen or so other couples drifting in lazy circles, and Alice supposed the hard-worked musicians were also relieved to be playing more familiar fare. Charlie's voice startled her out of a pleasant vacuum.

"I'm going to embarrass us both, Alice," he said, "but I need to know. Will you reconsider the decision you made six years ago?"

Alice sighed. She'd feared it would come to this. "Charlie, I refuse to believe you've been nursing a broken heart. You've kept a very handsome mistress these last few years."

"True," he said without embarrassment. "Are you holding that against me?"

"Of course not." In desperation, Alice returned to the argument she'd used six years ago. "I just don't love you, Charlie."

"I don't think I love you either," he said, which startled her considerably. "Not as the poets describe it, anyway. But I like you. I admire you. You were a charming girl, and you've grown into a beautiful woman. I need to marry, Alice, and I'd rather marry you than anyone else I know."

Alice looked up at him. "I'm not sure whether to be amused or insulted."

His smile was friendly but held some steel. "As you pointed out; it would be absurd for me to be protesting an undying passion. When you ended our engagement, I naturally assumed there was someone else. That appears not to be so. Since neither of us seems likely to be hit by Cupid's arrow, it would be sensible for us to marry. You can't really want to grow old as a spinster, and I still think we'd suit very well. Perhaps love would grow."

Put that way it did seem suitable. Alice was aware that in some secret part of her heart she'd been waiting all these years for Tyr Norman to return with an explanation and prot-

estations of love, but now he was back and clearly no answer
to her problems. "I don't know, Charlie," she said at last.
"May I think about it?"

"Of course. But not for another six years."

As the dance ended Alice was again aware of that steel
beneath his courteous surface, and she liked him better for
it.

When the music struck up again, she was swung into the
dance by Ivanridge.

She resisted. "Let me go!"

His arms were like iron. "We are in the hall, and I am
king. Dance with me."

Alice glared up at him and decided the time had come for
attack. She would not be his toy in this cat and mouse game.
She relaxed and allowed him to twirl her in the dance.
"What exactly are you up to?" she asked.

"Dancing?"

"I mean," she said, "why did you come here, why have
you stayed, and why do you keep forcing yourself on me?"

His eyes smiled down at her, full of hard-edged admiration. "The bold approach. But then that was always your
strategy, wasn't it?"

Alice couldn't bear his look and turned her head away.
"As a strategy," she remarked, "it leaves something to be
desired. It hasn't gained me an answer."

"Left you dissatisfied, you mean? We can't have that, can
we?" There was a weight of meaning to the words which she
could not fathom. "Let me see," he continued pleasantly, "I
came here because I was invited. I stayed because I found
unfinished business. I keep forcing myself upon you because
you seem to dislike it. If you can convince me you like it,
Miranda, I'll avoid you like the plague."

Alice looked at him in shock. "It's as if you hate me," she
whispered. "What have I ever done to you?"

"Very pretty," he approved. "It's all the theatricals, I suppose. Cuidad Rodrigo," he said, as he twirled them around.
"Badajoz. Albuera."

Alice's head was spinning and with more than the twirling. "Are you saying I drove you to war? You already had your marching orders when we met."

"Was that part of my appeal?"

She hit back. "I suppose we're all fools for a uniform."

"You must be grieving the war is over."

Alice fought him and stopped the crazy spinning. "You still haven't answered my question, Lord Ivanridge. If you found you didn't like war, you can hardly lay that at my door."

"There's war and war, Lady Alice," he said, and at that moment the music meshed with their action and stopped. "If you don't know that, your uncle certainly does."

He was gone and Lord Garstang was asking for a dance. Alice made an excuse and escaped into an empty corridor. What had all that been about? The uncle he referred to must be her mother's brother, General George Travis-Blount. As one of the senior men at the Horse Guards, he certainly knew all about war. Was Ivanridge suggesting that she ask him about it? Was he using the horrors of war as his excuse for the cruel way he was tormenting her?

There was no need for Alice to seek out her uncle. She had heard enough frank talk to have lost any romantic illusion about warfare. It was a bloody business usually prosecuted desperately in large amounts of mud. The most surprising thing was that the survivors often seemed to enjoy the memory.

Ivanridge, she suddenly remembered, had nightmares. She shuddered and hugged herself, though the corridor was not particularly cold.

But he could not possibly be accusing her of sending him to war. That decision had been made before they ever met. And whatever horrors he had seen and experienced did not excuse what he had done before he saw fighting at all.

Perhaps, she thought for the first time, he was mad. She had heard of men whose minds broke under the stress of war.

Major Ewing came strolling down the corridor, humming

a song, clearly a little on the go. "Ah, the lovely Salome! Damn fine dance, that."

"Thank you, Major." Alice linked arms with him. "I suppose you and Ivanridge know one another well."

He looked at her glassily and shook his head. "Different regiments. Anyway, Tyr Norman was a hero. I kept my head down."

Alice felt there was a mystery here that she had to solve. She steered the major to a window seat and he seemed happy enough to collapse there.

Alice sat beside him. "What do you mean, a hero?"

Ewing made a generous gesture. "Derring-do. Single-handed exploits . . . Sort of fellow who seeks out the most hellish spots." He shook his head. "Madmen, usually. Don't last long. But then they seem to have a death wish."

Death wish? Alice began to examine the notion that Tyr Norman had been so guilt ridden over his treatment of her that he'd tried to get himself killed. No matter how she looked at it, it didn't fit. If he'd felt guilty, he could have tried to make amends. He certainly would have no reason for assaulting her now as if she were the enemy.

Ewing was humming again and she guessed that he was soon going to drift off to sleep. "Major Ewing," Alice said to catch his attention. "How do you think Ivanridge survived?"

"Luck," he said simply. "There's a devil of a lot of luck in war. And he came to his senses. Last few years, I never heard of him acting crazy." He gazed, without focus, at the tapestry on the opposite wall. "Could have just been a way to make it up the ranks, if he was desperate enough. Hear there wasn't much money there . . . Made it to colonel with his craziness, so . . . crazy or not?"

His lids began to droop, and Alice left him there. So much for her melodramatic imaginings. He hadn't been awash with guilt. He'd just been ambitious.

So, what had he meant when he'd mentioned her uncle? Did he know that Uncle George would be coming after New Year's Day to enjoy the last few of the Twelve Days?

Alice looked into the hall. Couples were still dancing. She saw Roland flirting with Bella and Charlie dancing with Rebecca but no sign of Ivanridge.

She couldn't make herself enter the half-lit chamber, where he might be waiting in the shadows to pounce on her. She went quickly to her bedroom, a fugitive in her own home.

By employing tactics worthy of her uncle the general, Alice found it possible to avoid Lord Ivanridge.

It was no longer necessary for her to sit by his side at the high table, for after Christmas night the king and queen were expected to command whom they willed to sit there, and it was custom that the honor be spread around.

Alice complained to Rebecca of the waltzing so that she not be in danger of that intimacy again, and she ensured her safety by escaping from the hall revelries as often as she could. When Roland questioned her, she told him tartly that it was his fault for inviting Lord Standon. Then she felt terribly guilty about maligning Charlie's behavior.

Through days of skating and treasure hunts, charades and riding, she maneuvered with the sole purpose of avoiding Ivanridge even though she had no clear evidence she was being stalked. She resented it deeply. The man was completely spoiling her Christmas. Even her father noticed how strangely she was behaving.

"Anything up, Alice?" he asked her on New Year's Eve. "You don't seem to be in the thick of things like you used to be. Not feeling quite the thing?"

"I feel perfectly well, Father," she said, knowing that any other answer would have the doctor at the door. "I just feel I have to keep an eye on things."

"Nonsense!" declared Lord Raneleigh. "Everything's going marvelously. No more of it, now. Roland's organizing Snapdragon for midnight. I expect to see you in there grabbing a few, my girl. All right?"

Alice sighed. "Yes, Father."

That night as everyone waited for the approach of midnight and the beginning of the Year of Our Lord, 1816, Roland entered the hall bearing a great shallow earthen dish. Rebecca followed with a lighted taper. There was clapping and cheering, but all Alice's attention was on Ivanridge to be sure he stayed on the other side of the room from herself. He seemed fixed in the company of Lord Garstang and Miss Travis, however, and so she relaxed a little and allowed herself to join in the fun.

Her brother ordered the lights extinguished. Soon the room was plunged into darkness, except for the glow from the fire at the far end and that from Rebecca's taper. There was expectant silence as she touched the flame to the bowl. When the eerie blue flames danced up, Roland carried the dish of flaming brandy-soaked raisins to the high table and Alice started the traditional chant,

Here he comes with flaming bowl.
Don't be mean to take his toll,
Snip! Snap! Dragon!

Rebecca blew out her light and the lurid flames of burning alcohol were the only illumination as everyone gathered round to see who would be the first brave soul to risk their fingers.

Looking suitably devilish in the strange light, Roland flexed his hand. Quick as a flash he grabbed a raisin and popped it still flaming into his mouth and bit down. There was a cheer.

Take care you don't take too much,
Be not greedy in your clutch,
Snip! Snap! Dragon!

Major Ewing went next, then the Duke of Portsmouth who fumbled and burnt his fingers. There was a groan of derisive sympathy.

With his blue and lapping tongue
Many of you will be stung.
Snip! Snap! Dragon!

Alice was about to demand a turn when she thought to check on Ivanridge again. He wasn't where he'd been before.

3 QUICK STEPS
TO RECEIVE YOUR "THANK YOU" GIFT
FROM THE EDITOR

Send back this card and you'll receive 4 Arabesque novels!
These books have a combined cover price of $20.00 or more,
but they are yours to keep for a mere $1.99.

There's no catch. You're under no obligation to buy anything.
We charge only $1.99 for the books (plus $1.50 for shipping
and handling, a total of $3.49). And you don't have to make
any minimum number of purchases—not even one!

We hope that after receiving your books you'll want to
remain an Arabesque subscriber. But the choice is yours to
continue or cancel, anytime at all! So why not take us up on
our invitation to receive 4 Arabesque Romance Novels, with
no risk of any kind. You'll be glad you did!

Call us
TOLL-FREE
at 1-888-345-BOOK

THE EDITOR'S "THANK YOU" GIFT INCLUDES:

- 4 books delivered for only $1.99 (plus $1.50 for shipping and handling)
- A FREE newsletter, *Arabesque Romance News*, filled with author interviews, book previews, special offers, and more!
- No risks or obligations. You're free to cancel whenever you wish... with no questions asked.

BOOK CERTIFICATE

Yes! Please send me 4 Arabesque books for $1.99 (+ $1.50 for shipping & handling, a total of $3.49). I understand I am under no obligation to purchase any books, as explained on the back of this card.

Name _____

Address _____ Apt. _____

City _____ State _____ Zip _____

Telephone ( ) _____

Signature _____

Offer limited to one per household and not valid to current subscribers. All orders subject to approval. Terms, offer, & price subject to change.

Thank you!

ANQ2OR

Accepting the four introductory books for $1.99 (+ $1.50 for shipping & handling, a total of $3.49) places you under no obligation to buy anything. You may keep the books and return the shipping statement marked "cancel". If you do not cancel, about a month later we will send 4 additional Arabesque novels, and bill you a preferred subscriber's price of just $4.00 per title (plus a small shipping and handling fee). That's $16.00 for all 4 books for a savings of 33% off the cover price. You may cancel at any time, but if you choose to continue, every month we'll send you 4 more books, which you may either purchase at the preferred discount price. . . or return to us and cancel your subscription.

THE ARABESQUE ROMANCE CLUB: HERE'S HOW IT WORKS

ARABESQUE ROMANCE BOOK CLUB
P.O. Box 5214
Clifton NJ 07015-5214

She searched the crowd, but it was amazing how different people looked in the strange blue light. She felt a prickling between her shoulder blades but stopped herself from looking behind. She'd had enough of letting him spoil everything. If she wanted a raisin, she'd take one!

She stepped boldly forward and plucked a raisin from the flames. There was a cry. Before she could pop the raisin in her mouth it was slapped away. She was grabbed from behind, spun, and crushed to a hard chest.

"Damn you!" she cried in disbelieving fury that he would attack her so in public. She kicked at him, then understood.

The smell of burning silk and velvet told the story. He relaxed his arms cautiously, and they both looked down to where her loose silk sleeve had burned away, singeing his velvet where he'd smothered the flames.

Alice swayed with the shock of what might have been. She looked up at him numbly.

"Are you all right?" he asked as if he cared.

She nodded.

"Are you burnt?"

She felt a mild pain and looked down. "Just a little. It's nothing."

He relaxed. "Getting off lightly again," he said, the familiar edge returning to his voice. "You never learn, do you?"

By then her family and others were gathered around. "Good Lord, Alice," said Roland, "I didn't think I had to remind you to beware of trailing sleeves!"

"I didn't think—"

"I don't know what's the matter with you, Alice," said her father testily, which showed he was upset. "You're not yourself. Our thanks to you, Ivanridge. Damn quick thinking."

"I just happened to be closest."

"Nonsense. Fine bit of work. Learned it fighting Boney, I suppose." Lord Raneleigh looked at the younger man closely. "Fancy you were here a few years back in Hussar uniform, yes?"

Alice wondered if the sudden tension came from Ivanridge or herself. It was only then she realized that though she'd turned to face her father she had done so within the circle of Ivanridge's arms. She made a move to escape, but his hold was like steel and no inconspicuous movement was going to free her.

"Yes, Lord Raneleigh," said Ivanridge levelly. "That was before I inherited the title."

"Ah, that explains why I didn't recognize the name. Been bothering me. Don't usually forget people. Norman!" he announced with satisfaction. "That's it. Tyr Norman. Fine name for a fighting man. Thought so at the time. The Norse god of battle and the warlike race that conquered this island. Heard you lived up to your name, too. Good show. Good show."

Roland had turned back to supervise the game again and cheers and squeals indicated success or singeing, but Alice's father had put his considerable bulk between her and the table so she could not see what was going on. It also meant that the small amount of light was blocked. In that private darkness, Tyr Norman's arms settled more thoroughly about her. Again she thought about struggling, but instead she gave in to temptation and relaxed back against his hard body.

"Thank you, Raneleigh," Ivanridge said smoothly, as if nothing was untoward. "But it was more the case of seeming to find myself in situations which called for heroics. I did not set out to gain a reputation."

"Just lucky, hey?"

Though she knew she shouldn't, Alice raised her hands and laid them on his over her midriff. Sweet heaven, but this felt so right. There was no reaction.

"You could put it that way, I suppose," said Ivanridge dryly. "Certainly my destiny was shaped by some force, malign or otherwise."

She wanted to turn in the circle of his arms and taste his lips again . . .

"Otherwise, my boy!" declared her father. "Look where you are today. A fine reputation, a title, and a pretty woman in your arms." He peered at Alice. "Still look a bit shaken, my girl. But you can't cling to your rescuer all night." Alice hastily moved her hands. "Let him at the raisins before these greedy people have them all!"

Ivanridge took his arms from around her, but before she could gather her wits, he grasped her uninjured wrist and pulled her forward to the bowl.

"I deprived you of your raisin," he said. "I'll get you another one."

Knocked off balance by the sweetness of those intimate moments, Alice didn't know what to say, and she still couldn't read him. Had he really been concerned for her safety? Had there been sincerity in that cherishing hold? "There's no need," she said.

"I don't want to be in your debt. Ready?"

Without waiting for her consent, he reached out and snatched a flaming raisin. He brought it rapidly to her mouth. Alice hesitated for a fraction of a second, thinking it would serve him right to burn his fingers but then repented of such petty spite and opened her mouth. She closed it quickly on the delicious burned-brandy sweetness.

He sucked his fingers, but she had no way of telling whether he was soothing a burn or enjoying the remains of the brandy. He looked at her and in the uncertain light appeared much more the warm-hearted young man with whom she had fallen in love. She recognized the danger of it. No, she told herself desperately. She wouldn't play the fool again.

"Now you should get one for me," he said.

"After I was almost burnt to a crisp?"

"You were only slightly singed." He smiled slightly and without bitterness. "I'd be interested to know whether such a brush with danger puts you off or whets your appetite for more."

He *was* trying to seduce her again. Alice lost control of her breathing. "I'd be mad to want to catch fire a second time . . ."

He released her wrist and slid his hand around her until it rested in the small of her back as if they were alone in the world, as they might as well be in this dim light and playful mayhem. "Rather depends on the fire, doesn't it, Miranda?"

His hand felt like a burning brand there, and flames were spreading from it along her nerves. *No, she wouldn't let him do this to her!* She moved away from the heat, but that only took her a step closer to his body. She looked up at him. "What do you want?" she whispered desperately.

"Sweet, spicy fire in my mouth," he said softly. "I thought you were a courageous lady."

Alice was at the end of her strength. "If I pick you a raisin, Tyr, will you please leave me in peace?"

Something flashed in his eyes—anger? pain?—then dark lashes shielded it. After a moment he looked at her again and all she saw was kindness. "Yes, Alice. The war's over, isn't it? We all deserve some peace."

Alice nodded. He released her and she stepped close to the almost empty bowl. This time she made sure that her sleeves were well out of the way, then she picked a raisin and popped it in his ready mouth.

"Mmm," he said, as he swallowed. "Delicious." He caught her hand and slowly licked the trace of sweetness there. "You have to admit, Miranda," he said almost wistfully, "we are very good together." His smile was gentle as he kissed her knuckles. *"Pax tecum, deliciae."*

With that he left her and Alice knew the persecution—if it had ever existed at all—was over. Everything was over, except the Twelve Days. There were six more to go.

Alice moved through the days as if her head, her heart, and her body were separate. Lack of comment told her that her body was doing all the appropriate things. Her head struggled with the fact that she still loved a rogue and would go to his bed again if he snapped his fingers. Her heart ached because she wouldn't allow herself to do it.

She survived by counting away the days until he'd be gone. But she couldn't stop watching him like someone who stores scraps against a coming famine.

She could see no dark side to him now. He was still harder and tougher than he had been six years ago, but he was more relaxed. He was very popular and was kind and warm to everyone.

Except herself. He ignored Alice as if she didn't exist.

On the fifth of January Rebecca came to Alice's room to share morning coffee again. With Rebecca being Queen of the Revels, they had not found much occasion for chat.

"So here we are at the twelfth day," said Rebecca. "I must say that you work your guests hard, Alice."

"The penalty of being a monarch," said Alice, staring into the fire.

"Are you sure you are quite well, Alice?" Rebecca asked with concern. "You seem in very low spirits."

Alice looked at her friend, knowing Rebecca would see more than most. "I am perhaps a little tired, Becca. But please don't fuss."

"It's only that we care, dearest. I wondered whether you had burned yourself more seriously than we thought on New Year's Eve."

"No, honestly. It was nothing." Alice pulled back her sleeve. "See. There's not even a mark."

"Lord Ivanridge acted so quickly, didn't he? At first I thought him a little cold, but having to be with him to think up new mayhem, I have developed a warm regard for the man."

Alice looked at her friend in horror, aware of a stabbing pain suspiciously near her heart.

"Why do you look like that?" asked Rebecca, then she laughed. "Oh, not in that way, Alice, though why you should look as if I'd suggested self-immolation, I don't know. We have just become friends. I like him, and I think he's a man I could trust if I needed to."

"I suppose so," said Alice, feeling she had to say something.

Rebecca considered her. "It is my opinion that the gallant hero is not indifferent to you, Alice. I've seen him look at you once or twice in a very meaningful way. And it's amazing how often he turns the conversation to the topic of one Lady Alice Conyngham."

Alice felt her face flame. "You must be imagining it."

Rebecca grinned triumphantly. "You're *not* indifferent! I knew it. Why on earth are the two of you avoiding each other? It would be an excellent match on both sides."

"Heavens! Do you have us married already, and we've scarcely shared a sentence?"

" 'Methinks the lady doth protest too much.' "

Alice scowled at her friend and sought a retaliatory weapon. "And what of you and Charlie, then? You're living in one another's pockets."

Now it was Rebecca's turn to blush. "I . . . I do find I like Charlie very much." She looked anxiously at Alice. "I have no desire to hurt you, though."

Alice gaped. She had taken in the fact that Rebecca and Lord Standon were often in company without truly absorbing it. "I have no interest in Charlie," she assured her friend. "But you said you liked Ivanridge, too. Are you becoming a flirt, Becca?"

Rebecca smiled thoughtfully. "I like Ivanridge, but if I were to never see him again after tomorrow, I wouldn't give a fig. If I never saw Charlie again, I . . . I would miss him."

Alice absorbed her friend's words and stared into the flames again. She realized her feelings were the exact reverse of Rebecca's. The thought that Tyr Norman would leave Conyngham tomorrow, possibly never to be seen again, was unendurable.

"Oh, Alice," Rebecca said, interrupting these anguished thoughts, "you *do* care. You must know that I would never steal Charlie from you."

Alice felt as if she had been dreaming and had suddenly woken up. What had she been thinking of? She couldn't let Tyr Norman leave her life a second time or not without a battle. And she desperately needed to know what was behind the dark bitterness he had brought to Conyngham. She sensed that there she would find the key to her heart's desire.

She looked directly at her friend. "I don't want Charlie. I want Ivanridge."

"What?"

Alice leant over to take her friend's hand. "Becca, you are not to tell a soul. Promise?"

A wide-eyed Rebecca nodded.

"I jilted Charlie six years ago because I'd fallen in love with Tyr Norman."

Rebecca gasped. "But why did you never tell anyone?"

Alice lied without twinge of conscience. "My mother wouldn't permit such a mésalliance." In spirit it was true. The Countess of Raneleigh would have had to be tortured in her own dungeons before she would have agreed to her only daughter marrying a mere captain.

Rebecca knew this and nodded. "But everything's changed now, dearest. Why are you avoiding him?"

"Because everything's changed," said Alice cryptically, rising to her feet. She felt as if she were singing with new purpose and power. "But I can't give up without a fight. I intend to use every weapon in my arsenal. Don't ask questions, Becca, but will you be ready to help if I need it?"

"Need you ask?" Rebecca chuckled. "But this has the feel of one of those scrapes you were forever leading me into in our schoolroom days."

Alice shared a grin. "It does, doesn't it? But I promise, this one is going to be a lot more exciting. And a lot more rewarding."

The first thing Alice did was cut Charlie free. She drew him aside after breakfast. "Charlie, I am very flattered that you are still willing to consider me as a wife, but I think we both deserve better than mild affection." She did not miss the flash of relief in his eyes.

"I think you're right," he said, adding perceptively, "Is there finally someone else, Alice?"

Alice smiled. "Perhaps. You can be sure, if you hear of my nuptials, the relationship will not be based on mild affection." She reached up and kissed his cheek. On impulse she said, *"Pax tecum,* Charlie."

"Peace be with you too, Alice," he said and went off to speak to Rebecca.

Having tidied her house, Alice considered the next part of her strategy. She couldn't be sure that simply throwing herself in Tyr Norman's arms was going to do any good, despite the declaration of armistice, and she still had to solve the mystery of his behavior.

That was necessary in order that she know how to approach him. It was also necessary for her own peace of mind. Love, she discovered, had little use for pride, and she would forgive and forget his treatment of her if she had to. She would prefer, however, to at least understand it.

The obvious point of attack was General George Travis-Blount who had arrived two days before. She ran him to ground smoking a pipe in her father's study. He was a sinewy, hawk-featured man who bore a great resemblance to Alice's mother.

"Ah, Alice," he said without particular warmth. He'd never been a demonstrative man, and his manner to her had become stiffer as she had left girlhood behind.

"Good morning, Uncle," said Alice, taking a purposeful seat opposite him and arranging her flowing blue skirts. "I wanted to talk to you about warfare."

He scowled at her. "What the devil for? Not a suitable subject for a lady."

"Since men fight to keep us safe, Uncle, I would have thought it appropriate that we take an interest."

"Nonsense. Men manage war best without women dabbling their fingers in it."

That seemed to be said with some meaning, but Alice couldn't fathom it, so she stuck to her guns. "But when men return from war, it is often women who have to cope with the consequences." At his blank look, she added, "Wounds."

"Oh. I suppose so." He scowled at her. "Not thinking of marrying a wounded soldier, are you? Damned stupid thing to do."

Alice realized she didn't like Uncle George very much. "I would have thought it noble," she said.

The only reply he made was a snort of disgust.

Refusing to permit a distraction, Alice continued her advance. "Is it true, Uncle, that some soldiers are wounded in mind as well as in body?"

He puffed on his pipe. "Only weaklings."

"But some of the things that happen in war must leave horrible memories. Perhaps," she added, "give people nightmares."

He took his pipe out of his mouth and glared at her. "And what do you know, missy, of men's nightmares?"

At that moment a number of terrible revelations came to Alice in a flash. She was silent as she struggled to sort through them.

"Eh, missy!" her uncle barked. "Been up to your old tricks? Eh?"

Alice was too shocked to be embarrassed. "Mother told you."

"She did indeed. I'm pleased to see you have some decency and haven't taken your shame to an honest man's bed."

Alice felt as if her mind was like a blade—clean, sharp and deadly. She easily ignored his words and aimed for the heart. "Why did she tell you?"

"Eh? What?"

"You and my mother were not so close. She would not have told you without a reason."

His eyes slid away, and he made a business of fiddling with his pipe. "She was considerably distressed," he muttered.

Alice arranged her information like the battalions of an army: her mother's nature and her uncle's; Tyr Norman as she had known him six years ago and as she knew him now; his words as they danced on Christmas night. Major Ewing's description of his military career.

She waited, absorbing it all, until her uncle uneasily turned to look at her.

"You tried to kill him," she said.

His face twitched angrily, and he muttered words too foul for her to truly understand. "I'd have called him out but that your mother feared the talk. Don't know how he survived."

Alice wanted to scream foul words back at him, to claw at his sharp-boned face, but she was icy as she asked, "Why did you stop?"

"Wellington!" her uncle spat. "Damned jackanapes took a fancy to the rogue. It was made clear that I was to cease my meddling, so don't screech at me, girl. I did my best. You and your mother near broke me, and none of it would have come about if you'd just kept your knees together."

He was upset because he'd failed, not because of what he'd done. Alice could see no purpose in talking to him further. She stood stiffly. "He's here," she said.

Her uncle was goggle-eyed. "What! Tyr Norman?"

Alice nodded. "He's Lord Ivanridge now. You played billiards with him last night." Some of her anguish escaped. "Didn't you even know what he *looked* like, this man you were trying to kill?"

"Why the devil should I?"

Alice held his eyes. "If," she said with cool precision, "Tyr Norman has a heart big enough to forgive this family for what they have done to him, I am going to marry him. If you ever harm a hair of his head again, Uncle, I'll kill you myself."

With that, she left her uncle gaping.

Alice's urge was to run to Tyr and pour out the whole story, to persuade him that she'd known nothing of the foul plot, but she sensed that would be disaster.

For one thing, the Twelfth-Day tournament was underway, and the King of the Revels would be busy all day with the arrangements and taking part. For another, it would be better to consider her approach carefully, for there were traps to avoid.

It would be easy, for example, to slip into upbraiding him for leaving her without a word. It would be equally easy to scold him for his cruelty during this visit, even though she now understood. These things were irrelevant when set beside the horror which had been visited on him.

She remembered his words, now so meaningful. "It was more the case of seeming to find myself in situations which called for heroics." "My destiny was shaped by some force, malign or otherwise." She wondered when it had dawned on him that the fact he constantly found himself in the most hellish situations of the war was not simple bad luck.

No, she simply wasn't ready to talk to him yet. Tonight. She would speak to him tonight. On Twelfth Night. It seemed appropriate.

Before she went down to the tournament, she changed into her most becoming gown, a flowing gold wool worked with brown embroidery. She set a filmy veil of silk gauze edged with gold over her long plaits, fixing it with a gold circlet. She added a gold collar around her neck and heavy gold bracelets of medieval design. These bracelets had more commonly been worn by warriors, but that seemed appropriate. Alice was dressing for the fight of her life. The fight for love.

The tournament was held in the large meadow below the east walls, and a stand had been erected for the ladies and the elderly gentlefolk. Around the other three sides, ropes held back the local people who were all cheering for their favorite knights.

Even though the lances and swords were blunt, Alice had her heart in her mouth as she watched her beloved fight. She almost burst with pride at the sheer skill of the man. Roland was fit and trained for this medieval warfare. Major Ewing was a hardened, competent soldier. But Tyr had a spark of genius in the way he handled weapons and mount so that he carried all the prizes.

No wonder Uncle George had found him so hard to kill.

Rebecca slipped into the seat beside her. "Could I guess, perhaps, why you are dressed so beautifully?"

Alice took in Rebecca's very fetching blue and cream costume. "Doubtless the same reason you look your best."

Rebecca blushed and laughed. "But I fear Lord Standon

is not cut out for bloody warfare." They both winced as he was neatly unhorsed by Roland.

Next, Roland fought Tyr. Tyr won.

"Alice," Rebecca said softly, "you're looking at the man as if he were a flaming raisin you want to snap up."

Alice burst out laughing. "A flaming raisin! Becca, what a thing to call such a magnificent specimen."

Rebecca smiled and shook her head. Alice looked back to find that Tyr's attention had been caught by her laughter, and he was looking at her. She wished he were the sort of man who could be read.

He had been once, before her uncle and her mother had put him through hell.

She swallowed tears. The desire to run down and enfold him in her love was almost overpowering, but she controlled it. She must wait. She could never let him go, though. She'd tear her clothes off again, if that was what it took.

The light was going by the time the last tournament prizes were awarded. Now the huge bonfire was lit—the final celebration of light in this midwinter festival which was as much pagan as Christian.

Whole carcasses of ox, sheep, venison, and pig had been roasting all day. Now the mulled cider and the wassail bowl came out and a feast began for all—servants, tenants, tradesmen, neighbors. Anyone who cared to attend. There were all ages, from babes to centenarians, and all having a good time.

Alice kept a longing eye on Tyr, her need to be with him warring with her self-control. It wasn't practical to think of speaking here of meaningful things. He was always the center of a merry crowd, and she had her duties to perform, ensuring that all the guests were content.

A band of fiddle, pipe, and drum tuned up, and country dancing started. Alice danced with whomever asked as a clear full moon rose up to light the crisp winter landscape.

Alice noted that Bella Carstairs had finally gotten some sense and dressed herself in a becoming but warm, red woolen gown. She had apparently abandoned hope of Lord Ivanridge and was flirting purposefully with Lord Garstang.

Susan Travis was pretty in a cream and brown outfit from the Conyngham wardrobes and had come out of her shell considerably. Alice saw her dancing with Tyr and looking radiant, but it didn't bother her. She knew it was just the glow of being relaxed and admired and a sign of Tyr's kindness.

Rebecca and Charlie were together more often than not. It was not in their characters to be demonstrative, but Alice, who knew them well, could sense the warmth that was comfortably growing between them, and was delighted.

It was clear that Tyr was deliberately avoiding her.

After a while, this became intolerable and, fortified by a considerable amount of cider, Alice seized her beloved and dragged him into the circle for the next dance. It was just a country dance, but at least they were together and able to touch now and then.

After a momentary resistance, he didn't fight her, but it was as if he were walled off from her by glass. There was a polite smile on his lips, but she couldn't read his eyes. It was frustrating and frightening how little she could read him. It was alarming and exciting how even the fleeting unavoidable touches of his hand against her waist or fingers was turning her dizzy.

She was going to have to break through this barrier soon, to discuss delicate matters with this intimate stranger, and the thought terrified her.

He seemed to sense her unease and cautiously lowered his guard. "What's the matter?"

"I need to speak to you before you go."

The barrier slammed up again. "I don't think that's a good idea, Lady Alice."

The dance ended, and he was gone. Alice wondered if she would have to take him prisoner and lock him in the dungeons to speak to him. If that was what it took, she would, though she didn't know how she was going to explain it to her accomplices. And she certainly would need accomplices to overcome Tyr Norman.

Close to midnight the fire began to die. With the end of

the fire, the Twelfth Night would be over. When the Twelfth
Night was over, the Twelve Day Festival would be over. Everyone would leave, including Tyr.

Lord Raneleigh and the farmers went off singing to do
homage to the trees and assure good fruiting in the coming
year. As the midnight bells rang from the village church, gun
shots and horns were heard from the orchard as the men
saluted the oldest apple tree. The Reverend Herbert studi-
ously ignored this pagan rite.

Slowly, sated people began to drift home, either to village
or castle, still singing as they went.

It was time. Alice looked around for Tyr.

He had disappeared.

In a blind panic, she ran to the stables, imagining that he'd
already whipped a team up to speed to carry him away from
Conyngham. But when she arrived, she found everything
peaceful. She leant against a stall to catch her breath, wondering if she had finally run mad.

A sleepy groom came to see what the matter was, and she
had no sensible answer for him. She merely shook her head
and headed up to the house.

On Twelfth Night everyone was a little reluctant to admit
it was the end and go to bed. People were scattered all over
the castle—a few in the billiard room, others in the library,
some playing instruments in the music room, others playing
cards in the Chinese Room. There was even a supper laid out
in the Great Hall for the few with an inch or two of space in
their bellies.

Alice could not find Tyr.

Casting desperately along a first-floor corridor, Alice
came across a couple twined together in a window embra-
sure. Without hesitation, she interrupted them.

"Rebecca, have you seen Tyr?"

Rebecca was rosy with embarrassment, and Charlie
looked cross. "Damn it, Alice—"

But Rebecca stopped him with a gentle touch. "He said
he was retiring," she said.

"Oh, Lord," muttered Alice.

Rebecca looked understanding. "Charlie could go and tell him you want to speak with him."

After that earlier rebuff, Alice knew that would do no good. "No," she said. "It's all right. Sorry to have interrupted."

Charlie watched her hurry away. "I'm beginning to worry about Alice."

Rebecca gently regained his attention. "There's no need, love. She'll be fine. Now, before we were interrupted . . ."

Alice progressed briskly towards the chamber she had allotted to Lords Standon and Ivanridge, not allowing herself time to lose her nerve. This all felt eerily like that night six years ago, except then she had been much more tremulous. Tonight she felt like tempered steel.

At the polished mahogany door she raised her hand to knock but decided that would be a poor tactic. She turned the knob and walked in.

He was lounging on the bed with only the fire for illumination, cradling a glass of brandy. He looked up sharply, then sighed. "Go away, Alice."

Alice shut the door and leaned against it. "I need to talk to you."

"This isn't the time or the place."

"Last time you left at the crack of dawn."

He looked down and swirled the spirit. "With the passing of Twelfth Night, the magic fades . . ." He looked up at her somberly. "What do you want? An apology for living?"

Alice gripped her hands together. "I have come to offer an apology, Tyr. An apology for all that has been done to you by my family."

There was no reaction. His gaze rested on her steadily. "Accepted," he said at last. "Now go."

Alice bit her lip. "Tyr, I knew nothing about it!"

He closed his eyes and leant his head back against the headboard. "Alice, I came here full of bitterness with thoughts of revenge. I've managed to rid myself of it. It's over. Just leave me in peace."

Alice walked forward until she was standing by the bed.

His eyes remained closed. "If you don't listen to me," she said, "if you don't talk to me, Tyr Norman, I'll start tearing my clothes off again."

Those dark eyes snapped open. "You never did fight fair, did you?"

"I don't want to fight at all, Tyr. I love you."

Their eyes held as if locked. "You said that six years ago, too."

He was frighteningly hard, impervious. Alice could feel minute tremors shake her body and wondered how long she'd be able to stand, what would happen when she collapsed onto the bed. "I meant it six years ago," she whispered, "and it never changed, though I hated you at the same time."

"That doesn't make much sense."

"Six years ago you said you loved me. Did the love die when you started to hate?"

He broke the gaze and looked down. "One tends to displace the other."

"Which is in you now?" she asked softly.

He took a swig of brandy. "I am gratefully numb with alcohol."

Alice grabbed the glass and sent it crashing to flare in the fireplace. *"Talk to me!"*

His eyes flashed and he grabbed her, pulling her down to his lap. "What of, Miranda? Love? War? What the hell do you *want* from me?"

Alice knew she should be scared but she felt as if she was finally back where she belonged. "I'm asking you to marry me," she said.

His grip relaxed in astonishment.

Alice grasped the initiative and placed her hands on his shoulders. "I fell in love with you six years ago, Tyr, and it seems to be a permanent affliction. I can't bear to let you go without using every weapon I have."

"Do you know you have a very warlike turn of phrase?"

The muscles beneath her hands made no movement, gave her no indication of his feelings. She tightened her hold.

"Do you know you are the most shielded, guarded person I have ever met? *Show* me something of yourself, Tyr, before I lose my nerve!"

His mouth came down on hers, hot and spicy with brandy. He wasn't gentle, as he had been six years ago. Instead he crushed her to him and seared her with a passion capable of destroying both of them.

When the kiss ended, Alice looked up at him, shaken almost to fainting. "Thank you," she whispered.

With a crack of laughter, he pushed her aside and leapt off the bed to stand by the window. He rested his head on his hands there. After what felt like an endless silence, he said, "Tell me exactly what went on six years ago, as you know it."

With wisps of hope and considerable fear that heaven might yet escape her, Alice obeyed. When she'd finished she added, "I have to admit that I started this by telling my mother what happened." There was no response from that broad back, and so she carried on, determined to get it over with. "I must also confess that I didn't quite tell her the whole story."

He turned then, a touch of humor in his shadowed face. "I suppose you omitted little details such as declaring your undying love and tearing your clothes off."

Alice nodded ruefully. "But I never imagined she would seek revenge. I feared Roland or my father might call you out, but Mother . . ."

He leaned back against the window frame arms crossed. "First rule of life. Never underestimate a woman."

His protective shell was cracked, but Alice was far from sure of success. She still couldn't tell what was in his head. "Don't you believe me?" she asked.

"I just wonder why you had this insane urge to confess to your mother at all."

Surprise brought her up to her knees. "You abandoned me! I needed to talk to someone. I was terrified I was going to have a baby!"

He stared at her blankly. "You thought—For God's sake,

Alice, you couldn't be that naive." He walked over until he stood by the bed. His gaze was both searching and disbelieving. "Miranda," he said gently, "I never even took my breeches off."

Alice gaped. "You never . . . ?" She searched her memory, seeking detail amid dizzy ecstasy. "It was all rather hazy . . ." She felt hot color flood her cheeks and hid them in her hands. "Oh heavens, I fear I was just that naive." Then she looked up again, wide-eyed. "You mean there's *more?*"

He started to laugh. He leaned against one of the solid bed posts and laughed; there was more than a little wildness in it. At last he regained control of himself but kept his head against the post. He shook it now and then.

Alice swallowed. "Is there any point in saying I'm sorry?"

He looked at her, his eyes still damp with mirth. "It's always worth saying you're sorry. I should have realized, I suppose. You were such a darling innocent. But how could you think I'd leave you without a word if I'd taken your maidenhead?"

Alice was swamped with guilt for that lack of faith. She hesitated then put the question. "Why didn't you . . . ?"

He sat on the bed, leaning against the post, arms around one raised knee. Ghosts of humor still relaxed his features. "I had my orders, Alice. I sailed for Lisbon on the tenth. You enchanted me from Christmas Eve on, but I had to keep my wits for both our sakes. Not only were you a Conyngham while I was nothing, but you were engaged to marry a fine, wealthy, titled man. The only thing I could do for you was to spare you my inappropriate devotion." He smiled wryly. "I'd have done it too, if you'd behaved like a proper maid."

"I fell in love," she said softly, sending words across a gap she didn't quite dare to bridge. "I couldn't bear the thought of you leaving me. How could you bear the thought of leaving?"

"What choice did I have?" he asked simply.

"I would have broken off with Charlie in a moment. I did break it off with him. You should have known that."

"I never did have much faith in miracles. The closest I ever came to one was when the girl I adored came into my room and shyly begged for my love. I knew I mustn't take everything she offered, but I couldn't resist something to carry away to war. I was honored to be the first to show you the magic of love, Miranda."

Alice rose to her knees and worked her way down the bed until her legs brushed his. At last she dared to tease. "And succeeded so well that I never even noticed you kept your breeches on. Truly noble restraint, my lord."

"I'm glad you finally appreciate that." He plucked off her gold circlet, slid back her veil, and began to unravel first one plait then the other.

Alice's heart was thundering. "What are you doing?"

"In filthy mud, when deafened by cannons, choked by smoke, and surrounded by the dead and dying, I held a picture in my mind. Miranda with her hair long and loose around her . . ." He threaded his fingers through the heavy mass of it, letting it drift down around her so the ends trailed softly on the counterpane.

His hands slid beneath to circle her neck, cradling her skull. "Do I get to set the date, then, since you proposed? Not that it was much of a proposal . . ."

Joy bursting within, Alice pulled out of his lax hold and fell to her knees beside the bed. "Oh noble hero, mighty warrior! Honor this humble maid by giving her your name and heart in return for her everlasting devotion and love. Shield me in your strength and let me wrap you in the warmth of my tender love . . ." She had begun in parody but ended in honesty. "Please, Tyr, let me chase all the shadows from your eyes."

In a heartbeat he was on the floor beside her, and she was in his arms, wrapped again in the power of his kiss. After a satisfying interval Alice fought free to gasp, "Does that mean yes?"

"Did I ever have a choice?" His eyes were warm with laughter as his lips hungrily sought hers again.

The door burst open. Lord Raneleigh, Roland, Charlie, and Rebecca all pushed into the room.

"Damme!" spluttered Alice's father.

"Rebecca!" accused Alice. She began to scramble to her feet.

Tyr snared her and kept her in his lap. "Very comfortable carpet you have, Lord Raneleigh. Won't you join us?"

"Damme!" said Lord Raneleigh again. Roland and Charlie began to laugh.

"Sorry," said Rebecca unrepentantly to Alice. "I thought I'd make sure you didn't muff it this time."

"Muff what?" bellowed Lord Raneleigh. "Damn it, girl, get out of his lap!"

"I can't, Father," said Alice. "He's very strong. And anyway, since we're to be married, I suppose I should obey him."

Her father glared at her. "Well, of course you're going to be married when I find you rolling on the bedroom floor with him. What I want to know is why you couldn't go about it in a more normal manner. First you throw over Charlie, now this!"

Tyr suddenly stood, carrying Alice with him, then setting her on her feet. "You're completely correct, Lord Raneleigh," he said. "The only thing for it is to get her married before she changes her mind again. I think two weeks from now would do nicely."

"Two weeks," said Alice's father blankly. "You can't be married in a fortnight!"

"We don't want a big wedding, Father," said Alice, "and it's long past time I was wed." She smiled up at Tyr. "In fact, I think twelve nights would be quite long enough to wait."

His arms tightened. "Twelve nights it is. Did I ever tell you twelve is my lucky number?"

"Mine too," said Alice against his lips. "In fact Twelfth Night will always have a very special place in my heart."

"Damme," said the earl. "They're at it again!"

Dear Readers

Even as a child Christmas meant more to me than simply waking up Christmas morning to find presents under the tree. I loved the lights, the carols, the anticipation of gathering with family that came from far and wide to rejoice in the magic of the season. For me it was a time for miracles.

But as wonderful as those childhood memories are, they cannot come close to the thrill I feel as an adult with children and grandchildren of my own. The fulfillment of experiencing their excitement at decorating the tree, singing carols, snooping through wrapped presents, and snitching cookies I bake to leave on the hearth for Santa, is the greatest Christmas miracle that God has ever granted me.

I wish everyone Joy, Peace, and Love. May God's miracles bless you now and always. Merry Christmas!

Katherine Sutcliffe

HOME FOR CHRISTMAS

Katherine Sutcliffe

One

Another Christmas.

Big deal.

Once, Virginia Valemere had looked forward to the holidays with an ardor that made her parents, and everyone who knew her, shake their heads in amusement. The Glenn Miller Orchestra's "Silent Night, Holy Night" had ushered in September. "The Little Drummer Boy" and "Jingle Bell Rock" had greeted trick or treaters in October, and by Thanksgiving night the seven-foot spruce trucked in from Canada had flashed like neons from Vegas in the dark.

By the first of December her shopping had been completed and the countdown was on. For the next three weeks she would pray, as she had every year since she was five, for a horse of her own and a white Christmas . . . both of which were impossible, considering that she lived with her mother and younger brother, Jeff, in a three-bedroom, zero-lot-line condominium in Dallas, Texas, with a mean December temperature of sixty-five degrees.

That had changed the day of her thirteenth birthday, however. Her mother had been killed in a three-car pileup on Central Expressway. Her father had shown up the day of the funeral to usher her and Jeff away to his horse farm in Pilot Point, an hour's drive north of Dallas, and suddenly her life had changed drastically. No more overcrowded schools, peer pressure, dance lessons, or select soccer games. She and Jeff were plopped down amid Dick Valemere's Arabian training and breeding facility, Renaissance Farm.

In 1975, heaven had found her at last. Not only was she surrounded by the country's most incredibly beautiful horses, there were nearly a thousand acres on which to enjoy them: lush rolling hills and pastures dotted with trees and ponds, horse barns with red-carpeted aisles and arenas large enough to accommodate the local schooling shows. Horse enthusiasts had traveled to Renaissance from all over the world: Saudi sheiks, Japanese investors, Armand Hammer, and Hollywood movie stars—all willing to pay millions for her father's incredible mares and stallions.

Then the 80's oil bust hit, as did the Internal Revenue Service, which considered breeding and showing horses too much fun for the American populace—God forbid that they should enjoy the fruits of their labor. The millions doled out on horse flesh, *once* tax deductible, could be better spent on thousand-dollar toilet seats for the President's luxurious Air Force One and programs studying the breeding habits of the tsetse fly. By 1985 her father had filed for bankruptcy, as had most of the horse breeders and trainers across the country. By 1990 he'd been forced to sell the majority of his land and horses to developers in order to keep the hounds of foreclosure off his heels, as well as to pay for her and her brother's education.

By 1991 it was finished. Gone.

Virginia closed her eyes at the memory. At thirty years old she was *too* old to dwell so on the past. The old "what might have beens" wouldn't accomplish anything but depressing her further. That was *not* why she had ridden out here to Roberts Hill, the highest point in Pilot Point, where she could look out over the far-reaching, wave-tipped stretches of Lake Ray Roberts. She had come here to feel the nip of December wind on her cheeks, to allow the power of the Arabian gelding beneath her to invigorate her. Perhaps this evening she would feel like shopping for a Christmas tree— a small one to put on the fireplace hearth. She might even splurge on a few new baubles and lights . . . and maybe not.

Locomotion shifted beneath her, danced in place, raised his arched neck suddenly, and pointed his ears down the meandering wooded trail. Virginia hardly noticed. The first reluctant strands of "I'm Dreaming of a White Christmas" had crept into her thoughts, lazily coiling in her memory like smoke on a windless day.

The motorcycle came sailing over the hill's crest like a giant bat out of hell, straight for Virginia and the terrified horse. Locomotion screamed and reared; Virginia clutched at his black mane to steady her seat, and as he made a move to bolt down the hazardously steep path, she forced his head around so his momentum drove him in a circle. She did her best to speak soothingly. "Whoa, boy. Good boy. Good Loco. Easy, easy."

Only when the horse had calmed enough for Virginia to look up did she discover that the motorcycle from hell, and its helmeted, blue-jeaned driver, were perched atop the crest, motor growling like a dragon.

"For the love of God," she shouted, "turn that detestable machine off before I wind up with a broken neck!"

The driver regarded her in silence for what felt like an eternity before he killed the engine. Still, the horse continued to dance and snort, to back away from the metal monster he was certain would devour him at any moment.

"Thank you," she snapped.

"You're welcome," came the muted reply, just as caustic, very deep, and more than a trifle surly.

"Just what the devil do you think you're doing tearing through here on that despicable piece of junk? I should call the police. You're a damned menace and should be arrested."

"Be my guest."

She narrowed her eyes, noting once again the faded jeans tucked into calf-length, mud-spattered boots; the jeans were worn thin at the knee. He wore a blue denim work shirt, which he filled out across the shoulders to perfection, its sleeves rolled up above the wrists. She could just make out the fringe of shaggy black-brown hair peeking out from beneath the black astronaut-looking helmet and brushing the tops of his shoulders. He wasn't a kid, not by any stretch of the imagination. His arms were hard, with well-defined muscles bulging beneath his sleeves. More like a slightly toned down version of a Hell's Angel.

"Well?" came the voice again, taunting this time and hinting of impatience. "Do you intend to perch there all day giving me those go-to-hell stares or can I get on with my ride?"

"You have no business up here, mister."

"Who says?"

"*I* do. I . . . my *father* . . . owns this property. He has for the last twenty years."

Silence, then, "Is that so?"

Her face turned hot, her throat tight. It was a lie, of course. All Dick Valemere owned now were ten acres adjacent to these, a stable that had once been his own hay barn, and a tiny clapboard house once occupied by one of his Mexican hands. He'd lost their magnificent home, training facilities, and the last five hundred acres to foreclosure four years before. It had all been bought by some arrogant multimillionaire back East who hadn't bothered to occupy the estate until a few months ago. Rumors had run rampant that he eventually intended to bulldoze the entire farm and construct another shopping mall.

God forbid.

The cyclist said nothing for a moment, then he kickstarted the machine, filling the woods with a roar like a 747. With little regard for her dancing horse, the man slowly drove by her, obviously watching her from behind the shatterproof plastic, his facial features obliterated by the black shading.

"Merry Christmas," he shouted just before he gunned the motorcycle and took off down the hill.

"You look like Darth Vader!" she yelled after him.

By the time Virginia reached home, her horse was lathered and so was she. She had barely cantered through the gates when Rachel Ellison, a dead ringer for a young Elizabeth Taylor, appeared at the barn door, her hands on her hips, her small foot tapping. "You're late," the girl said, her blue eyes twinkling with mischief. "Might I remind you that the greatest priority of every serious and dedicated equestrienne is punctuality."

"No, the greatest priority of every serious and dedicated equestrienne is paying their starving instructors on time." Virginia smiled pointedly at her student, slid off the horse, and thrust the reins toward her companion. "See that he's rinsed thoroughly and put on the walker for half an hour. He needs time to cool out physically as well as mentally."

"By the look of you he's not the only one." Rachel fell in beside Virginia, who removed her riding gloves as she strode toward the barn.

"Is it that obvious?" Virginia asked.

"Like a neon sign. Care to talk about it?"

"What would a twelve-year-old know about adult problems?" Virginia paused at the barn entry, allowing her eyes to adjust to the dim interior. The smell of rich Bermuda hay and crimped oats momentarily filled her with a sense of well-being. All was as it should be: aisles swept clean, stalls mucked, hayracks swelling with loose green grass. No spiderwebs cluttering up the rafters in *her* barn, no sir.

"I have a few of my own problems," Rachel declared with exasperation. "I'm not that different from you, you know."

"Only about eighteen years," Virginia said as she tucked her gloves in the back pocket of her riding jeans and helped the struggling young woman back Locomotion into the wash stall.

"Trivialities. We're both women, right? Both of our mothers were killed in car accidents . . . and we both love horses more than we love food . . . and speaking of food . . ." Rachel ducked into the office and returned with a cold cola. She popped the top and dropped down on a bale of Bermuda, long legs crossed Indian fashion. "I'll remind you what you told me when we first began to ride together: 'A true athlete intent on winning never allows personal problems to effect his main objectives: performance and winning.' So tell me . . . is it sex?"

"What do you know about sex?"

"Hey, I watch the soaps."

"How could it be sex when I haven't even dated in six months? The closest I've come to an eligible man recently is seventy-year-old Chester Baxter at Baxter's PicNPac."

"I rest my case."

Virginia shot her with the water hose. "If you must know, Marcia Clark, I'm simply going through my bah-humbug period. It's Christmas. I'm broke, and besides that, I was nearly thrown from my horse thanks to some maniac tearing over my trails on a motorcycle the size of the Starship *Enterprise*."

Rachel's eyes widened.

"The idiot came wheeling at me from nowhere. He didn't even have the grace to apologize."

"The *arrogance* of *some* people. Was he cute?"

"How would I know? He was hidden inside a big black bubble that made him look like Robocop. Besides, pretty is as pretty does. The guy was a jerk."

Virginia stepped into her office and dropped into a chair. The desk before her was littered with papers: pedigrees of horses for sale, glossy, full-color magazines, *Arabian Horse Times* and *Arabian World* that reminded her that there were farms and trainers out there that had managed to make it through the bust and were on their way back to the top. Then she reminded herself that Renaissance might well have made it, too, if only—

There came a trumpeting call from the far end of the barn. Virginia moved to the office door and gazed remotely down the barn aisle to the distant double stall where the stallion paced, eager for his morning exercise. Rachel moved to the stall and gazed dreamy-eyed at Lindale, her young face a mixture of adoration and hope. Virginia knew that look, knew what the girl would ask before she asked it.

"No," Virginia said, stepping from the office. "You're not ready to ride him yet."

"But—"

"No buts. He's too much horse for you, Rach."

"He would never do anything to hurt me. You said so yourself. He has the finest mind and disposition of any stallion in the country."

"Agreed. But a horse is only as good as his rider. If the one up is nervous and overly excitable, the horse will be, too. They're dependent on the rider to assure them that there is absolutely nothing to be frightened of."

"I know, I know. Horses are prey and therefore their only defense to what they perceive as danger is flight. An out-of-control horse can hurt you unintentionally. But I'm not afraid of him, GiGi. I never would be."

"No."

The girl's face fell and for an instant Virginia was tempted to saddle up the stud and allow Rachel a few turns around the arena, perhaps to satisfy her own curiosity as much as to appease her favorite student. But she had never been one to take chances with her students—especially with this one. Rachel had become very special to her since she'd discovered the young beauty straddling a fence and trying her damnedest to mount Loco bareback. That had been four months ago. The girl had since become a fixture around the place, showing up every day after school, paying for her lessons out of her allowance and lunch money, doing odd jobs around the barn just for the opportunity of being as close as possible to the horses. The fact that the child and her grandfather, and occasionally some fractious on-again, off-again father, occupied what once had been Virginia's home had never entered into it.

Smiling, Virginia waved a flyer in the air. "This should make you happier, Miss Ellison."

"The only thing that would make me happy right now is learning that Santa intends to stuff my stocking with this horse," Rachel declared, then kissed Lindale on his velvety nose.

"You've been doing so beautifully on Equator and Loco, I thought it time for you to participate in your first show."

Rachel turned her head. Her round eyes looked like blue china. Her black, slightly curly hair, cropped off at her jawline, framed her flushed face like a swirling cloud.

"Well?" Virginia waved it again. "Mystic Acres Christmas Show. Two weeks from today. You'll ride Loco in saddleseat and Equator in hunter. We'll sign you up for high point youth. High point prize is a new saddle. How about that? You can finally stop abusing mine and own your own."

"Great." The word was about as emotionally charged as a eulogy.

Virginia frowned. "Of course . . . I'll need your father's permission."

Her cheeks suddenly colorless, Rachel hurried to Equator's stall and proceeded to halter him.

"What's up?" Virginia asked.

"I was just thinking . . . maybe I'm not ready yet to show."

"Oh?"

"I wouldn't want to embarrass you by making you or the horses look bad."

"Wait a minute . . . this coming from the girl who, just minutes ago, was ready to climb aboard a sixteen-hand stallion? If it's simply nerves over riding before a judge—"

"That's not it." With a sigh, Rachel slid the halter off the gelding's head. "I guess I won't be riding today, not after I tell you what I have to tell you." Rachel closed the stall door and latched it. Her head leaning against the grill, her small body looking suddenly as if it might collapse in on itself, she gazed down at her dusty boots and appeared to work up her courage. "Remember that release form my father signed giving me permission to take lessons and do odd jobs?"

Virginia nodded.

"Well . . . I sorta forged his name on it. The truth is, GiGi . . . Dad knows nothing about my riding here. The one and only time I ever asked him for permission to ride he forbade it."

Virginia turned away, crumpling the flyer in her hand.

"Please don't be mad."

"Mad? For God's sake, Rachel, I could be sued for this. And have you any idea of the consequences had something, however minor, happened to you while you've ridden and worked here?"

"I just needed time to convince him—"

"In the meantime, I'm wide open to litigation."

"I'll talk to him. I'll convince him. Please, don't make me stay away from Renaissance and the horses, GiGi. Please."

She almost relented. The child's adoration of horses was more than apparent—had been every day for the last many weeks. Before school, after school, the weekends, and holidays were spent in Virginia's barn, grooming, mucking, or simply sitting under an oak tree, her small hands clutching the lead rope as the horse of the day munched contentedly on grass. Only another equine devotee could understand the almost spiritual bond a horse lover shared with their animal.

"I'm sorry, Rach. Without your father's approval, I simply can't allow you around the horses. I can't afford to lose what little I have left. I'm sorry."

"Merry Christmas to you, too, Mrs. Scrooge. Don't tell me—a horse has thrown a shoe or chipped a hoof, God forbid. Say, Baxter's has just received a new shipment of Christmas trees, one of which would look spiffy in the den, hint, hint. By the way, ol' Chester sends his regards." Jeff stretched his long legs out before him and smiled wearily at Virginia.

He still wore his green hospital scrubs. He needed to shave, not to mention sleep. His brown hair obviously hadn't seen a clipper in several months, making Virginia almost smile as she remembered finding her younger brother passed out cold from sipping too many suds with his group of semi-delinquent friends, climbing into his bed while he slept it off, and proceeding to shave one half of his head with horse clippers. That, of course, had been years ago. Now, as a Resident at Dallas's largest, most prestigious public hospital, his forty-eight-hour shifts left him with only enough energy to drive himself home before falling into bed.

"You look like a lady who's just lost her last friend," he said.

Virginia poured herself a cup of coffee and watched Rachel disappear over the hill on her bike. "Lost her most talented student, to be precise. That young woman pedaling away has the potential to go champion at Youth Nationals next summer. I'm not certain I've ever come across a rider who caught on so quickly, or who loves horses as much as she does—aside from myself, of course. She's the type of rider who could go a long way in making an instructor's career."

"So what's the problem?"

"An overly protective father."

"Hmm. There are shades of familiarity here, methinks. I hope she respects her father's wishes better than you do. And speaking of Father . . ." Jeff left the chair and joined Virginia at the window. He reached for a bottle of spring water he had put on the countertop earlier. "So how is he?"

"Same as usual."

The television chattered in another room.

"He continues to stare at that screen like some mindless statue. Occasionally he rouses enough to talk back to it."

"How are the headaches?"

"They come and go. As long as he behaves himself, they're minimal." Virginia tossed the coffee dregs down the sink disposal. "He grows angrier and more remote every day, Jeff. The medication Dr. Swenson prescribed for his depression doesn't seem to be helping much."

"Maybe we should try increasing the dosage. I'll talk to Swenson when I see him tomorrow at the hospital. Now for some good news . . . I understand there's a new doctor on staff, a big-shot neurosurgeon specializing in traumatically induced pseudoaneurysms."

Virginia rolled her eyes and shrugged her brother's arm away. "Don't start, Jeff. I can't handle getting my hopes up again. We've contacted every specialist in the field and not one of them would guarantee results—"

"There are never any guarantees when it comes to surgery, GiGi."

"Spoken like a true doctor covering his butt from malpractice."

"He's not going to get better on his own, Sis. The more the pressure builds in his head the worse the consequences. The paralysis is only the beginning. Eventually his eyesight will be affected as well as his ability to speak. I needn't remind you that the aneurysm could blow at any moment for no reason at all."

"You don't need to remind me, Jeff. I live with that reality every day. I live it twenty-four hours a day, remember? Every morning I stand outside Dad's bedroom door, terrified of going in to discover he's died during the night. I walk on eggshells around here for fear of doing or saying something that will upset him when it doesn't really matter because he's so furious at the world over what's happened to him he's like a short-fused stick of dynamite. I can't say or do anything that he finds remotely acceptable."

Jeff slid his arm around her and hugged her close. "This is really getting to you. You can't keep up this pace much longer. You've lost too damn much weight and look as if you haven't slept in a month. You need some help around here."

"Help? How do we manage that, Jeff? I give lessons five hours a day, seven days a week. Four hours each day are spent going from one farm to another, training horses that won't ever see a *polka-dot* ribbon, much less a blue, unless someone mistakes them for a child's birthday game and pins the darn ribbon to its butt. Dad's medication alone runs us five hundred a month. Another fifteen hundred goes on hospital bills and therapy. If you want to shell out advice, why don't you talk to your peers at the hospital and convince *them* that charging ten dollars for an aspirin is just a tad bit steep, especially for those of us with no insurance."

"Oh, so now this is all my fault."

Her tone softening, she shook her head. "It's no one's

fault, Jeff. Any more than we can point the finger of blame for Dad's accident at any particular source."

"The source is out in that barn, Sis. If I'd had my way I'd have sold that damn stallion to the packers for fifty cents a pound."

"It was a freak accident—"

Jeff walked away and angrily flung the empty water bottle in the garbage. "Jesus, I can't believe you still defend that—"

"I was there, Jeff. I saw the whole thing. Dad knew how Lindale reacted to the whip, yet he took the bat to him anyway. And besides, the horse didn't intentionally fling himself to the ground; he spooked at the whip, tripped, and fell. Lindale was barely green broke, Jeff. He was a baby and terrified of being hit."

"Yeah, well, that baby pulverized Dad against the rail in the process of pitching a tantrum. Can you blame Dad for forbidding you to ride him?"

"If Dad was in his right mind he'd acknowledge that Lindale isn't dangerous. He bred that horse, Jeff. He loved him as much as I do. He truly believed that Lindale would return Renaissance to its former prestige. So do I, for that matter."

"The only thing that damned horse has brought us is heartache and bankruptcy."

"That'll change when my mare foals. The cross between Lin and Born Famous is going to be incredible. There won't be a mare owner in the world who won't want to breed to him."

Jeff shook his head, then ran one hand through his brown hair. "You horse people are all alike. Why don't you just toss your money into the toilet and flush? You've got about as much chance of collecting on that dream as you have of winning the lottery." He moved to the hallway, pausing to look into the living room. "I'll talk to you later, Dad," he said in a voice loud enough to be heard over the blaring television. He waited. When there came no response, he moved down the short corridor and disappeared from sight, closing the bedroom door behind him.

For a long while, Virginia remained in the kitchen, her arms crossed fiercely over her breasts. She forced down the frustration she could feel working its way up her chest, then she moved to the den.

Her father sat in his wheelchair, one hand wrapped around the TV remote, his eyes gazing fixedly at the screen. Once upon a time Dick Valemere had been a fine-tuned machine, as graceful on a horse as a dancer on his toes. There hadn't been a woman in the industry who hadn't been attracted by his virility. There hadn't been a trainer in the industry who could best Dick Valemere in the ring. It was a given that if Dick thought a horse good enough to show . . . that horse would exit the gates with the championship.

Virginia bent over her father's shoulder and lightly kissed his cheek. "It's a beautiful morning, Pop. I don't have an appointment for another fifteen minutes. Would you like me to take you to the barn today?"

He wouldn't, of course, and she knew it. He hadn't visited the barn in three years . . . not since the day of the accident, though there had been times when she had glanced toward the house to find him sitting at the window, staring down at the barn and the horses he had loved so devotedly.

Dick aimed the remote at the television and turned up the sound. A group of talk show guests screamed at one another and hurled accusations while a Christmas tree in the background glistened with red and green lights.

Blah, blah, blah.

Things are tough all over, she thought.

Finally, she went down on one knee beside the chair and tightened her fingers around her father's useless hand, the action throwing open a flood of memories that cascaded over her mind's eye like shimmering sparks from a Roman candle. As a child, she thrilled at the moment that this very hand, then so powerful and leathered by the long years of working in weather, would wrap around her own. She was the daughter of Richard Valemere, and that had been something to be proud of.

"Pop, Jeff tells me that Baxter's has got in a selection of

Christmas trees—the blue spruce that you like. Thought I'd pick one up before I head for the Hayeses'. I might even splurge and buy a carton of eggnog and some of that Corsicana fruitcake you like so well."

"Hayes," he muttered, and turned up the volume again. His face contorting slightly, he shouted, "You ain't training his horses, are you? You better not be training, GiGi—"

"No, Pop. Calm down. Please. I'm not training. I'm simply giving lessons to Tim Hayes's two girls. They ride those Halflinger ponies, remember?"

His eyebrows drawing together, he leaned toward her. "I better not hear you've been on that stallion. He'll kill you like he did me."

"Pop, you're not dead. Lindale would never—"

"Might as well have put a bullet to my head."

"It was an accident, Pop. You know it as well as I do."

"You've got no business on those horses, GiGi. A woman your age should be married by now and raising my grandbabies. Had you finished vet school—"

"I didn't want to be a vet, Pop. I want to train horses. I want to teach children to ride those horses safely and responsibly."

"And look where it's got you. Noplace, that's where. Just like me. I dedicated my entire life to building the finest training facility next to Chauncey's and what the hell have I got to show for it? The friggin' IRS cut off one nut, that stallion cut off the other. I'm fifty years old and washed up as a man, much less a human being. Jesus, I wish you and your brother had let 'em pull the plug on me and just let me die right then and there."

"We love you."

He focused again on the television, tuning her out as easily as hitting the mute button.

Resignedly, Virginia stood and moved to the door. "Is there anything special you'd like from the store, Pop?"

A television commercial blared in response—a car dealer dressed like Santa's elf tap danced on the hood of a Japanese-made sedan, the tiny bells on his pointed shoes jingling "Deck the Halls."

As she turned to go, he said, "How do you expect to get a husband when you smell like a horse? Slap on some makeup and for God's sake brush your hair. You're a woman, not some plug-spittin' bronc rider."

"I love you, too," she muttered under her breath.

Two

The return address on the envelope read, *Ride with Pride Arabian Horse Club of North Texas.* There was a cameo of an Arabian horse's head wearing a Santa cap. Even before Virginia shifted the truck into neutral and tore open the envelope, she knew what to expect. Several times a year the local horse club held benefit auctions and exhibitions, the proceeds of which were mailed to Virginia and her father to help meet his medical expenses. Once, Dick Valemere had been actively supportive in the local riding clubs, judging and donating money for the upkeep of the show facilities. A time or two he had even donated breedings and young geldings to be auctioned off to help other trainers who had fallen on hard times.

The check was for $285.47. Phyllis Aynsworthy, the club President, had signed it, punctuating her signature with a smiley face. Virginia gave the check a quick kiss and tucked it into her pocket. No, $285.47 wasn't a great deal of money, but considering the bank had bounced her last check for half of that amount, it would go a long way toward paying the mounting electric bill.

Shifting into first, she pulled out on Blackjack Road and headed for Highway 377. To her right, the grounds which had once belonged to Renaissance stretched like a lush golf course as far as she could see. There were sprawling ponds and wide-stretching oaks, some of which were a hundred years old. At the top of the highest rise sat the barns, red-brick, chateau-looking structures that would rival the most beautiful homes in the world. Several hundred yards beyond that sat the house . . .

Focusing her eyes on the road ahead, Virginia crammed the stubborn gearshift into third and hauled it toward the highway.

Baxter Grocery and Milliner, Est. 1878, had, through the last century, changed very little, thanks to the generations of Baxters whose aspirations for success were exceeded only by their desire to nap away the afternoon on cots in the back of the store. In the late 1960's, Chester, then a man of forty-odd years had begrudgingly changed the name to Baxter's PicNPac, hoping to woo back the clientele who had, over the last decade, drifted up 377 to purchase their foodstuffs at the shiny new PacNSave, with its eat-in deli featuring fresh fried chicken, barbecue, and mustard potato salad—not to mention their frozen food department, offering stores of TV dinners and packaged vegetables crammed into little square boxes. The only refrigeration system Baxter offered was a red and white 1935 cola machine and an icebox where he kept eggs and bottles of milk . . . along with the containers of worms and catfish bait he stocked for the folk on their way to the lake to "wet their corks."

A group of octogenarians, all in overalls, straw hats shoved back on their balding heads as they lounged under Pilot Point's oldest oak, the communal ground where old friends met to discuss the gradual corruption of the world, looked up as Virginia pulled off the highway onto the gravel parking space outside the store. Their lined faces broke out in big smiles as she slammed the truck door and waved.

"Howdy, young lady," called Frank Handling, lacing his fingers across his barrel belly. He'd propped his big, booted feet on a rusted plowshare while his closest companion, a scrawny, bewhiskered farmer named Barney Millcoat, perched on an overturned well bucket and whittled on a block of soft pine. "How's yer pa?"

" 'Bout the same, Frank. How's your wife?"

"Fair to middlin', I reckon, though she don't git 'round too good these days. Rheumatism in her knees. You ready for Christmas?"

Virginia glanced at the old tin rain gauge and thermometer nailed to the porch post. "Hardly seems like Christmas, does it, when it's pushing seventy degrees."

"Almanac reckons the weather's gonna change come Christmas. Gonna be a bitter one, it says."

"I'll believe *that* when I see it, Frank."

"That's the trouble with your generation, GiGi. Don't nobody believe the almanac no more."

"Show me a white Christmas and I'll never doubt it again."

"All right," he replied and smiled again.

Virginia paused at the open door, allowing her eyes to adjust to the interior. Above the door were the dusty, original white and red signet faces painted by medicine and milling companies years ago. But it was the inside of Baxter's which compelled her to return again and again. The dim interior was a compilation of sights and odors, a threshold that would, the moment she stepped inside, sweep her back to a less complicated time. The scents of tobacco, onions, and neat's-foot oil; the musty smell of potatoes, the tangy scent of sweet feed, bananas, and the wax on consignment cutting saddles were a melange that filled her with a sort of euphoria.

"Afternoon, Miss GiGi."

Virginia stepped into the store. The sagging wood floor creaked and rang like a hollow drum as she moved toward the counter. "Afternoon, Chester."

"How's yer pa?"

"No change."

"No change is good sometimes. How's your brother?"

"Getting by."

"He comin' back up this way to practice?"

"I don't know."

"I tol' him when I seen him last that I would rent him an office upstairs real cheap."

Virginia glanced toward the rickety stairs leading to the store's upper floor.

"We could use a good doctor in these parts, not like some we got now who don't give a squat 'bout anything but the almighty dollar."

Baxter owned two grocery buggies, both of which had obviously been filched from the PacNSave. Virginia dropped her bag into one and started toward the back of the store. The front left wheel squeaked and wobbled so badly she struggled to keep it rolling in a straight line, but it didn't matter. The sooner she could make her way out of Chester's range of sight and hearing the better. Otherwise, his conversation would eventually lead to his asking her to dinner again. While Rachel Ellison considered her over the hill and man-desperate, she wasn't so old and needy that she would succumb to groping by a man with no teeth who smelled like Bull Durham snuff.

Chester kept his rounds of greasy yellow cheese on a flat board stretched across two sawhorses. Patrons were obliged to slice their own, to wrap it in butcher paper, and tie it closed with string. Chester would weigh the cheese upon checkout, being sure to subtract three cents for the paper and string. She estimated a pound and wrapped it, then struggled up the narrow aisle littered with canned goods, pencil tablets, laundry soap, and women's personal items . . . which were nestled far too close to a store of moth balls and epsom salts.

Obviously, Chester had shifted the wine again. Not that he kept a great deal in stock, and certainly nothing requiring a cork remover. His selection would taste a lot like grape juice; if she was lucky there would be her favorite blackberry flavor. She'd discovered years ago that by heating it slightly she could subdue its cough-medicine-like flavor.

Chester had tucked the wines behind the castor oil and turpentine. Virginia swiped up the last bottle of Blackberry Royal, kosher for Passover, and dropped it into the buggy, then swung the buggy around, slamming headlong into Baxter's second grocery cart.

"Oh," she gasped. "I'm terribly sorry. I didn't see you . . . there."

It was *him*. Darth Vader on a motorcycle.

She was certain of it the moment she glanced down at his boots . . . the same boots he'd been wearing that morning, thick-soled things that hit him mid-calf. They were scuffed and dusty.

Her face turned warm. Her stomach suddenly hurt.

"We have to stop meeting this way," he said in that recognizable, deep, and gravelly voice tinged with sarcasm.

Reluctantly, her gaze shifted up, up to his face. He looked a hell of a lot bigger off his motorcycle. Downright menacing. And terribly cute. No, not just cute . . . That dark beard stubble across his sunken cheeks and jaw could not be deemed *cute* by any stretch of the imagination. *Cute* was a word to describe chubby-cheeked, freshly shaven bank officers and bespectacled computer nerds.

"Hello?" he said pointedly and waved one hand over her eyes. He didn't quite smile, just raised one heavy dark brow and stared at her with disturbingly fierce blue eyes.

"You again," is all she managed and tried to tear her buggy away, only to discover, to her discomposure, that they were coupled like passionate dogs.

"I see you bought the last bottle of my favorite. Blackberry Royal. What a shame. Guess I'll have to settle for spring water again . . . unless you'd like to share that one?"

"Not on your motorcycle." She yanked on the cart again, to no avail.

"Cheese and wine." The stranger picked up her package of cheddar and sniffed it. "Mite pungent, isn't it? Not exactly the sort I'd pick out to nibble on during a romantic evening. Then again, vinegary grape juice impregnated with a splash of blackberry flavoring isn't my idea of impressing that special someone either."

His hair was a thick, dark mane of loose swirls and waves. A tiny gold stud glittered on his left earlobe. He had a magnificent mouth. She couldn't stop staring at it.

"My name is Neil," he said.

"Congratulations." With a last effort, she dislodged the buggies and turned to leave. The wheel squawked and gyrated. She nearly plowed into a stack of canned sardines and oyster crackers before she managed to turn the corner, slowing only long enough to glance around. The man in the faded jeans was staring down at the dusty bottles of wine as if caught in some life-altering decision.

She hurried to the icebox, grabbed a gallon of milk and a quart of eggnog, then battled the buggy to the checkout counter where Chester was perched on a three-legged stool, his attention focused on the twelve-inch TV screen where the Dallas Cowboys were trouncing the Buffalo Bills. Draped across the wall behind him, laced among candy bars and cigarette soft packs, was a solitary string of Christmas lights twinkling red, orange, and green.

The Christmas tree. She had almost forgotten.

"How 'bout them Cowboys," Chester said with a shake of his head.

She refused to look back down the center aisle of the long, rambling building. *He* was there, somewhere, setting her nerves on end and making her feel agitated over nothing. Who the devil did he think he was to scare her horse out of its wits . . . then to show up here, of all things—*her* place of refuge—*her* place to daydream about bygone days—*her* escape from reality.

"Got your fruitcake," Chester said, and hauled the round cake tin out from under the counter. "The ten-pounder all the way from Corsicana. Don't mind if I had me a piece, do you?"

"Not at all."

"Will you be takin' a tree this year?"

"Yes." She nodded and glanced toward the back of the store. The biker was headed to the checkout, his buggy littered with milk, eggs, a six-pack of sodas, hamburger buns, and chocolate chip cookies. He'd opened the bag and was munching a cookie.

"I'm glad to hear it. It's a shame more folk don't put up real trees anymore. It's always them fake ones. Plastic.

Ever'thing is plastic now. Plastic Santas. Plastic angels. Plastic holly and mistletoe." He totaled the bill, then spat his snuff into a coffee can tucked behind the cash register. " 'At'll come to $79.39."

"Just put it on my tab, Chester."

Chester chewed his gums before shaking his head. "Can't do it, Miss GiGi, much as I'd like to. You ain't paid the last two months, you know."

The room turned hot. The man was standing directly behind her now, watching, hearing everything that was transpiring.

"Chester, I'm certain I'll be able to settle up next week, just as soon as my clients pay me."

"Miss GiGi, you know how much I think of you and your pa, and how I hate what's happened to y'all, but I got my own bills to pay—bein' Christmas and all."

She nodded. Her hands flat on the counter, she asked, "What is the total bill?"

"Two hundred twenty-five and some-odd cents."

She thought of the check in her pocket—the one from the riding club. With some reluctance, she pulled it out and handed it to him. "This will about cover it if you don't mind handling a two-party check."

He studied it as if suspecting it to be counterfeit, then his head wagged up and down. "Done. Git on out yonder and pick out your tree while I box up your goods."

Barely managing a hoarse thank you, Virginia exited the store as quickly as possible without looking back, knowing the man named Neil continued to watch her. The urge to jump in the truck and vanish around the nearest curve—to escape this utterly humiliating fiasco—overwhelmed her momentarily. Once outside the store, buried within the false forest of tottering trees, hidden from the gawking farmers' view, she covered her face with her hands and considered throwing up.

There had been more embarrassing moments than this, she told herself.

It wouldn't have bothered her in the least had *he* not been looking on—the tall, overly good-looking man with the bluest eyes she had ever seen. Everyone in Pilot Point was familiar with her and her father's situation, but the motorcyclist was a stranger . . . and the first man she had been remotely attracted to for so many years she had stopped counting.

That was a complication she didn't need or want at this time in her life.

"Nice selection of trees," came Neil's voice behind her. She turned to find him holding her box of groceries and eating a piece of her fruitcake. "I'm probably the only person in the world who likes these little green things in fruitcake. Where do you want the box?"

"In the back of the truck."

He sauntered off. She stared after him, forgetting the Christmas tree.

Upon depositing the groceries into the truck, he popped the remaining fruitcake into his mouth and started toward her again. Her eyes widened; she plunged into the trees like a fleeing squirrel, knowing even as she buried herself within the prickly green spruce needles the chances of her disappearing were as likely as hiding an elephant under a napkin.

"Picked one out yet?" he asked.

Grabbing the closest one at hand, she nodded.

Neil moved up beside her, his arm brushing hers. "Nah. Too little. Hard to crank up the old holiday cheer with something that small. How about this one?"

The tree was a generous eight feet tall, big enough to take up half of her small living room . . . but it was undeniably beautiful, full and round and fragrant. Christmas card perfect.

"Well . . . perhaps—"

"Sold. I'll load it on the truck."

He did so with little effort, tying it down with a roll of cord Chester had provided. Keeping her distance, gripping her keys and knowing full well that Chester, not to mention the gossip-minded group beneath the oak tree who were watching with curiosity, Virginia fought the temptation to jump in the truck cab and take off the instant Neil had anchored the tree to the truck bed.

Finally, he stepped away and brushed needles from his shirt. "That should hold her well enough. Be sure to cut the bottom two inches off the trunk just before you submerse it in water. You might try adding a couple of spoons of sugar to the water as well. Helps to keep it green a while longer."

Managing a tight smile, she said, "Thanks for the advice."

"Thanks for the fruitcake."

They stared at each other several eternal seconds.

"Citron," she heard herself say. "The little green things are citron. They dye them that color. I took a tour of the bakery once and watched as they made the cakes . . ." Her voice faded and she bit her lip.

"How about a date?" he asked.

"They don't use dates in fruitcake."

He pursed his lips and slid his fingertips into the tops of his jeans pockets. "I'm asking you for a date."

"Oh." Time to move and groove. As she made her way around him and started toward the truck, she said, "I don't date strangers. Sorry. I really have to go now." As she opened the truck door, he grabbed it with one hand. His fingers were long and slender and well-manicured. No mechanic's hands, these. They were too clean, too perfect. They looked like a pianist's hands.

Jumping into the cab, Virginia jabbed the keys at the ignition, fully aware that Neil remained holding the door. The engine coughed, groaned, and sputtered to life. She grabbed for the door handle; he held on fast.

"Please," she said. "I have to go."

"No can do, sweetheart."

"I'm not your sweetheart and yes I can."

"No, you can't. Not yet. You have a flat."

Fingers strangling the steering wheel, Virginia glanced at Frank Handling and his cohorts. All were leaning forward, elbows on knees, palms cupped around the backs of their ears in an attempt to eavesdrop on her conversation.

"Look," she muttered under her breath. "Nice try, but I don't have the time to chitchat, mister. I don't have the time or desire to date—nothing personal, you understand. I'm just not into middle-aged hippies."

With that, she managed to slam the door, grind the gearshift into reverse, and take off, tires slinging gravel and stirring up a cloud of chalky dust.

The truck listed like a sinking boat. Damn it. *She had a flat!* A bad one.

"Got a spare?"

Looking out the driver's window, she met Neil's eyes. He rolled up his shirtsleeves just short of his elbows and said in a tone that brooked no further argument, "Kill the engine, Virginia, and get out."

Three

The attendant at the service station directly across 377 from Baxter's scratched his head with a ratchet, spat a wad of chew toward the oil well, and regarded the nail-punctured tire. "That's gonna take some plugging. Can't guarantee it'll last, but it might—just long enough for you to get into Denton and buy a new tire."

"How long will it take?" Virginia asked and glanced at her watch.

"Don't rightly know. Jimmy ain't here right now—he's the one who does the plugging. He ran up to Tioga to get some barbecue for lunch."

"Great."

The man wiped his hands with an oily towel and squinted at Neil with one eye. "That machine don't work, mister. If you want a cola you'll have to go over to Chester's. Me and him cut a deal. He don't sell gas, oil, or sparkplugs and I don't sell cola or candy."

"Smart move," Neil said, and dropped the coins into his shirt pocket.

"I like to think so. Well, y'all just make yourself at home if you want. I got to get Max Peterson's brakes changed for him—went completely out this morning going over the Roberts spillway. That ain't good. Max could really have done some damage to that spillway if he'd gone off it, I told him." He snickered, tucked the towel in his back overalls pocket, and ambled into the reeking garage.

"Looks like you're stuck with me whether you like it or not," Neil said.

"I'm perfectly capable of waiting alone."

"I'm not capable of going off and leaving young ladies in need."

"My, aren't we chivalrous? I could have used a little of that chivalry this morning when you were terrifying my horse."

"Tell you what. To make up for my recklessness I'll buy you a cup of coffee and a piece of pie at Mom and Pop's Cafe."

A truck full of fledgling, adolescent cowboys pulled up. The radio blasted a Garth Brooks and Reba McEntire duet as the kids revved the engine and whistled at the service attendant. Sighing, Virginia said, "Why not?"

Three years ago a reporter from the *Denton Daily News* Sunday edition had come all the way out to Pilot Point just to take pictures and write a story on Mom and Pop's Cafe at Christmas. Mom and Pop Cochran believed in sharing their seasonal memories with all their friends . . . and they had seventy-five years worth of seasonal memories. Peg collected Santas. Jim favored ornaments. There were over two thousand Santas perched in every available nook and cranny, staring out at people as they ate. Jim's ornaments hung from a 60's aluminum tree in one corner of the room, and from the ceiling, windowsills, light fixtures, and Peg's earlobes. Tables were decorated with candy cane stenciled cloths, and even the toilet jingled "Here Comes Santa Claus" when it was flushed.

Dixie Brown, dressed like Mrs. Claus and wearing peppermint-scented perfume, greeted Virginia and Neil as they entered the cafe.

"Merry Christmas, y'all! A table or booth? Aw, don't tell me. A booth, of course. There's one here by the front window. Is that all right? Kind of warm today, ain't it? 'Course, you know what they say about December weather in North

Texas: If you don't like the weather just hang on a few hours—it'll change. Almanac says it's supposed to get real cold soon. I sent my better half down to the hardware store last night to buy up some insulation for the outdoor pipes. Ours bust last time we had a hard freeze—Lord, what a mess. Our specials for the day are hot apple cider and mince meat pie. Gloria will be by in a minute to take your order." Dixie hurried to the door as a cluster of new customers arrived and began her oration all over again.

Virginia gazed out the window and did her best to ignore her companion across the table. It wasn't easy. His virility sucked the air out of the room.

He relaxed into the red vinyl booth and regarded her. "Not into Christmas, huh?"

"I have nothing against it."

"Then why do I get the feeling this atmosphere is making you uptight . . . or is it just my company that annoys you?"

"I don't know you."

"And you're shy?"

She glanced at her watch. "I have appointments this afternoon."

"You're not going anywhere until that flat is fixed so you might as well chill a while and enjoy the coffee I'm about to order you. If you smile I might even buy you a piece of Mom's priceless mince meat pie." He tilted his head slightly, causing his hair to slide over his shoulder with abundant unruliness. In her mind, she saw him again as he was that morning, long legs spread and the motorcycle jutting out from between his thighs. Something had sprung to life in her then, but it was nothing compared to the unrest in her now.

Gloria Guice, in red spike heels with white, fluffy straps across the insteps, hurried toward the booth, two plastic-coated menus tucked under her arm. Her short, starched Claus skirt swung back and forth like a red velvet church bell with each sway of her curvaceous hips.

Her eyes locked on Neil. "Why, there you are, honey-bunch. I was wonderin' when you was goin' to drop by again. Hiddy, GiGi. How's your daddy? I keep meanin' to drop by and say hello to him, you know, talk about ol' times and all." She patted the back of her upswept platinum-blond hair and continued to smile down at Neil. "Last time you was in you promised to take me for a ride on that bike of yours."

Neil eased the menus from under Gloria's arm and handed one to Virginia, who did her best not to smile at his predicament. When Gloria latched on to the idea of nabbing a man, she didn't let go easily. She should know. Gloria had used every trick in the book to seduce her father.

"Sorry," he replied simply, and flipped open the menu. "I didn't bring the bike today."

"I know. I seen that car you got out of. That'd do, for sure. Bet that baby cost an arm and a leg."

Virginia glanced out the window and scooped out the sparse collection of cars scattered over the parking lot. Nothing special there.

Gloria plucked a pencil from behind her ear and smiled at him again. "I seen you yesterday down on 380 at that shop that specializes in foreign auto parts. Exactly where was that shiny black speed machine made, hon?"

"Italy."

"Well, it suits you, sweetie, to a T."

"I like to think so."

"How fast will she do?"

"Faster than I'm willing to go."

"Yeah?" Lowering her voice, she asked, "And how fast is that?"

"Depends on my mood," he replied, those blue eyes focused on Virginia, those lips curled just a little on one end, giving him a slight tomcat look. Virginia felt her face go warm again and focused harder on the goings-on outside the cafe. She saw it then, the car in question. It wasn't parked at the cafe at all, but next door, at Baxter's. He'd left it under a shade tree on the north side of the building.

As casually as possible, Virginia slid from the booth. "When you get around to taking our order, Gloria, I'll have coffee with cream and sugar. No pie for me today, thank you."

She retreated to the ladies' room. Thank God, it wasn't occupied. Locking the door, she leaned her forehead against the plastic sign declaring: ALL EMPLOYEES OF THIS ESTAB-LISHMENT ARE REQUIRED TO WASH THEIR HANDS BEFORE RE-TURNING TO WORK.

It wasn't enough that he was good-looking; she was just on the verge of getting over that.

But he was also wealthy. Very wealthy by the looks of that *speed machine,* as Gloria had so aptly described it. An *Italian* speed machine, which meant it undoubtedly cost him something just short of the national debt. Oh, yes, it was him, all right: long, sleek, and dark. Intimidating. Reckless. Fast. A playboy. Probably one of those millionaire movie or rock and roll stars who were buying up ranches in the area for weekend retreats.

Wearily, she turned to face the mirror.

Oh, God.

She should have listened to her father that morning before leaving the house. She was a mess: her hay-sprinkled brown hair, her makeup—except there was no makeup, only a smudge of dirt across her chin. She hadn't plucked her eyebrows in six months, and Jeff was right. She'd lost so much weight the last few months that her clothes hung on her.

There was a tube of lip gloss in the bottom of her purse, along with several pieces of cinnamon-flavored gum, a handful of loose change, grocery receipts, and a compact of Succulent Plum cheek blush. Virginia dabbed the powdered color across each high cheekbone, swiped the gloss over her lips, then dug for a brush, finding only a pick she used on the horses' tails. There wasn't much help for her hair; it needed trimming and had become more than a little faded by the sun. To say it needed a good washing and conditioning was putting it mildly.

Good grief. What was she doing? Why, suddenly, did she give a flying leap what she looked like? Glaring at her reflection in the mirror, she said, "You don't have time for vanities, GiGi. You don't have time for flirtations . . . especially with the likes of him. That one's been around a time or two. He's a heartbreaker. Love 'em and leave 'em Joe. Remember your priorities."

Someone knocked on the door.

"In a minute," she snapped, then for good measure flushed the toilet, regretting the instant she did it. "Here Comes Santa Claus" spilled out into the hallway as she opened the door to come face-to-face with Gloria, who smiled broadly, revealing lipstick-smudged teeth.

"Your friend ran across the road to check on your tire. Says to tell you he'll be back directly. So tell me, hon, you two a thing or what?"

"No, Gloria. I only met him this morning."

"Not many like him come through here."

Virginia wove her way through the clutter of vinyl-covered cafe chairs, then elbowed through the cluster of cowboys on their lunch hour crowded around the jukebox. Gloria followed on her heels.

"He tips real good. 'Course, you'd expect that from a man who drives a car like that. Then again, you never know with people. I've waited on some fellas drippin' money and they don't leave me squat. Don't make any difference to them that I got four kids to support. Now, take your dad, for instance. He was always one heck of a tipper. Twenty, thirty percent sometimes. Say, honey, don't you want your coffee?"

"Not today, Gloria, thanks." Slipping out of the cafe, Virginia cupped her hands over her eyes and watched Neil head back across the road. He'd donned a pair of reflective sunglasses. A rising wind whipped his dark hair back from his shoulders.

Meeting him at center parking lot, she said, "Good news?"

"Not very." He ran one hand through his hair. "There are two punctures and Jimmy still isn't back from Tioga."

"Good ol' Jimmy." She looked at her watch, which was better than looking up at him. She couldn't see his eyes behind those mirrored glasses, but worse yet, she could see herself, windblown and disheveled, looking more like a sixteen-year-old tomboy than a thirty-year-old woman who hadn't had a date in six months.

"If there's someplace you need to be I'd be happy to drop you," he said.

"Damn," she muttered. "Of all times. I promised the Hayeses I'd be at their place by one-thirty, and the Robinsons' by three. I've got to run by the house before—what's that?" She stared down at the keys dangling from his fingertips.

"Keys to my car. I'll hang around here for a while and wait for good ol' Jimmy to get back from Tioga. I'll bring you your truck this evening."

She almost laughed. "You're joking, of course."

"No." He tossed her the keys. She almost dropped them.

"I'll wreck it."

"It's insured."

"You're crazy."

"So I've been told."

"You don't even know me."

"Your name is Virginia Valemere. Your father is Dick Valemere and you have a brother named Jeff. You live at 3307 Saddle Trail."

"I suppose you know my phone number as well?"

"No, but I'd like to." Again that tomcat smile made her step back in reflex.

"Just keep her below one-sixty. She shimmies a little if you go much over that."

"You're crazy," she repeated, even as her fingers closed around the keys.

"Ho, ho, ho." He flashed her a smile that set fire to his eyes. "See you tonight, Virginia."

"I'm terribly sorry, GiGi, but Bob has the checkbook with him and he's run to Denton. Tell you what—I promise to drop the check in the mail to you first thing Monday morning."

Virginia looked beyond Karen Robinson, to the distant cavernous den with its towering artificial tree and wrapped gifts underneath. "I can drop by later to pick up the check," she said, focusing on the woman's immaculately made-up face.

Karen Robinson smiled tightly. "Gee, I really have no idea what time Bob is getting back. He really should've left your money, but his mind is always elsewhere, the poor dear. It's the holidays, you know."

"I know."

"Oh, before you go, I have a little something for you. Karen Robinson dashed to the tinseled tree and returned with a decorated glass jar of peppermints which she presented to Virginia as if they were one of the priceless pieces of art scattered throughout the Robinsons' three-story antebellum mansion. "Merry Christmas, GiGi. I hope you enjoy them and thanks ever so much for all your hard work with Bob's horses. Oh, my, there's the phone. See you next Saturday!" With that, Mrs. Robinson closed the door in Virginia's face.

Peppermints. Bob Robinson owed her for two months training—eight hundred dollars, and all she was handed were peppermints.

She counted backward from ten, then headed toward the car . . . the machine. The chocolate brown, kid leather seats wrapped around her as she slid behind the wheel. Lights flashed, digital gauges sprang into action like life support monitors as she switched on the ignition. Without so much as a tremor, the car purred. Michael Crawford's *Love Songs* oozed from a stereo system that would put the most sophisticated sound stage to shame. Sliding the gearshift into first, Virginia eased the car out onto the highway, then floored it.

"Peppermints. Bob Robinson owns the largest chain of restaurants in this frigging country and he won't pay his bills—at least not mine. I've a good mind to—"

The car phone rang.

She stared at it.

It rang again.

Hesitantly, she picked it up. "Yes?"

"Hi."

Him again. His voice sounded extraordinarily deep over the phone and oddly professional, conjuring up images of some Armani-suited attorney or CEO.

"Enjoying my car?"

"It's very nice, thank you."

"Are you watching your speed?"

She glanced at the speedometer. Her eyes widened and she eased off the gas. "Of course."

"Everything all right?"

"Oh, sure. I land on my backside attempting to break some pea-brain thoroughbred and all I get to show for it is a jar of peppermints."

Silence, then, "Your truck is ready. I'll swing it by your place around seven. 'Bye."

Seven. It was already four-thirty!

She stopped by the local discount store and bought hair color and lavender-scented milk bath—the sort that came in gallon plastic jugs decorated with contrasting plastic flowers. She bought raspberry-red nail polish for her toenails. And tweezers. And since the rack of imperfect clothes and merchandise was marked down an extra twenty percent for the holidays, she splurged and grabbed up the only size four jeans she could find—they were royal blue with a pair of red satin lips on the back pocket, but oh, well, they were still better than the worn-thin denims she rode in every day. Chocolate covered cherries were on special, too—Jeff would appreciate those—they'd give him a sugar boost when he needed something to keep him awake at the hospital, and her dad loved the caramelized popcorn that came in five-gallon tin containers depicting Santa shimmying down a chimney.

She paid for it all with a credit card, holding her breath as the overworked and less-than-Christmas-cheery checkout girl waited for her purchase to be authorized by some depersonalized computer. At last, the machine spit out the receipt; Virginia signed it and ran for the car.

The realization of what she was doing didn't occur to her

until she had soaked up to her chin in milk bath bubbles for ten minutes. With her hair plastered to her head with dye, she stared down at her red toenails peeking out of the water.

It wasn't as if he was picking her up for a night on the town . . . far from it. She had turned him down, after all, when he'd asked her out—she didn't date strangers, remember? He was only returning her truck and picking up his car.

Perhaps she would invite him in for a glass of Blackberry Royal and fruitcake. Or better yet, wine and cheese. Maybe she would put on a Christmas CD and they could decorate the tree together. Of course, she would introduce him to her father . . .

And maybe not.

Had she met him on the street face-to-face she would not have recognized him. Gone was the biker. In his place was the man belonging to the voice on the phone, an Armani-suited, Gucci-loafered fashion statement that smelled of Drakkar aftershave. The man named Neil—God, she had spent the last two hours primping for a man whose last name she didn't even know—was standing in the aisle of her barn, his hands in his pockets, the rich material of his coat caught behind his wrists as he regarded her horses.

"Nice animals," he told her. "Well taken care of."

"They're my future. And my friends. They bring me a great deal of pleasure."

"Ah, but woman can't live by horse alone." He moved to Famous's stall. "Pretty mare. Looks like she's due to foal soon."

"First week of January. I have to admit, I'm nervous as heck. The mare is nineteen. It took us three years to get her cleaned up enough inside to breed her with any hopes that she would take." The bay mare slid her silky muzzle between the bars and nickered softly. Virginia stroked her and blew gently into her nostril. "She's carrying this farm's future—I feel it in my heart, Neil. This foal is going to put Renaissance Farm back in business. We're going to prove to the industry that Lindale is the sire of the future. We'll be freezing and shipping his semen all over the world."

"Must be some stallion."

"As close to perfect as you can get conformation wise, with extreme intelligence and disposition."

"What's he worth?"

"There's no amount of money that could buy him right now. I need him too badly."

Raising one eyebrow, he glanced at her askew and grinned. "Everything has its price, Ms. Valemere."

"No."

"A few hundred grand could buy your way out of this stock barn and into something a little more impressive."

"I've had impressive. I'll have it again. When enough of Lindale's foals are on the ground and they're mopping up the futurities and the Arabian Triple Crown I'll have enough capital to buy back what rightfully belongs to me and my father."

"I take it you mean the farm up the road."

"My father's farm. He designed every square foot of the five barns, breeding labs, and arenas. There's not another facility outside of Chauncey's in Scottsdale that can come close to matching its grandeur."

He moved to Equator's stall. The gray horse turned its exotic head and regarded him with eyes as big and liquid as a llama's. "Must have been tough giving it all up," Neil said.

"That's putting it mildly. It broke my father's heart. The hardest part is watching it just sit there, going to waste. There hasn't been a horse on the premises since we sold it. We attempted to contact the owner once—inquired whether he would consider leasing one of the barns and indoor arenas to us—but the jerk's business manager responded that they had no interest in doing so . . . and wished us luck, of course."

"Cold-hearted bastard."

"Tell me about it."

He walked to her office door and nudged it open with his foot. Light poured out, spilling over his shoulders and reflecting off his hair. A look of studied indifference marked his features as he regarded the cramped but neat interior, then turned back toward her.

"Sorry, but I have to run. I have an appointment in Fort Worth."

"Oh." She lowered her eyes. "Gee, and here I was about to invite you in for Blackberry Royal, fruitcake, and Chester's cheese."

"Maybe some other time."

She nodded.

He left the barn. Virginia followed, keeping a respectable distance behind him as he walked to his car, unlocking it with the push of a button on his key chain. "Thanks again for the use of your car," she told him as he folded his long legs and dropped into the seat.

"No problem."

"Maybe we'll bump into one another again sometime."

"Undoubtedly." He flashed her a smile that made her stomach knot, then he started the engine. "Enjoy a glass of Royal for me," he said.

She nodded, stepping back as he reversed the sports car then shot down the long gravel drive like a black streak. For an instant, his brake lights beamed as he yielded to traffic, then he was gone through the dark, disappearing around the nearest curve.

Virginia stood in the driveway and stared after him, then returned to the house. Jeff stood inside the kitchen, hungrily eying the silver-plated serving dish of cheese cubes, fruitcake, and butter crackers she had laid out in the shape of a Christmas tree.

"So where is our mystery man?" he asked, popping a cheese into his mouth.

"Gone."

"Already?"

"He had plans."

Jeff nodded and swallowed his cheese.

"It doesn't matter, Jeff. You needn't look at me as if I've just learned I'm terminal or something. It wasn't as if we had a date or anything. He simply returned my truck. Besides, it serves me right for acting so snooty to him earlier."

"He'll call, right?"

She smiled and reached for a wineglass.

"And when he does you'll stop playing hard to get and go out with him. Right?"

"If it means getting you off my case," she declared in a falsely light voice, then prepared to pour him a glass of Royal.

"Thanks, Sis, but as much as I'd like to stay and help you put away this incredible display of munchies, I gotta run. The hospital called. They're a little short-handed in the ER tonight, and I figured—hey, we can use the extra money." Tweaking her cheek, he said, "Cheer up, GiGi. He'll call."

"Sure."

She poured a single glass of wine and watched her brother's car disappear through the dark, then she wandered to the living room where the mammoth Christmas tree took up one complete wall. There were old ornaments stacked in chairs and a cardboard box of tangled lights. Bing Crosby crooned "I'm Dreaming of a White Christmas" on the stereo, and the thought occurred to her that she had spent $52.60 she didn't have on jeans she normally wouldn't be caught dead in, lavender milk bath that was little more than dish detergent, and red nail polish that made her toes look like raspberries, and for what?

She tapped on her father's bedroom door, then pushed it open enough to see him propped up in bed, staring at the television atop his bureau. "Pop," she called softly. "Would you care to help me decorate the tree? I've cut up some cheese and fruitcake. I've bought you some eggnog. And listen . . . it's your favorite Christmas song on the stereo."

"Thought you had a date for a change," he barked without looking at her.

She shook her head. "I could use a little *friendly* company tonight."

He hit the volume control so the TV dialogue drowned out

*May your days be merry and bright. And may all your
Christmases be white.*

Closing the door, Virginia turned back to the living room
and gazed up at the dark, unadorned tree. *Merry Christmas
to you, too,* she thought.

Four

The office phone rang at ten A.M. It was Rachel Ellison.

"Don't tell me. Your feet are propped up on the desk and you're enjoying your fifth cup of coffee of the morning. The horses are begging to be fed and the stalls haven't seen a muck fork since I left yesterday. You're exhausted and regretting the fact that you sent me away from the barn in bitter tears. You're about to beg me to come back. Aren't you?"

Virginia mopped the sweat from her brow, glanced down at the muck fork in one hand, and grinned. "Try again, Chimp."

"Do you miss me a little?"

"More than a little."

"I can be there in fifteen."

"Fine. Just bring written permission from your father—"

"Okay, okay. I get the picture. I suppose it doesn't matter to you that I cried in my pillow all night long."

Virginia sat down on the edge of the desk. "I can relate," she replied wearily.

"Great! Then I propose that we do something about it."

"I'm game."

"I have a plan."

Virginia laughed. "Oops. I smell trouble."

"Trouble just happens to be my middle name—you said so yourself at least a dozen times."

"Yes, but I've never met anyone who took such pride in the fact."

The girl giggled, then her voice became conspiratorial. "The plan is this: Tonight. My place. Seven-thirty. I'll introduce you to my dad. You can sit down face-to-face—over a dinner which I will personally prepare—and explain that there is absolutely nothing dangerous about my riding."

"But riding can be *very* dangerous, Rach—"

"With *you* as an instructor?"

"Well, if you want to put it that way . . ."

"So you'll do it?"

She toed the fork with her muddy boot. It wasn't the aspect of facing some grouchy, gray-haired fizzle who had a thing against horses that bothered her most. It was the idea of walking back into what once had been her own home—of seeing it again for the first time in four years—and remembering how good it all had been then.

"Well?" came Rachel's hopeful voice.

"I suppose if I want to stand any chance at all at Youth Nationals next summer I should at least give it a shot, huh?"

"Yes!" Rachel shouted.

"Seven-thirty?"

"Come hungry and loaded for bear."

"He's that bad?"

"Depends on his mood."

"I'll bring a twelve gauge."

"How about an uzi. See ya!"

Jeff's eyes were red from lack of sleep. He needed to shave. He accepted a cup of coffee from Virginia and shook his head. "Five members of one family gone just like that and I had to be the one to break the news to a woman that her father and four of her children were dead."

"How did it happen?"

"Drunk driver. The idiot careened over the medium and plowed headlong into their car. The crazy thing is, the drunk walked away from it with a broken arm and a bump on his head. Go figure."

Virginia squeezed his shoulder reassuringly. "I'm sorry, Bro."

"If that wasn't enough, we had three gunshot victims— one a drive-by in Oak Cliff. Some eighty-two-year-old granny who'd taken her dog out for a whiz. She got it right between the eyes. Dead before she hit the ground. Merry Christmas." He shook his head and stared into his coffee. "Sometimes I wonder how much of this I can handle. Guys on the staff say I'll eventually get used to it, but how the hell can someone get used to so much senseless and stupid human destruction?"

"Not you. That's what's going to make you such an incredible doctor. I'm proud of you, Jeff Valemere, just you remember that."

He smiled tiredly and for the first time since returning from the hospital, focused his attention completely on her. "A dress? What's the occasion? Don't tell me 'the car' called and asked you out."

"No. I'm doing a favor for a friend. I'm going to attempt to convince Rachel's father to let her continue riding."

"I assume he's coming here."

She shook her head.

Jeff frowned. "Are you sure you can handle it, going home again? Seeing the place after so long, I mean."

"We all have to face our past eventually. Maybe I'll see it through an adult's eyes and it won't seem so impressive."

"Fat chance."

"Thanks for the encouragement."

As Virginia reached for her purse, Jeff caught her arm. "We need to talk, Sis. About Dad."

"If I don't leave now—"

"Look. I gotta get some sleep, I'm due back at the hospital at seven A.M. so I won't be up when you get back."

"Then it'll wait until tomorrow." She tugged on her arm. He shook his head. "No, it won't."

Looking up into her brother's troubled eyes, Virginia swallowed.

Releasing her arm, Jeff said, "His blood pressure is way

up. The pain in his head was bad this afternoon. I had to up his Demerol to ease it."

"So what are you suggesting?"

"I mentioned to you yesterday that there's a new doctor on staff—a surgeon specializing in trauma to the posterior lateral portion of the brain. He's good, GiGi. Very good. We studied his procedures in school. He's been written up in every medical journal in the country. The *Journal of the American Neurologic Society* claims he might well be the best in the country. I want to talk to him about Dad."

"Jeff, we've been told by every doctor who's examined him that his odds of surviving that surgery are too minimal to calculate."

"I intend to talk to him, GiGi."

"Fine." She turned for the door. "You do that."

The paved drive up to the house was a quarter-mile long and flanked by oaks. The house itself consisted of fifteen thousand square feet of luxury. It crowned the hill like a castle. She would never forget the day she and Jeff moved in with her father. Suddenly, her life had turned into a fairytale—everything young, starry-eyed girls dreamt of. Damn, but it was hard not to envy Rachel Ellison—or not to continue to harbor resentment toward the man who purchased Renaissance. Then Virginia reminded herself that Rachel would no doubt be glad to give it all up to be allowed to ride.

Taking a deep breath, Virginia rang the bell, which chimed deep and soft in the heart of the house. A moment passed, then the door opened, revealing an older man of medium build with basset hound eyes. He looked like Walter Cronkite.

"Mr. Ellison?"

"You must be Virginia." The man smiled and studied her appreciatively. "The kid never mentioned you were so pretty, or so young. Please, come in."

Here goes, she thought, and stepped inside.

She had forgotten how beautiful the twin staircases were. They swept in a graceful curve to the second-floor landing. She and Jeff were continually in trouble for sliding down the mahogany banisters—racing one another to the bottom.

"I must admit, I expected someone a bit more . . . substantial, Miss Valemere. And perhaps not so feminine. You really don't look like a tyrant at all."

Focusing her attention away from the overhead chandelier, each crystal prism hand cut in Rumania, she smiled. "Neither do you, sir."

His bushy eyebrows shot up and he chuckled. "Wicked girl is our Rachel. Never quite know what to expect from her. She doesn't fib, mind you, but has an extraordinary talent for skewing the truth. And by the way, you can relax, dear. I'm not Rachel's father. Grandfather. The name is Billings. Alfred Billings. Rachel's mother was my daughter."

Relaxing, Virginia offered her hand. "What a shame. I was beginning to hope that this conspiracy of Rachel's wouldn't be as difficult as I'd anticipated."

"Oh, it'll be difficult, all right, if I know my son-in-law. He's a mite overly protective where his daughter is concerned. I don't envy you your objective."

"Thanks for the encouragement."

"Not to worry. If it's any consolation, I'm in your corner, for whatever good that will do you." Motioning toward the nearest door, he said kindly, "I believe you know the way, Miss Valemere?"

Oh, yes, she knew the way. Knew every nook and cranny along the way to the den—her father's favorite room, with Brazilian rosewood paneling and ceilings with three-hundred-year-old beams he'd imported from an Irish castle outside Dublin. A troika of stained glass windows depicting Trojan horses stampeding to war was placed strategically on the west wall so the afternoon sun could set fire to the blaze of red, blue, and gold in the glass. It was all there still, just as it had been the day her family had packed up their belongings and walked away.

"GiGi!" Rachel sang from the kitchen doorway, then flew

across the room to fling her arms around Virginia's neck. "God, I thought tonight would never get here. How is Lindale?"

"Incredible."

"And Equator and Loco?"

"Missing you dreadfully."

"With any luck I'll be there to ride them after school tomorrow."

She smiled. "I'll do my best, Rach. I promise."

Stepping back, wringing a dish towel in her hands, Rachel said, "I hope you like lasagna. It's Dad's favorite."

"The old 'way to a man's heart is through his stomach' ploy, huh? So when do I meet the ogre?"

Rachel and her grandfather exchanged looks. Alfred proceeded to relax in his easy chair while Rachel chewed her lower lip. "Dad's running a little late, as usual. I told him that I'd be serving dinner at seven-thirty but he has a problem remembering to check his watch, I'm afraid."

"He does know I'm coming, right?"

"Well . . . not exactly. But he won't mind, I promise. Dad may be a bit of a mule but he's not in the habit of being rude to a guest."

"Unless, of course, she happens to be his daughter's clandestine riding instructor."

"Right." Backing toward the kitchen, beaming Virginia a less-than-believable smile, Rachel added, "The Christmas tree's in the study—through that door. I thought we all might decorate it after dinner. It'll give you and Dad time to get to know one another. Once you get to know him, I'm sure the two of you will become great friends."

Virginia crossed her arms and watched Rachel disappear into the kitchen. "Why do I get the feeling I'm being set up?" she said to Rachel's grandfather.

"Because you are."

"I was afraid of that. Should I escape now or take my chances of being eaten alive?"

"He's not so bad, just a mite moody occasionally. Being

a single father to a lass as precocious as that one isn't always easy."

Virginia walked to the study door. The room wasn't so different than when her father had occupied it, but instead of Rob Hess glossies of world champion horses on the wall there were groupings of Rachel in everything from a tutu to a baseball uniform. The towering tree had been placed before the plate-glass windows overlooking the pool.

"I understand Rachel's mother died in a traffic accident," she said without turning. "My condolences to you."

"It was hard," Al replied. "She was my only child."

"Then you're doubly lucky to have Rachel."

"I'm most fortunate that Rachel's father has allowed me the opportunity to participate in bringing her up. Most men in my position are forced to settle for a card on the holidays and a brief visit during summer vacation."

She scanned the walls, the tables, the desk for a photo of Rachel's mother. There were none.

"I take it Rachel's dad still has a difficult time dealing with her death?"

"Hmm." Al packed tobacco in a pipe bowl, his sad eyes never leaving Virginia. "It's been a difficult few years . . . for more reasons than one, I'm afraid."

Rachel appeared again, her face flushed, her eyes sparkling. "He's home! Now everyone remain calm. I'll talk to him first, sort of ease him in to this scheme." Flinging her dishtowel in the vicinity of the kitchen, she sprang from the room like a fleeing gazelle.

"Hi, Dad! You're late, but I forgive you. I fixed your favorite tonight. Lasagna. Gee, you look like you've had a rough day. I'll pour you a cola. Oh, by the way, I invited a friend to dinner, which explains the candles and good china. I thought we'd all decorate the tree together—that way we'd all get to know one another better."

Virginia looked at the floor. "You're babbling, Rachel," she muttered to herself. "Take a deep breath and slow down. He'll suspect something's wrong if you don't . . ."

"Well, well. Isn't this a surprise?"

She didn't have to look up; she knew the voice immediately. The deep smoothness of it wrapped around her throat like a velvet noose.

Oh, the irony of it all.

"I presume the two of you know one another," Rachel declared nervously as she planted herself between Neil and Virginia. He stood just inside the door, silk tie loose and askew, his coat, hooked on one finger, slung over his right shoulder. As always, he needed to shave. His hair was a riotous mess, as if he'd raced his cycle along Blackjack Road without a helmet.

Her face went from cold to hot as her gaze locked with his.

"We've met," Neil said, his eyes narrowing and his lips forming that not quite friendly grin that made him look infuriatingly smug—if not outright challenging. "I'm *Darth Vader*. A *menace* on a motorcycle. And the *jerk* who bought her father's farm. Hello, Virginia. Good to see you again. My, but don't you look pretty in a dress."

"I think I should go," she said, and moved toward the door.

"You can't!" Rachel cried, staring at Virginia pointedly. "Look, I don't know what's gone on between you two before, but can't you at least sit down like two responsible adults and have dinner together? I made lasagna, for Pete's sake! *Please.*"

It was hard to ignore Rachel's entreating expression, or the fact that her wide blue eyes were brimming with tears. But it was just as difficult to stand before her father, in what once had been her home, and acknowledge to herself that for a brief few hours she had come very close to having a crush on the very man whom she had decided long ago that she didn't like—for myriad reasons.

Alfred left his chair and cleared his throat. "I think I'll have my dinner upstairs tonight—I have some reading to catch up on. Looks like the three of you are going to need some time and privacy to work this out."

"Work what out?" Neil asked, and tossed his coat over the

couch. "The fact that Ms. Valemere happens to hate my guts and thinks I'm a middle-aged hippie?"

"We'll discuss it over dinner," Rachel said, then caught her father's hand and tugged him toward the dining room, even as he continued to regard Virginia with a look so belligerent she felt like slapping his face—just on principle. "Come on, GiGi. I promise I won't let him bite you. He might be a bit of a non-conformist but his bark's a lot worse than his bite . . . most of the time."

Non-conformist? *That's putting it mildly,* Virginia thought, then reluctantly followed.

The table was set nicely with blue and white china and a poinsettia arrangement. Rachel sat her father at the head of the table, herself to the right, and Virginia to his left, then she dashed to the kitchen to retrieve the food.

Virginia sat in silence, her eyes taking in the handpainted mural of the farm's scattering of ponds and rolling hills. As a fifteen-year-old, she had sat in the corner and watched the artist depict the lush landscape in minute detail. In the end, he had allowed her to paint her initials just below his in the corner. They were still there.

"I guess this means I shouldn't bother asking you out again," Neil said.

"You should've told me."

"You were cold and angry enough to me the first time we met. Why exacerbate the problem?"

"I would've found out eventually."

"By that time you might've realized that I'm not such a 'jerk' after all."

"No?" She smiled thinly and reached for her water glass.

"I bought a farm that was for sale. So what? Was it my fault that your father went belly-up?"

"Keep my father out of this."

"That's what this is about, right? You're angry at me because I'm living here and you're not. You're angry because I have money and you don't."

"Why, you—"

"Food's on!" Rachel hurried into the room, hefting a pan

of steaming pasta which she placed on a trivet, then she reached for Virginia's plate. Their eyes met briefly, but long enough for Virginia to note the mounting despair on Rachel's face. Taking a deep breath, Virginia relaxed against the back of her chair, clasped her hands in her lap, and bit her lip.

"So tell me," Neil said, raising one eyebrow at his daughter. "To what do we owe the pleasure of Ms. Valemere's visit?"

Rachel sat down. "Well . . . it's Christmas, after all. We should be neighborly at Christmas, right?"

"Too shallow, Sweet Cheeks. You're up to something. What is it?" Neil said.

"I've come here tonight to ask your permission for me to instruct Rachel in riding," Virginia announced, preferring to get to the point so she could, as gracefully as possible, make a break for it at the first opportunity.

He looked at Rachel. "We've been over this months ago."

"I assure you, Mr. Ellison, that I take every precaution—"

"No."

"But, Dad—"

"The risks are very minimal," Virginia argued. "She's required to wear protective headgear at all times—"

"No."

"But, Dad. I'm a great rider. GiGi says I'm a natural. That I could even go national champion in equitation."

Virginia closed her eyes.

Neil looked first at Rachel, then directly at Virginia. His jaw worked. His face became dark and his blue eyes hooded. "Then I take it my daughter's been riding already."

Rachel sank in her chair with a groan.

"Mr. Ellison, this means a great deal to your daughter," Virginia said as calmly as possible.

"Miss Valemere, my daughter means a great deal to me."

"I can understand your concerns . . . considering the loss of your wife—"

"Don't bring Rachel's mother into this. My feelings regarding Rachel's welfare have nothing to do with Charlotte."

His lips curled as he added, "Far from it." Then staring at Rachel, he added, "And you're grounded."

"What? You're being an ass, Dad."

"I told you in no uncertain terms that you were not to get anywhere near those horses. And as for you . . ." He turned again to Virginia and pointed a spoon at her nose. "I could sue you for this. I could take everything you own."

"You already have," she replied smoothly, and stabbed her lasagna with a knife.

"Why do you have to be this way?" Rachel cried and jumped from her chair, small hands clenched and tears streaming from her eyes. "I'm sorry you're so angry at the world, Dad. I'm sorry for what happened between you and Mom, and I'm sorry for everything terrible that's happened with your job, but none of that is my fault. Why are you so angry at me? Sometimes I think all I am to you is a reminder of everything that's brought you unhappiness—is that why you hate me so? Because I remind you of Mom?"

She turned to run from the room. Neil caught her arm and swung her around. His expression went from anger to an intensity of emotion that was almost palpable. "I don't hate you, Poppet. I didn't hate your mother, either."

"You've got a funny way of showing it." She yanked her arm away. "You're never here and when you are you're barricaded off in your stupid office brooding away your life. No wonder Mom was so miserable being married to you. No wonder she went off with that other man—"

"Enough." Rachel's grandfather walked into the room, his pipe in one hand, a magazine in the other. "Is that any way to speak to your father?" he said. "In front of our guest, no less. Such behavior—were you a year younger I would put you across my knee, but considering I'm partially to blame for spoiling you rotten I'll forego the spanking for a good dressing-down. No one was responsible for your mother's unhappiness except herself, young lady. Your father did everything in his power to please and appease her, but she, too, was far too accustomed to getting her way, thanks to *her* mother's penchant for excess," he added in a disparaging tone. "Now apologize to your father and Virginia. You've embarrassed them both as well as yourself."

For an eternal minute Rachel refused to speak. Her only show of emotion were the tears flowing down her cheeks. Finally, she turned and walked out of the room into the study and closed the door behind her.

Virginia gently lay her hand on Neil's, which was fisted fiercely on the table; it was reflex, pure and simple—her usual need to comfort, to nurture. She understood pain and anger, and the bitter bite of disillusionment and disappointment.

Then he opened his hand and laced his fingers through hers.

She swallowed and forgot to breathe.

"What the hell is going on with her, Virginia?" he asked wearily.

"It's called puberty, as I recall." Her gaze drifted to their entwined hands. What was she doing? And why?

Al moved up beside Neil and laid a reassuring hand on his shoulder. "She adores you, son. You know that. But in case you haven't looked lately, she's growing up. She feels she should be allowed to make a few decisions on her own. Aside from that . . . it's Christmas. The child in her still craves to experience that holiday jolly. She's still hoping Santa will show up with his bag full of miracles and make everything the way it was before Charlotte died."

Neil sat back in his chair and briefly closed his eyes. He looked immensely tired, suddenly, and sad. Drawing his hand from Virginia's, he laughed bleakly. "Sorry, Al, but you'll have to agree it was never good between me and Charlotte. Ever."

"But Rachel doesn't know that. In the beginning you and Charlotte did a respectable job of hiding your problems. All that child can remember is that her life changed drastically Christmas Eve three years ago and it's never been the same. I've seen morgues with more holiday spirit than this place has at Christmas."

Al dropped the magazine onto the table next to Virginia's

plate: *Journal of the American Medical Association*. A photo of Neil, sans hair and ear stud, surrounded by an army of suited, briefcase-toting officials stared back at her. The bold headlines read:

"WHEN ICONS FALL
The Case of Dr. Neil Ellison"

She scanned the article. "My God," she whispered, her gaze drifting back to his. "You're a surgeon."

Five

"Was a surgeon. I haven't picked up a scalpel in three years." Neil pushed away from the table and headed for the liquor cabinet across the room. Grabbing a decanter of sherry, he removed the stopper, then stood with his back to Virginia and Al a long while before reluctantly setting it aside. "Not again," he said. "I can at least do that much for her."

"Talk to Rachel," Al said. "For the love of God, man, she's your daughter. She worships you. She's old enough to know the truth. It's imperative that she understand the situation between you and Charlotte before this breach between you gets any wider."

Virginia put aside her napkin and left the chair. "You're welcome to practice on me," she offered tentatively. "I have an incredibly strong shoulder to lean on. And I love to give advice. Besides that . . . I adore Rachel. How about it, Doc? Just you and me. We'll go for a walk. You'll give me a tour of the barns. I've almost forgotten what they look like."

Slowly, he turned to face her, looking like a man on the verge of shattering—hardly the arrogant menace on a motorcycle, or the tomcat flirt who had sent her fleeing to the bathroom at Mom and Pop's Cafe. "Why the hell should I confide in you?" he asked.

"Good question. The same reason I spent my last few dollars on a pair of discounted jeans with a pair of red satin lips embroidered on the butt, I suppose. There's something about each of us that makes the other one just a little crazy."

His blue eyes narrowed and his lips thinned. "Yeah, you *do* make me a little crazy at that."

Clearing his throat, Al said, "I'll wrap up the lasagna. We'll eat when you get back."

Virginia followed Neil out of the house, falling in beside him as he moved down the red-bricked path through double iron gates sequestering the house from the sprawling paddocks and work arenas. They walked in silence—he with his hands in his pockets, she with her arms crossed, slightly shivering from the chill . . . and the odd sense of anticipation she had come to experience in his company. A short time ago—sitting across from Neil Ellison at Mom and Pop's Cafe—she'd convinced herself that that feeling of anticipation was nothing more than extreme dislike; she'd never been one to appreciate such flagrant arrogance, after all. Heaven help her, but now she wasn't so sure.

The grounds and buildings were dark. Reaching the door of what once had been the stallion barn, Virginia flipped open a breaker box and hit several switches, flooding the vicinity with illumination.

Memories washed over her, as pure and iridescent as the buzzing, blinding lights, and she smiled. "It's been so long," she whispered. "Isn't it beautiful—all the lights, the bleachers. When I first came to Renaissance I thought it all looked like a circus. I learned to ride in that arena there. Late at night, after Dad had finished working horses, I would bridle Locomotion and pretend I was a bareback rider for Barnum and Bailey's, standing on Loc's back while he trotted around the arena. Even then I dreamt of becoming the world's greatest trainer.

"Every two months Dad invited the local horse clubs to use the facility for schooling shows. Dressage would perform there." She pointed to a distant rectangle of earth, now grown over by grass. "Jumpers used that arena, but this one was special." Virginia walked to center arena and for an instant she heard again the cheer of the spectators and the voices of the ring stewards calling, "Gates Open! Enter at the trot, please!"

She smiled and turned back toward Neil, though she couldn't see him—not in the least. Like a performer on stage she could see nothing beyond the glare of the lights.

"Every Christmas my father had a twenty-foot tree delivered from Canada. He would put it here, center arena, and invite his clients from all over the world to join us. We would drape the tree with tinsel and lights and gold ornaments engraved with the horses' names and their winnings for that year. Every barn, every fence, every building glowed with Christmas lights. We were a great blaze of red and green that could be seen for miles. We would present our yearlings for sale there, beside the tree. We'd drape a garland of poinsettias around their necks and parade them around the arena at a trot. The horses loved it as much as the clients, I think."

A light flickered overhead and went out.

So did the memories.

A sudden cold wind swept over the show ring, stirring up eddies of sand. Neil emerged from the lights, a silhouette at first, then materializing like a bold spectre, his hands still in his pockets and the first two buttons of his dress shirt open.

"I'm sorry," she said. "We came out here to talk about you and here I am rambling on about the good ol' days."

He stopped a hand's width from her. His eyes were dark as storm clouds, his features rigid with a kind of emotion that sent a spear of thrill through her. She should back away. Turn and run. He was the enemy, after all. The representation of all her father had lost.

"You're beautiful," he said softly. "You're radiant when you talk of the past, and when you're with your horses. I can't help wondering what you're like when you're with a man. I wonder if your eyes flash as brightly, or your face flushes with such intensity. I know one thing: You look damn good straddling a horse . . . and I'm going to kiss you whether you like it or not because that's what I want and I'm damned stubborn about getting what I want."

He wrapped one arm around her waist and drew her close. His body pressed against hers felt hard, and hot, and big. He smelled of expensive aftershave.

She struggled—briefly. She opened her mouth to protest and nothing came out.

"Shut up, Virginia," he said in a voice like a growl. "Don't even think about talking or shooting me with one of your verbal barbs again. Not right now. I've thought of nothing but kissing you since I saw you on that hillside, your hair in your face and your brown eyes flashing with anger . . . and those damned long legs hugging that horse like a lover. Christ, I've never known a woman who was so unaware of herself as a woman. Now hush and part your lips. I don't intend to kiss a piece of marble—that's not what I need tonight, sweetheart."

He lowered his mouth to hers, gently at first, tentatively, as if he expected some unpleasant reaction. His lips were warm, moist, and demanding, making her knees go weak, her body supple. His tongue slid inside her like a soft, hot flame—urgent, but not invasive. It penetrated slowly and deliciously, turning the chilly air warm and caressing as eiderdown.

Much too soon, the kiss ended. Forcing her eyes open, Virginia did her best to focus on his face. Impossible. The world was spinning like a carousel.

He made a sound deep in his throat, then backed away. Turning, he walked toward the stallion barn, pausing only long enough to glance around and raise one hand in invitation.

Taking a deep breath, making sure her legs were strong enough again to carry her, Virginia followed.

The stallion barn was a plush suite of richly paneled stalls larger than most hotel rooms. Each stall boasted an oversized grilled window that afforded the studs the opportunity to gaze out over the far-reaching facility and pastures. There were automatic waterers and swing-out feed doors. Covering the double-wide center aisle was plush, ruby-red carpet, and overhead were a string of crystal chandeliers, now dusty and laced with spiderwebs.

The old pain surfaced, and so did the anger.

"Why in God's name did you buy Renaissance if you had

no intention of running a horse business?" She swept one hand over the dust-covered stall grill. "What a damned waste of a dream."

Neil dropped down on a bench seat and stretched out his legs, crossing them at the ankles. "I intended to turn this barn into a medical clinic."

"A clinic." She closed her eyes and sank down on the bench beside him.

"Yes, a clinic. A free clinic for desperately ill children whose parents can't afford the high cost of medical care. Believe me, Virginia, there are a great many of them out there."

"So what happened? Why haven't you done it?"

"Things got in the way."

"Such as?"

"My wife." He shook his head; his features became bitter, his shoulders rigid. "She couldn't understand why I would give up my position at Boston General to waste my time on a lot of indigents who couldn't pay to keep her living comfortably in the lifestyle to which she had grown accustomed. Mind you, my intentions weren't motivated purely for altruistic reasons. At thirty-five years old, I was burned out. Shot. The idea of walking into an OR turned me inside out.

"You see, Virginia, I was too damned good at what I do . . . or did. My profession turned me into God. Every minute of every day I was responsible for the lives of sick and dying people—desperate people who would sacrifice everything they owned to give me the opportunity of saving their lives or the lives of loved ones. I had to pick and choose which of those lives I would save, and when I started refusing to do that, the hospital did it for me. Their decisions, of course, were determined by the patient's insurance coverage . . . or their standing in the community.

"I couldn't take any more." His voice grew deeper, wearier. Leaning back against the wall, he stared straight ahead his eyes and features oddly blank. "Things hadn't been good with Charlotte in a very long time—since I figured out that her greatest aspiration in life was to belong to three country clubs and have unlimited credit on her platinum charge cards. She didn't want kids. Rachel was the result of a night of drunken spontaneity on her part. I got her pregnant on purpose, then was forced to threaten to cut off her allowance if she went through with an abortion.

"Then came Rachel." Breathing deeply, he appeared to relax. A smile toyed with his lips. His eyes grew warm and liquid. "Suddenly I had a daughter to think about. I did my best to provide the stability I felt she deserved. I tried to make things work with Charlotte, and did my best to deal with the stress of my job, but it didn't work. The final straw came four years ago this week."

Leaving the bench, he walked down the carpeted aisle, his head down, his shoulders burdened. The air, suddenly, became charged and she regretted having encouraged him to confide in her; she wasn't comfortable witnessing this sort of raw pain . . . she wasn't comfortable with the distress she, herself, was experiencing because of his pain. The thrill she'd experienced from his kiss had left her shaken enough.

"There was a car wreck—a bad one. Two families were brought to General's ER. There was a girl about Rachel's age with extreme head trauma—you could tell by looking at her and her family, the Evansons, that there would be no insurance to cover even the simplest medical care, much less surgery.

"The other family was a different story. The Woodwords were upper class—pillars of Society—an old boy from one of Boston's founding families. Problem was, when good ol' Brad Woodword and his wife and daughter were hauled in on stretchers, his blood alcohol level was way beyond the legal limit. His daughter had suffered a few broken bones, a punctured lung, some scrapes and bruises, questionable internal bleeding. She was conscious and stable.

"The powers that be inferred that she was priority. I disagreed and ordered the Evanson girl to the *OR*." He swallowed and ran his hands through his hair. "There was nothing I could do to save her. She died in surgery two hours later.

"I quit my position at the hospital that night, went home, and informed Charlotte that I had no intention of ever picking up a scalpel again, or working for that hospital. I told her we were moving here where I would do General Practice work and devote my time to the clinic and to Rachel. Charlotte told me to go to hell, packed her suitcases, and drove off in the night.

"A week later she was broadsided by a train—or rather, she and her companion were broadsided by a train as they departed the Harbor Motel. Her companion was a colleague of mine at the hospital—the head of pathology, whom I lunched with frequently and occasionally played racquet ball. He was married with three kids, and had been screwing my wife for two years. You know what they say . . . the spouses are always the last to know.

"Three months later I was sued by the Woodwords for malpractice, citing my decision to perform surgery on the Evanson girl. They called it a blatant act of reckless defiance, poor judgment, and abandonment of my sacred oath as a physician. They said it resulted in needless distress and an extended hospital confinement due to the fact that their daughter was attended by a physician who was less skilled than I . . . I won the case, after a three-year battle."

At last, he turned back to Virginia, and his face looked ravaged. "Rachel is all I've got, Virginia. She's my sanity. My grip on reality. There've been times over the last years that I would have gladly put a gun in my mouth if it hadn't been for her. Call me overprotective or a tyrant about her well-being, but, as a doctor, I've seen more than my share of head injuries due to riding accidents."

"There's a risk in everything we do, Neil . . . riding a bike, driving a car, walking across a busy street. How many injuries have you seen due to football or skateboarding?"

"You can continue to defend the sport after what happened to your own father?" His tone was disbelieving if not outright belligerent.

"Yes," she replied calmly. "I can." She walked to him, then stopped several feet from him; her knees were shaking again, and her palms were moist. Focusing on something other than the memory of his embrace got more difficult the nearer she was to him. Best to stand away—far away. Focus on the business at hand and not on the core of heat doing a slow somersault somewhere in her nether region.

"There's a show at Mystic in less than two weeks. Rachel will need to ride several times before then—come to my place and watch her. If you're not comfortable with her abilities after that, I won't pursue it."

He raised one eyebrow.

"I promise," she stressed, regarding his lips.

"Is that what I have to do to see you on a regular basis?" he asked softly.

A reluctant smile teased her mouth. Tilting her head, she regarded him from behind her lowered lashes, and the realization occurred to her that she was flagrantly flirting with the doctor—her student's father, the man she had despised since the moment he'd slapped a NOTRESPASSING sign on what once had been her own paradise on earth. God, what a difference a few days—and a kiss—made.

"Yes," she finally replied in a silken voice. "I suppose it is."

"That's blackmail, Ms. Valemere."

"Whatever it takes, Dr. Ellison."

Virginia down-shifted the truck into second gear and sped up the drive, spitting gravel and dust behind her. Lights blazed in the tiny house, as did the red and green tree lights twinkling in the window.

Her brother's car sat beneath the twisted live oak near the front porch. Great! She'd have someone to confide in. She'd break open the new bottle of Blackberry Royal on the seat beside her and confess that she might, just possibly, have fallen in love tonight. Imagine that. She'd returned to Renaissance with one motive in mind . . . helping Rachel. She'd accomplished that—Neil had agreed to give Virginia and Rachel the next two weeks to convince him that Rachel was a natural at riding—but she'd come away feeling like a giddy teenager who'd been kissed for the very first time.

Oh, but *what* a kiss. The memory of it still gave her butterflies.

"I'm home!" she called as she entered the kitchen. As usual, Jeff had abandoned his dinner dishes on the table and in the sink, but tonight she didn't care. Life was good—for a change. For the first time in years there was a light at the end of the tunnel and it *wasn't* a freight train.

"What an unbelievable night. This calls for a double shot of Royal with a splurge of lemon—you'll have one, too, of course. This is a night to celebrate. I met the most incredible man, Jeff. Well, actually we had already met—you're not going to believe this in a million years."

Jeff was sitting in what once had been their father's favorite recliner, his gaze fixed on the blank television screen. He barely appeared to notice as Virginia sat down on the sofa across from him and offered him a glass of iced Royal. Her mood sank like a stone in water.

"Something's happened," she said, her chest constricting with dread. "Dad—"

"Is fine now. He's asleep. We had a rough few hours, though. The pain in his head has become unbearable. I wanted to take him in but he wouldn't have it. Says if it's his time to go he'll do it in his own bed in his own way."

He reached for a stack of papers and magazines on the floor near his feet, then handed them to Virginia. "I've been collecting articles on the surgeon I was telling you about. There's no doubt in my mind, GiGi. If ever there was a surgeon who could attempt this sort of delicate operation with any hope of success, Dr. Neil Ellison is the man."

Virginia put aside the wine and stared down at the collection of articles in her lap.

Jeff said, "He's a goddamn genius. The best in this country. And he's on staff at my hospital. Once you've read those articles you'll be convinced—"

"I don't need to read the articles." She put them aside and sank back into the sofa. Raising her eyes to her brother, she said, "I just finished having dinner with Dr. Ellison. He's Rachel's father."

For a moment, Jeff's face went blank with confusion. Then, like someone rousing from unconsciousness, he slowly sat forward, his hands fiercely gripping the chair arms. "Jesus. He's 'the car?' "

"The menace on a motorcycle. The middle-aged hippie. Mad Max at Thunderdome. The bastard who bought our father's farm for a song and dance. The mystery man I've loathed for years for no particular reason other than that he existed. He kissed me tonight and I melted into a puddle at his feet."

Jeff left his chair and dropped onto the sofa beside her. "This is incredible. The guy's crazy about you. He'd do anything for—"

"Not *that*."

"I'll talk to him."

"It won't do you any good." She left the sofa and walked to the tree with its meager sprinkling of ornaments, lights, and tinsel. "He hasn't picked up a scalpel in years. He wants nothing to do with it any longer. Besides, where do you propose we get the money for a specialist such as Ellison? Not to mention the hospital expenses. We're talking tens of thousands of dollars, Jeff, on top of what we already owe."

"I'll tell you where we'll get the money." Jeff left the room then returned with a paper which he held up in front of Virginia's face. "I took a call this afternoon from Pam Locke of Equine Management out of Woodenville, Washington. Seems she has several parties interested in that stallion of yours—Lindale. When I questioned her about what she thought the horse could be valued at, she said minimum one hundred and fifty thousand—maybe more if you took him to auction. Seems he's got one helluva pedigree."

Virginia took the paper from him and turned away. Jeff moved up behind her. In a gentler voice, he said, "I know how hard you've been working to keep Dad's business afloat, but it's over, Sis. It's never going to be what it used to be any more than Dad will ever be what he once was. As a physician—not as your brother—I have to say that if something's not done soon for our father he's going to die. The chances of his surviving that surgery may be slim, but not nearly as meager as his going on the way he is now."

"Have you spoken to Dad about it?"

"I intend to tomorrow, when he's up to it."

At half-past two in the morning, Virginia put aside the last article concerning Dr. Neil Ellison. No doubt about it, he was highly regarded in the medical profession, and that was putting it mildly. His techniques were lauded in every medical school across the country. He had even been awarded the Annual Prize by the American Society of Neurologic Surgeons. Virginia sat up in bed, massaged her throbbing temples, and sighed wearily.

Sometime during the last hours a front had moved in. The air felt frigid. Condensation had formed on the windowpanes and wind whipped the trees outside in intermittent bursts. Virginia reached for her terry robe draped over the foot of her bed, tiptoed from her room and down the hallway, and stopped at her father's closed bedroom door. The silvery white light of the television spilled from beneath the door, as did the muted volume of a classic oldie. Nudging open the door, she peered inside.

Her father lay propped up on pillows. She couldn't tell immediately if he was awake, or if, as usual, he had drifted off while watching Letterman or reruns of *I Love Lucy* and *Bewitched*—he'd always had a thing for Elizabeth Montgomery.

His blanket had slid from the bed. Virginia swept it up and carefully spread it over his legs, then tucked it around his chest. He appeared to be asleep. Taking the remote control from his relaxed hand, she was about to turn the television off when he said, "Don't you dare. *I Dream of Jeannie* is on next."

She smiled. "Heaven forbid that you miss another incredible episode of Jeannie."

"I keep hoping I'll catch a glimpse of Barbara Eden's belly button."

"No chance, Pop. Women were forbidden to have belly buttons in the 60's."

He chuckled and caught her hand. "What the devil are you doing up at this hour, little girl?"

"Just catching up on my reading."

"That reading wouldn't happen to have something to do with one Dr. Ellison, would it?"

"Jeff's talked to you already."

He nodded and squeezed her hand. "Sit down and listen to me."

Virginia sat down beside him.

"I won't beat around the bush," he said. "I want the surgery. I want this Ellison to do it."

"Pop, he wants nothing to do with this sort of responsibility any longer."

"So you'll convince him."

Virginia looked away. "I assume Jeff's told you about Neil and me as well."

"Your brother seems to think Ellison is quite fond of you."

"I've only known him for a few days."

"What difference does that make? I knew your mother two weeks before we got married."

"And look how that ended up."

"Not so bad. I got two beautiful children out of the relationship before we decided that what we each wanted out of life was too damned dissimilar. We were still friends up until the day she was killed. I've never loved another woman like I loved her . . . and continue to love her. I've no doubt that had she been alive and still with me during the rough times in the business I might have weathered the storm a bit more successfully. She was a strong, determined woman. You're a great deal like her, GiGi. And for that I thank God every day of my life."

He closed his eyes briefly. His features became weary, the hold on her hand a bit weaker. "I can't continue like this, sweetie, floating in and out of consciousness, so medicated to obliterate this pain in my head that I become mindless. You think I like spending my days watching reruns of *Press Your Luck* and *Gilligan's Island?* Do you think I'm proud of my behavior toward you and Jeff? I'm not a man—I'm a flipping piece of cheese."

"Don't say that."

"You're not a kid any longer, Virginia. It's time to get on with your life. You can't do that when you're struggling every day to bring in enough to meet my medical expenses—much less to pay Baxter's grocery bill. You can't even go out on a proper date without worrying about your old man back at home who might decide on that particular night to peg out."

"You always had a way with words, Pop." She smiled.

"Damn right. I had a way with horses and women, too." He turned off the television, casting the room into near darkness—the only illumination coming from a nightlight near the headboard. "I've instructed your brother to speak with Ellison tomorrow," he said.

"If that's what you want, Pop."

"That's what I want."

Six

Jeff paced the corridor, occasionally glancing at his watch, then into an office where a middle-aged woman with graying hair sat behind a desk typing data into a computer. He'd asked his supervisor at the hospital for a half-hour break to see Dr. Ellison. The half-hour wait had dragged on to forty-five minutes, then an hour, and he'd yet to get in to see him.

The receptionist peered up at Jeff from behind her bifocals as he stopped once again at her desk. "I'm sorry, Dr. Valemere. Dr. Ellison is still tied up in a meeting. If you'd care to leave your name and number—"

"I've tried that already. He hasn't returned my calls."

"Dr. Ellison is a very busy man."

"Tell me about it." He glanced at his watch again. "Aren't we all?"

In that moment Ellison's office door opened. A group of gray-haired, suited men emerged, their faces somber. Some carried briefcases, others held stacks of files and X-rays.

"Stubborn son of a bitch," one of them murmured.

Another said, "Can you believe that guy? What a damn waste of talent."

"Damn waste of the hospital's money, if you ask me. There are a dozen other surgeons in this country who would give their right nut to hold Ellison's position at this hospital."

"Yeah, the problem is, they're *not* Ellison."

"So who the hell is? If any of us were, we sure as the devil wouldn't be in that office begging favors, would we?"

"I'd like to hold him down and cut that goddamn hair."

"Careful. He might run you over with his motorcycle."

They all laughed and filed out of the office.

The intercom buzzed. Ellison's deep, perturbed voice crackled over the machine. "Hey, Molly, are those donkeys' rear ends gone yet?"

Molly smiled before catching herself, then she punched a button and replied, "Yep. They've gone to purchase a rope to hang you, I think."

"Then I'm outta here for lunch before they get back."

Molly glanced up at Jeff. "Ah, Dr. Ellison, I should remind you that someone has been here waiting to see you for the last hour."

Silence.

"I don't think he intends to leave until he's spoken with you," she added.

Silence.

"It's a Resident, Doctor. His name is—"

"He knows who the hell I am," Jeff interrupted, and made for the closed door despite Molly's protests.

Neil looked up as Jeff burst in. Punching the intercom button, he said, "Make me a reservation at Atlantic Cafe, Molly. This shouldn't take long."

"Whatever you say, Doc."

Reaching for a bottle of aspirin, Neil relaxed into his chair. "This better be important, Dr. Valemere. I've just spent two hours arguing with a lot of vultures who would like nothing more than to pick out my eyes with a dull butterknife—and do you know why?" He poured two aspirin into his hand, then a third for good measure. "Because I refuse to operate. You see, when I agreed to hang out my shingle at this hospital, it was with the understanding that, while agreeable to consultation regarding certain of my colleagues' patients, I would not, under any circumstances, go into another OR."

"Then what the hell are you doing here?" Jeff said.

"Because this hospital pays me a hell of a lot to be here. Because my name looks good on their letterhead. Because my name on their letterhead makes them a great deal of money."

"That stinks."

"Welcome to the world of medicine, as in *big business*. If you remember anything, my aspiring and starry-eyed young doctor, remember that this particular hospital, and ninety-nine percent of them across this country, are not charitable institutions. If they were . . ." He popped the aspirin into his mouth and swallowed them dry. "Then these grotesque-tasting little bastards wouldn't cost ten dollars a pop."

"If you hate it so much then why do you continue it?"

"I don't hate the practice of medicine. I hate the business of medicine." Dropping the aspirin bottle into a desk drawer, Neil regarded Jeff with an intensity that made him frown. Finally, he said, "You look like your sister. How is she, anyway?"

"I didn't come here to talk about GiGi, but as long as you've brought it up . . . not great. She expected you to call. You were supposed to drop by to watch your daughter ride. You haven't done either. Considering I've left you messages for the last week, to which you haven't responded, I have to assume your sudden disappearing act is due to your avoidance of me."

"Maybe you assume too much, Dr. Valemere."

"Yeah? Then why the hell haven't you returned my phone calls?"

Neil stood and moved across the room to a triple-tiered set of oaken file cases. "I don't have time for chitchat."

"Chitchat?" Jeff laughed disbelievingly. "My father's life is hanging in the balance and you call that chitchat?"

Neil yanked open a drawer and fingered through the files.

"What the hell kind of doctor are you?" Jeff demanded in a raised voice. "What the hell kind of human being are you, for that matter? Do you think you can just play God with people's lives and dreams?"

Slamming the drawer closed, Neil slowly turned. "Playing

God is exactly what I'm *not* doing," he replied through his teeth, then held up a file labeled with his father's name. "Even before your first attempt to contact me, I acquired your father's medical records—everything from the day he was first brought in three years ago to his last visit six weeks ago."

Neil opened the massive file, withdrew the most recent collection of X-rays and, one by one, snapped them onto the lit viewbox behind his desk. The eerie outline of Dick Valemere's skull and brain shimmered before them.

"Take a good look, Valemere. Even if I did the surgery, I'm sorry to say your father's chances of surviving are one in a hundred."

"His chances with another doctor are one in a thousand, and his chances without surgery are zero."

Neil flipped off the light and turned away.

"So that's it? You can just turn off a man's life and walk away as if it were nothing more than a negative on glass? Christ almighty, Ellison, you're cold. I hope to hell I haven't turned into a zombie like you by the time I'm your age."

Opening his office door, Neil looked at Jeff and said simply, "So do I, Dr. Valemere."

Lindale lowered his head as Rachel brushed his forelock, then planted a kiss on his nose. The horse nickered and nudged her, making her laugh. "You sweet-talker. I know what you want—another molasses cookie." Digging into her pocket, Rachel produced a horse treat, which she fed to the stallion. Lindale wagged his dished head up and down in appreciation, then nudged Rachel again.

Watching from the adjacent grooming stall, tightening the girth on Equator's saddle, Virginia shook her head. "You're spoiling him rotten, Rach."

"He deserves to be spoiled. A horse as incredible as Lindale should be pampered like a king."

"Absolutely." Virginia slipped Equator a cookie, then walked to the closed barn door to check the weather conditions. The temperature over the last few days had continued to plummet. Rain had threatened all day. Virginia and Rachel had prayed the inclement weather would hold off another two days so it wouldn't interfere with the Mystic show tomorrow.

Virginia opened the door and stopped abruptly.

Neil stood at the threshold, hands shoved in his coat pockets, his woolly coat collar turned up around his ears.

"What do you know," she said dryly and loudly enough for Rachel to hear. "Look what the Italian sports car has dragged in."

"Hello to you, too, Virginia." His eyes narrowed.

"Dad! You came!" Rachel flung herself on her parent and danced up and down. "You're just in time to see my lesson."

He smiled thinly. "I can't wait."

"I'm going to prove to you that you haven't got a thing to worry about."

"Promise?"

"On a stack of Bibles this high." She waved one hand above her head, then turned to Virginia and dragged her down to whisper in her ear, "Take him out to the arena. I want to enter at the trot like I'll do at the show."

"Showoff," Virginia whispered back.

Rachel dashed back into the barn. Virginia turned back to Neil, saying nothing, just walking past him toward the arena.

"You look cold," he said behind her.

"It's thirty-eight degrees."

"That's not what I meant."

"Don't take it personally, Dr. Ellison. It's just bad business to get too involved with clients. When friendship walks in the door, good business sense walks out the back."

"Are we talking about me or you?"

"Both."

He moved up beside her, his arm brushing hers. She moved away, slightly, and focused on the hazy mist slowly swallowing up the surrounding hills and trees and settling over the arena.

"Are you angry with me for not calling, not coming, or

for virtually tossing your brother out of my office on his ear?" He touched her cheek; she turned away. "I've missed you," he said.

"You don't know me well enough to miss me."

"Are you saying you haven't had the desire to see me the last two weeks?"

"I don't have the time to dwell on what might have been. I have a business to run. Which reminds me—I'll need money up front for the show tomorrow. There are stall and drug fees. I'll bill you later for the class fees since we haven't decided yet just how many classes we'll do. You *do* intend to be there, don't you?"

"I said I would."

"You say a great many things, Dr. Ellison."

There came a noise from the barn. Rachel exited the building, her horse prancing high as they trotted through the arena gates. Only it wasn't Equator that Rachel was riding. It was Lindale—blowing, snorting, hooves clashing upon the gravel path, nostrils elongated and red as embers.

"Rachel!" Virginia cried, and scrambled up the arena fence. "Get off of that horse this instant!"

"He's incredible!" she called, her little body rising and falling at the post trot, her hands easily manipulating the double reins as they made the first bend in the arena.

"Jesus Christ!" Neil leapt up on the fence beside Virginia. "What the hell do you think you're doing allowing her to ride that stallion?"

"I haven't 'allowed' any such thing."

The stallion made the second bend of the arena. His knees breaking level, his neck arched at the poll, he thundered toward Virginia and Neil, his breath a vaporous mist in the cold.

"Rachel!" Neil yelled. "Get off that damned—"

"Hush," Virginia snapped, then crawled up another rung of the fence, her breath caught somewhere in her chest as Rachel and Lindale flashed by. "Check him back just a little," she called. "Remember, left, right, left with your hands—not much—use your little fingers. Yes! Now drive him into it with your legs. Rock him back, Rachel, and let him go!"

Like a well-tuned machine, Lindale slightly lowered his back end, lifting his front. His legs pumped up and out, hooves flashing, muscles straining and rippling as the animal park trotted around the ring.

"My God, they're incredible together." Virginia shook her head. "Do you know how rare it is to find a stallion as levelheaded as Lindale, Dr. Ellison? Look at him—he's doing everything she asks, and yet doing it as if he were carrying china on his back." Turning to Neil, she regarded his profile while he watched his daughter. "You should be very proud, Neil. Rachel is one of the most gifted young riders I've ever come across."

"She makes it look easy."

"The sign of a good rider, not to mention a good horse."

"I suppose that says something for the trainer and coach."

Cupping her hands around her mouth, Virginia yelled, "Bring him down to a walk and cool him out. It's beginning to rain. We don't need either of you getting chilled!" Relaxing, she stepped away from the fence and up against Neil. His arms closed around her before she could move away.

"Be still and be quiet," he said in her ear. "I want to know that I have your undivided attention. I don't care how long we've known one another, I've missed you a lot the last week because I enjoy your company. I like the flash of your eyes and the blush on your cheeks when you're aggravated—like now. You don't give a damn about impressions—you're not impressed by my money or my occupation. You look damn good in a pair of jeans and you're intelligent. Your idea of a good time is to relax with a bottle of Blackberry Royal instead of Dom Perignon. You'd rather muck out a stall than spend an evening at the country club. You have hay in your hair and yet smell like French perfume.

"My daughter is crazy about you. So is her grandfather. So am I. I came to that conclusion last night when I was forced to take a sedative for the third night in a row because all I could think about was the taste of your lips when I kissed you and the sparkle in your eyes as you stood in that big arena swimming in the memories of your childhood."

"Please, Neil. I . . . I don't want to hear this."

"Why? What the hell have I done to turn you so against this relationship?"

At last, she pulled away, backing into the arena wall. Her chin began to quiver. Her throat became tight. "Damn you. Don't make this any harder than it has to be. You're Rachel's father—"

"So it's best to keep our relationship strictly business? I don't buy it, sweetheart, not after the way you responded when I kissed you."

"Don't remind me." She tried to push by him.

He grabbed her arm. "If I'm going to be dumped like a sack of horse dung, Ms. Valemere, I'd like a feasible explanation."

"I don't have time for this. My father needs his dinner and I have a hundred things to do to get ready for the show tomorrow."

"Is this tantrum about your father?" he demanded. "Are you pissed because I refuse to take his case?"

She attempted to twist away.

"Answer me, dammit." He shook her.

"Yes!" she shouted. "Yes, because after three horrifying years of searching for, waiting for, the right surgeon to come along, he did and he's so damned caught up in his own self-pity he's wasting his God-given talent, not to mention the lives of desperately ill patients."

"Christ." He ran one hand through his hair and shook his head. "You sound like my ex-wife."

"This has nothing to do with money. But while we're talking about money, has your decision got anything to do with the fact that you believe we can't pay your fee?"

He blinked and laughed disbelievingly. "You can ask that after everything I've told you?"

Feeling her cheeks turn hotter, she said, "Because if it is, you can relax. We'll have the money, Dr. Ellison. I'm selling Lindale. He's going to auction and if Pamela with Equine

Management is right, we'll come away with more than enough to meet our financial responsibilities."

There came a soft gasp. Virginia and Neil turned to discover Rachel.

Still astride Lindale, Rachel fixed Virginia with a stunned look, her eyes filling with tears. "You're selling Lindale? But you can't. GiGi, you always swore he wasn't for sale for any price. This horse is your future. He's my dream. You can't sell him. You can't!"

Rachel dug her heels into the stallion's flanks; as the horse lunged forward, she drove him out through the arena gates and toward the distant rolling hills.

"Rachel!" Neil yelled after her.

Virginia grabbed his arm and said, "Get in my truck. Quickly!"

The keys were in the ignition. Virginia slammed the gearshift into first even before Neil managed to scramble into the passenger side and close the door. Directing the truck through the open paddock gates, Virginia was forced to turn on the wipers to clear away the freezing mist on the windshield.

She slammed on her brakes as they topped a hillock. A few yards away, she saw Lindale standing calmly amid a patch of brown grass, head down as he grazed. Rachel, thank God, was still on his back.

Neil was the first out of the truck. His long legs carried him effortlessly over several fallen tree trunks and clumps of brush. Virginia followed, the fear that had clamped around her chest gradually lifting.

Rachel wiped the tears from her cheeks and before her father could utter a word, said, "Don't waste your breath. I know I was stupid. I could have been hurt. But since the minute I first saw Lindale, I always dreamt that someday he would be mine. Now he's leaving and I won't ever see him again."

Virginia laid her hand on Lin's warm neck and gazed up through the mist at Rachel. "There's a difference between fantasies and dreams, Rach. At some point in our lives we have to decide for ourselves what those are, and which are reasonably obtainable. No matter how old we get, we all want to believe there's really a Santa Claus—some magical little fairy who'll make everything good and right in our lives without our having to sacrifice. But life's not that way. There's no big bag of miracles someone can just open and disperse at a whim."

Virginia smiled, though not bravely. "I always believed Lindale came along for a special purpose. I truly believed that purpose was to breathe life into Renaissance. Now I know it was to help my father."

Rachel sniffed, then wiped her frosty-red nose with the back of one hand. Neil raised his arms to her, and with a little hiccough, Rachel slid from Lindale's back down into her father's arms. Father and daughter stood in the swirling, freezing mist, clinging to one another fiercely.

Gathering Lin's reins, Virginia said to Neil, "Take her back to the house. Get Rachel out of those clothes. There's a terry robe hanging on the back of the bathroom door. There's some cocoa in a canister by the stove. While you're heating the water I'll bed down Lindale."

"Right," he replied softly, still gripping his daughter tight. Then, with Rachel's arms wrapped around his neck and her legs around his hips, he returned to the truck, leaving Virginia to watch them drive off into the gray December twilight.

Seven

It was a scene straight off a Norman Rockwell painting. Rachel, wrapped snugly in Virginia's terry bathrobe, her dark hair a riot of curls around her face, stood near the towering Christmas tree, tinsel dripping from her head, ears, and shoulders. Neil had started a fire in the infrequently used fireplace and sat on the hearth, elbows on his knees, his shoes removed, allowing his feet to warm and dry. Her father, as usual, sat in his wheelchair, but instead of clutching the television remote, he carefully gripped a cup of eggnog in his good hand.

Bing Crosby crooned "White Christmas" in the background.

"Seems the party started without me," Virginia declared and kicked off her rubber muck boots without taking her gaze off her father. His cheeks were flushed with color; he was smiling. "Pop." She moved to his chair and stooped to look at his eyes. "Are you soused? Have you spiked your nog again? You know what the doctor said—no smoking, no liquor—"

"No sex. No nothing. I ought to be a confounded monk," he announced, then gulped his nog again and licked his lips.

Her eyebrows went up and she slowly stood, glancing toward the kitchen. "What's that smell?"

"Cookies." Rachel flung another handful of tinsel over the star on the top of the tree. "I found a roll of refrigerated sugar cookie dough while I was raiding the fridge for the eggnog. I figured, what's a house without Christmas cookies baking in the oven?"

Stretching out his legs and wiggling his socked toes, Neil raised a steaming cup toward Virginia and grinned. "Hot Blackberry Royal. I discovered that if you heat it and add a touch of lemon juice it tastes almost like grape punch."

"You all look ridiculous," she declared, on the verge of laughing.

Partially turning his chair, Dick said, "Aw, climb off that high horse, GiGi, and have a drink. You look like hell."

Narrowing her eyes and running her hands self-consciously over her damp hair, Virginia wandered toward the fireplace and reached for Neil's offered drink. She glared. He grinned and shrugged one shoulder.

"Speaking of horses," her father said, "how are ours?"

"I can't believe what I'm hearing. Pop, you haven't asked about the horses in three years."

"You're usually too tired in the evenings or too damn glum. How's that mare? She's due to foal in a few weeks, isn't she?"

"Fameous?" She sipped her Royal, her gaze dropping to Neil's feet. He wore woolly gray socks embroidered with tiny red Santas. There was a hole working its way onto the little toe of his right foot. "She's fine, I suppose," she said thoughtfully, her mind on Neil Ellison's feet, then drifting for what seemed to be the millionth time to the memory of his kiss . . . and his earlier confession of missing her. "I'm a bit concerned because she's bagged up so soon. I may call Dr. Starr tomorrow, just to be on the safe side. We simply can't take any chances where that foal is concerned."

Dick attempted to shift in his chair. His face contorted briefly in discomfort; one side of his mouth appeared to twist, then droop. His right eye began to twitch ever so slightly. As Virginia made a move to assist him, he waved her away.

"Quit fretting, Ginny Lea. I'll be fine in a minute or two."

"You haven't called me Ginny Lea since I was a child," she said softly.

"You'll always be my little girl." He caught her arm with his weak and trembling hand. Turning to Rachel, he declared, "I believe I smell cookies burning."

"Oh!" Rachel tore off toward the kitchen, Virginia's robe flouncing around her ankles.

Dick chuckled. "There's nothing like a child's laughter to lift a house out of the doldrums, eh, Doc?"

Neil drank his Royal and agreed with a smile.

"I'd always looked forward to bouncing a few grand-babies on my knee," Dick went on. "Ginny Lea was always good with kids—had more patience and common sense by the time she was twenty than most women do by the time they reach my age. So tell me, Doc. You plan on having any more?"

"I really haven't given it much thought." Neil glanced at Virginia. That tomcat look was back in the curl of his lips and the lazy lowering of his lashes over his eyes. A heat sluiced through her and she wondered if it were the wine, the shock of finding her father in such a garrulous mood, or the heart-stopping flirtation twinkling in Dr. Neil Ellison's eyes that made her feel the slightest bit tipsy.

"So how about it, Ginny Lea?" came her father's voice through her fog.

Dragging her gaze from Neil's, she turned to her father. "What?"

"I was just saying to Doc that he and Rachel should stay for dinner. I imagine that if you set your mind to it you could scrape up enough for two more."

"We're having warmed-over pot roast." Tossing back her head, she quaffed the last of her wine and turned for the kitchen. "I'm certain Dr. Ellison already has plans for dinner."

"On the contrary," Neil replied. "Dr. Ellison hasn't got a damn thing to do for dinner. He and his daughter would like nothing better than to join you for leftover pot roast."

Virginia closed the double louvered doors, obliterating the sight of Neil sitting on the hearth in his stocking feet schmoozing with her father. Pressing her head against the door, she muttered, "What the hell does he think he's doing?"

"He likes you," came Rachel's voice behind her, causing Virginia to jump and turn. Rachel smiled and offered up a plate of hot cookies. "Go on. Take one. You need it. Take two. You're too thin."

She took two.

"He won't stop talking about you, you know. Always asking how you are when I get home from my riding lessons. He's like a little kid—probing me about whether or not you mentioned him."

"He does?" She nibbled as the cookie sprinkled her lips with fine granules of powdered sugar.

"I've never seen him like this—not even with my mom. Then again, he wasn't very happy with my mom."

"I'm sorry."

"So am I." Nudging the door open with one shoulder, allowing Brenda Lee's "Jingle Bell Rock" to flow into the room, Rachel regarded Virginia with a half-smile that looked uncannily like her father's. "If this is the kind of hell grown-ups go through as they're falling in love, I'm not so sure I want to do it."

"Is that what we're doing, Rachel? Falling in love?"

For a brief moment the child's features went melancholy and her eyes clouded over, then her face was radiant again and her blue eyes—so much like her father's—flashed with impishness. "If Santa won't deliver Lindale into my Christmas stocking maybe he'll make up for it and bring you." With that, she bounded from the room, allowing the door to swing closed behind her.

There was plenty of leftover pot roast, roasted potatoes, and carrots. Virginia dumped it all in a Dutch oven, turned on the stove, and shoved the pan of food inside. Then she left the house, hugging herself against the cold as she ran to the barn, flipping on the dim lights that spilled a yellow tinge over the barn aisle and stalls.

She blanketed each of the horses.

Keep busy, she thought, then she wouldn't have to think

about what Rachel had said. Children! They could say the darnedest things. Obviously, Rachel had allowed her vivid imagination to run away with her. Imagine Rachel believing that her father was actually falling in love with her. The idea was absurd. Just as ridiculous as the idea of her falling in love with him.

Neil Ellison was a selfish, self-centered genius egomaniac who, though he would deny it until his dying breath, played God with people's lives.

How dare he have the audacity to come into her home and face her father after so coldly refusing to help him?

How dare she experience the tiniest twinge of thrill when she looked into his eyes? How dare she, even for a fraction of a second, contemplate the possibility of their falling in love after he had virtually sentenced her father to die?

"You're going to wear a hole in that saddle if you're not careful."

Not only had he invaded her life and her house . . . now he was here, in her oasis, her private world where all her problems, no matter how monumental, became insignificant.

Not bothering to look up, she rubbed the creamy leather conditioner all the harder into the saddle. "I've a show to prepare for. One doesn't enter the ring without being properly turned out."

"Your pot roast burned."

Her head came up.

"Not to worry." He moved toward her, his attention drawn to the array of tack hanging from nails on the walls. "I managed to scrape enough off the bottom of the pot to feed your dad and Rachel. Personally, after three cups of Blackberry Royal I'm not particularly in the mood for so wholesome a fare."

"There's bologna in the fridge. Help yourself. You've already made yourself at home."

He stood in silence, watching as she rubbed the leather furiously with an oily cloth. "Put down the saddle, Virginia," he demanded in a silky voice.

"Why?" Flipping the lightweight English saddle over in her lap, she proceeded to oil beneath the knee flaps.

"I want your undivided attention."

Looking up at last, her shoulders tense and her teeth clenched, she said, "How can you sit in that room with my father after you've so flagrantly shirked your responsibility as a physician?"

"He's not my responsibility unless I make him my responsibility."

"Which obviously you have no intention of doing."

Jumping up from her stool, slinging the saddle onto the aluminum caddy, she walked to her office and flipped on the light. Neil followed, then closed the door behind him.

Virginia moved across the room to a refrigerator, yanked it open, and stared inside at the half-eaten goose liver sandwich on a paper plate, a jar of bread-and-butter pickles, and a grape soda. There was a brown bottle of Regumate, paste wormers, and salves, along with a box of baking soda.

Neil turned off the light.

Standing in a pool of illumination pouring from the fridge, Virginia looked around. "If you dare get fresh I'll slap your face," she told him pointedly.

He grinned. "You sound like one of those hysterical, men-hating women in romance novels."

"I happen to like romance novels, Dr. Ellison."

"So you like the idea of being swept off your feet by some swaggering, dominating cad."

She backed away. "That would depend on the cad, of course."

"Take me, for instance."

"You're a cad, all right. I'm just not certain you're hero material."

A grin curled one end of his mouth. One eyebrow drew up. Profiled by the shimmery white light from the fridge, he looked like some deity of Greek mythology. "Now that, Ms. Valemere, is a challenge if I ever heard one."

Her eyes widened. "That's not what I intended—"

"Isn't it?" Wrapping one hand around the nape of her

neck, his fingertips curling roughly into her skin, he pulled her close and lowered his face over hers. "You don't lie any better than you pretend to be angry, Ginny Lea."

He kissed her—not like before, not gently, but fiercely. Nothing tentative about this one. His mouth was hard and warm and wet, rousing sensations of pleasure that made her skin grow moist with heat. She was swimming, drowning, suffocating, yet she had no strength to stop it. She didn't want to. Leaning her body into his, she kissed him back, her tongue dancing with his, her body bold and supple, molding into his hard curves and inviting more—much more.

Sliding one arm around her waist, he spun her toward the couch in a move as lithe and graceful as if they were two dancers. The cushions were soft and draped with a cotton throw. She sank into them, sprawling into the pool of soft illumination from the refrigerator neither of them had bothered to close. His body was heavy on hers and insistent, his hands eager, searching, deftly unbuttoning her shirt and laying it open, exposing the lacy lavender French-cut bra that cupped her breasts into generous globes. His gaze swept them, and his eyes became inflamed.

Fighting for breath and reason, she angled her face away and groaned, "No, no. Please." Yet, when he opened his mouth and breathed his hot, moist breath upon her breast she made a sound in her throat that was neither guilt nor regret—and far from denial.

He unhooked her front-closure bra and slowly peeled it back with the tips of his fingers, then slid one thumb over the nub of her erect nipple before sliding his tongue over the tip—lips, hot as a flame, drawing it into his mouth with a slight but demanding tug. His teeth nipped her, grazed her, then feathered the sensitive tip rapidly, making her catch her breath and clutch him to her, wanting more—oh, God—needing more. When he drew away, rising on his knees to unsnap and unzip his jeans. The thought of further denial came and went fleetingly. She could only watch, mesmerized, as the blue denim rolled back to expose the dark line of hair running from his navel into his briefs where his swollen sex thrust against the frail cotton material with an eagerness and enormity that was shocking.

She curled her fingers into the waistband of his briefs and dragged them down.

He caught his breath. "I knew there was nothing shy about you, Ginny Lea. Not the way you look and walk, and ride those damn horses. You like having a stud between your legs."

Closing his hands around her arms, he raised her to her knees, opened her jeans and slid one hand into them while the other played with her breast, squeezing and releasing in rhythm with his fingers sliding in and out of the wet, warm, and aroused cleft between her legs.

Wrapping her arms around the back of his neck, burying her hands in his hair, she pushed him down, kicked away her jeans and the filmy bikini panties he had nudged down to her knees, and mounted him. He grabbed her buttocks and lifted his hips, impaling her, filling her, his sex like warm, pulsing iron inside her, and she swiveled her hips round and round, causing him to hiss through his teeth and whisper rough, coarse sex words that made heat waves of pure, unfettered thrill radiate through her.

The climax came in a rush of pleasure so intense she cried out and went rigid, her head thrown back, her nails digging into his chest with each rhythmic contraction of her body gloving his.

At last, totally drained of the ability to move, she sank onto him, so weak and replete that breathing seemed an incredible effort. Eternal moments passed before she finally managed to lift her head from his shoulder and look at him. His face and hair were damp with perspiration, despite the bracing coolness of the room. The tomcat grin was back, only now it was a picture of satiation.

"That, Ginny Lea, was one hell of a ride." Twisting a tendril of her hair around one of his fingers, he gently tugged her down so he could brush a kiss across her mouth. "Care to try it at the hand gallop?"

"I thought that *was* a hand gallop." She kissed him back.

"The canter, I think. My back end didn't come close to engaging like it should."

She laughed and tweaked his cheek, but when she began to roll away, he closed his arms around her again and held her hard against him. "Gin, I—"

The phone rang. The answering machine clicked on. Virginia's request for the caller to leave a message sounded eerily loud in the closed room, then came the response:

"Hi, Virginia, this is Pamela with Equine Management. I've made all the arrangements for the auction. The interested parties have been notified that I'll begin taking bids on Lindale tomorrow evening, December 23. There are five very interested clients who will be participating for sure: one overseas, another in California, one in Florida, and a couple in your area. So take a deep breath and relax. I have no doubt that we're going to get enough for Lin to go a long way toward paying for your father's surgery. Merry Christmas! Talk to you tomorrow night after the sale."

Virginia slid her legs off the sofa and sat up. As if rousing from sleep, she blinked and glanced at the open refrigerator, at the half-eaten sandwich, and the stream of light slicing through the dark and laying like a weightless blanket across her lap.

She reached for her jeans. "I must have been out of my mind."

Neil gently caught her hand.

She yanked it away. "Of course, there isn't going to be any surgery, is there, Dr. Ellison?"

"Gin—"

"Don't call me that." She dragged her pants up her legs, then fumbled with the closure on her bra. "I think I'll go bathe. I smell of a coward."

Neil jumped from the sofa and grabbed her arm. "Goddammit, will you listen to me? I've made arrangements for your father to have a new set of X-rays taken. I've set up a meeting with some of my colleagues to discuss his condition. If we all concur on the prognosis we'll discuss the best way to deal with it in terms of surgery."

She froze. Her heart beat in her ears. Staring up into his dark face she opened her mouth, but nothing came out.

"That's why I came here to see you," he confessed in a much wearier voice. "I wanted an opportunity to visit with your father, to see for myself what sort of mental and physical shape he's in . . . whether or not he could hold up to the operation psychologically as well as emotionally."

"And what did you discover?"

"That while he might grumble occasionally about wishing he had died three years ago, he wants like hell to live. Without that desire to go on, Virginia, not even God himself could get him through that surgery alive."

"And what else did you discover?"

"That since his last checkup his paralysis has gotten much worse. It's affecting his speech, his sight, and motor functions. In the course of our visit I counted five minor seizures—"

"Seizures?"

"The drawing down of his mouth, the curling of his hand, the rapid blinking of one eye. His right cheek ticked periodically. To put it bluntly, the pressure of the clot on his brain is causing a sort of short circuit. It's only a matter of time before the burnout."

She dropped heavily onto the edge of the desk and covered her face with her hands. Neil slid one arm around her shoulder and she laid her head against his chest. He rubbed her back and stroked her hair. Finally, she collected herself enough to ask, "When have you scheduled the tests?"

"I thought you might want to wait until after Christmas."

"And when will you do the surgery?"

A moment passed before he said, "I'm not doing the surgery, Virginia. That will be done by Dr. Richard Melgrave. He's one of the best in Texas."

Coming off the desk, shirking aside his arm, she shook her head. "No way. No way is my father going into that OR with anyone besides you."

Running one hand over his eyes, Neil backed away. "I'll agree to assist Dr. Melgrave—"

"I want *you,* Ellison. Only the best. Had I wanted to risk just any hacker opening his head I would have dragged out the Yellow Pages."

"I trust Melgrave implicitly."

"But *he's—not—you.*"

She left the office and stormed out into the night. The temperature had dropped drastically. The mist had become an icy film that covered her face by the time she reached the back porch. Snatching open the door, she came face-to-face with her brother. Jeff's jaw tensed and his hands clenched as he looked beyond her to Neil, who emerged through the dark, shoulders hunched against the cold, his long hair fast becoming damp.

"What the hell are you doing here, Ellison?"

"Freezing my ass off." Neil made a move to mount the steps. Jeff pushed past Virginia and skidded on the slick porch before grabbing a support.

"You son of a bitch, you've got some balls coming here. And you—" He focused on Virginia. "I thought you had better taste."

"Jeffrey!" came their father's voice from the kitchen. Dick wheeled his chair to the door; his frame was silhouetted against the light pouring over his shoulders. "Is that any way to speak to our guest? I thought I'd taught you better manners."

"Dad, this pitiful excuse for a man is—"

"I know who the devil he is. And I know what he's doing here."

"Oh?" Jeff crossed his arms and stared again at Neil. "Then why don't you enlighten me?"

"Aside from so slyly attempting to assess my condition . . . he's in love with your sister."

Virginia felt her cheeks go hot.

Jeff raised both eyebrows.

They both stared at their father as if he had suddenly leapt from his chair and tap danced across the floor.

Dick shook his head. "The pair of you are biting at the man like a couple of rabid jackals. Give him a break, for

God's sake, and think about what you're asking of him. He's damned if he does and damned if he doesn't. If he stands back and does nothing to help me and this messed up gourd of a head, Virginia will blame him the minute I drop dead as a mackerel. Not a promising prospect for a would-be love interest. If he agrees to operate and I die on the table, which, as I understand it, is the most likely scenario, then my darling daughter will never look at him again without recalling that I died under his care. Also not a promising prospect for a would-be love interest. I wouldn't blame the man if he turned his back on us all and walked away.

"He won't, however. Because whether he wants to face reality or not, he's a consummate professional, as dedicated to the science of saving lives as a priest is to saving souls. He's willing to assist Dr. Melgrave during the surgery and that's good enough for me."

"He's discussed this with you already?" Virginia asked.

"And why shouldn't he?" Her father's face became contrite. "For the last three years I've festered in this damn chair because I was told that if I so much as stubbed my toe my head would explode. I allowed the two of you to make me into a bodiless, mindless potato, wasting away my days in a kind of self-pitying stupor.

"Last night I lay in bed and contemplated blowing my brains out. And even though I've never been much of a religious man, I asked God to give me the strength to do it—else he'd better do something quick to give me some reason to keep hoping.

"Then this evening *he* walked through the door—Ellison. I knew who he was immediately. I recognized him from those journals you left by your bed, Ginny Lea. No offense to either of you kids, but I'm taking back control of my own destiny. If I choose to go under a knife wielded by Jack the Ripper himself, by God, I'll do it if it means I have the slightest chance of living a half-normal life again."

He rolled his chair away from the door. "Now, there's another cup of spiked eggnog in here with my name on it.

And I do believe I hear Gene Autry singing 'Rudolph, the Red Nose Reindeer.' I suggest the lot of you get in the house before you freeze to death."

Eight

"This is class forty eight: Hunt Seat, Walk-Trot-Cantor: Twelve and under championship. Our champion is . . . Equator AA. Owned by Dick and Virginia Valemere and ridden by Rachel Ellison. Equator is a five-time U.S. and Canadian Top Ten Champion by Bandos. Congratulations, Rachel and Virginia. Don't forget that championship neck ribbon and trophy as you leave the arena . . . as if you would."

Virginia smiled her thanks to the crowd of well-wishers huddled in their parkas and earmuffs at the exit gate. As Rachel, for the third time that day, made her victory lap around the ring, Virginia glanced across the crowd in the stands, then toward the parking lot outside. Overnight, the weather had turned from bad to worse. Sleet fell intermittently. The fog was as dense as gray cotton.

Thank God for enclosed arenas. She only hoped the ice would hold off until after the show.

"Way to go, Rachel!" The spectators cheered as Rachel and Equator rode through the gates.

Her face glowing, smiling ear to ear, Rachel gave Virginia a high-five, then wrapped her arms around Equator's neck. Virginia led the horse to his stall, where Locomotion remained cross-tied and saddled, ready for Rachel's Saddle Seat Championship class.

Rachel searched the long barn aisles as she removed her black velvet hunt cap. Her expression was pensive. "Dad's not here yet, is he?"

Virginia shook her head and led Equator into the grooming stall.

"He promised, GiGi. He swore he would come see me ride."

"I'm sure he's on his way, sweetie. Perhaps it's the weather. The Interstate between here and Dallas can become pretty treacherous when it's like this."

"If he doesn't hurry he'll miss me all together."

"While you loosen up Loco in the warmup pen, I'll give him a call."

"Try my house. If he doesn't answer there, try the car phone."

"I promise."

Donning a navy blue English derby, Rachel took charge of Locomotion and led him toward the warmup ring where another six horses were being tuned for the upcoming class. Watching her go, Virginia couldn't help but experience a flutter of her heartbeat. The girl's eyes, her smile, her hair were reminders of her father, and the passionate moments Virginia and Neil had shared the night before.

So where was he?

How would she manage to conceal the desire to touch him again? How did one successfully mask this absurd elation over the very real possibility that they were falling in love?

Falling?

Who was she kidding? She'd fallen already. Hard. She'd been kicked in the stomach once by a rambunctious colt and felt less winded. She'd gone through the motions all day of preparing horses to show, coaching Rachel from the sidelines, and talking with friends and prospective clients, all the while allowing her mind, and senses, to recall the scent of Neil Ellison's body, and the feel of it inside her own.

Virginia slid on her coat, tugged a knit cap down over her ears, and made for the outside phone booths.

As instructed, she called the Ellisons' residence first. The phone rang twice before the answering machine came on. There were sleighbells ringing, then a child's choir came on, singing "The Little Drummer Boy." Rachel's voice joined in. "Merry Christmas! Sorry we can't take your call—"

Virginia hung up. She blew on her numb fingertips, slid another quarter in the slot, then, reading from a piece of paper, punched in Neil's car phone number. "Come on, Neil," she muttered, clutching the receiver to her ear. "I'll never forgive you if you let Rachel down." Six rings later, the mechanized voice came on: "Your call cannot be completed at this time. The mobile customer you've called has turned the mobile unit off or has traveled beyond the service area. This is a recording."

"No joke, Sherlock." She slammed the phone down and stomped her feet to warm them. The loudspeaker announced the third call for class fifty, Country English Pleasure Championship, thirteen and under. It wasn't until the system crackled to silence that she heard her name being called.

Phyllis Aynsworthy, the club president, stood at the facility door, waving her arms.

Virginia shoved aside the booth door and stepped out.

"Phone call!" Phyllis shouted. "Your brother!"

Jeff?

No, not Jeff.

She must have misunderstood. Jeff wouldn't be calling her here unless . . .

Oh, God.

"There's an emergency!"

She ran toward the barn, her gaze fixed on her friend's face that was pinched with an obvious attempt to appear as normal as possible. Her tight smile and creased brow, however, gave her emotions away.

Panting, each word punctuated by puffs of air in the biting cold, Virginia grabbed Phyllis and shook her. "It's my father, isn't it? Something's happened—"

"Jeff's on the phone, GiGi. Hurry."

A strange, stilted silence greeted her as she entered the normally busy office. The cluster of men and women working the show all regarded her with blank expressions, their eyes not quite meeting hers.

He's dead. He's dead, was her only thought. *He's died and I wasn't there for him.*

Forcing her trembling fingers around the phone, she raised it to her ear. "J-Jeff? Is he—"

"Listen to me very carefully, GiGi. I'm at the hospital. Dad's going into surgery—"

"What happened?"

"He walked out to the barn—"

"He *what?*"

"I found him collapsed in one of the stalls. How long will it take you to get here?"

She tried to focus on the wall clock.

Four-thirty.

Dammit, she'd hit Dallas during rush hour.

No. No. It was Saturday.

Thank God.

Someone moved up behind her and put a comforting hand on her shoulder. "We'll make certain your horses are taken care of. We'll get Rachel home as well. Get going, GiGi, before this weather gets any worse."

"An hour," she said dryly into the phone. "Maybe longer, depending on the condition of the roads."

Another eternity of silence, then, "Then you'd better leave now, Sis."

She hated hospitals—the smell of them, the sterility of them, the sights and sounds of pain and fear and the heavy hush of dread that draped like silken webs from every wall. She'd heard once that hospitals were painted that sickly pale green because someone somewhere had decided the color was soothing to peoples' troubled minds and souls. How anyone could conceive that foam green would somehow alleviate the trauma of an emergency room was beyond her ability to understand.

There were beds lined up along the corridor; most were occupied. She saw an old woman who had slipped on ice and no doubt fractured a hip. A child lay squirming on another, his mother trying frantically to keep him still while a nurse applied a cold compress to the egg-sized swelling on his forehead.

The doors burst open behind her and a cluster of paramedics wheeled in a man strapped to a stretcher, his clothes peeled back exposing his big, white belly that had been laid open by a bullet. An attendant straddled the unconscious patient and pumped his bloody chest with his hands while another ran alongside with an IV, shouting orders to the nurses who scurried to attend.

Focusing on a bedpan on the floor, Virginia considered throwing up.

"GiGi!" Jeff elbowed his way through a crowd of hysterically babbling East Indians.

She almost collapsed.

Jeff caught her and hugged her fiercely. "Thank God, you made it all right."

"How's Dad?"

"Stabilized for the time being. He's scheduled for surgery in . . ." He checked his watch. "Half an hour."

A group of police emerged from an office, their walkie-talkies crackling with static and voices of dispatchers. Virginia shook her head and briefly closed her eyes. "I don't understand how you can stand here so calmly amid this bloody bedlam."

"Neither can I, sometimes," he replied gently.

Catching her hand, he led her down the hall and around a corner where it was quieter, then he ushered her toward a door. Her steps slowed. Jeff's face became somber as he hesitated, his hand closing more tightly around hers.

"He's conscious. That's a positive sign. There's a great many monitors, tubes, needles, and IV's. Just . . . don't expect too much."

She nodded and braced herself emotionally.

Jeff nudged open the door.

A doctor stood at her father's bedside, his back to the door. He was dressed in OR garb—again the nauseating green—and he held a clipboard of papers and spoke softly to a nurse at his side. At the sound of their entry, he looked around.

Their eyes met.

"Hi," Neil said gently.

She tried to smile. And move. She thought of flinging herself against him. When he held out his hand to her, she stared at it as if it were a life-preserver and grabbed it, allowing herself to sink into the comfort of his presence. Then she focused on her father.

She wanted to be strong for him. But she couldn't.

She tried not to cry, but she did, quietly and as controlled as possible.

There were tubes running from his mouth and nose, lines connecting him to a cardiograph and an oxymeter. A scattering of IV's stood around his bed like sentinels.

He opened his eyes.

"Hey, Pop."

"About time."

"You always said my middle name was Tardy." She glanced at the cardiogram; its line seemed horrifyingly weak.

"How . . . show?"

"Leave it to you to want to discuss business at a time like this."

"Rachel . . . ?"

"Three championships."

He winked and attempted to smile. His fingers opened and encircled hers. "Watch . . . that mare. Showing signs of premature . . ."

"Pop, don't worry. Fameous isn't due to foal for another week."

"Waxed . . . dripping colostrum. Call that woman vet— what's her name? The one with the nice butt . . ."

"Dr. Starr."

He grinned again and licked his lips. "Wouldn't mind sippin' a nog or two with her."

"You'll get your chance when you get home."

"Call her now . . . check that mare."

"If this were any other time I'd be thrilled that you're showing such interest in the business again. However, I think it best if you simply rest—"

"Beautiful, Ginny Lea. So proud of you. Such a . . . fighter. Sorry for being such a bastard the last few years. Forgive me?"

"Of course I forgive you, Pop. I never took it personally."

Jeff moved up beside her, as did several nurses, all dressed the same, their hair tucked up under mesh caps. They moved around the bed like an efficient squadron ready for war. "Time to go," Jeff whispered, his voice breaking slightly. Then he bent over his father and kissed his brow.

Virginia turned away, aware, suddenly, that Neil no longer held her. She ran into the corridor, searched the scattering of nurses and doctors, feeling desperate to find the one person who could assuage this overwhelming anxiety—this need for reassurance that her father would pull through.

But Neil was gone.

Although Jeff insisted that she take a sedative and lie down in a vacant hospital room, she lay in the dark and stared at the ceiling, her heart hammering in her ears, her nerves expanding with each noise outside the door. Repeatedly, she attempted to think of anything other than what was going on in the OR down the hall, but that was impossible. The three men she cared most for in life were there—fighting for life—her father's life, the outcome inevitably to change their futures for the better or, God forbid, the worse.

Why had she heard nothing from Jeff? Although not participating in the actual surgery, he had been allowed to sit in the balcony to view the proceedings. He'd promised to keep her abreast of the progress, yet hours had passed and she'd heard nothing.

Her head groggy from the sedative, she left the room and wandered down the hall to the small waiting room with its ring of couches and chairs, end tables with stacks of tattered magazines, and discarded Styrofoam coffee cups. There were a dozen or more people there, milling about the tiny room, chatting amiably, laughing quietly. They all looked around as Virginia walked in.

There was Chester Baxter, Frank Handling and his old pal Barney Millcoat, Peggy and Jim Cochran from Mom and Pop's Cafe, along with Dixie Brown and Gloria Guice. Phyllis Aynsworthy and several of her friends from Mystic were crowded around a small Christmas tree blinking on a table. Rachel's grandfather sat on the floor, Rachel's head resting on his lap as she slept.

Virginia closed her eyes briefly, willing back her emotions.

Gloria, dressed in a pair of reindeer-imprinted leggings and a baggy T-shirt boasting a sequin Santa face, was the first to step forward. "I hope you don't mind that we all came down, GiGi. But you know that Dick has always meant a lot to all of us. He's been a real friend and supporter to each of us at one time or another."

"That's a fact," Peggy said, and walked to a half-barrel keg placed on the floor with a big red ribbon tied around it. It was heaped with silver coins and dollar bills. "Since last Christmas we've taken up collections at the cafe to help with Dick's medical expenses. By my last reckoning there's just short of six thousand dollars here. We planned to bring this over to the farm on Christmas Day, but I figured this was just as good a time as any."

Phyllis joined her. "And this is from the club. We managed to see around six hundred from the last few shows and raffle. I know it's not much, but I guess every little bit helps."

Virginia took a deep breath and managed a shaky smile. "Of course it will. You're all so very kind. Such wonderful friends. Hopefully, our financial situation won't be too staggering . . . I've sold Lindale."

"Oh, no," someone moaned.

"I'm so sorry," someone else whispered.

"We'll miss him," said Virginia. "But I'm certain he'll go to a farm that can promote him more capably than we can at

Renaissance. Besides, Fameous is due to foal soon. With any luck she'll give me a colt as incredible as his father."

She turned away and moved down the hall. Her eyes burned. Her throat felt raw. The effects of the medication Jeff had given her made her brain feel hazy and heavy. Her body felt numb.

There was a tiny plastic Santa on the floor. She picked it up. A child's toy, obviously, with rosy cheeks and a flocked red suit, his beard of curly nylon. She pulled the string at the top of his head and he lit up with a glow as warm as a firefly's.

A man walked from a room, leaving the door slightly ajar behind him. It was the chapel, with several short rows of pews placed before a statue of the Virgin Mary holding the baby Jesus in her arms. Virginia went in, sat in the back pew, and allowed the dimness and quiet of the sanctuary to envelop her.

The Santa in her hand continued to glow.

Closing her fingers around it, she shut her eyes.

Perhaps she dozed. She couldn't be certain. But as she opened her eyes someone was sitting near her—an older man dressed in a checkered flannel shirt and dungarees. He had silver hair swept back from his forehead and a kindly smile that somehow made her feel warm and oddly secure.

"You must be Virginia," he said. "Oh, don't look so startled. I just heard your friends in the waiting room talking about you and your father. Sounds like you've had a rough go of it the last few years."

She nodded.

He glanced at the glowing Santa in her hand. "What have you got there?"

"I found it." She rubbed it with her thumb and tugged on the string, yet it continued to glow.

"How refreshing to see someone your age still believes in Santa Claus. Do you believe in God as well?"

Virginia gazed up at the Holy Virgin. "I suppose I've always considered them the same person, Santa and God."

The man's eyebrows went up. "What a fascinating theory. Why say you?"

"They're both the quintessence of goodness and of giving. Of rewarding the virtuous and charitable." She laughed self-consciously. "I always believed that the Christmas holiday was a time when God could masquerade as a mortal and frolic amid His human flock. The gifts we received on Christmas Day were *His* way of celebrating His Son's birthday."

The man nodded thoughtfully. "Tell me, Virginia, when you were a child . . . what did you wish for most for Christmas?"

"To find a horse beneath my Christmas tree," she replied dreamily, her mind drifting to some strangely peaceful place where images of her own childhood sparkled before her like lights on a Christmas tree. "And to experience a white Christmas," she added with a light giggle.

"And what do you ask for now, as an adult?"

"I want my father back . . . and to experience a white Christmas."

The stranger laughed softly. "Would you care to rest your head on my shoulder, Virginia? You look very tired. Close your eyes a few minutes, my dear. That's the girl. Just relax. Everything is going to be fine. Just fine."

"Virginia? Ginny? Love? Wake up."

She lifted her head and forced open her eyes. A figure stood beside the pew—tall, silhouetted against the light pouring through the door behind him. Then he touched her cheek with his fingertips and bent to kiss her lips. "Good morning," he whispered.

"Neil? Oh, God, Neil." She stood up, her fingers grabbing his smock and clenching. "My father—"

"Came through the surgery beautifully." He smiled. "Jeff's with him now in recovery."

She wobbled.

He caught her.

She clung.

He held her. Close. And stroked her hair.

Finally, she roused enough to say, "We have to tell the others."

"They've been told already. They're waiting to share the good news."

Virginia turned toward the door, then stopped and looked around, her gaze sweeping the tiny chapel, empty but for herself and Neil. "The gentleman . . . the stranger . . . where did he go?"

Neil frowned. "There wasn't anyone—"

"He was just here. We spoke. He was an older man with gray hair . . . I dozed on his shoulder."

Cupping her cheek in one hand, Neil kissed her again. "You must have been dreaming, sweetheart. I've been here a while watching you sleep and there was no one with you."

Frowning, she took one last glance around, her gaze falling to the floor where her toy Santa lay, still glowing. She swept it up and held it in her hand, her sleepy mind struggling with the image of the stranger who had so comforted her those moments before . . . the memory oddly drawing away as if down a tunnel. A dream. Yes, it must have been a dream.

She tugged the string, and the light went out.

Her friends burst into applause as Virginia and Neil left the chapel. They flooded around her, hugging, kissing, and offering her their best wishes.

Then Jeff appeared through the crowd, swept her up in a bear hug, and spun around. "It was incredible! That was the most beautiful, inspiring performance I've ever witnessed in an OR."

"Where is Dr. Melgrave?" she asked. "I have to thank him."

A look of surprise crossed Jeff's face. "Didn't you know? Melgrave didn't perform the surgery—he's attending a conference in Chicago. Sis, Dr. Ellison did the surgery."

"Neil?" She looked around. He stood in the distance, a nurse at his side as he looked over a patient's chart. Virginia walked to him, her heart skipping as he looked up, that infamous grin returning, but tired. She didn't hesitate, but slid her arms around his neck and pulled his head down, kissing him with her open mouth, her hands twisting into his soft hair.

Applause erupted again. Dixie shouted, "Atta girl, GiGi. Go for it!"

Backing away at last, she smiled up into his blue eyes and whispered, "Darling, how can I ever thank you enough?"

"Oh, I can think of a number of ways," he whispered back, then slid both arms around her.

The phone woke her.

Virginia sat up in bed, her heart pounding, her brow sweating. From her living room came a deep voice speaking quietly—too softly for her to make out the words or tone. Then there was silence.

Her bedroom door eased opened. Neil walked in.

"Was that the hospital?"

He nodded and sat down beside her on the bed. "It was Jeff. Your father's awake and cantankerous as always." He grinned. "I told Jeff I'd relieve him first thing in the morning."

With a sigh, Virginia fell back on the pillows. "I can't believe it's all over. After all this time of fearing the outcome . . ." Taking his hand, she held it to her lips. "Sometimes I think you were God-sent, Dr. Ellison."

He bent and kissed her lips, her nose, her eyes, then breathed softly in her ear. "If it were a little later in the evening I might try to seduce you, Ms. Valemere. But since my daughter could pop in at any moment, I should do my best to behave. While I encourage an open and honest dialogue with Rachel on any matters sexually related I'm afraid show-and-tell is a little beyond even *my* scope of indulgence."

She made a soft, disappointed sound in her throat.

"However, I could explain that since it's Christmas Eve she should get to bed early or Santa won't come . . . no pun intended."

She gasped and hit his arm. Laughing, he fell beside her, wrapped his arms around her so she lay her head on his shoulder, and listened to his heart murmur in her ear.

"Can you stand my thanking you one more time?" She nuzzled his chest.

"Yes."

"A thousand times—thank you."

"Just doin' my job, ma'am."

"No, you weren't. You walked away from the OR a long time ago. You did this for me."

He was silent for a moment, then said, "Maybe. Or maybe I was doing it for us."

Lifting her head, she searched his eyes. "For us?"

His lips curled. He caught her face in his hands. For an instant he looked on the verge of saying something; then, just as quickly, he rolled away and left the bed.

"Fickle!" she called after him.

Reaching the bedroom door, he stopped and turned. Forearm propped against the doorframe, his hair a mess, his shirttail hanging out of his jeans, he was the pseudo-Angel again. Mad Max. The menace on a motorcycle leering at her from behind the shield of his Darth Vader helmet.

Sexy—and tempting as hell.

She wanted him like hell.

"You have a couple of messages," he told her.

"Oh?" She patted the bed beside her.

He didn't smile. "Both from Equine Management. The first came in last evening around seven. Lindale went to the highest bidder for two hundred and twenty-five thousand. The money was wired into your account within a matter of hours."

"Two . . ." Briefly, she closed her eyes. Two hundred and twenty-five thousand dollars. She wasn't sure she was more staggered by the unbelievable sum . . . or the realization that Lindale—her pride and joy, the future of her farm—now belonged to someone else.

"The second message was left early this morning. Ryder Horse Transport would be picking him up today."

"Today?" She swallowed and glanced at the clock. Eight P.M. Her eyes flashed back to Neil's, and she leapt from the bed in her bare feet and ran for the door. He caught her arm.

"He's already gone, Ginny."

"Gone. He can't be—"

"The transport came around three this afternoon."

"Why wasn't I told?"

"We thought it best this way, that it would be easier on you."

"We? Who is this 'we' you're referring to?"

"Myself and Jeff."

"Jeff hated that horse! And as for you, who gave you the right to make that sort of decision for me? I helped bring that horse into this world. I bottle-fed him after his dam died of colic. He was my best friend, Neil, and you allow those people to take him away without my saying goodbye?"

"GiGi!" Slamming the back screen door, Rachel skidded to a stop at the living room threshold, her eyes like two blue china saucers. "It's Famous. Something's wrong. She's gone down and won't get up. I'm not sure, but I think she's foaling."

"No. No, she can't be. She's not due for another week." Pushing by Neil, Virginia grabbed her parka from the peg on the wall, crammed her sockless feet into her muck boots, and followed Rachel into the night.

The air felt bitter and biting and wet, stinging her eyes and skin so even a breath burned her lungs. A thin film of ice covered the ground. She slid once and almost fell as she hurried toward the distant barn with its lights pouring through the open doors and office windows. Upon entering the barn, she ran down the long aisle, her step slowing as she passed Lin's empty stall.

The stalled horses whinnied at the sight of her and paced rapidly from side to side, stirring up shavings of dust, banging against the stall sides with their hooves.

Rachel disappeared into Famous's stall, and there came a heart-stopping cry. "GiGi! GiGi, come quick."

The bay mare was on her side, ribs heaving, body sweating, tail curled up over her back as she groaned and strained. Lips pulled back, exposing her teeth, the mare lifted her head slightly to better see Virginia, the whites of her frightened eyes showing. She lay in a pool of bloody fluid and tissue. A pair of tiny front hooves protruded from her body, as did a muzzle.

Cautiously, unable to breathe, Virginia caught Rachel's arm and pulled her back. "Dr. Starr's number is written by the phone. Call her. Tell her to get here as soon as possible."

As Rachel dashed away, Neil moved up behind her. "Is there anything I can do?" he asked.

"She seems to be handling it nicely," she whispered, and flashed him a smile. "A bit premature. Hopefully it doesn't mean there's a problem."

"On Christmas Eve? It wouldn't dare."

Virginia stepped from the stall and closed it as quietly as possible, casting the stall into deep shadows again. Wearily, she sank against the door. "God, what else could possibly happen?"

"One thing about it, Ginny Lea. This is a Christmas you'll remember for a long, long time."

Virginia smiled. "I'm sorry I was so angry with you. It's just that people who don't own horses can't appreciate the bond we have with them. They're our children. Our companions. Occasionally, our confidantes. When we're riding our horses, it's the purest sense of freedom we can ever experience. It's the closest thing to actually flying we'll ever know. It's an odd, spiritual thing. In some strange way they become part of us."

Rachel returned. "Dr. Starr says she'll be here in ten minutes. Can we stay and watch?"

Virginia slid her arms around the child. "Of course. I don't think Fameous will mind."

The three of them stood together, their arms around one another as they watched the miracle of life take place before them. Little by little the foal emerged, struggling, its hooves rending the protective sac until it lay curled in the fragrant, warm straw.

Virginia went to her knees beside the foal, removed her parka, and covered its wet, trembling body, then ran her hands over its face, ears, chest, and legs. "It's a colt! It's a beautiful, perfect colt!" Laughing, she hugged the bone-weary baby in her arms. "This calls for a celebration. Break out the Blackberry Royal, my darling Dr. Ellison, and don't even bother to heat it!"

"I'm afraid it's a bit too early to celebrate," came the vet's voice, and Virginia looked up, smiling at the petite brunette with a stethoscope around her neck. Dr. Leah Starr crouched at Neil's side, her expression concerned as she ran a hand down Fameous's lathered neck.

"What's wrong?" Virginia asked her friend.

Dr. Starr shook her head and slid her hand into the mare up to her elbow. A moment passed, then she withdrew, a grin sliding across her face. "Holy cow. I'm not believing this. Ho, ho, ho, and Merry Christmas to you, too."

With a gush of fluid, another pair of feet appeared from the mare's opening. Neil began laughing. Rachel let loose a squeal that caused the horses to set up a chorus of whinnies. "It's a miracle!" Rachel cried and jumped up and down. "Twins!"

The second colt slid easily into Dr. Starr's arms. Marked almost identically as the other, the colt kicked and squirmed, its long legs scrambling before it settled down to rest in the straw.

With that, the mare let go a tired, relieved groan and closed her eyes.

"Congratulations." Dr. Starr smiled and shook her head. "Incredible as it may be, they're normal size and absolutely perfect."

It took a great deal of coercing from Neil and Rachel, but Virginia finally agreed to spend the remainder of Christmas Eve night at their place. Rachel couldn't imagine waking up on Christmas morning unable to open her gifts, she'd pointed out. Besides, it was tradition: Granddad Albert served crushed cranberry pancakes for Christmas break-fast—the only day of the year he prepared them!

The smell of coffee woke her. Sleepily she gazed up at Neil, who waved a steaming cup under her nose.

"Don't you ever sleep?" she asked him.

"Too busy watching you. Are you aware you smile when you sleep?"

"Maybe because I'm deliriously happy."

"You look good in my bed, Ms. Valemere."

"Oh? I wasn't aware this was your bed, Dr. Ellison."

"Where else would I put you?"

"Have you spoken with Jeff?" Shifting up against her pillows, she smiled her thanks and accepted the coffee.

"Your father's awake and wondering where the devil you are."

"Seriously?"

"Would I lie to you?"

A door slammed. Neil raised one eyebrow. "Any minute now. Brace yourself."

Rachel burst into the room, eyes flashing, cheeks a burst of color. "I've got it," she declared, jumping onto the bed by Virginia.

"You've got what?"

"What you can name the twins." Beaming a smile, she said, "Celebration for the first . . . and Miracle for the sec-ond."

"Celebration and Miracle." Virginia smiled and nodded. "I like that."

"Yes!" With a whoop, Rachel cried, "Last one to the Christmas tree is rancid eggnog!"

"You're on," Virginia replied, then flung back the bed-covers and jumped from the bed.

"Not so fast." Neil looped his arm around her waist, bur-ied his face against the curve of her throat, and groaned. "Damn but you smell good in the morning."

Her eyelids fluttered closed. His warm breath and lips upon her skin made her heart quicken. "If you don't stop, Dr. Ellison, I'm afraid my nog is going to curdle."

Laughing, still holding her tightly, he drew her to the draped window. "Ready for your Christmas present?" he murmured in her ear.

She nodded.

He opened the drapes, revealing deep white snow blanketing the hills and trees as far as she could see. Icicles dripped from the bare tree limbs and sparkled like crystal. "Merry Christmas."

Melting back against him, she smiled. "For me?"

"All for you, Ginny Lea."

Sitting amid discarded Christmas wrappings and ribbons and bows tinkling with tiny bells, Rachel opened her final gift. Her eyes grew large. Her lower lip trembled. "A saddle? You actually got me a saddle?"

"Why not?" Neil replied with a shrug. "My motto is, if you can't lick 'em, join 'em."

As Rachel ran her hands caressingly over the soft brown leather, Virginia regarded her father, long, denim-clad legs stretched out by the tree, a big red bow taped to the top of his head, Rachel's gift to him dangling from around his neck: a bright purple tie depicting stampeding horses. She felt weak and trembling, and shockingly in love. The irony was, she had spent Christmas Eve night in what once had been her home, and she hadn't cared for anything other than counting the hours until she could see Neil again—to be a part of this familial scene with him and Rachel and Al. She'd experienced the anticipation of looking forward to Christmas morning as if she were ten years old again.

Oh, if only her father could have been here.

Thanks to Dr. Neil Ellison, he would be, very soon.

Slapping his thighs, Alfred hefted himself out of his chair. "Looks like that fire could use some more logs, young 'un. Give your grandpa a hand and let's let the lovebirds have a few minutes alone."

"Sounds like a plan," Rachel declared, then wiggled her eyebrows at Virginia, making her laugh. Leaping up on her grandfather's back, the girl slapped him on the rear and yelled, "Get the right lead, you ol' donkey, or it's the cannery for ya tomorrow!"

After they'd left, Virginia settled back in her chair. "She's precious, Neil. I adore her."

"Feeling's mutual, I assure you."

"You've done a wonderful job raising her."

"It's not easy being a single parent."

"You were lucky to have Al."

"It's not the same as having a mother, though, is it?"

"No." Her cheeks warming, she lowered her eyes.

Neil got up, scattering paper and tinkling bells. Al appeared at the door at that minute, his eyes round and fixed on Virginia. "There's someone here to see you, dear. You'd better hurry. He seems a trifle impatient."

Frowning, Virginia glanced at Neil, then followed Al through the kitchen and out the back door. The snow had begun falling again, dusting the trees like powdered sugar. There was no one waiting at the back door, and she was just about to question Al when her eye was caught by the towering spruce Christmas tree in the center of the distant arena. In a wink, the red and green twinklers came on, the star atop the tree beaming in the gray, snowy light.

She stepped into the snow, remotely feeling the wet cold close around her ankles.

The horse, with Rachel astride, emerged from behind the tree, ears pointed, nostrils wide and blowing, a garland of poinsettias around his arched neck. Rachel waved, and her distant voice called, "Merry Christmas, GiGi!"

"Lindale?"

She spun back toward the house.

Neil stood above her, smiling down at her through the snowfall. "Yes, Virginia, there is a Santa Claus."

"You?" She shook her head in disbelief. "You bought Lindale?"

"Rachel wanted a horse for Christmas. What can I say? I spoil her rotten. Problem is . . ." He stepped from the porch, sinking into the snow with her. "She'll need a good trainer.

Someone willing to live on the premises. Be willing to share the house . . . not to mention my bed," he added more softly.

Blinking snowflakes from her eyes, she managed at last to catch her breath. "That's some opportunity, Dr. Ellison . . . for the right person. Just how long does this contract extend?"

He slid his arm around her and lowered his lips to hers. "Nothing short of a lifetime . . . welcome home, Ginny Lea."

Dear Readers,

I am so pleased that Kensington has decided to reissue "The Miracle" in this collection of short stories. I still receive numerous letters in response to "After Innocence," and in almost every single one of them, you have begged me to tell the story of Lisa Ralston and Julian St. Clare. Well, "The Miracle" is their story, a story of two people who come together in an act of fate, against their will, with wonderful consequences. Set just off the rugged coast of Ireland shortly after the turn of the century, be prepared to be swept away by the Marquis of Connaught and his fiancée. I hope you enjoy reading "The Miracle"—because it was sure fun to write.

As always, I am hard at work on a new novel. This year I have three new releases, *The Third Heiress* in paperback, *House of Dreams* in hardcover, and *Deadly Love* by B.D. Joyce. Please visit my website at www.brendajoyce.com for more information—and I always answer my e-mails.

Happy Reading!

Brenda Joyce

THE MIRACLE
Brenda Joyce

One

It was Christmas Eve, and Lisa had never been as miserable or frightened in her entire short life.

She was hiding from her fiancé, the Marquis of Connaught. She had run away from him two months ago, on the night of their engagement party. But now she was desperate. She did not know how much longer she could continue to hide like this, alone and cold and hungry—and so terribly unhappy and afraid.

Lisa shivered. She was wrapped in a mohair throw, for she was only wearing a white poplin summer dress. When she had fled her engagement ball, she had fled without any clothes except for the evening gown she was wearing. That had been discarded immediately. And it was frigidly cold outside, the sky dark and threatening, and as freezing inside her parents' huge summer home. But she did not dare make a fire for fear of alerting a local resident or a passerby to her presence. For fear of alerting Julian St. Clare to her presence.

How she hated him.

Tears did not come to Lisa's eyes, however. On the night of her engagement party she had cried so hard and so thoroughly that she doubted she would ever cry again. Julian's betrayal had been a fatal blow to her young heart. How naive she had been then, to think that such a man had come courting her out of love and not more sanguine reasons. He had only been interested in her because she was an heiress. He did not want her, had never wanted her; he only wanted her money.

A loose shutter began banging wildly against the side of the house. Lisa was huddled on the floor in a corner of her bedroom. The shutters there were open, as were the blue and white drapes, so that the faded winter light could filter into the room. The house was low on supplies. Although there were gaslights, Lisa dared not use them, using only candles. The candles were all but gone. She was almost out of food, too, as there were but a few canned items left in the pantry. Yesterday she had begun using the last bar of soap.

Dear God, what was she going to do?

Lisa wiggled her toes, which were numb from the cold. She stared out the window. It had begun to flurry.

Even though the window was closed and made of double-paned glass, Lisa could hear the thundering of the surf on the shore not far from the back of the house.

It was Christmas Eve. Lisa imagined the cozy family parlor of her Fifth Avenue home. Right now her father was undoubtedly poking the logs in the fire, watching the flames crackle, clad in his favorite paisley smoking jacket. Suzanne, her stepmother, would be descending the wide sweeping stairs, dressed formally for supper. And Sofie, who had returned from Paris with her beautiful baby daughter, was she there, too? Lisa's heart twisted. She missed her father and stepmother and stepsister terribly. A sense of loss swept through her, so acute it made her breathless and dizzy.

Or was she faint from hunger and lack of sleep?

Lisa slept fitfully at night, her dreams deeply disturbing. As if she were a child, she dreamed of being pursued by monsters and beasts. She was always running in terror, afraid for her life, for she knew if the beast caught her, he would coldly, cruelly destroy her. He was a shaggy, wild creature, horrific and not human at all. Until she saw his face.

The beast always had a face. He was blond and gray-eyed

and coldly patrician. He was devastatingly handsome. His face was Julian St. Clare's.

Lisa listened to the banging shutter and the pounding surf. His face had fooled her. His face and his kisses. How stupid she had been. Lisa knew now from overhearing the gossips at her engagement party that his reputation was vast and well known—he was impoverished, reclusive, and he disliked women. He was only marrying Lisa because she was an heiress. And Julian had not denied it when Lisa flung the accusation in his face.

Lisa shivered again. This time the cold was far more than bone-chilling—it wrapped icy fingers around her heart. According to Sofie, St. Clare was more coldly furious with her each and every passing day. And more determined to find her. He had hired detectives to aid him in his quest.

Would he never grow weary of this game? Lisa prayed daily that he would give up, find himself another American heiress, and return to his ancestral home in Ireland.

The banging of the shutter was louder now, more forceful and rhythmic.

Sofie knew where she was. If St. Clare left, Lisa was certain that Sofie would reveal that fact to her immediately so Lisa could go home.

Bang. Bang. Bang.

Lisa's brief reverie of returning home and being swept into her father's arms was rudely interrupted. Something was not right. She strained to hear.

Bang. Bang.

Lisa sat up straighter. The shutter was still banging wildly in the wind, but something was banging downstairs, too. A new noise, a different noise. It was rhythmic, forceful.

Lisa was on her feet. Panic washed over her. Was someone knocking on the front door?

No! Of course not! But she dropped the throw and ran down the hall to the second-floor landing. Hanging onto the smooth teak banister, she peered down into the foyer. This time there was no mistaking the sound of someone banging on the front door. Every drop of blood drained from her face.

Bam. Bam.

And then the brass doorknob rattled.

Lisa was frozen. It crossed her stunned mind that St. Clare had found her.

Suddenly the glass window beside the front door shattered. Lisa started to scream, but her mouth was so dry with terror that she could not utter a single sound.

A heavy broken branch poked through, sweeping glass shards from the frame. And then St. Clare's head appeared in the opening.

Their gazes met.

His gray eyes glittered with anger.

Lisa's teeth chattered and her knees buckled.

"Open this door," the Marquis commanded above the howling wind.

Lisa whirled and began to run back down the hall.

"Lisa!" he shouted.

She did not know what to do, where to go. As she raced towards her bedroom she realized she would be trapped if she returned there. She ran past it, panting, her heart pounding. Lisa skidded down the back stairs. She realized that he would find her if she attempted to hide in the house. As she flew across the back foyer, she could hear him running down the corridor upstairs.

She had to escape.

Lisa threw the bolt on the back door. As she flung it open, a gust of freezing wind and snow blasted her. Lisa did not notice as she raced outside.

She was stumbling down the stone steps which led to the back lawns and tennis courts and ultimately the beach when she heard him shouting her name. Lisa flung a glance over her shoulder as she ran across the snow-dusted lawn. St. Clare was just barreling out of the house.

Lisa screamed as she slipped and fell. She pushed herself up from her knees, but got caught on the frothy lace hem of her skirts. Stumbling, she wrenched at her skirts and took another step forward. And then a hand clamped down hard on her shoulder.

Lisa's slipper-shod feet continued to move, but her body was hauled backwards. A pair of muscular arms wrapped around her. Lisa did not hesitate—she sank her teeth into one of those arms.

But all she got was a mouthful of his overcoat, while he did not appear to notice anything. A moment later St. Clare had thrown her over his shoulder and was hurrying back to the house.

He was tall and muscular and Lisa was petite, so her eyes were level with the small of his back. She did not give up. "No!" she shouted, beating his back with her fists, her cheek rubbing against his wool coat. If he noticed her wild resistance, he gave no sign. Lisa pummeled him harder as sobs choked their way out of her throat.

St. Clare strode into the back hall, kicking the door closed. To Lisa, the kick seemed brutal and violent. Her fists uncurled, stilled. Abject fear seized her again.

He did not pause. He strode purposefully through the house, kicking open both doors to a front parlor. Without breaking stride he entered the dark room and deposited Lisa on the sofa. Their gazes met.

Some of the cold fury dimmed in his eyes. His gaze swept her from head to toe and widened.

Lisa realized her teeth were chattering. She was shivering uncontrollably, not just from fear. From the freezing cold.

"Good God," he said grimly, his jaw flexing. He shrugged out of his overcoat and flung the coat on top of Lisa. Before Lisa could protest, he tucked it firmly about her. "You little fool," he said.

Lisa burrowed into his coat, which was wonderfully warm, trying not to notice the musky male scent that clung to it. She never removed her eyes from his. Her teeth chattered more loudly than before, and her shivering continued unabated.

His mouth tightened. St. Clare immediately turned on a gaslamp. The room was flooded with light. He went to the hearth, knelt, and began to make a fire. Within moments flames began to dance, but he wasn't through. Soon the hearth was blazing.

Lisa remained on the couch, staring at his broad back, filled with dread and too stunned to think coherently. She could not believe that she had been caught.

Finished with the fire, he turned and strode to her.

Lisa could not help but flinch, pressing herself against the back of the sofa.

His gaze darkened. "You're blue," he said flatly. "Has it not crossed your mind that you might catch pneumonia and die wearing a summer dress like that in this weather?"

Lisa's reply was instantaneous. "Then you would have to find another heiress, wouldn't you?"

He started, eyes wide.

Lisa wished she had kept silent.

His expression hardened. "Yes, I would."

Lisa inhaled. "I hate you."

"You have made that very clear." Suddenly he reached for her.

Lisa cried out.

He lifted her into his arms. "I am not going to hurt you," he said coldly, moving back to the fire. "You may have a suicide wish, but I do not share it." A shadow Lisa did not comprehend clouded his expression.

Lisa was tense, acutely aware of being cradled against his broad, hard chest. His masculine scent assailed her. Lisa squirmed. She despised him, and she was not going to marry him, but he was a devastatingly attractive man, and she could not forget the few times he had kissed her when he was courting her—before she had learned the truth about him. Lisa had had many beaux before St. Clare, even though she was just eighteen. Young men had always flocked about her, vying for her attention. But only one young man had dared to kiss her before St. Clare, a friend who had confessed at the time that he was miserably in love with her. His kiss had been chaste and totally unremarkable. Julian's kisses had seared not just her body, but her soul. And they hadn't been chaste at all.

Lisa realized that he had halted in front of the fire with her in his arms. He was staring at her almost fixedly.

Lisa prayed her thoughts did not show. Flushing, wetting her lips, she said hoarsely, "Put me down."

His temples throbbed visibly as he tore his gaze away and laid her on the rug in front of the hearth.

Terribly relieved to be out of his arms, Lisa resolved to forget the past and the dreams she had once had for them, no matter how difficult it might be. She would never allow him to kiss her again, and she certainly wasn't going to marry him, no matter what he and her father had planned.

But she was acutely aware of him standing beside her just as she was acutely aware of the tension simmering between them.

Lisa was determined to ignore him, and in spite of the roaring fire, she had never been colder in her life. She refused to think that he was being kind. Clearly he was not a kind man. He was only concerned about her because he wanted her fortune.

"You may ignore me if it pleases you," he said from beside her, staring at her again. "I had planned to return to the city tonight, but will wait until the morning. I will send my driver into town to bring us a hot supper and anything we might need. And some suitable clothing for you."

Lisa sat up, facing him. A momentary feeling of light-headedness afflicted her, but she ignored it. "You may certainly return to New York City tonight. Don't linger on my account."

His eyes darkened. "Lisa, you are returning with me."

"Then you will have to act forcibly, sir."

"You are a stubborn bit of baggage," he said coolly. "And I suggest that you cease trying to antagonize me in this childish manner."

"Oh, so now I am a mere child?" Lisa felt hurt, bitterly so. "You did not treat me like a child, St. Clare, when you were courting me—and kissing me!"

His fists found his hips. His stare found her mouth.

Lisa wished she had not brought up the subject. "Just go away and leave me alone," she said, staring at the floor.

"I cannot do that, Lisa."

Her head flung up. "I am not marrying you," Lisa said vehemently. "Were you the last man on this earth, I would not marry you!"

He folded his arms and looked down at her. "Ahh, so now we get to the gist of the matter."

"Yes. The gist. The gist is that you are a cold, uncaring man. You are a fraud, St. Clare." Unfortunately, Lisa's tone was tremulous. She hoped all the hurt she was feeling was not showing in her eyes. She had never been a good actress.

His expression was impossible to read. "Let us finish this once and for all. I am sorry. I apologize to you for not being forthright from the start. Perhaps if I had been honest and explained to you the reasons I sought your hand in matrimony, we would not be at this impasse now."

Lisa was incredulous. She got to her feet abruptly, leaving his coat on the floor. But instantly she was assailed with a wave of dizziness and she could not respond as she wished to do.

St. Clare gripped her arms. "You are ill."

Lisa allowed him to steady her. "No, I am fine. I am just hungry," she said, as her vision cleared. Then, realizing that his warm palms gripped her bare wrists, she shrugged free of him. "Stop touching me," she snapped.

Shadows crossed his eyes, but he dropped his hands. "You are ill," he repeated, staring closely at her.

"I am fine. I am tired, that is all. And I do not accept your apology, St. Clare."

He eyed her. "I see. You intend to fight me to the bitter end?"

"Yes. Nor do you see. I doubt you see anything at all except your own selfish wishes. You are a cold, ugly man. Your face might be beautiful, but you have no heart—and you toyed with mine, which is unforgivable!" To Lisa's dismay, hot tears suddenly filled her gaze.

He was silent. "You are so very young," he finally said.

"I also apologize for hurting you, Lisa. That was not my intention."

"What was your intention?" she cried. "Other than to marry an unsuspecting heiress."

His jaw flexed. "I am tired of your accusations. It is very common for an heiress to seek a title, just as it is common for a nobleman like myself to seek an heiress. You are acting like this is a crime akin to murder. We are not the first to find such an accommodation, Lisa."

"No!" Lisa shook her head. Her long, dark hair, which had long since come loose of its coil, fell like black silk across her shoulders.

"This marriage can be a success if we reach an understanding, you and I."

"No," Lisa said fiercely. "No. When I marry, I am marrying for love."

Something flickered in his eyes. "I am afraid that is not possible."

Lisa did not like his tone. "I shall beg my father to break this off. Surely now that he knows how resistant I am, he will not force me to wed you. My father loves me."

"It is too late," Julian said quietly.

"Of course it's not too late!"

He hesitated, staring. "Lisa, we were married by proxy last week."

Lisa could not move. Surely she had misheard?

His mouth was a thin, tight line. "We are already man and wife."

Two

Lisa had maintained a stoic silence ever since Julian had informed her of the fact of their marriage. He did not want to feel guilty, and he certainly did not want to feel sympathetic toward her, but it was very hard for him to maintain his distance whenever he looked into her expressive amber eyes. She could not hide her feelings of hurt and bitterness and despair. She was only eighteen—so very young.

He almost cursed himself for what he had done, but he had not had any choice. He was only a man, he could not change God's will, and he had been desperate.

Julian could not eat. He sat at the dining table with his bride at a long, oval table that could accommodate a dozen diners with ease. Lisa had chosen to sit opposite him at the table's far end, a foolishly defiant gesture, and she refused to look at him or speak with him. But then, she appeared to be starving, and she had not stopped eating since his manservant had laid out the repast.

He watched her help herself to another serving of roasted chicken and boiled potatoes. He could not believe how thin she had become in these past two months. He kept remembering how, when he had lifted her in his arms, she had been as light as a feather. Dark circles were etched beneath her eyes. He could not ignore his responsibility in this affair, or the guilt which filled him as he faced it.

He knew he should have chosen a different bride.

Lisa was too young, too vulnerable, and if he dared be honest, far too pretty as well.

She did not suit him, and she would hate his home, Castleclare, when he took her there.

He shut off his thoughts. They were becoming distinctly painful. He knew he shouldn't think about faults, especially not his own, for then his thoughts would take him backwards in time, to a place he dared not go. Not ever again.

Lisa suddenly sighed.

Julian knew he was staring at her, and now that she was finally finished eating, she lifted her head and their gazes collided. He felt unbearably tense. He suddenly knew he could not take her with him to Castleclare. His every instinct warned him against it. She was trouble.

Suddenly she was slapping her napkin down and rising to her feet, a clear breach of etiquette. Coolly she said, "I am retiring to my room." Her gaze flickered with hostility.

He chose to stand politely. "Good night, madam," he said, inclining his head.

Giving him half a glare, for the effect was ruined by the hurt in her eyes, she shoved back her chair as noisily as possible and marched from the room.

Julian sighed and collapsed in his seat. He was well aware that she was trying her damnedest to provoke him. He was, perhaps, relieved that she had gone.

O'Hara appeared magically in the room. Short and round and old enough to be Julian's father, he was Julian's single manservant, acting as butler, valet, footman, and coachman as need be. He had insisted on accompanying Julian to America.

"That poor lass be starvin', m'lord," O'Hara said accusingly.

Julian leveled him with a cool stare. "I am well aware of Her Ladyship's condition."

Without asking, O'Hara filled Julian's wineglass. "Ain't right, m'lord. Her bein' so unhappy an'—"

"O'Hara," Julian said calmly, "you are going too far."

O'Hara ignored the unveiled warning. "Mebbe y' should court the lass just a tiny bit."

Julian stood up abruptly, scowled, and left the dining

room, taking his red wine with him. In the library he stared out the window, for no one had thought to draw the brocade draperies. It had begun to snow heavily and the sky was opaque, the front lawns already covered with several inches of snow. He hardly cared. His bride was upstairs, hurt and unhappy, all because of him. Why did he keep thinking about her?

Ever since he met her, he'd had no peace, none at all.

Julian set the wineglass down. Unwelcome images invaded his mind—images of Lisa curled up in her fourposter, her mouth full and red and inviting, her small nose tilted upward, eyes closed as she slept, her black lashes fanning on her pale cheeks. Her dark hair would be rippling across her shoulders, her naked shoulders . . .

Julian swallowed and turned away from the window. His groin was suddenly, shockingly, full.

He had no right to such thoughts.

But it had been so goddamn long.

Lisa woke with a cry of fright.

Morning sunlight was streaming into her bedroom and a fire blazed in the hearth, warming it. But she was not alone.

Julian St. Clare, the monster of her dreams, stood beside her bed, staring down at her, his face impossibly handsome—and impossible to read.

Complete comprehension struck Lisa immediately. She recalled all of the events leading up to that moment in the space of a single heartbeat. With that realization came dread and despair. Sitting up, brushing loose strands of hair from her face, she realized she was wearing nothing but a thin, sleeveless summer nightgown.

Lisa yanked the covers up to her chin, her face flaming. Julian had seen her breasts. Her heart raced alarmingly. "What are you doing in my room?"

A flush also colored his cheeks. "I knocked several times but you failed to awaken. I came in to tend to the fire," he said stiffly.

"Well, now you can get out."

Julian's eyes flashed. "I suggest that you moderate your tone, madam."

Lisa hugged the covers to her breasts, wondering how long he had been staring at her while she slept in such a state of immodesty. "My rudeness only matches yours," she managed, more meekly. "No gentleman would invade a lady's bedroom, sir, for any reason."

He sighed, clearly annoyed. "It is freezing cold, Lisa, and you have suffered greatly in the past two months. Do you wish to ruin your health?"

"What do you care?" Lisa shrugged. And received an angry look which somehow pleased her immensely.

He began to leave, then halted, facing her again. "We are snowed in."

"What?"

"It snowed all night. The driveway is impassable, and the roads can be no better. We are snowed in."

Lisa stared at him in growing horror.

"I will see you in the dining salon," Julian said. "O'Hara has prepared breakfast." His smile was cool. "I am afraid we will have to remain here for several days, Lisa, you and I, together."

When he was gone, Lisa sagged against her pillows. "No," she whispered miserably. "Oh, no!"

There was only one way for Lisa to survive the next few days until Julian took her home and that was to remain inside her bedroom, avoiding his presence and company completely. Except, however, for meals.

Lisa had no intention of starving herself now that there was food in the house, not after these past two very lean months. She arrived at the breakfast table at a quarter to ten. Julian was reading a day-old newspaper he had brought from New York. As she entered the room wearing a pale pink day dress, he rose to his feet. In spite of herself, Lisa had to admit that his manners were impeccable.

And that, even though he was wearing very old riding boots, breeches which fit him like a glove, and an equally old houndstooth riding jacket, he exuded an intensely masculine appeal. Lisa was careful to pretend to be oblivious of him as she took her seat at the other end of the table. Of course, it was impossible—she felt him looking at her with frightening intensity.

Surely he was wrong, she thought in sudden despair. They could not be married by proxy. It was an intolerable thought.

O'Hara came bustling into the room carrying a platter of sausages and eggs and freshly toasted muffins. "Good morning, m'lord, m'lady," he said jovially with his thick lilting Irish brogue. He beamed. "Merry Christmas!"

Lisa froze. She had forgotten what day this was.

Julian also remained immobile at the other end of the table. Their gazes clashed instantly.

Lisa quickly looked away, murmuring, "Merry Christmas," to the servant but not to Julian, a man who might be her husband, feeling awful about being so petty. Christmas was a special day, a day of love and joy and celebration. Yet this day was a day of sorrow and despair. Lisa yearned to be at home with her family. How she needed her father and stepsister now.

And although Lisa had been famished, she suddenly lost her appetite. She lurched to her feet. "Excuse me. I . . ." She could not continue. Vaguely aware of Julian's riveted gaze— and the fact that he was also standing—she turned and rushed from the room.

"Wait, Lisa," Julian said, hurrying after her.

She whirled in the corridor. "Please, just leave me alone," she begged.

He froze. "Lisa, it is time for us to talk."

"No," she cried and shook her head fiercely. Her thick braid swung like a rope against her back.

He gripped her elbow. "Come with me." His tone was soft but firm; it was a command.

Hating him intensely, Lisa realized she had no choice and allowed him to lead her into the library. He released her but did not bother to shut the doors. He turned his back to her and stared out at the snow as it was blown into an odd assortment of puffy shapes on the lawn.

Lisa hugged herself. This was the worst Christmas she could imagine. Her heart felt broken all over again. How alone she felt.

Slowly Julian faced her. "You deserve some explanation." Lisa said nothing. There was nothing to say.

"It was not my choice to remarry, Lisa. In truth, had I a choice, I would never have married again."

Lisa swallowed, feeling quite ill. "You are definitely making me feel better, St. Clare."

"Please. Take off the gauntlets for a moment, Lisa."

She blinked and finally, reluctantly, nodded. Even though she despised him for his deception and treachery, she wanted to know what he was thinking, wanted to hear what he would say.

He coughed to clear his throat. "Circumstance forced me to wed."

"An heiress like myself?"

"Yes." His gaze found hers. He appeared regretful.

"This hardly exonerates you, St. Clare," Lisa snapped. "Another woman might be happy with this kind of arrangement, but not I."

"My brother is ill."

Lisa stiffened, all ears now.

Julian's jaw was tight. He avoided her eyes. "Robert is my younger brother, my only brother. Our parents died years ago. He is the only family I have, and his welfare is my complete responsibility."

Lisa did not move. But Julian's anguish was a vivid thing, shimmering in his eyes, consuming him. She wished she were unaware of it.

"He has been diagnosed with consumption," Julian said.

Lisa stared. Consumption was fatal. His brother would, sooner or later, succumb to the disease and die. "I am sorry."

His head swiveled, his stare pierced her. His expression was stoic, except for his burning gray eyes. "Are you?"

"Of course."

He coughed again before speaking. The tip of his nose had grown pink. "He is at a spa in Switzerland and he must remain there for the rest . . . for the rest of his life. The treatment is very costly."

"I see," Lisa said, beginning to understand.

Julian abruptly turned his back to her. "I cannot pay the bills. But the Irish climate does not suit him. Robert, of course, prefers London, but that is as bad. He must remain in Switzerland. Yet I have no funds."

"So you came to America to marry an heiress."

He did not face her. Lisa thought he shuddered very slightly. "Yes. I had no choice. My brother's health is at issue."

His health, his life. Lisa did not want to feel Julian's pain, but it was so palpable that she did. She took a deep breath, wanting to flee the room, wanting to flee him. "I am sorry, St. Clare, about your brother. But your explanation changes nothing."

Slowly he faced her. "I see."

She took a step backwards, away from him. "I still don't want to be your wife."

"It's too late, Lisa," Julian told her. "It has been done. We are married." For a single moment, before he lowered his gaze, Lisa saw the burning intensity in his gray eyes.

Her heart was hammering madly. What had that look meant? It was not the first time she had glimpsed it. And should she really care to decipher his innermost feelings? She wanted nothing to do with him.

Lisa clenched her fists. "Take my money and return to Ireland and pay your brother's bills. But leave me here."

He stared at her dispassionately. Yet behind his stoic expression, she felt a fresh wave of anger building.

Lisa did not wait for him to respond. She ran from the room.

* * *

Lisa found solace in her bedroom. She flung herself face-down on the bed. She was acutely aware of the man downstairs, a stranger she despised, a stranger who was her husband—a man who was hurting because his brother was dying. Lisa told herself that it was not her affair, that she must not feel sympathy for him. She did not care. She must not care.

And surely he would agree with her final suggestion? Surely he would leave her in New York with her family and take her money instead? After all, he had not wanted to remarry in the first place. How hurtful that statement had been.

But St. Clare was full of surprises. What if he felt it his duty to import her to Ireland and his rundown ancestral estate?

What could she do? Defy both her father and St. Clare yet again? Lisa was exhausted from the past two months of hiding. She did not fool herself. Her strength—and bravery—were sapped. She could not run away again.

Which meant she must accept her fate. And if her fate was to go with Julian to Ireland . . .

St. Clare's image swam before her mind. When he had first come calling, she had been overwhelmed with his masculine beauty, his formal bearing, and his utterly aristocratic demeanor. Lisa was no longer deluded. He was only pleasing on the surface; he was a cold, heartless man.

He was not the knight in shining armor she had dreamed of and yearned for ever since she was a young girl.

Lisa felt like weeping. If only he were as ugly on the surface as he was on the inside.

A light rap sounded on her door. Lisa jerked, knowing who it was. She sat up, flinging her braid over her shoulder, but said not a word. Maybe he would think that she had fallen asleep.

"Lisa, it is I. Julian. There is more which we must discuss."

Her heart beat at a gallop. "There is *nothing* more to discuss," Lisa cried at the closed door. "Go away, St. Clare."

He opened the door and stepped inside. Lisa regretted not locking it, too late. He eyed her. Lisa realized her skirts were billowing about her legs in utter disarray. And that she probably looked quite indecent, lounging about the bed. She slipped to the floor.

His jaw flexing, he said, "We must finish this once and for all. You cannot hope to avoid me."

To hide her roiling emotions, she cried, "I can do my best to avoid you, St. Clare. And I intend to avoid you as much as possible from now until death do us part!"

He stared at her, first at her defiant face, then at her mouth, and finally his gaze slid down her bodice and skirts to her toes. "You are a contradiction, Lisa, for you are far tougher than you appear—and you appear a delicate beauty, fragile and ephemeral. I would never have dreamed you capable of running away and hiding from me for two full months. Your determination and courage are astounding."

"I do not think you are complimenting me," Lisa said.

"I am not complimenting you." His gaze was piercing. "You *are* far stronger than you appear, yet I sense you are not really as tough as you try to seem. I think that defiance runs against your true nature."

"So now you are an expert on my true nature?" Lisa scoffed, but she was alarmed. This man was also astute. Defiance was not characteristic of her. She had never been defiant before in her life. Lisa's temperament was basically even and pleasant. She was not strong. Her stepsister, Sofie, was strong. These past two months had taken every ounce of courage she possessed and then even more, a resolve which she had not even known herself capable of.

Lisa moved to a plush red chair and sank down, clasping her hands tightly in order to hide their trembling. She did not want St. Clare to guess how unnerved she really was. What did he want now? And why did he have to seek her out in the intimate confines of her bedroom?

He turned and slowly closed her door, worrying Lisa even more. Then he faced her, leaning one broad shoulder against it. His stare was unyielding.

And Lisa wanted him out of her room. She leapt to her feet. "What is it that you want?"

His gaze narrowed. "Why are you distraught, Lisa? You have no reason to fear me. I will never hurt you. I am a civilized man."

She lifted her chin. "I am not afraid of you."

"You are quaking."

"Hardly," Lisa lied. "I am . . . cold."

His mouth seemed to ease into a smile. Briefly it transformed his face, making him far more stunning than should be possible. "I only wish to discuss the future with you."

Lisa's eyes flashed. "We have no future!"

"You are being childish again. We are married and that is not going to change. However, I think you will be happy to learn that I am leaving for Europe the moment we return to New York City."

Lisa stood up. She wanted him gone, she did, but that meant that he would be leaving in a few days. She was too stunned to speak.

"Sorry to see me go?" he mocked.

"I am glad to see you go!" she cried, but her words felt like a contradiction, like a lie. Then she jerked, stricken with another inkling. "Wait—you are taking me with you?"

He shook his head. "No. I did not say that *we* were leaving. I am leaving. I have matters to attend to that cannot wait. I will send for you in the spring."

It took Lisa a full moment to grasp what he was saying, and even then, she did not comprehend his words completely. He was going to do as she had suggested. He was going to leave her in New York, taking only her money with him. Lisa knew she should be elated. Instead, she was strangely dismayed.

Clearly he had told her the truth earlier, that, given a choice, he would never have remarried; clearly he did not care for her at all.

It should not hurt. Her heart was already broken. Then why did she feel so bruised and battered now?

He returned her shocked gaze. "This is what you want,

isn't it, Lisa? For me to take your money and leave you behind?"

Lisa's bosom began to heave. "Yes," she managed, without any conviction.

"I *will* send for you in the spring," he said firmly.

Lisa shook her head. "B-but I won't come."

His stare remained on her face. "Do not think to defy me another time, Lisa. Do not force me to return to America to fetch you." His words were soft and filled with warning.

Lisa was trying to imagine the next six months, being married to him, yet residing worlds apart. Why wasn't she thrilled? "I will not obey your summons like some well-trained and docile lackey, St. Clare, when it comes next spring. Do not bother sending for me."

He stared at her tightly folded arms. "Then I shall come to fetch you."

"Why?" Lisa cried. "Y-you don't want me—so why?" And even she heard the hurt in her tone.

He had turned toward the door, but now he froze. Her words seemed to hang in the air . . . *you don't want me.*

"I shall send for you in the spring because, madam, you are my wife, for better or for worse."

"Oh, God," Lisa whispered. "I am doomed."

He hesitated, suddenly appearing uncertain and far younger than his thirty years. "Lisa, perhaps in six months time you will grow up and realize that your lot could be much worse."

She waved a hand at him, unable to speak, hot tears burning her eyes, wanting him to go. When she found her voice, her tone was both bitter and hoarse. "I want to be alone."

He finally nodded and walked to the door. But he did not pass through it after he opened it and Lisa could not resist having the last word. "Julian."

He started at the sound of his given name.

Her smile flashed, tearful and bitter, in her pale face. "Merry Christmas, St. Clare."

He blanched, staring. And left without another word.

Three

Castleclare, Clare Island, 1903

Clare Island formed a buffer between the roiling Atlantic Ocean and the wild western Irish coast. Its windward side was impassable, a jumble of soaring cliffs and jagged hills that were mostly bare, constantly buffeted by the wind and the sea. But the island's leeward side was lushly green and fertile; the high, sloping hills were dotted with sheep capable of nimbly maneuvering amongst the stony slopes and twisting paths that dissected the countryside. On a good day, the shepherds could just make out the sandy beaches of Connaught County on the far side of Clew Bay.

Castleclare was perched on the northernmost side of the island, facing Achill Island. Built in the thirteenth century by the first Earl of Connaught, the original keep had been added onto many times since. Pale stone walls enclosed numerous rambling structures, but the turreted towers of the castle itself rose above it all. Julian had not been home in over six months. But he was hardly soothed by the sight of the ancient barbican and the central tower looming beyond it. He had been all over Europe on a wild-goose chase.

Julian stared grimly ahead as his carriage rolled down the dirt road towards the castle. He intended to wring his brother's neck if he found him at Castleclare, and as he had looked everywhere else, he expected to locate him there.

The old, rusted iron portcullis was open, as always. Julian's coach rumbled through. O'Hara braked far too abruptly, the two bays squealed, and Julian was thrown off his seat. Sighing, he flung open the door, its hinges protesting noisily. His coach was as old as his manservant. He wouldn't mind purchasing a new conveyance, but he was loath to let the old family retainer go, no matter how annoyed he might occasionally be.

"M'lord, beg yorr pardon," O'Hara wheezed, panting and out of breath.

Julian gave him an impatient look and did not wait for him to dislodge himself from the upper driving seat. Stepping from the coach, he strode across the dirt and gravel drive and pushed open the heavy and scarred front door. He paused inside the cavernous central hall.

It was a part of the original, thirteenth century keep. As such, it was entirely composed of stone, thus cold, and being windowless, dark. Pennants hung from the rafters. Swords, maces, and a crossbow hung on the walls, all weapons from another, earlier era. Julian glanced around. The centuries-old trestle table, heavily scarred, was coated with dust. The oversized hearth, set against the far wall, was devoid of a welcoming fire. The stone floors were bare and frigid. Julian could feel the cold seeping up through the worn soles of his riding boots. Last week he had discovered the beginnings of another hole on his left sole.

"Robert," he barked.

There was no answer, nothing except the echo of his own voice, but he had not expected one. His home was far too large. He passed through the hall, seeing not a soul. He had cut his staff down long ago to the all-purpose O'Hara, two equally generic maids, and a cook. Because his staff could hardly keep up with his immense home, he ignored the dust motes hanging in the air and the cobwebs in the corners. He could not help thinking about the bride he had not wanted to begin with. She would hardly find his home pleasant after the pomp and splendor of New York City's highest society. His pulse raced disturbingly at the thought.

Julian traversed another dark, unlit corridor, leaving behind the keep. The wing the family inhabited had been built in the sixteenth century. The floors were parquet, the windows wide. Numerous works of art lined the walls, including a Botticelli, a Velasquez, and a Courbet. Julian had never been able to part with the art his family had accumulated and admired for centuries.

At the door to his brother's chamber he paused, just long enough to hear a feminine giggle. Julian's eyes widened and he shoved open the door.

Robert sat on his four-poster bed, which showed signs of recent activity. He was dressed only in a pair of fine gray wool trousers. His arm was around a local girl Julian vaguely recognized. Julian's stare hardened.

The girl was also half-clad. She squealed, pulling her dress up to cover her abundant breasts. Robert took one look at Julian and turned a ghastly shade of white. He jumped up from the bed while the girl fled. "Julian! You're home!"

"How clever of you, Robert," Julian ground out. He stared. "You are supposed to be at the spa."

Robert ran a hand through his thick chestnut hair. "Julian, can you blame me for wanting to have fun? Before it's too late for me to enjoy myself?"

Julian felt a stabbing all the way to his soul. "No, I do not blame you, but your hedonistic tendencies must be modified, Robert." His gaze had already found the empty bottle of port on the bedside table. "Dammit, the doctors told you to drink less, and not to exert yourself."

Robert smiled slightly. "A little bedsport, brother, is hardly an exertion." Suddenly Robert's expression changed. Julian tensed as he began to cough, uncontrollably, for several moments. Very grim, Julian waited until the fit had passed before speaking. Walking to the bedside table, he poured his brother a glass of water and handed it to him.

"How often have I told you to stay away from the local girls?" he asked quietly.

"She's a widow," Robert said mildly. "I'm hardly as noble or as clever as you, but I'm not stupid."

Julian studied his brother. They were very different men, and not just because Robert was seven years younger and

gravely ill, and not because Robert was fair and auburn-
haired. Robert had always been a charming, reckless rake.
He had left a trail of broken hearts from Clare Island to
Dublin and then to London as well. Julian's eyes narrowed.
Although Robert's cheeks were flushed, he had not lost any
more weight. The last time Julian had seen his brother he
had dark circles under his eyes, his skin had been pasty
white, and he had looked terrible. He appeared to have improved. "You look very well."

Robert smiled, his gray eyes guileless. "I have had a very
good week, Julian. I think the doctors are wrong. I think this
climate is less damaging than they say."

"I want you to return to the spa," Julian said flatly. "No
ifs, ands, or buts about it."

Robert was dismayed. "Julian, I know you have an open
mind. We must speak of this at length. I do not want to spend
my final days in the goddamned spa!"

Julian's chest heaved. "You are hardly at Death's door!"
he snapped furiously. "Do not talk that way!"

Robert's expression was mulish. "I want to enjoy the last
years of my life."

Julian stared. Aching.

Robert smiled and walked over to his brother and slipped
his arm around him. "I am feeling so much better ever since
I came home. My spirits are as important as my health."

Julian felt himself relenting. "They say you only stayed at
the spa for a month. The moment I sailed for America you
left."

Robert shrugged guiltily. "I took advantage of your ab-
sence." He hesitated. "Have you come home alone?"

An emotion Julian had no wish to identify swept through
him. His entire body stiffened. "Yes. But have no fear. I have
done my familial duty. I merely left my rich little bride in
New York until the spring."

"You are married!" Robert was elated. His eyes danced.
"Julian, that is wonderful—tell me about her!"

"There is nothing to tell." Julian looked away as Lisa's
lovely image filled his mind.

But Robert was not about to be put off. He flung his arm around Julian, still grinning. "Is she pretty?"

"Yes."

Robert waited, and when no elaboration was forthcoming, he shook Julian lightly. "Well? Is she fair or dark? Plump or slender? What is her name?"

Julian felt his temples throbbing. "Her name is Lisa. She is Benjamin Ralston's only daughter, and she has the kind of fortune we need to provide your medical treatment and keep up this estate."

Robert stared at him searchingly. "Why don't you send for her now?"

Julian shrugged free of his grasp and paced to the window—only to realize his mistake. From Robert's room there was a perfect view of the shimmering lake. Immediately he turned away. "I have no wish to send for her."

Robert stared; their gazes locked. The silence was tense and laden with unspoken denial. "You need her here, Julian. Don't deny it."

"That's absurd."

"It's been ten years!" Robert cried.

Suddenly Julian was enraged. "Don't tell me how long it has been!" he shouted, his face a dark, furious red.

Robert's eyes widened and he stepped back, as if fearing Julian would strike him.

Julian wanted to hit him. He realized that his fists were clenched, painfully so.

"Julian," Robert said, braced for a blow.

Julian became aware of the rage that threatened to consume him, body and soul. He began to shake. He was terrified of his feelings. But he was a man of iron will, and that will had been honed and strengthened for ten long years. He forced the rage down, forced the fury back to the place where it had been born. When he had gained control, he was drenched with sweat and gasping for breath.

All the while, Robert watched him, tears in his eyes. "Let go," the younger man finally whispered. "Let go. *They're dead.*"

Julian refused to look at him. He left the room.

Robert felt a tear trickle down his cheek. "Goddamn it," he said to himself. "I want my brother back."

It was a prayer.

London

Lisa felt that she was traveling to her doom. She stood motionless at the steamer's railing, staring blindly as London's jagged skyline emerged into view. She had traveled abroad numerous times as a child and as an adolescent with her parents. Once she had loved the sight of St. Paul's needlelike cathedral soaring above the city. Now she did not even notice it.

Lisa gripped the railing with both gloved hands, her pale blue parasol forgotten at her feet. Oh, God. In a few moments she would finally come face-to-face with St. Clare again.

Lisa closed her eyes, feeling quite dizzy and very ill. In the past six months, she had tried very hard to pretend to herself and the world at large that she was still Lisa Ralston, and not St. Clare's wife. But it had quickly proved impossible. At every social occasion, she was introduced as Lady St. Clare, the Marchioness of Connaught, Julian St. Clare's wife. At every tea and soirée the ladies flocked to her, oohing and aahing over her successful marriage to the blue-blooded and oh-so-noble Marquis. "How could you let him leave without you?" she was asked again and again. The ladies thought Lisa so terribly lucky. Not only had she married a title, but her husband was also astoundingly handsome.

She had not wanted to obey his summons when it had come, just as he had promised. But her father was adamant. He had betrayed her with the proxy marriage, and now he had betrayed her yet again, insisting that she join her husband.

How she despised St. Clare.

Yet he haunted her thoughts constantly. Not an hour went by that Lisa did not recall one of their hostile exchanges and his too-handsome face. At night, he frequented her dreams. Too often, then, Lisa was swept back to an earlier time, when he was courting her and she was falling in love, blithely unaware of his motives. She would awaken strangely elated until reality claimed her, leaving her ill and shaken by her comprehension of the truth.

Glumly, Lisa stared over the railing of the steamer. She finally noticed the rowboats floating by the river banks, where parasoled ladies flirted with gentlemen in their derbies and shirtsleeves. The steamer was just passing the London Tower. Two swans drifted by the wharf, and redcoated soldiers guarded the riverside entrance. Lisa stared at the thick, dark walls. Today, the Tower reminded her of a prison. And that was where she was going—to a prison of her own, a prison with no escape. Her spirits had never been lower.

Yet she was trembling, too, her heart racing uncontrollably. In a few more minutes her ship would find its berth. St. Clare would be waiting. Not for the first time, Lisa thought about leaving the ship and fleeing into London's midst. Yet she had failed to escape Julian in New York; she was convinced he would find her if she dared to run away again. His will was far stronger than hers.

The ship was guided to its dock by belching tugboats. Lisa scanned the waiting throngs as the anchors were lowered, the vessel secured, and the gangplanks thrown down. She gripped her parasol so tightly that her gloved hands ached. She did not remark a tall, golden-haired man standing a head above the rest of the cheering crowd.

The passengers began to disembark. Lisa had traveled with her maid, a plump and pretty blond girl Lisa's own age. Betsy loved to chatter, but she was silent now, her blue eyes as large as saucers as she stared at the city of London. Lisa was relieved. Betsy had talked ceaselessly for the entire trip, and Lisa was not in the mood now for her inane conversation. Betsy following, they walked down the gangplank.

There was pandemonium all around them on the wharf.

Passengers were embraced and greeted by relatives and friends. Ladies wept. Children jumped up and down. Gentlemen grinned from ear to ear, and Lisa espied a couple passionately entwined. She recognized the gentleman as a fellow passenger, and suddenly she was envious.

If only . . .

She shoved aside her thoughts.

"Lisa?"

The man's voice was unfamiliar, but unmistakably Irish. Lisa turned to see a tall, handsome gentleman. "Lady St. Clare?" he asked, his gaze sweeping over her so thoroughly that she became aware of being hot and disheveled and probably quite untidy as well.

"I am Lisa *Ralston* St. Clare."

Suddenly he smiled. "And I am your brother-in-law." He gripped her gloved hands tightly, giving Lisa the distinct impression that he wanted to embrace her. "Robert St. Clare, in fact. It is wonderful to finally make your acquaintance."

Lisa managed a wan reply. So this then was the brother with consumption. She had expected a pale invalid, not this charming and flamboyant rake.

Robert did not give her a chance to gather up her thoughts, other than to wonder where St. Clare was. "Good God, how beautiful you are. Julian never said a word!"

Lisa turned red. Her heart banged painfully against her breast. Of course St. Clare hardly thought her beautiful; in fact, he probably described her as a hag.

"I am sorry." Robert tucked her arm in his. "Forgive me. But you know Julian." He laughed uneasily.

Lisa could not hold her tongue. "No. I do not know your brother, not at all." Her tone was acerbic.

Robert stared at her searchingly.

Lisa flushed again and glanced away, reminding herself that she was a lady and she must not allow her ill will towards her husband to make her act in any other manner.

"Perhaps, in time, you will understand Julian better," Robert said at last.

Lisa glanced around carefully. "He is not here." She refused to be disappointed. He had not even come to greet her after her week-long journey and their six-month separation.

"No," Robert protested, "Julian went to make certain that all of our arrangements at the hotel were satisfactory. He should be here at any moment."

Lisa did not comment upon the fact that Robert could have checked upon the arrangements, allowing Julian to greet her. How eager he was to see her again.

But Julian suddenly pushed through the crowd, materializing before her very eyes.

Lisa froze at the sight of him.

His strides faltered as well.

Lisa was momentarily stricken. She had forgotten how stunning he was, how patrician and how elegant—how incredibly masculine. Her heart skipped a beat as their gazes caught and held.

He too appeared stunned by her presence, yet he was the first to look away.

It was then that Lisa noticed the woman he was with. Tall, willowy, and blond, she was as patrician as he. In fact, she might have even been his sister. She was only a few years older than Lisa. Did Julian have a sister?

St. Clare moved forward, taking one of her hands and bowing over it, avoiding her eyes. "I hope your journey was not too tiring," he said, his tone formal. And then he glanced up.

Lisa could not look away. For one moment she felt that she was drowning in a sea of gray. The very same magnetism which had captivated her so thoroughly when they first met pulled at her now—the same magnetism and the same soul. Something stirred deep inside her. But Lisa had been determined to avoid this pull ever since his deception. She would avoid it now by reminding herself of the short history they had shared.

Lisa extracted her hand from his. His palm was hard and warm, even through her white cotton gloves. "The voyage was fine."

"Good." His glance wandered to hers again. And raked

over the bodice of her short, fitted jacket and the length of her narrow skirt, both the palest blue muslin and the latest fashion, to the very tips of her white patent shoes. He turned abruptly, leaving Lisa shaken, and the blond woman stepped forward.

"May I introduce my neighbor, Lady Edith Tarrington," Julian said. "Edith is also staying at the Carleton. When she learned that I was meeting you at the wharf, she expressed her desire to join me. Edith, my . . . bride, Lady St. Clare."

Edith Tarrington smiled at Lisa. "I am so pleased to meet you," she said. "The whole county has been in quite a state since Julian returned home and declared that he had wed. We have all been eagerly awaiting your arrival, Lady St. Clare."

Lisa managed a faint smile. She did not know what to think. Who was this neighbor of Julian's? She was far too beautiful for Lisa to be at ease. Then Lisa realized that Julian was regarding her intently again.

His gaze quickly lowered. "A hansom is waiting. We will spend the night in London, then take another steamer to Castleclare."

At first Lisa failed to reply. She glanced from Julian to Edith Tarrington and back again. Surely Julian would not introduce her to a woman who was significant to him. Surely not. "That is fine."

They stared at one another, almost helplessly.

Robert coughed, grinned, and slapped Julian's shoulder. "To the Carleton then, my friends. Your beautiful bride is surely tired and eager for the finer comforts of life!" His smile faded slightly. "Of course, you will join us, Edith, if you have no other plans?"

Her expression cooled. "How kind of you, Robert. In fact, I am free this evening, and I will gladly join your group."

Lisa felt dismayed, but she told herself that she was being foolish.

Then Edith touched Julian's arm. It was a brief gesture, yet it bespoke years of familiarity. "If it is all right with you, Julian." Her tone was low, intimate.

But Julian was looking at Lisa. "Of course," he said. Then

he stepped aside, gesturing for Lisa to precede him. "After you, ladies," he said formally.

And as Lisa walked forward with Edith Tarrington towards the line of waiting carriages, she felt his eyes on her back, burning with the intensity she had somehow forgotten.

Four

Supper was at eight. St. Clare had reserved a private room for the four of them that was just off the Palm Court, an exalted, palm-filled atrium which replicated the famous interior of the Paris Ritz almost exactly. The Carleton Hotel had been opened by Cesar Ritz three years earlier, and he had done his best to bring France in all of its glory to London.

Lisa was in a state of nervous tension as she exited her rooms. The last person she wished to see was Edith Tarrington, but the other woman was just departing her suite across the hall as Lisa shut her door. The two women paused, looking uncertainly at one another. Lisa forced a smile. "How lovely you look, Lady Tarrington." It was hardly a fabrication. Edith was one of those rare women who looked superb in pale pink, and her evening gown revealed far more of her willowy figure than it concealed.

Edith smiled slightly. "Thank you. Your gown is stunning. I am sure Julian will be impressed."

Lisa had found it almost impossible to decide what to wear. She was loath to dress for the husband she did not want, but she had chosen a silvery chiffon gown that she knew was superb, far more low-cut and provocative than she was used to wearing. Yet she muttered, "Julian will not notice this dress, I assure you of that," before she could think better of it.

Edith started.

Lisa wished she had reined in her unruly tongue. She felt

her cheeks burning, yet could not come up with a comment
to distract Edith Tarrington. Fortunately, Edith resumed her
usual genteel expression, and gestured for Lisa to precede
her. Lisa was glad to do so.

A moment later she came to the head of the stairs, which
looked down on the Palm Court. She tripped.

Edith steadied her with a gloved hand under her elbow.
"Careful—" she began, then instantly followed Lisa's gaze
to the two gentlemen standing on the landing below.

Julian and his brother were a magnificent sight in their
tuxedos, apparently waiting to escort the ladies through the
atrium to the private dining room. Robert had been speaking,
while Julian had seemed restless. Now they were both motionless, staring up at the women.

Lisa had seen Julian in evening clothes before, of course,
but the impact was still shattering and physical. Her heart
skidded to a stop. Her mouth became unbearably dry. In his
black tailcoat and trousers and snowy white shirt, Julian St.
Clare was utterly devastating.

Lisa wished, she desperately wished, that he were an ugly,
old man. She could not continue to fool herself. She despised him, oh yes, she did, but whenever she looked at him
her heart stopped and her body tightened. She remembered
every single one of his soul-shattering kisses. Oh, God. How
had she come to this impasse? To be married to a man she
despised—one so terribly beautiful—a man who did not care
for her at all?

Then Lisa thought about the beautiful blonde beside her,
and she peeked at her. Edith appeared as mesmerized by
Julian as Lisa was, and Lisa's heart sank. Were her suspicions correct?

Yet Julian was staring at Lisa—she was certain of it. And
when their gazes connected, there was no more doubt.

She had become utterly motionless, poised on the stairs
with one hand on the smooth wooden banister. She could not
seem to direct her slippered feet to move. His eyes had
drained her of the ability to function.

Julian finally looked at Edith with a small smile. His jaw

was flexed and he had jammed his hands in the pockets of his tuxedo.

Then Robert came forward. "Ladies, you are a sight for sore eyes. How lovely you are!" He smiled at Lisa, ignoring Edith.

Lisa came down the last three steps. "Thank you."

Julian faced her, extending his arm somewhat stiffly. His glance included Edith. "My brother is correct. You are both lovely. Shall we? Our room is ready."

Lisa's heart sank even further, dismay welling deep inside her. She had wanted some small sign from him that he found her attractive. Clearly he was unimpressed. Or equally impressed with Edith. She forced a smile, giving him her arm. She reminded herself that she did not care. If she should care now about what he thought of her she was forever doomed.

But she noticed that Robert shot his brother a dark look. And in that moment Lisa knew that they would be friends.

Julian escorted her through the hotel lobby. Lisa was aware of the guests, the men in their tailcoats, the ladies in their brilliantly hued evening gowns, turning to stare at them as they passed. What a couple they must make, Lisa thought, suddenly saddened. So clearly at odds with one another. So clearly miserable together.

Julian held out a chair for her, putting Lisa on his right. As she sat, one of his hands accidentally brushed her shoulder blade. She stiffened, shocked by the feeling of his palm on her bare back.

She glanced up at him. His eyes were wide and riveted upon her as well, as if he were as surprised and shaken as she.

Abruptly he turned away.

Robert seated Edith across from Lisa. The men sat down between the ladies, facing one another. Robert leaned toward Lisa. When he spoke, his tone was low, so no one could overhear him. "You make a striking couple. Everyone in the lobby is whispering about the two of you. They want to know who you are."

Lisa could only stare at him; then she realized that Julian

was frowning at them both—and that Robert's hand was covering hers.

Julian fingered his glass of wine, unable to ignore Robert as he leaned close to Lisa, regaling her with story after story about his university days. He had been amusing her all evening. Lisa was smiling, as she had been most of the night. Smiling at Robert.

But then, his brother was a charming rakehell with a reputation half as big as London. Of course Lisa was charmed and amused. Robert was an expert when it came to seducing women.

Julian was relieved, of course, that his brother was being his normal amiable self. Robert, of course, had no interest in Lisa other than a familial one. His gallantry allowed Julian to be a silent observer—it also allowed him to brood.

He had forgotten just how pretty Lisa was.

No, not pretty, breathtaking. So tiny, so dark, and so lovely.

So entirely different from Melanie.

Julian slammed his gaze to the table, lifted his glass, and drained it. He reminded himself that he had no right to any feelings other than formal ones, that she was his wife in name only, and he intended to keep it that way.

"Julian?" Edith's voice was soft with concern. Her gloved fingertips rested briefly on his arm. She had also spent most of the evening silently watching Robert flirt with Lisa. Although most of the county thought that Edith hankered after Julian and was heartbroken over his marriage to another woman, Julian did not believe it—he never had. "Are you all right?" she asked quietly.

Julian surprised them both by answering Melanie's younger sister honestly. "Given the circumstances, I am faring as well as possible." He turned his gaze directly toward her. "And you?"

Edith held his eyes, her own shadowed with unhappiness.

"I suppose my answer is precisely the same." She turned her head and glanced at Lisa and Robert again.

Julian thought that his suspicions about Edith were correct. Having known what it was to love and lose, he pitied her. And Robert, the fool, did not even guess.

His glance strayed yet again across the table to his bride. To his lovely bride, whom he did not want. Not in any way.

Then Julian's grip tightened on his wineglass. Whom was he fooling? The French burgundy he was drinking, and had been drinking steadily all night, had caused a gentle unfurling of warmth in his gut. But it had also caused another reaction, one he was determined to ignore: an incipient fullness in his loins. He had ignored it for some time now, and intended to do so forever if need be.

Then Julian realized that Lisa was not listening to Robert, who was talking about the opera. She was staring at him, her expression frozen. Julian realized that Edith's fingertips still rested upon his arm.

He flushed, realizing what Lisa must be thinking.

Edith must have realized at the same time, because she paled, dropping her hands to her lap.

Lisa turned to Robert abruptly, her face stricken with hurt although her lips formed a stiff smile. Robert said, "Of course, the very next day I woke up on the sofa and couldn't remember where I was. It was downright embarrassing."

Lisa laughed, but this time the sound was shrill and hollow. Her eyes turned to Julian.

Julian could not look away. Her gaze was filled with silent accusation and profound hurt.

He wanted to tell her again that he was sorry. Not for the misunderstanding about Edith, which was ridiculous, but for marrying her against her will, for spoiling all of her girlish dreams. He wasn't an expressive man. He wondered if he could find the right words. Suddenly he knew he had to reassure her. He shoved his chair back abruptly, surprising everyone, even though they had long since finished dessert. "Lisa, would you care to join me for a breath of air?"

The color drained from Lisa's face.

* * *

Lisa was surprised by Julian's invitation, surprised and anxious. He did not hold her arm as they wandered into the hotel's gaslit garden which fronted on Haymarket Street. High brick walls enclosed the garden from the public's view. Lisa was immediately assaulted by the fragrance of lilies, which were on display everywhere. Julian paused by a marble water fountain. Goldfish swam there, catching the light of the tall gaslamps and a beaming full moon.

Lisa stepped away from him, her heart pounding. What did he want?

She had tried not to look at him all evening, to concentrate on Robert, whom she already liked, but it had been impossible. Not when he was seated directly across the table from her, not when his presence was so virile and commanding. And not when Edith and he seemed to share a deep and sincere friendship. But surely they were not lovers. Surely not.

Lisa flushed, because if Julian were in love with Edith Tarrington it would explain so much. It would certainly explain his disinterest in Lisa herself. The possibility had distressed her all night, yet she knew she shouldn't care. Why was she torn this way? She didn't want St. Clare. Yet she was jealous of another woman.

And what did he want now? Lisa could not imagine why he had asked her outside. Certainly not to talk, and certainly not for any other intimacy.

Her thoughts quickly became fixated. He was her husband, and if he was not involved with Edith, he might very well intend to kiss her now, or even later, in her rooms.

Lisa's pulse raced.

And what might happen later? They were man and wife, but they had never consummated their marriage. Did he think to come to her room tonight—to come to her bed? Surely he must do so eventually.

Lisa felt faint at the thought. She had no real desire to let him into her bed—not under these circumstances, dear God.

But she was not immune to his virility. A part of her yearned for his caress, his kiss. Oh, damn her secretly passionate, unladylike soul!

"Lisa?"

She was so lost in her thoughts that she jumped at the sound of Julian's deep voice. She looked up at him, wide-eyed and breathless. "Y-yes?"

He folded his arms across his chest. "I wish . . . I hope you enjoyed supper tonight."

She nodded, unable to look away. "Everything was fine."

He continued to stare at her face. Or was he staring at her mouth? Lisa began to tremble. She could not think of a thing to say. His relentless stare was causing her heart to ricochet inside her chest.

Lisa wrung her hands, certain he was thinking about kissing her. She tried to get a grip on reality by reminding herself that he had married her for her money, regardless of her will. But the night was warm, the moon benevolent, enticing. The scent of freesia and orange blossoms mingled with that of lilies. Lisa was a captive of her husband's charisma, and she could not look away. She wet her lips desperately. "Wh-what is it th-that you wish to say, Julian?"

His jaw was tense. His eyes seemed smoky, warmer than before. He cleared his throat. "There are several matters we must discuss."

Lisa was paralyzed by the increasingly husky sound of his voice.

Julian shoved his hands into his pockets. "I asked you to join me outside because I wished to apologize yet again."

Lisa started. "Apologize?"

"We have gotten off to an exceedingly bad start, you and I. We must rectify this."

"Y-yes," Lisa whispered, hope burgeoning in her breast. Perhaps they might start anew. Perhaps they might even fall in love.

He inhaled. "I have already explained to you about Robert's health and his medical bills." He hesitated. "What is done is done, Lisa. We are married, and surely we can be civilized about this."

Lisa was stiff. She did not like his use of the word "civilized." Nor did she like being reminded of his motives in marrying her in the first place. She waited, hoping he would tell her he cared for her in spite of his need for her money, that he found her pretty, that he wanted to make their marriage a real one . . . a happy one.

Julian swallowed. "Many couples find themselves in a situation similar to the one we are in. Surely you realize that."

Lisa managed a nod, her heart banging like a drum.

"I am not the beast you think me to be—not completely, anyway. For instance, I am prepared to accept the fact that you will not like Castleclare. This evening it occurred to me that if you wish, I will not mind if you reside half the year in New York."

Lisa managed, "I . . . I see." But she was dismayed. How could they build their future if she was away half of the time?

"No, I don't think that you do see." Julian was flushing now, high up on his cheekbones. "What I really want to say is that we must make this marriage a civil one, an amicable one. I shall try to understand you. Thus, if you wish to spend half the year in New York, I shall not prevent you from doing so."

Lisa did not know what to think. What did he mean by an amicable marriage? "I . . . I also wish for this marriage to be amicable, Julian," she said tremulously. "I wish for us to be friends." She could not smile. Her entire future seemed to be hanging in the balance of their conversation.

He stared at her. "I do not think you understand. What I am trying to say is that I will not make any bestial demands upon you."

Lisa could not move. "You are right—I do not quite understand," she whispered finally, but she was lying. Her temples began to throb as the realization of what he was trying to tell her began to sink in.

"God," he cried, raking his short blond hair with one hand. "You are so naive, so innocent. You cannot hide a single one of your feelings!" He faced her squarely, his legs braced wide apart, as if prepared to do battle. "I am not trying to hurt you again."

"You are not hurting me," Lisa lied, praying she would not cry. Something warm and wet trickled down one cheek.

"You don't understand, do you?" He was suddenly bitter. "You are young and you have a full life ahead of you. My life is over. I do not want you to suffer on my account. In fact, if you wish, you can return to New York tomorrow."

Tears filled Lisa's eyes. She heard herself say, "I want to try to make this marriage a successful one. Even you suggested that in New York. We are man and wife—there is no other choice."

"If you mean what I think you mean then the answer is *no*. It is impossible."

Lisa was desperate. "Nothing is impossible. Surely we can become friends."

He spoke thickly. "We cannot become friends. Not in your sense of the word."

"But one day I will have your children!" Lisa cried.

He turned white. "You don't understand!"

"No, I don't. I don't understand *you* at all."

His chest heaved. "Lisa, I think I failed to make myself clear in New York. Our marriage will be successful if we respect one another and treat one another with decency." He paused. *"There will not be any children."*

Lisa had already sensed that this was coming, already dreaded it. She shook her head helplessly.

"This will be a marriage in name only."

"No," Lisa cried, aghast.

"There is no other alternative," Julian said flatly. But his gaze was agonized. "Lisa, you must try to understand."

"No! I do not understand!" Lisa sobbed and fled the garden.

Julian almost called her back. Instead, he sank down on the edge of the marble fountain, covering his face with his hands. He had the distinct feeling that he had just destroyed the last of her innocence without even laying a hand upon her.

Five

Castleclare, Clare Island

"These are your rooms, my lady," O'Hara said happily.

Lisa stared. From the moment they had arrived on Clare Island, she felt as if she were entering an ancient world. The small village where the ferry docked had mesmerized her—thatched-roof cottages of stone and timber appeared to have survived for centuries. There were no gaslines or telephone poles, no motor cars or even horse-drawn trolleys. Smoke puffed out from each and every stone chimney, even on this cool but pleasant May day. A man guided a donkey laden with wooden faggots down one street, a carter drove a shaggy pony down another. A woman stood on one unpaved corner, her plaid apron full of fresh, warm eggs. Barefoot women washed their laundry in a lazy river. And St. Clare's coach had to meander through a flock of sheep crossing the town's largest thoroughfare, an unnamed main street.

But perhaps the most shocking element of all was the silence. Except for the occasional bark of a sheepdog, a baby's cry, and the song of treetop birds, the world of Clare Island was stunningly quiet.

Castleclare belonged to the era of knights in shining armor and their damsels in distress. When St. Clare's coach had finally topped the highest hill, Lisa first glimpsed the castle. Her heart skipped a beat. This was St. Clare's home?

Beige stone walls guarded the castle, a half-dozen square watchtowers rising from them at intermittent intervals. The entrance to the castle consisted of a real barbican—even if it was half in ruin—and an ancient portcullis remained dubiously aloft. Behind those walls a single round tower soared above all the steeply pitched thatch and slate interior rooftops.

Lisa only had to blink to see mailed knights riding through the barbican and archers in their jerkins. With another blink she could see the lady of the castle standing on the imposing front steps of the keep, waiting for her warrior husband to return.

"My lady?" O'Hara intoned.

Lisa did not hear the beaming old man. Eyes wide, she glanced around the huge bedchamber which was now hers. A fire blazed in a huge hearth below an exquisite green marble mantel—one in need of polishing. A beautiful antique gold clock graced it, two standing Grecian statuettes guarding the timepiece. The clock needed a good cleaning. A faded Aubusson rug covered the parquet floor. Lisa noticed several holes. The walls were covered in yellow silk, worn and stained in places, and even torn. The moldings on the ceiling were the most intricate Lisa had ever seen, and above her head, in a trompe l'oeil window, cherubs floated in a blue sky blowing gold trumpets. Tired gold damask draperies adorned the oversized windows. Through them, Lisa had a stunning view of the rolling countryside of Clare Island.

She stared at her canopied bed. It appeared to be a bed of state. It was huge, the coverings mostly gold and purple, the velvet curtains tied back with tasseled cords. Lisa could not imagine sleeping in such a bed. She wondered who had slept there before her, which statesmen, which royalty.

The rest of the room's furniture was as tired and as old, but every faded chair and scratched table reeked of history. Lisa was used to wealth—her father's house was one of the finest in New York—but this was entirely different. She felt as if she had been swept back in time. She could hardly believe that Castleclare was her home, that this was her room.

Yet she liked the room. Very much, in fact.

She liked Castleclare.

For the first time in two days, for the first time since Julian had shocked her with his announcement that he intended no real marriage between them, Lisa felt a rush of excitement. She would spend hours and hours exploring the island and the castle. She could hardly wait to begin.

"M'lady, I am sending up one of your maids with a spot of tea and muffins. Will you be needin' anythin' else? A hot bath, mayhap?"

Lisa started. She had forgotten the butler was there. Then her quick smile faded, because the very bane of her existence stood in the open doorway behind O'Hara.

Her gaze on Julian, Lisa heard herself say, "That will be fine. Thank you, Mr. O'Hara."

He bowed, beaming, patting his worn jacket as he exited.

Lisa's eyes narrowed. O'Hara needed a new suit. His clothing was a disgrace.

Lisa realized now that she was alone in her room with St. Clare. She did not like the intimacy. Not at all. Her gaze lifted to his.

Julian stared at her. "I realize that this hardly meets with your satisfaction," he said impassively. "But you have carte blanche. Please feel free to redecorate this and any other room that you think needs such care—with the exception of my private apartments, of course. Relay your instructions to myself or O'Hara, and they will be carried out."

Lisa lifted her chin, her eyes flashing. "I don't want to redecorate this room."

"Sulking will not improve things," Julian said, his eyes far too probing for comfort.

Lisa did not like looking into his turbulent gray eyes, but could not glance away. The silence grew between them. Stunned, she realized that, in spite of what Julian wished, there was a bond between them—a bond of tension and heat. Ducking her head and angry with herself for wanting him as a man, she said, "I like this room just the way it is."

He started.

"Now, if you will excuse me?" Lisa knew she was being unforgivably rude, but she marched to the door and held it, making it clear that she wished him to leave. His proximity unnerved her. That and her own treacherous thoughts.

Julian looked at her one last time, a sweeping glance that began at her eyes and finished at her toes, then he bowed and strode away. For some reason, Lisa thought that he seemed angry. That pleased her to no end.

Lisa was lost, but she did not mind. She was deep within the castle in yet another, newer wing, a long gallery lined with dozens of portraits of St. Clares. How handsome the men tended to be, handsome and commanding, she mused, and how pretty and elegant the women. But not a single ancestor could compete with Julian's patrician looks.

She wondered where his portrait was, and if it was even in the gallery. She strolled down the length of the narrow room until she found it. She faltered. If the gilded label on the frame had not read "Julian St. Clare, thirteenth Earl of Connaught," she would not have recognized him.

He was smiling.

Her heart hammering wildly, Lisa moved closer to the portrait, her eyes wide. It had probably been painted ten or eleven years ago. Clearly Julian had been a much younger man. But God, he had been so different! His smile was genuine. It reached his eyes, it came from his soul. It was the smile of a happy man.

Lisa wondered what had happened in the past ten years to turn him into such a cold, aloof man. She could not help being disturbed. She would have liked to know the man in the portrait. She sensed that she never would—that he was gone forever. Inexplicably, she was sad.

Lisa decided to leave the gallery, too disturbed to remain. But as she turned her eye caught a glimpse of the portrait besides Julian's, that of an extraordinarily pretty blond woman.

Suddenly filled with dread, Lisa came closer, already certain of what she would find, certain of who that woman was.

"Lady Melanie St. Clare, the thirteenth Marchioness of Connaught," Lisa read aloud.

She stared grimly at the young woman. Lisa could not help noticing how utterly different Julian's first wife was from herself. Not only was she blond, she had a fragility about her, an ethereal quality that made her beauty astounding. Upon closer inspection Lisa saw that her eyes were a robin's egg blue, her complexion perfectly porcelain. And the way that the portraits were placed, it appeared that she and St. Clare were smiling at one another—for all eternity.

Oddly enough, Lisa's heart sank.

What had happened to her? Lisa only knew that she had died. Had Julian loved her? That thought was distinctly upsetting. Worse, Lisa remarked now that Melanie St. Clare bore a distinct resemblance to Edith, although Edith was a much stronger version of the dead woman. She did not like the fact of their resembling one another, not at all. Lisa turned and left the gallery, her stride swift. She had little doubt that Julian had loved his first wife completely.

Was Edith related to her? A cousin or a sister, perhaps? Did Julian see his first wife in the other woman every time he looked at her? Did he yearn for Edith now because of her resemblance to Melanie?

In the corridor outside, Lisa paused, trying to shake both her thoughts and her distress. To make matters worse, she was uncertain about which way to go. Finally she bore left, passing numerous closed doors as she did so. The castle was completely silent except for the harsh echo of her own footsteps.

The corridors were dark. She began to grow uneasy when she did not find the stairwell. She started to feel that she was not alone, which was ridiculous. She began to start at her own shadow. It occurred to her that a castle like this might very well be haunted. Lisa had never faced a ghost before, but she now knew that she believed in their existence.

She finally knocked on a door, not expecting a response.

When she dared to open it, she found a dark, dusty bedroom, the furniture covered in tattered sheets. How many apartments, she wondered, did Castleclare contain?

A movement made her screech. Lisa gasped in relief when she spotted a mouse scurrying across the floor.

Waiting for her pounding heart to still, Lisa realized that she would like to renovate Castleclare. Not redo it, but open and air all the rooms, refinish the furniture, clean the rugs and drapes. Restore the castle to all of its original magnificence and ancient glory.

Lisa hurried on. Relieved, she finally spied a staircase, quickly following it down. She was certain now that she was on the castle's second floor, the floor where her own apartment was.

She could not help wondering, not for the first time, if Julian's rooms were on this floor as well.

Lisa tried another door. It opened with a noisy protest and she barged in on Robert.

He was reclining in bed, fully dressed, but his shirt was open halfway down his chest. He wore his socks but no shoes. He was reading.

He started when he saw her, exactly as Lisa did. She blushed. "I am so sorry!" she cried. "I am lost."

"Please, don't be sorry," Robert smiled, closing the book and standing. "I am glad to see you. Come in."

It wasn't proper, not at all, and Lisa hesitated.

Robert's eyes widened. "I thought we were friends."

"We are," Lisa said firmly. Still blushing, she entered the room, wondering if she dared ask Robert about Julian's first wife. She hovered close to the door.

"Were you exploring your new home?" Robert asked, sauntering over to her.

"Yes. This castle is vast. How many rooms does it contain?"

"I forget whether it's fifty-six or fifty-seven," Robert said lightly. "A hundred years ago the St. Clares were very wealthy and powerful. We had numerous estates, here in western Ireland and in southern England. But my father and grandfather were both gamesters, and between the two of them, they gambled away everything except Castleclare."

"Oh," Lisa said. "That is terrible."

"I believe my brother could turn our fortunes around if he wished to." Robert smiled. "He is a clever man. Many years ago he made some successful investments. But these past ten years, he has lost all interest in the estate."

Lisa wondered if Julian's loss of interest had to do with the obvious change in his character. She hesitated, wetting her lips. "I found the portrait gallery."

"Ah, yes. Did you have a nice visit with all the St. Clare ghosts?"

"It was very interesting." Lisa fidgeted, dying to ask him what was really on her mind while dreading his answer. Then she blurted, "I found Julian's portrait."

Robert had ceased smiling. His gray gaze was curious. "Yes. That was done a dozen years ago. Julian was eighteen and newly wed."

Her heart was hammering. "He was a happy man then."

"Yes. He was. And he was my hero." Robert smiled pensively. "He was seven years older and could do no wrong. I worshipped him. I followed him everywhere. He did not mind. Until . . ." He paused, his glance fastening to hers.

"Until?" Lisa prodded.

"Until he met Melanie."

"His first wife."

"Yes."

Lisa paced across the room and stared out of the thick, grayish window at a small, shimmering lake. She realized she was hugging herself. She turned. "What happened?"

"She was Anglo-Irish. Although her father had an estate here, just across the channel, Melanie was raised in Sussex. The summer she was sixteen she came here with her parents, and she and Julian met and immediately fell in love. She refused to leave her father's Irish estate, and Julian began courting her in earnest. They were wed the following year."

"So he really loved her," Lisa said, feeling miserable. "She was very pretty."

"She was very weak," Robert said, his tone harsh and accusing.

Lisa jerked.

"Yes, Julian loved her, but she was as fragile as hand-blown glass." Robert's stare was chilling. "You don't know what happened, do you? How she died? He hasn't told you, has he, about the accident?"

Lisa shook her head. She was perspiring in spite of the castle's ever-present chill.

"But he wouldn't. He won't speak about it. He's never spoken about it, not to anyone. It happened ten years ago, and Julian has never been the same. When they died, I lost my brother." Robert's voice had become thick.

Lisa trembled. *"They?"*

"They had a child. A little boy. Eddie. He was two years old, blond and beautiful, a little angel. He drowned in the lake."

"Oh, my God," Lisa whispered, turning to look at the jewel-like lake. In spite of the leaded glass, it was the color of emeralds, sparkling in the spring sun. A place of peace—a place of death.

Robert's eyes were filled with tears. "Julian was bereft. Hysterical. As was Melanie. Instead of comforting one another, they retreated from one another. Melanie locked herself up in her rooms, Julian in his. And there was anger. So much anger with the grief. I begged Julian to come out. I was so frightened. Although Melanie had taken Eddie to the lake that day, Julian blamed himself for the tragedy."

Lisa was breathless with dread. *"What happened?"*

"Two days after Eddie died, Melanie left her rooms. No one knew—it was at sunrise. She went down to the lake clad only in her nightclothes." He stopped and brushed his eyes with his fist.

"No," Lisa said, already understanding, horrified.

"Yes," Robert said softly. "She drowned herself."

Six

Lisa had to sit down. She was vaguely aware of Robert guiding her to a chair. She covered her face with her hands. She ached for Julian with every fiber of her being. And now she understood.

Oh, God, how she understood.

"He has never recovered," Robert said, kneeling on the floor beside her. He took her two hands in his. "I know you are angry with my brother for marrying you without love, against your will. He told me how you ran away. You are a brave, strong woman, Lisa, and a beautiful woman—exactly the kind of woman my brother needs."

Lisa wiped her eyes, unable to put the tragic double death out of her mind. She stared at Robert. "I am not sure what you mean. Julian doesn't need me. He did not marry me out of choice. I thought he was falling in love with me, fool that I was. I had no idea that he had come to America to wed an heiress." She was careful not to mention that she knew about Robert's consumption. She wasn't sure if he would be pleased that she was aware of his ill health.

"That is the past. What is done is done. He does need you, Lisa," Robert said in an urgent tone.

Their eyes met. For an instant, Lisa was unable to move. "What are you saying?" Her pulse was racing. Surely Robert did not mean what she thought he meant.

He gripped her hands more tightly. "I have no doubt that you will thaw his icy heart. And bring back the man we have all lost."

Lisa laughed in disbelief. "Me?" She was strangely out of breath. "How on earth could I thaw his heart?"

"The way all women thaw all men, Lisa, sweet. By making him fall in love with you."

Lisa was so stunned that she could not make a sound. She did not even blink.

Robert chuckled. "Surely you are up to the task?"

"T-task?" she squeaked. She found her tongue. "He doesn't even think I'm pretty!"

Robert snorted. "You are beautiful. No man could think otherwise, and that includes my brother."

"I . . . other men have found me attractive," Lisa said hesitantly. "Robert, this is absurd! Julian truly does not know I exist!"

"He knows."

Lisa trembled. She was frightened—exhilarated. "What about Edith?"

"Edith?" Robert's tone was strange. "She is Melanie's youngest sister, you know. But she is nothing like Melanie. Julian never considered marrying her. I know that for a fact."

"Are they . . . close?"

Robert hesitated. "They are friends. Forget about Edith. Julian is an honorable man. He is not dallying with her, Lisa. I am certain of it."

Lisa studied her hands. Robert's proposal had left her breathless.

"The alternative is to give up on him, to let your relationship flounder, to remain perfect strangers," Robert pointed out.

Lisa was afraid. The stakes were so high—if she dared attempt what Robert suggested, if she dared to try to tame the beast and set Julian free. "Just what is it that you expect me to do?" she whispered. "How would I even start to make him . . . fall in love with me?"

Robert's grin was reckless. "That's easy, sweetheart. Seduce him."

Lisa opened her mouth to protest, but no sound came out. Her eyes were as round as saucers.

"You could do it, Lisa," Robert said fiercely, his gray eyes flashing. "And I would help you. I know all there is to know about seduction."

Seduce Julian. Seduce him—win his heart—make him fall in love with her. Lisa was in shock.

It was a monumental task. She did not know the first thing about seduction—she was no temptress. She would make a fool of herself, she was certain, if she dared to try what Robert was so firmly suggesting. "Perhaps," she said huskily, "I might befriend him first?"

Robert's wide grin flashed. "Seduction is the way to a man's heart—especially in my brother's case."

Lisa was frozen. Her mind raced. Panic warred with excitement, despair with hope. And her anger was gone. It had drained away, leaving in its place a deep, abiding compassion. He had loved once and lost everything. How could she turn her back on him now, ignoring what she knew, no matter how afraid she was of his rejection?

"Well?"

Lisa was suddenly quite faint with the prospect. "You are mad," she managed in a rough whisper. "We are both mad."

"Is that a yes? Do you agree?" Robert asked exultantly.

Lisa nodded.

They stared at one another, the first bonds of conspiracy forming between them.

"I will tell you exactly what to do, even what to wear," Robert told her in a low, confidential tone.

But Lisa did not hear him. Images danced in her head of herself, clad in one of her lacy peignoirs, sauntering over to Julian, who was reading in front of the fire. She would sashay just a bit, the way the hussies did on stage in theatrical productions, and suddenly he would realize that she was there. He would be stunned. His gaze would slide over her. Lisa would smile seductively, and as she turned to face him, her silk jacket would open . . .

Lisa sighed. Who was she fooling? Not once in her life

had she sashayed around in her peignoir, and she knew nothing about seduction, nothing at all. Even with Robert's help, she would probably make a fool of herself. "I am going to need a lot of help."

"Have no fear," Robert said with absolute assurance.

Lisa was not soothed. And her trepidation increased when Robert's door swung open and Julian entered. She stiffened as her cheeks turned red.

"Robert," Julian said irascibly, not having seen Lisa yet, "do you know where my little bride . . ." He stopped in mid-sentence, his eyes widening as they found her.

Robert dropped his hand from Lisa's shoulder and rose to his full height. "Yes?"

Julian looked from Robert to Lisa, his expression one of utter surprise—and then one of stern displeasure. "I see," he said slowly.

Lisa got to her feet. Her nerves were rioting, her face burning. Surely Julian did not think that she and Robert were carrying on in any illicit manner? Her gaze met his. His was cold and dark and seemed angry. Lisa regretted being closeted with Robert in his bedroom.

"Hello, Julian," she said unsteadily. "I was lost and I had no idea that I was outside of Robert's room."

Julian's expression was set in stone. "You are hardly outside of my brother's room." He looked again at Robert. "What were the two of you discussing with your heads so close together?"

Lisa could not think of a suitable reply.

"Your bride was exploring. She has been in the portrait gallery. We were talking about the family, of course." Robert smiled and walked over to his brother, then smacked his shoulder. "What's wrong? Are you jealous, Julian? Am I not allowed to converse with your bride?"

Julian flushed. "Do not be absurd," he snapped. He directed his cool stare at Lisa. "The cook wishes to discuss the evening's menu with you, Lisa."

"Of course," she managed, fingering the fabric of her skirt. She could not force a smile, not even a small one. She desperately wanted to tell Julian that she understood, that she was sorry. She also wanted to explain that there was nothing improper between her and Robert, and that there never would be. Suddenly feelings she had thought dead and buried were welling up inside of her—feelings of wild, aching love. Lisa was shocked to recognize them.

Robert seemed amused. "I am not feeling very well. I think I will take a nap. Why don't you show Lisa to the kitchens, Julian? She won't be able to find the way herself."

Julian nodded curtly. He gestured, and Lisa preceded him from the room. She was acutely aware of him directly behind her.

They traversed the corridor and went downstairs in silence. Lisa had to hurry to keep pace with Julian. As they crossed the cavernous central hall, she drew abreast of him and dared to peek at his face. Was he angry? Or had she imagined it? Was he jealous?

Could it be possible?

A man had to have strong feelings in order to be jealous. Julian had never given her any indication that he had any feeling towards her at all.

Lisa could stand it no more. She plucked on his sleeve. When he failed to halt, she gripped it more firmly. "Julian, stop!"

He paused, his hands on his hips. It was an intimidating posture. "You have something to say to me?"

Lisa dared not think. "Yes. Julian, Robert and I were only talking, and surely you don't—"

"Of course I don't," he said coldly.

Lisa flushed. "I have displeased you."

"No. To the contrary, I am glad that you and my brother are such good friends." His tone did not soften.

Lisa was afraid to bring up the subject of his first wife and son. But she stared up at him, hurting for him, feeling for him, consumed with the love she had thought lost forever. "Julian?"

He waited, his gaze upon her upturned face.

Her heart pounded explosively. "Julian, I saw your portrait in the gallery," she began.

Julian's head shot up, his entire body stiffening. "I am sure that you had an amusing afternoon," he said, cutting her off, "but the cook is waiting." He turned abruptly, crossing the hall with long, hard strides, not even waiting for her.

Lisa was frozen. Had he guessed what she wanted to discuss? Had his rudeness been intentional—and meant to prevent her from raising the subject she so desperately wished to explore? Lisa could not help but think so.

Slowly, she followed him to the kitchens. Now that she understood what the shadows in his gray eyes meant, she could not stop thinking about him and his tragic loss. Her mind was made up.

Lisa paced her bedroom, still in her purple evening gown, an immodest iridescent affair which Robert had chosen. She was trying to decide what to do. Supper had been tense. Julian had not noticed her gown; in fact, Lisa thought that he had hardly noticed her. Julian had spent the evening studying his wine and pushing his food around. His mood had never been darker. Thank God for Robert, who had chatted with Lisa for most of the night.

She had not been able to take her eyes from Julian, who was so incredibly handsome even while so taciturn. Whenever she had thought about what she must do later that night, she had shivered with an odd combination of terror and excitement.

There was a soft rapping on her bedroom door. Lisa quickly opened it and Robert slipped into her room.

"What are you waiting for?" he asked, but he was not smiling. "Julian has gone to his rooms."

"Oh, God," Lisa whispered, suddenly so terrified she was ready to give up their plan before even starting.

Robert gripped her arm. "You have to do this."

She looked into his intense gray eyes and slowly nodded. "Tell me how to—start."

He smiled briefly. "Tell him that you wish to discuss the castle's condition. Choose a chair and sit down. Lean forward a bit. Do not worry if he looks down your dress."

Lisa felt her cheeks turning red.

"Talk about hiring more staff and spring cleaning. Look up at him with wide eyes. You have wonderful eyes, Lisa, so very expressive. Don't be afraid to use them."

Lisa nodded fearfully.

"At some point go up to him and place your hand on his arm and ask him in a soft voice if he truly minds what you intend to do. Be as soft and feminine as possible."

"I don't know about this, Robert," Lisa said. "How do I get him to kiss me?"

"Tonight is not a night to entice him into kissing you," Robert said. "Don't even worry about it, unless he kisses you. If he does, be receptive. Respond naturally. I am sure I don't have to tell you what to do." Suddenly he appeared anxious. "Has Julian ever kissed you, Lisa?"

She blushed. "When he was courting me."

His gaze was direct. "Did you like his kisses?"

"Robert!" Lisa protested.

He smiled briefly. "Well, that is a relief."

"He hasn't kissed me since I ran away from him the night of our engagement party," she said somewhat miserably.

"He will." Robert sounded confident. "Forget about kissing tonight. I just want you there in his room, looking so beautiful and innocent. You will stir his heart and soul, Lisa, as well as his body. I am sure of it."

Lisa gnawed on her lip. "I seem innocent?"

"Very."

Feeling as if she were about to face the hangman, Lisa turned towards the door. Robert halted her. "One more thing," he said, his hand on her shoulder, "don't talk about the accident."

Lisa started, about to protest, as Robert opened the door and gave her a gentle push. She found herself in the dimly lit corridor.

Her heart thundering in her ears, she refused to deliberate.

She had already learned that Julian's suite was at the other end of the floor. Quickly she traversed the hall. Suddenly quaking with fear, Lisa knocked on his door.

It was opened instantly.

Seven

Julian stood on the threshold of his suite in his shirt-sleeves, which were rolled up to his elbows to reveal muscular forearms dusted with golden hair. His shirt was unbuttoned to his waist. Lisa almost gasped at the breadth of his chest and the tense lines of his abdomen. He was still wearing his black wool trousers, but his feet were bare. She had never seen a man in such deshabille before. She could hardly tear her gaze upwards to his face.

But she did. And when their eyes met, time stood still. Lisa could actually hear her own racing heartbeat.

Julian's expression shut down. He took a step backwards, his lean, broad-shouldered body blocking his doorway as effectively as any physical barrier. "You wish to speak with me?"

It was very hard to formulate the single word, "Yes." Lisa's voice was a shaky whisper.

His gaze darted to hers again, searchingly. As he stared at her, Lisa thought he would refuse her request. Instead, his expression hard and somehow stoic, he stepped aside. Lisa entered the sitting room of his suite.

She did not notice its appointments other than the hearth containing a blazing fire and a pale, worn rug that covered the wooden floors. Her senses were rioting and focused only on the tall, golden-haired man standing beside her. Lisa was trying to remember Robert's instructions but her mind remained a solid blank. Only one word was engraved there—seduction.

"Lisa," he said harshly. "You wish to speak to me?"

Lisa jerked. Panic filled her. What was she supposed to say? Oh, yes, the castle! "The castle," she whispered hoarsely, beginning to feel flushed.

"The castle?" he echoed, his gray gaze riveted on her.

Lisa tried to unscramble her brain. "Castleclare."

"I know the name of my home," he snapped.

Lisa flinched.

He turned away, his shoulders squared. He ran a hand through his short, golden hair, then faced her grimly. "You wish to speak to me about Castleclare. What is on your mind?"

Lisa had been staring at his mouth. His mobile, surprisingly full mouth. Flushing hotly, she nodded, still attempting to gather her wits. She was supposed to sit down and lean forward. Relieved, she suddenly darted across the room, aware that Julian was watching her like a hawk, and perched stiffly on a faded red velvet settee with gold trim and tassels. Julian stared at her, his brow furrowed.

"We need staff," Lisa blurted. And then she remembered to lean forward.

His stare did not waver. "Yes, we do," he said slowly. Suddenly his gaze slipped below her throat.

Lisa could not believe that Robert's plan was working. Julian was actually looking at her decolletage. Her heart skidded to a stop.

His eyes rose abruptly, and for a split second, their gazes locked. His gray eyes were distinctly bright. A scant instant later he wheeled and was pacing the room. Lisa took a deep, fortifying breath. She could not tear her own gaze from him. The muscles in his thighs and buttocks kept pulling the fabric of his wool trousers taut.

But she was less afraid now, even growing elated. Robert's plan was working, for she was almost positive that Julian's expression meant he did desire her.

He faced one of the triple-sized windows, speaking without turning to face her. "You may hire more staff. Draw up a list of the servants you require. I shall glance over it to-morrow."

Lisa did not move. But she recalled the rest of Robert's instructions now and knew that she was supposed to get up, sashay over to him, and place her hand on his arm. She was so nervous she felt frozen.

Julian whirled. "Is there something else?" His tone was like the lash of a whip. His gaze remained riveted on her face—as if he were afraid of looking anywhere else.

Slowly, Lisa stood up.

Julian's expression turned slightly comical—as if he knew what was about to happen but just could not believe it.

Lisa began to walk towards him, feeling as if she were in a trance. Then she remembered she was supposed to sashay. She swung her hips. Julian's eyes widened. Feeling re-warded, she put more effort into each pelvic tilt. Forward and back, then side to side. Julian stared at her, wide-eyed and motionless.

Lisa reached him, panting from her efforts. She looked up at him, recalling what Robert had said about using her eyes. She batted her lashes, something she had never done before. Julian stared down at her, a flush high upon his cheekbones.

Lisa placed her small, soft palm on his hard, bare forearm. Touching him caused a quick thrill to sweep over her; it left her breathless, even giddy. "Julian?" Lisa whispered, batting her lashes again.

His chest rose and fell. His nostrils flared. His eyes blazed. *"What the hell do you think you're doing?"* he mut-tered furiously.

Lisa felt as if she had been socked. In the abdomen. For a moment, as their gazes locked, she thought she had mis-heard him. But there was no mistaking his anger.

"Lisa?" he demanded. Suddenly his hand closed on her wrist, yanking her palm from his arm. He flung her hand aside. *"Just what the hell is going on?"*

Lisa jerked, realizing with horror that she had not en-thralled him, only enraged him.

He towered over her, his hands on his hips. "I think you should return to your room," he said tersely.

Lisa's eyes filled with tears. Oh, God! She had made a fool of herself—as she had known she would! Lisa turned to flee. Instead, she tripped on the flounced hem of her gown and crashed to the floor, landing on her hands and knees.

"Lisa!" Julian cried, the anger gone from his tone.

She was intent on running away to the sanctuary of her room. She should have never listened to Robert. She tried to get up, but her skirts made it an impossible task, and she was also hampered because she couldn't see clearly, her vision blurred by tears. She was still on her hands and knees when she felt Julian kneel beside her. She froze.

Suddenly he gripped her waist, his hands hard and strong and large. Their effect was like a red-hot iron brand.

Julian had frozen as well.

Stunned by the suddenly explosive feeling pervading her, Lisa shifted slightly so she could look into his eyes. His were glittering and hot.

For the space of a single heartbeat neither of them moved. Julian's hands still held Lisa's waist, but his gaze was fastened on her mouth.

Lisa wanted his kiss. She had never wanted anything more. His name was on the tip of her tongue. It rode her soft, trembling breath. *"Julian."*

He tore his eyes away. "Let me help you up," he said thickly.

Lisa found herself on her feet a moment later, Julian having put a safe distance between them. She could not seem to slow her rioting heart, or calm her rampaging senses.

Julian's fists slammed into the pockets of his trousers. Lisa's eyes widened and she couldn't help but stare. There was a long, thick protrusion behind his button-front fly.

"Lisa, it is time for you to leave."

Lisa dared not look at him again. She walked to the door, her knees weak and buckling. She paused, her hand on the knob, feeling his eyes burning holes in her back. She jerked around. "Julian . . ."

She could not continue. In truth, she did not even know what she wanted to say. His eyes ensnared her again, their ferocity frightening her, thrilling her.

"I am asking you to leave now," he said very forcefully.

She met his stormy eyes. "Why won't you kiss me?"

He inhaled, the sound sharp and ripe.

"Julian?" Lisa said desperately.

His temples pounded visibly. "I thought I made myself clear," he ground out, "that this marriage is one in name only."

"Why?" Lisa implored. "Julian, why?"

"Because," he said, perspiring, "it is what I wish."

Tears filled Lisa's eyes again. "So you shall be loyal to a dead woman for the rest of your life?"

He stiffened abruptly.

Lisa could not stop. "I am sure that you loved her, and that she was wonderful as a woman and a wife. I do not think to compete with her—I would not dare—but can't you give me a chance?"

One word, rasped. "No."

Lisa recoiled.

"No!" Julian shouted.

Lisa was frightened, for Julian was furious. She fought with a bravery she had never known she possessed. "She is dead, Julian. Melanie and Eddie are dead. Your loyalty won't bring either of them back. It accomplishes nothing. Please think about what I have said."

"Do not say another word," Julian cried in a dangerous voice.

But Lisa was compelled. She had to finish what she had begun. "Julian, do not misunderstand. If I could change the past and make things right for you, I would. I would give her back to you if I could, her and your son. I don't know why I have this desire, I don't know why I care at all when we are perfect strangers and I have been so hurt and betrayed by you. But I do care, I do. About you. It is time to let them go. I am so sorry, Julian. So sorry."

Julian stared at her, incredulity and rage suffusing his

face. "Get out," he said, bracing himself on one of the bed's posters, his body shaking.

He was in pain. Terrible, terrible pain. Lisa saw it, sensed it—felt it. She wanted, desperately, to gather him to her breast as one would a hurt, frightened child. She moved across the room. She did not think. She wrapped her arms around him from behind and laid her cheek against his trembling back.

He whirled violently, the movement throwing her across the room. Lisa almost fell again, but managed to regain her balance.

"Do not interfere! Get out! Leave me alone!" he roared.

Lisa jumped backwards, cringing against the bureau.

He suddenly moved forward, towards her. Lisa pressed her spine into the wood, suddenly regretting everything, realizing the jeopardy she was in. He towered over her. "Never dare to speak to me about them!" he shouted. "You have no right!"

Lisa wanted to tell him that she had every right. She was his wife now, his flesh-and-blood wife, not the ghostly Melanie. But she did not dare. Tears streaked her cheeks, tears of despair, of fear. She quite expected him to strike her.

But he suddenly turned away with a soft, ragged moan. Covering his face with his hands, he whispered, "Get out, Lisa."

She was immobilized, wondering if he was crying.

"Please," he said, his back to her, his shoulders sagging.

Lisa's heart broke. She slipped past him and fled.

Eight

No matter what, he was going to stay away from her.

At all costs.

Julian's room was immersed in darkness, lit only by the glow of the dying fire in the pale, marble-manteled hearth. He was not in the stately canopied bed. He stood motionless by one of the windows, staring out into the moonless night. From his bedroom window, he could just make out the flash of whitecaps on the pitch-black bay.

If only he could stop thinking about her.

Her. Lisa. He refused to think of her as his wife.

Yet her image haunted him. What had she intended? To seduce him? The idea was almost laughable. Instead, a wave of grief rose up in him, so intense that it almost choked him.

He covered his face briefly with his hands. A tremor swept through his lean body. He realized, too late, his mistake. He had married a girl who was charmingly innocent, naturally good-natured, and far too beautiful. How could he have been such a fool?

He should have attached himself to a skinny, older woman like Carmine Vanderbilt, who had been in the market for a titled husband for more years than anyone could count. Then, he would not have been so terribly tempted.

Julian cursed his body for its betrayal.

He paced. Lisa knew nothing about seduction, and her efforts might have been comical if they had not been so utterly original and somehow so damn enticing in spite of her bumbling. Dammit. He couldn't laugh, and he couldn't cry, not when he was filled with such lust.

It had been so goddamn long.

He paced, cursing himself for being a mere man.

The real problem was that Lisa was not just innocent and beautiful, but compassionate and kind. He had chosen her thinking her nothing but a hothouse flower, a spoiled and spineless debutante. How wrong he had been. She possessed nerves of steel, iron-willed determination, and the courage of an entire pride of lions. Yet she was naive, innocent and, except for her amateur attempt at seduction, incapable of manipulation. Her every emotion was expressed on her face and in her golden-brown eyes. Tonight Julian had hurt her yet again, as unintentionally as all the other times.

How he hated hurting her.

But she had felt far more than hurt, and far more than compassion. Julian recalled a single shared look, after Lisa had tripped and fallen, when he was helping her to her feet. God, she had wanted him then, too.

Julian's hand slipped, once, and he touched himself. In his mind he pretended it was Lisa touching him and he could not stand it.

How could he survive like this?

He had to stay away from his bride. Dear God, he had to.

But a tiny voice taunted him, saying, so what? So what if you take her to your bed? *So damn what?*

The rage came so quickly that Julian did not recognize it until it was too late. His hand flew out, striking the vase of flowers from the corner table. Blue and white porcelain hit the floor, shattering loudly. Wildflowers lay strewn on the old Arabian rug amidst the broken shards and the puddle of water.

Julian groaned. Regret seized him, body and soul. Not just regret for breaking the vase his mother had cherished, a gift from Julian's grandmother, but a vast, deep, bitter regret.

He regretted the past, he regretted the present—and he feared the future.

Breathing harshly, ignoring his sex, Julian walked to the

sideboard and poured himself a shot of Irish whiskey. It was a poor substitute for what his body needed.

But he had no choice.

Passion was to be denied at all costs. Forever. Just as he must forever deny himself his heart.

Lisa had not seen Julian in days. The morning after her humiliating effort at seduction, he had left Castleclare, leaving her only a brief note. *Matters of business require my attention in London immediately. Regretfully, Julian St. Clare.*

Lisa did not believe him for a moment.

He was running away from her and their problems.

She sat on a red plaid blanket with Robert, a picnic of roasted chicken, vegetable salads, and hot buns laid out beside them. She could not stop thinking about Julian, wishing desperately that there had been a different ending to that other night.

Lisa knew now that Robert was wrong. She was not going to seduce Julian and make him fall in love with her. He was a man stricken with dark demons, and she was only a young, sheltered woman hardly capable of exorcising them.

How she ached though, wishing that she could.

A part of her still yearned to try.

Robert tugged playfully on her hair. "A penny for your thoughts, sister-in-law?"

Lisa smiled wanly. "I am not sure that they are worth that."

Robert was stretched out on his side, his jacket was open, hatless, as the May sun beat down on his pale face. Had he not been so pasty, with dark circles under his eyes, Lisa would never have thought him a man soon fated to die.

"Then I'll guess," he said, grinning. His smile faded. "You are thinking about my pigheaded brother."

Lisa hugged her knees to her chest, her blue and white skirt belled out around her. "Yes."

"He is afraid of you, Lisa. Afraid of his own feelings. That is why he has run away."

"It would be nice if you were right, but after the other night, he probably cannot stand the sight of me," Lisa replied. She had told Robert almost everything.

"After much reflection, I have decided that the other night actually went well."

"How can you say that?" Lisa gasped. "It was so horrible—you have no idea!"

"Surely you are not ready to give up?"

Lisa stared at Robert's cheerful face. How *could* she give up? After a few days respite, she felt far less humiliated than she had, but she could not shake Julian's image from her mind. Sometimes she even imagined him looking at her with his hot eyes. At other times she saw him with his hands covering his face, his body wracked with a pain that was not physical.

"Why did he love her so much?"

Robert was somber. "Lisa, when she took her own life, they were still newlyweds. She was beautiful but very simple. She was sweet and uncomplicated. Yet he is a very complicated man. I am not sure Julian would fall in love with Melanie if he met her today, but they truly suited each other then."

"That hardly matters," Lisa said morosely. "Julian is in love with a ghost."

Robert sat up with a wry smile. "Do you really think he is still in love with her, Lisa?"

Lisa sat up straighter, her heart pounding. She thought about what Robert had said. "There are probably many feelings locked up inside Julian. Love may very well be one of them."

"I think there is a single feeling inside my brother, and it is not love. It is rage."

Lisa stared, her fists curled by her sides. "Yes," she said slowly, "Julian is certainly angry. But I am not sure that your plan will work. In fact, I doubt it. I do not think I am woman enough to mend his soul and steal his heart."

"I think," Robert said lazily, picking up a handful of cherries, "that you are precisely the woman for the task."

Julian had stayed in London for a fortnight. He had taken care of several affairs, most of which involved paying off debts acquired over the past ten years and re-establishing his and his brother's personal credit. A gentleman survived with credit, and Julian had been tardy in rectifying matters since his marriage to Lisa.

But the closer he came to Castleclare, the more tense he became. Lisa's image had stayed with him during the entire trip. He had not been successful in forcing it to the back of his mind. Now, as he strode through his home, he could think of little else. Inexplicably, he wanted a glimpse of her. Or had she left him while he was gone? Julian would not be surprised. He would be relieved—he would be dismayed.

O'Hara met him in the library. "Her Ladyship is out with your brother, m'lord," he said blandly. "Cook made them a hearty picnic."

Julian felt a stab of jealousy, but was rational enough to realize that it was misplaced. Robert had only brotherly feelings for Lisa. In the next instant, the jealousy returned with a vengeance. But what if Lisa fell in love with Robert?

Many women had succumbed to his gallantry and charm. Tersely, Julian asked, "Are they alone?"

"Yes, m'lord." O'Hara smiled. "Y' know yer brother. Robert said he had no need of grooms. Guess he wants the lass all t' himself."

Julian was well aware of O'Hara's prompting. He tamped down a scowl. "Where are they?"

"They took the small gig and drove out towards the lake."

Julian halted in mid-stride, a feeling of nausea rising in him. He ignored it and it subsided. A moment later he was hurrying outside and ordering his favorite mount brought around. While he was waiting for the seventeen-hand sorrel, he saw a rider enter Castleclare through the barbican. It was Edith Tarrington.

Julian mounted as she rode up to him at a canter. Edith was a superb horsewoman who often hunted with the hounds. "Hello, Edith."

"Julian, have you just returned?" She reined in beside him.

"Yes."

"Where are you off to in such a rush?" she asked, studying his face. She was wearing a pale green riding habit that set off her porcelain complexion perfectly.

"Robert has taken my bride on a picnic," Julian stated, aware of how frequently he now thought of and referred to Lisa as his bride. He refused to wonder why.

"I see," Edith said somberly.

Julian looked her in the eye. "Why don't we join them?"

Edith nodded, her face reflecting a tension that was hardly characteristic of her. In unison, they wheeled their mounts and cantered down the drive and through the raised portcullis. Julian could not enjoy the fast ride. He kept thinking about Robert and Lisa sharing the picnic, imagining Robert's amusing quips and Lisa's honest laughter. He kept imagining her smile, her dimples, and her shining eyes.

A moment later he and Edith topped a rise. Julian's reaction was immediate. He halted his cantering horse far too abruptly, causing the animal to rear. Below, he saw the shimmering, emerald green lake where Eddie had drowned and Melanie had taken her life.

"Julian?"

It was a moment before he could speak. The nausea seized him again; he ignored it. "I am fine," he lied. He had not been to the lake since their deaths.

He spurred his sorrel forward, having spied Robert and Lisa as small figures beneath several trees. Edith followed.

He cantered down the slope. Robert and Lisa heard him approaching and turned to watch. Julian halted his gelding but did not dismount. He barely glanced at Robert, who rose to his feet, grinning amiably. Julian could not take his eyes from Lisa.

As she returned his stare, a warm pink crept up her cheeks.

Julian could not ignore it. Desire stabbed him harshly, directly in the loins, and with it, a soul-felt yearning far more potent.

Lisa remained motionless.

The devil inside him taunted, *Why not? Why not let go of the past?*

Then Edith came cantering up behind Julian. Reining in, her gaze swept everyone. "Hello, Lisa, Robert."

As Robert replied, Julian slid to his feet, his jaw set with the resolve he had lived with for a decade. He left his horse drop-reined and moved slowly towards her. Lisa began to rise as Julian extended his hand. Their palms clasped. As he pulled her to her feet he felt his pulse racing uncontrollably. He had not planned to approach her this way.

And he knew, *he knew,* that he should release her hand, turn around, and go—but he was incapable of behaving rationally.

She wet her lips. "Hello, Julian. Did you have a pleasant trip?"

He knew he was staring, but he could not tear his gaze away. She was so perfect and so lovely, and her lips were full and ripe and meant for kissing. If only he could forget those few times he had plundered there when he was courting her in New York City. "Yes."

Lisa looked at her toes, fidgeting.

Suddenly Julian heard himself say, tersely, "Walk with me."

She started, her eyes wide and wary. Wincing, he remembered his previous rejection of her. Julian tried to force a smile and failed. He held out his arm.

Slowly, Lisa placed her palm in the crook of his elbow.

They walked away from Robert and Edith in a strained silence. Julian's heart was drumming. He knew he should speak, any trivial subject would do, but instead, he was consumed with the idea of kissing her, just once. Dammit. He wanted to kiss her, badly, so badly, but knew he did not dare.

He would never be able to stop with a single kiss.

"Julian?" Lisa asked in a nervous tone. "Are you all right?"

Julian paused beside a pile of boulders which blocked his view of the lake. He raked a hand through his hair. It was trembling. "Why do you ask?"

"You keep staring," Lisa said tersely.

Julian's jaw ground down. It was on the tip of his tongue to tell her that he kept staring because she was impossibly lovely, but that kind of talk did not come easily to a man like himself—and he had not flattered any woman since Melanie. "I am sorry. I am just . . . tired."

Lisa licked her lips again. "Perhaps we should all go back to Castleclare."

"Yes," he said, when he really wanted to say no. Lisa turned to walk back to the picnic area. Julian had to clench his fists to stop himself from seizing her—and pressing her body tightly against his.

Reluctantly, torn as never before and acutely aware of it, Julian followed her. Over Lisa's shoulder, he saw Robert and Edith standing in awkward silence. Then he looked at Lisa's rigid back.

Oh, God, he thought with an inward groan. He should have stayed in London. Returning to Castleclare was a mistake. He wanted her so fiercely—he could not remember ever wanting a woman this much before. But surely that was because of the physical state he was in. Surely that was because he hadn't had a woman in ten achingly long, lonely years.

Not in ten goddamn years.

Nine

Although Julian had returned home, Lisa did not see hide nor hair of him in the next few days, except at suppertime. He remained locked in his library or he rode out across the island. After the fiasco Lisa had caused with her miserable attempt at seduction, she did not dare intrude when he was closeted with his business affairs, or ask to join him when he galloped through the castle gates.

But she would watch him ride away through her bedroom window, a magnificent figure astride his sorrel, and her heart would twist, hard. His misery had affected her greatly—she could not bear to witness it. If only he would extend his hand even halfway towards her, Lisa would meet him the rest of the way.

She could not stop thinking about him. Could not stop imagining how it might be if only he would bend just a little. Lisa could imagine passion bursting between them—and the following blossoming of love. If only . . .

To soothe her injured soul, to heal the ever-present hurt in her heart, and to distract herself from what was fast becoming an obsession, Lisa focused her efforts on restoring Castleclare. Through O'Hara, Julian had approved her plans, although Lisa was not certain he had really paid any attention to them. She and Robert hired a dozen carpenters and twice as many maids, several gardeners and groundskeepers, and eight new permanent staff, including a housekeeper. Lisa now awoke every morning not to cheerful birdsong and the quiet country silence of Clare Island, but to the sound of banging hammers and rasping saws.

Lisa hugged her arms to her breasts and watched the men working in the ballroom. Julian had agreed that, when Castleclare was ready, they would have a ball. One entire wall was being repaneled, as a centuries-old leak had destroyed the original woodwork. Maids were waxing the parquet floors. Tapestries had been taken outside to be beaten and aired and when needed, repaired. Two young men stood on ladders and were painstakingly cleaning every crystal on the Louis Quatorze chandelier.

"You should be proud of yourself, little sister-in-law," Robert said, entering the room. The windows were open and the fresh, mid-May air was filtering into the huge, bright room. He sniffed appreciatively and sighed. "Castleclare has needed a woman's loving touch for a long time," he declared.

But Lisa hardly heard him. She was wondering where Julian was. She had seen him riding away very early that morning at a near-gallop. Did he despise her so much that he could not remain in his own home with her? Or was he, possibly, tempted by her presence, and thus seeking to avoid her almost desperately?

"You should be pleased with yourself," Robert repeated softly.

Lisa faced him, forcing a smile. "I love Castleclare. I am happy to see the beauty of this place restored."

He studied her and said softly, "Julian will come around."

She bit her lip. "He hasn't paid me any attention since the day he returned—not since the picnic." She could not hide her wounded feelings from Robert. "He hasn't even noticed the changes in his own home—or bothered to thank me for my efforts."

"I am certain that he notices everything," Robert said with a smile. "It is time for you to make another move, Lisa."

She stiffened. "I hope you are not suggesting what I think you are suggesting," she said huskily, her cheeks flaming.

"This time when you go to his room, wear a peignoir. I

happen to have the perfect garment for you, something made in Paris."

Lisa was frozen; then her color increased. "I can't."

"Yes, you can," Robert said, laughing. "You can and you will and this time, my beauty, I daresay you might succeed in taming the beast."

Lisa was filled with dread. She knew she was a miserable excuse for a temptress.

But she could not stand the status quo. She had never been more unhappy. She could not continue living with him and being so thoroughly neglected, so ignored. She had to do something to get Julian's attention.

A movement caused them to glance up. Lisa stiffened. Edith Tarrington stood on the threshold of the ballroom, regarding the two of them, her brows knitted together. In her pale gray riding habit she was impossibly beautiful.

Robert did not greet her, so Lisa went towards her. She had already overheard three new maids talking about Edith's unrequited love for the Marquis. Apparently she had comforted Julian after Melanie's death when she was a blossoming young woman of fifteen.

"Hello, Edith. How nice of you to call," Lisa managed with a smile.

Edith nodded, glancing around the room, but not at Robert, who still did not move or make any effort to greet her. "You are doing a wonderful job here, Lisa," she said softly. Her gaze finally fastened on Robert. "Hello, Robert."

His jaw flexed. "Edith. I am afraid that Julian has already ridden out. You have missed him." His gray eyes flashed.

Edith twisted her riding crop in her gloved hands. "I . . . I had heard there was renovation here, and I was curious to take a look," she said. She appeared to be lying. She was not good at deceit.

Robert made a harsh sound, like a snort.

Although more dismayed than before, Lisa said gamely, "I would be happy to give you a tour, Edith."

Suddenly Robert moved forward, his stride aggressive. He inserted himself between Lisa and Edith. "Aren't you needed in the kitchens, Lisa? I need some air myself. Why don't I escort you back to Tarrington Hall, Edith?" His tone was hostile.

Edith paled.

Robert gripped her elbow firmly. "Come." Without waiting for her answer, he began propelling her from the room.

When they had left, Lisa thanked her stars for Robert, a real friend and ally, and walked slowly after them. Her heart was drumming wildly. Did she dare do as Robert suggested?

But what if Julian rejected her yet again?

Lisa did not think she could stand it.

On the other hand, the romantic fool within her wondered what would happen if he did not reject her this time.

"You are hurting me," Edith cried, yanking her arm from Robert's grasp. They stood outside the stables in the bright morning sun, Edith's mount tied at the post rail a few yards away.

"I do apologize," Robert said coldly.

Edith's mouth trembled but her eyes flashed. "You are a boor, Robert. I do not know why the ladies find you so attractive when you are so rude!"

Robert's eyes narrowed. "I hardly care what you think of me, Edith."

"That has been made very clear," she said, as she turned her back on him.

He whipped her around so that she faced him again. Her face paled as his head ducked close to hers. "But I am very tired of your chasing after my brother," Robert said through clenched teeth.

Edith was frozen for a single instant, then her gloved hand shot out. In spite of the soft deerskin, the slap to Robert's face cracked loudly. His head jerked back and his eyes widened. So did Edith's.

The sound still reverberating between them, they stared at one another in shock.

Edith took a step backwards and cried breathlessly, "Oh,

God! I am sorry! I—" But she never had the chance to finish.

Cursing, his face tight with tension, Robert seized her by her shoulders, pulled her up against him, and ground his mouth down on hers. Edith was so stunned she could not move. Robert clamped one arm around her waist and deepened the kiss, forcing Edith's lips open.

Edith's hands slowly gripped his shoulders, not pushing him away but not clinging either.

Robert tore his mouth from hers. He was panting. Angry. "Maybe now you will stop chasing after my brother."

Edith stared at him, touching her swollen mouth with her gloved fingertips.

Some of Robert's anger faded as he stared into her blue eyes. Suddenly he realized what he had done. "Edith . . . God," he murmured softly. "I am sorry."

Edith squared her shoulders, her eyes glistening with tears. She turned her back on him abruptly, hesitated—then she whirled. Very distinctly, she said, "I am not chasing Julian." Then she about-faced and rushed to her horse.

Robert watched her mount, making no move to help her. He stared as she urged her dappled mare into a canter and then galloped across the ward and through the barbican.

He cursed.

When Julian returned to Castleclare, the sun was just beginning its descent. He reined in his sorrel outside of the gates, briefly admiring the orange-red sun as it hung over the crenelated roof of the central tower, the bay glistening darkly blue just behind it. Then, tension he could not escape mounting inside him, he spurred his sorrel forward.

A few moments later he had entered his home. The hall was empty and silent, but a cheery fire blazed in the hearth. He looked around, almost grimly. The ancient trestle table had been polished until it gleamed. The stone floors had been waxed; they glistened like silver. Even the coat of mail in one corner had been tended to, and he saw no dust motes in the air nor any cobwebs in the corners. His mouth tight, Julian crossed the hall.

He turned down the corridor and entered that part of the castle which had been begun in the sixteenth century and completed at the turn of the seventeenth. His footsteps slowed as he approached the ballroom.

He paused on the threshold, taking a deep breath. God, it looked the way it had when he was a small boy of six or seven, before his father had gone so deeply into debt when his mother had had the resources to keep the place up. Julian's heart twisted as Lisa's image filled his mind.

All because of the little bride he did not want—yet wanted far too badly.

Julian stared at his reflection in the Venetian mirror above a small Chippendale table on the opposite side of the room. He glimpsed himself standing in his oldest riding jacket and threadbare boots in the magnificent room. Overhead, the chandelier sparkled, even in the fading twilight. How alone and forlorn he appeared. His face was a mask devoid of emotion, stern and patrician.

This was not going to work.

Lisa was no vain, shallow society heiress. She was sweet and lovely and she loved his home and dear God, she was willing to give him another chance. He knew it. Every time he dared to look at her he saw her every emotion shimmering in her amber eyes.

"Julian?"

He whirled, steeling himself against her. He nodded without speaking, but could no more stop himself from glancing at her thoroughly, from the top of her head to the tip of her toes, than he could stop the sun from setting.

Her gaze was fastened upon his face. "I . . . saw you ride in," she said hesitantly.

Had she been watching for him? His pulse raced; his heart tightened; his loins filled. He clenched his fists tightly so he would not reach out, grab her, and do the unthinkable—so that he would not kiss her.

"Do you . . . like it?" she asked.

His jaw flexing, he forced himself to respond. "Everything is fine."

Lisa's gaze searched his, as if trying to read past his words to delve into his heart and his soul.

Abruptly Julian strode past her, his face a harsh mask. It was either that or succumb to temptation.

Lisa wrung her hands, trying again and again to decide what she had done to anger Julian so. Why wasn't he pleased with her efforts to restore Castleclare? Had she somehow offended him? She covered her racing heart with her hand. It hurt her so much. How could she go on this way, loving him, aching for him, wanting to be with him—while he avoided her so completely?

She walked over to the Victorian mirror to survey herself in the peignoir Robert had left for her.

It was white silk trimmed in white lace. Breathtakingly beautiful, it was also scandalous. Lisa's nude body was almost visible through the fabric. When the jacket opened, she could see her nipples through the thin silk.

He will not be able to resist you. So Robert had said. And what did she have to lose? She wanted him so much. She was so desperate, she would welcome the briefest of embraces, the shortest of conversations, a single touch.

Screwing up her courage, terrified of failure, Lisa walked to the door. Supper had been over hours ago; the household was asleep.

But not Julian. Robert had assured her that his brother stayed up late, reading.

Barefoot, Lisa walked silently down the hall to his apartments, her heart banging like a drum. She could hardly breathe.

She poised herself to knock, then she decided against it. If he saw her like this, he would never let her into his rooms. He would guess her intentions immediately.

Flushed and breathless, Lisa tried the knob. The door opened and Lisa glided inside.

The sitting room was lost in darkness, except for the fire dying in the hearth. A quick look assured Lisa that Julian was not within. Did she really dare enter his bedroom?

Wetting her dry lips, Lisa crossed the small salon. She peeked into his bedroom.

Julian sat in bed, wearing nothing but the gray trousers he had worn to supper that night. His chest formed thick slabs of muscle, his stomach was concave and flat. Lisa could not tear her eyes from him.

He was not reading. A book lay by his hip, but it was closed. He was staring at the fire.

Suddenly his head jerked around and he saw her. His eyes shot open, traveling up and down her nightgown.

Lisa could not move.

Julian remained staring, wide-eyed and frozen.

Lisa forced her legs to function and entered his room. "Julian," she said hoarsely.

He swung his strong legs over the side of the bed, his thighs straining the fabric of his trousers, and rose to his feet. He was still staring at her, stunned.

Lisa hugged herself. Her mind was failing her, and she could not think of what to say or do.

Julian's gaze dropped to her breasts, pushed into prominence by her folded arms. He immediately looked at her face, jamming his hands into the pockets of his trousers. His erection was impossible to miss. "What do you want?" he snapped.

Lisa felt a moment of pure panic. She cried, "Julian, don't send me away! At least let us talk! I cannot continue this way! Please!" she heard herself beg.

His gaze again slammed down her breasts and thighs, lingering on the place where they joined. He jerked his eyes to hers. A tremor passed visibly through his body. "No."

One single word, filled with steely resolve, and Lisa felt as if it were the first nail in her coffin. *"Please."*

"No!" he shouted, his eyes blazing.

Lisa choked on a sob. She was frightened of his anger and

knew she must flee. But instead her feet carried her forward, to him. Incredulity changed his expression.

Ignoring his disbelief, Lisa gripped his bare arms. "Julian, why are you doing this? Why?" she asked, begging hysterically. And as she gripped him she felt his heat and his power, both utterly male. A searing sensation filled her loins—never before had she been overcome with such physical desire.

Lisa wanted him. She wanted to take his face in her hands, devour his mouth, then open her thighs and accept his big body inside of hers.

Suddenly his hands closed on her shoulders. Lisa saw the savagery in his eyes and felt a flash of fear, thinking he intended to push her away. Instead, his palms tightened. Lisa cried out. Their gazes locked, and the sound of their harsh breathing filled the room.

"Damn you!" Julian said, and then Lisa was crushed against his hard, hot body, while his mouth seized and opened hers. His tongue swept deep. His hands slid down her back, then up, and down again, finally gripping and spreading her buttocks. Unthinkingly, instinctively, Lisa pressed her pelvis against the massive ridge of his erection.

Julian froze, holding her up against him, his mouth still fastened on hers, their tongues entwined.

And Lisa knew that he would leave her.

She locked her hands around his neck, pressing shamelessly against him, kissing him frantically, trying to express all of her love.

Then Julian ripped his body from hers.

Lisa stumbled, falling against the bed. She caught herself before she fell to the floor, lifting her head just in time to see Julian striding from the room, his face stark with lust, with anger, with denial.

Ten

Her room was bathed in moonlight.

He stood on the threshold, the corridor behind him dimly lit, staring at her sleeping form. She appeared, in that moment, to be an angel.

An angel sent from heaven to aid him, to heal him.

Julian closed his eyes. He was trembling. He dared not move, afraid to leave, so afraid, and worse, terrified to go closer. He did not trust himself. He was losing control.

He reminded himself that she was no heavenly angel, but a flesh and blood woman who had somehow managed to turn his carefully constructed life upside down.

Lisa. How had she managed to break the steel bonds surrounding him? He wanted to send her back to New York City. God, he did. But if he did, the small spark she had stirred inside his breast would die, and suddenly he did not want to be a dead man again.

God, no.

But he was also afraid to live.

What would happen if he allowed himself to respond to her? What if he allowed himself to love her? Julian choked. He did not dare. Once upon a time he had loved so much and lost everything, even himself. He could not withstand such tragedy and grief again.

Julian turned and left Lisa's room.

* * *

"Why aren't you smiling when you are so lovely to-night?" A soft male voice said in Lisa's ear.

Lisa shifted in order to see Robert. It was the evening of the ball, but Lisa felt no excitement. Instead, the hurt of rejection filled her breast, and she ached with it. "How can I smile when he has avoided me like the plague these past few weeks?"

Robert sighed, putting his arm around her. The guests were just beginning to arrive, one grand covered coach after another rolling up the drive and pausing by the open front doors to allow their passengers to alight. Lisa stood with Robert in the great hall, acutely aware of Julian standing by the doorway in his elegant black tuxedo. His back was to her, his shoulders squared.

"He did not even say hello to me when I came downstairs," Lisa said, her mouth trembling. "The tension has worsened between us. I do not know how I can go on."

Robert hugged her to his side. "He is fighting himself, Lisa. When you enter the room, he cannot keep his eyes off you."

"I don't think so," Lisa said in a tight voice.

"When you look at him he turns away, but when you are oblivious, his eyes devour you," Robert said. "I know you will break down his resolve."

Lisa no longer believed Robert, even though she knew his intentions were good. "I have to join Julian to greet the guests," she said sadly, pulling away from her brother-in-law. "And somehow pretend that our marriage is not a miserable sham that is destroying me."

Before Robert could reply, Lisa spied Edith Tarrington and her father entering the hall. Edith had never looked lovelier than she did in her silver chiffon gown. Lord Tarrington and Julian shook hands. Lisa watched Julian lean towards Edith, kissing her cheek while she gripped his palms. Lisa's heart sank. Robert was also regarding them, and he muttered something that sounded suspiciously ill-mannered under his breath.

Lisa lifted her chin and sailed forward. This was her

home, her ball, these were her guests. As she came abreast of Julian he finally looked at her; their gazes collided, held, locked. Hurt and anger vied for predominance in Lisa's heart and soul. It was very hard to tear her gaze away.

But she did and said gamely, "Hello, Edith, Lord Tarrington. It is so wonderful that you could join us for Castleclare's first ball in so many years." Smiling in a manner which she desperately hoped was gracious, her back to Julian, Lisa extended her hand.

She did not have to look at Julian now to know that he stared unblinkingly at her.

"The first dance is ours," Julian said in her ear.

Lisa jerked. His warm breath sent unwanted heat unfurling throughout her body. All the guests had arrived and were mingling in the newly renovated ballroom. The ladies were ravishing in their rainbow-hued gowns and glittering jewelry, even if some of it was glass and paste, the men resplendent if not always elegant in their black tailcoats and white shirtwaists. Two buffets had been set up at the far end of the room, and waiters were passing flutes of champagne. The orchestra awaited orders to begin.

Lisa stared up at Julian's handsome but grim face. Her heart was pounding madly. He stood so close to her that their bodies almost touched. "I beg your pardon?"

"The first dance is ours." Not waiting for her acceptance, he took her gloved hands in his. Lisa stiffened in shock, not so much at his presumption after these past miserable weeks, but at the sensation engendered by his touch. Her mouth turned dry.

His jaw flexed. "It is traditional, Lisa, nothing more."

She felt like wrenching her hands free of him, in spite of all their guests, and slapping him silly. Slapping him until he told her why he refused to look at her, why he was determined to avoid her, why he was such a coward. Until he told her why they could not have a wonderful life together. Instead, Lisa plastered a smile on her face and moved into

Julian's arms. He nodded to the orchestra which immediately began a waltz.

As he began to sweep her effortlessly around the floor, she closed her eyes, acutely aware of every powerful inch of him, and of the extraordinary tension filling them both.

If only she could stop loving him.

If only her heart could be as cold as his.

The crowd applauded them.

Tears stinging her eyes, Lisa met Julian's gaze. Seeing his expression she stumbled, but he caught her. His eyes were twin mirrors of warmth and concern. His next words startled her. "Don't cry," he whispered.

His unexpected sympathy and sudden tenderness undid Lisa. Tears spilled down her face. Julian halted in mid-stride. Trying to break free of his embrace, Lisa began to weep. She realized that Julian was watching her, apparently horrified. The crowd was utterly silent.

Lisa lifted her gown and whirled and ran from the room. She could take it no more.

"This is all your fault," Robert said harshly.

Edith stiffened. "That is unfair. What's more, it is untrue!"

They stood shoulder to shoulder near the entrance of the ballroom, and Lisa had just run past them, sobbing. Julian stood alone in the center of the dance floor, his face white. Glaring at Edith, Robert jerked his head at the orchestra, and followed that unqualified gesture with an upward slash of his hand. The conductor could not misunderstand and immediately the band began the same sedate waltz again. None of the guests moved as an astonished silence filled the ballroom.

Suddenly Robert seized Edith by the elbow and led her onto the dance floor. She cried out as he put one hand on her waist, gripped her other palm, and began to whirl her about. "Relax," he snapped, his gray eyes blazing.

"You are hurting me," she gritted, her blue eyes heated.

Robert eased his hold fractionally. "Someone ought to turn you over his knee," he said grimly.

She jerked as he spun her around. "How dare you suggest such a thing."

"Perhaps I'll be the unfortunate soul to administer such a painful lesson?" Robert's smile dripped vinegar.

"I need no lesson, especially from a rogue like you!" Edith cried. But then Julian strode through the ballroom, his face flushed, and he disappeared across the threshold. Other couples began to filter out onto the floor.

"Poor Julian," Edith said softly, her gaze still on the open doors through which he had vanished.

"I have had it!" Robert shouted, causing a couple to falter and gawk at them. But Robert did not care. He had halted in mid-stride; he held Edith hard against his chest. "Leave my brother alone. He is falling in love with his wife! Do not interfere."

Tears filled Edith's eyes and she nearly spat, "I don't want your brother! I never have! How many times must I deny it?" She wrenched free of Robert, very much as Lisa had moments ago, and hurried from the ballroom.

Robert stared after her, uttering a string of curses no well-bred gentleman should ever express in polite society.

Lisa lay weeping in a heap on her huge canopied bed, her gold satin ballgown crushed beneath her. Julian stood in the doorway, overwhelmed by her pain, acutely aware that he was the cause of it. "Forgive me," he said harshly.

Lisa stopped crying. Slowly she sat up, staring at him. Julian met her glistening amber eyes and felt the blow all the way to his stomach. Despite his bitter regret, he was thoroughly aware of how gorgeous she was, even disheveled and teary-eyed, her ebony hair rioting about her bare shoulders. How gorgeous and good, how vulnerable and young. "Lisa . . ." He did not know what to say.

"Get out," she said tremulously.

"Not until you forgive me," Julian said firmly, his gaze

fastened upon her. "Lisa . . . please. I never meant for any of this to happen."

"But it has!" She lifted both hands as if to ward him off. "I want to go home. I give up. I concede defeat. Take my money. Just let me go."

Julian was aware of his heart slamming to an unpleasant stop. Her words had caused another blow, one even more physical in sensation than the previous time. He could not respond. An image of Lisa leaving Castleclare pervaded his mind.

"I am going home. You cannot stop me."

Julian was overcome with tension, immobilized by it. Grief welled up out of nowhere. "I will not try to stop you," he said hoarsely. But his mind screamed at him—*Don't let her go!*

Lisa stared at him, a beseeching look suddenly in her eyes.

Julian wanted to speak, but did not dare, afraid he would voice his traitorous thoughts. Afraid he would beg her to reconsider, to stay. She was right—she should go. But . . . Oh, God. Could he survive her leaving him? Suddenly he wiped his eyes with the back of his hand. He was shocked to realize that he was crying.

"Julian?" Lisa whispered, poised as if she intended to rise and rush to him.

"You are right. This has been a disaster. It is best that you leave," he said unsteadily. His heart was hammering, each blow so painful that he could hardly think. He was almost ready to refute what he knew was best, and call her back.

Somehow he bowed. Somehow he kept his face devoid of all emotion. "I apologize, madam, for all the inconvenience." He turned and left the room.

"Julian!"

In the hall, his strides faltered.

"Julian!"

He began to run.

Eleven

The ball continued, the sounds of the orchestra and the laughing, conversing guests filling the castle, but Julian did not care. He felt as if he were in some kind of living nightmare, and he was both horrified and shocked.

He shoved open the front doors, ignored the footmen, and left Castleclare.

His strides long and hard, he walked rapidly past the coaches and broughams double- and triple-parked around the circular drive, across the ward and through the barbican. He did not know where he was going; he did not care. One thought drummed in his mind: Lisa was leaving and he had to let her go.

His strides lengthened. The night was starry and bright and in a few more days there would be a full moon, so Julian had no trouble seeing the rough ground. Lisa's tearful image remained stamped upon his mind. Of course she wanted to leave him. And he, of course, wanted her to.

Didn't he?

Yes, he did—he wanted nothing more!

Suddenly Melanie's face swam before his eyes, and as always, Julian forced her image away. But this time he realized that her face was blurred and indistinct, as if he could not quite recall precisely what she had looked like. And then, Lisa's fine features were transposed upon Melanie's.

Julian's strides quickened until he was running. He welcomed the exertion. He pumped his arms and legs, gulping in the cool, early June air. Sweat streamed down his face and body. Still, he could not seem to outrun Lisa's crystal-clear image or Melanie's faded one.

He had destroyed his marriage. But he had not wanted another marriage in the first place. The first one had ended in tragedy, which haunted him to this day. Why did it seem as if this second one was ending in another tragedy?

Julian halted, out of breath and panting. He had topped a painfully familiar rise. Below him, the lake shimmered in the starlight, wet and shiny and black, streaked with silver, the landscape around it dark and shadowy and vague. Julian's heart lurched.

The words came up, without thought, erupting before he even understood them. *"Damn you, Melanie."*

He froze, stunned by the sentiment. Worse, he was aware of a seething hatred welling up inside of him, a hatred directed at his first wife.

Julian could not move. This was all wrong. He *loved* Melanie. He had loved her from the moment he had first laid eyes upon her. And he still loved her, even now, ten years after her death.

Julian's blood was pumping violently now, and he did not feel any love inside of himself; no, he felt a furious hatred—oh, God.

Everything, dammit, was *her* fault.

Eddie's death, her suicide, the endless torment of his life, and now Lisa's desertion.

Lisa. Julian covered his face with his hands. His shoulders shook. He felt torn—torn between a dead woman who had betrayed him by taking her own life and a live woman whom he had hurt again and again when she only wanted to love him.

He turned his back on the lake abruptly, the lake where Melanie's body lay with that of his only son. He had a vicious urge to destroy everything in his path. He wanted to rant and rave at the moon. He wanted to exhume her body from the bottom of the lake and wring her neck.

Julian gasped, then shut his eyes in dismay. How could he feel this way towards Melanie? What was happening to him?

It wasn't her fault. She had been weak, frail. He had
known from the beginning she was as fragile as glass. He
hadn't cared. He had loved her completely. It was his fault,
wasn't it, his and his alone?

He should have prevented her death!

Julian shuddered, rage and guilt twisting up inside him,
seething and confusing and overwhelming him until he
could hardly remain upright. And from where he stood, Julian could see his magnificent home, splendidly alight because of the ball Lisa had insisted on having, a ball he had
not given a damn about. His home, which she had restored
to its former magnificence because she loved Castleclare
even though she was an outsider—because she loved him.
And he could just faintly hear the band, the pretty, happy
strains of the piano and violins on the Irish sea breeze,
sounds as pretty and happy as his second wife. Suddenly he
began to choke, because his home was alive now, alive the
way it had been in the first years of his marriage and in all
the time prior to that, when it had been nothing but a haunted
tomb for so very long.

For a moment Julian remained motionless. The lake
which held all the secrets and tragedy of the past rooted him
in place, yet Castleclare beckoned him in a way he felt almost incapable of resisting.

Julian found himself walking back towards Castleclare.

But he was acutely aware of the lake behind him where
Melanie was entombed, and as acutely, he stared at the castle
ahead of him where Lisa wept in grief.

Lisa had dried her red, swollen eyes, but she had no
intention of returning to her guests. How could she? Julian
had destroyed her. Never had she loved this way before,
never would she love this way again. It was hopeless. To
love such a complex man, a man so determined to cling to
the past, yet filled with such anguish, was impossible. Lisa
wanted to comfort and hold and cherish Julian until death
parted them naturally fifty years hence. Yet he would not

even speak to her, was determined to ignore her. God, it wasn't worth the pain.

Tomorrow she would go home.

Lisa had made up her mind.

Her bedroom door suddenly swung open. Lisa stiffened in utter surprise. Julian stood on the threshold, his eyes hot and wet, his trousers streaked with dirt and mud, his shirt open to the waist. He stared at her. Lisa's mouth became completely dry, because she saw something in his eyes that she had never seen before—the whole man, complete with his soul.

"Julian?" she whispered, her insides fluttering with hope.

His body began to shake. "I came . . ." he began, and could not continue. He licked his lips. "I came," his voice was harsh and low, "to say goodbye."

Tears filled Lisa's eyes. She gripped the bedding so tightly she was sure she was shredding it. She must try to reach him one last time—something had changed. "Julian, perhaps I don't have to leave," she whispered, her gaze locked with his.

He was trembling, and he almost appeared to be crying. He shook his head. "You must go. I . . . understand."

Her heart exploded with his pain. Lisa was almost certain that he did not want her to leave him. She was on her feet before she could think otherwise, rushing to him. But Julian raised both hands, halting her in the center of the room. "Don't!" he shouted. "Can't you see? I am trying so very hard . . ." Tears suddenly spilled onto his cheeks. "So very goddamn hard to let you go!"

Lisa froze as she recognized the extent of his conflict. He wanted her, she knew he did, and she was joyous. But the fury she saw in his eyes terrified her. Instinct made her whisper, "Let me help you, Julian."

"You cannot," he shouted, his eyes blazing. He raised his fist and shook it at Lisa. "You cannot help me, Lisa—no one can."

She pursed her lips, choking on a sob.

Then Julian shouted, "Dammit! Damn her! Damn Melanie!"

Lisa inhaled hard, wanting to go to him but afraid to. Julian covered his face with his hands, his body shaking.

Lisa said softly, "Curse her again Julian, if you must. She left you, Julian. She was weak—she left you."

Julian dropped his hands from his face and stared at her almost blindly. "I hate her." Abruptly he turned and struck out, his fist hitting a pitcher on the bureau and sending it crashing to the floor.

Lisa jumped away from him.

Then he faced her, shaking with rage. "I hate her," he said, each word distinct. "I hate her!"

"Julian . . ."

"Dammit!" he cried, and with the sweep of his arm he sent everything on the bureau crashing to the floor. "She let Eddie drown! And then she took her own life! She left me— damn her!"

"Julian!" Lisa cried, frozen in the center of the room.

But if he heard her, he gave no sign. He went berserk. With the strength of several men, he upended the huge oak bureau. Lisa watched, mesmerized and terrified, as it crashed over in the center of the room. But Julian did not stop. His expression twisted with rage and madness, he pulled out the top drawer and flung it clear across the chamber. Lisa fled to the other side of the bed as the four other drawers were also heaved at the far wall.

Julian ripped the hangings from her bed, tearing them apart with his bare hands, while Lisa cringed, unable to look away or even flee and hide. He tore the draperies from the window on that side of the bed and kicked over the bedstand, surely damaging his foot. The gaslamp spilled as he sent books flying in every direction. A man possessed, he finally lifted the beautiful standing Victorian mirror and sent that thudding against the opposite wall where it broke apart, glass shattering all over the floor.

Lisa watched and wept as he expelled a decade of pentup rage. She was very afraid, for she could hardly trust him now, but she also knew that he had to finish this, until the rage was gone, or she would never have a chance to love him and be loved by him.

When Julian was finished—and it could not have been more than five or six minutes—her room was destroyed. He stood gasping in its center amidst the jumble of broken chairs, drawers, the upended bureau and bedstand, the ripped bedding and draperies, the broken vases and lamps and cosmetics. His face was red with exertion; his tuxedo jacket was torn between the shoulders and arms. An unnatural silence filled Lisa's room, broken only by the sound of Julian's harsh breathing.

Lisa swallowed. She was as rigid as a board, unable to react or speak.

Julian remained unmoving, his head hanging. Suddenly he said, "It's my fault, too."

Lisa jerked.

Julian whispered, *"My fault."*

Lisa cried out, "No. It's not your fault. God took Eddie, Julian, and I cannot explain why. No one can, but Melanie was a grown woman—her suicide was *not* your fault!"

"She was a child," Julian moaned.

Slowly, Lisa began to weave her way across the room, through the chaos, toward him.

Julian covered his face with his hands. Tears streaked through his fingers.

Lisa did not hesitate. When she was close enough to touch him, she wrapped her arms around him. "Oh, Julian, dear, it is not your fault. Melanie was old enough to know better. Don't blame yourself."

For one moment, his body stiffened in resistance against hers. But Lisa held him hard, stroking his back, his hair, murmuring endearments, telling him that it was not his fault, that if anyone was at fault, other than Melanie, it was God. And suddenly his body melted against hers and he was crushing her against him and murmuring her name. The tears fell yet again from Lisa's eyes; his hard palms

stroked down her back and up and down again. They clung
to each other.

For a very long time.

Lisa knew that she had found ecstasy at last.

But then Julian finally moved, shifting her in his arms.
"Lisa," he whispered roughly.

She lifted her face upwards. His gray gaze was shining.
When their eyes finally met, so did their souls.

Very tenderly, he cupped her face with his palms, his
hands strong and filled with barely controlled intensity.
Then, slowly, he leaned over her. Lisa's heart soared as his
mouth touched hers gently. For a brief moment, their mouths
brushed. And then Julian claimed her.

Hungrily, without control, his mouth seized hers while he
locked her against his rigid body; Lisa did not protest. She
strained against him so that her softest parts met his hardest
ones, while their mouths fused. His tongue sought hers and
she opened wider, accepting all of him. As desire coursed
through every inch of her body, joy infused her entire soul.

Suddenly Julian lifted her in his arms, stepping over the
drawers and bureau. He carried her to the bed and laid her
down, his hot eyes meeting hers, a question there. Lisa held
her arms out to him. "Yes," she whispered, beaming. "Oh,
yes!"

He came down on top of her, wrenching off his torn tailcoat, never taking his eyes from hers. Lisa reached up and
laced her hands behind his head, smiling at him happily.

His eyes brightened and a beautiful smile transformed his
handsome features, until his head dipped and he took her
mouth again.

Lisa sighed.

Tenderly, his lips moved over her face, cherishing each
eyelid, her cheekbones, and her nose. Lisa did not move. Her
body had become boneless, melting into the bed, while wet
heat flared deep inside of her. Julian began nuzzling her
neck, her shoulders, and the bare skin of her upper chest,
then lower, where her bodice ended. His breathing filled the
room, harsh and male and impatient.

Lisa moaned softly, recognizing his need because it matched her own. He rubbed his cheek against her breasts and he was moaning, too.

His head moved lower. One of his arms became an iron band beneath her, lifting her slightly. "Lisa, how I want you," he said, kissing her stomach through her satin ballgown. "I have wanted you for a very long time, from the moment we first met."

Lisa's pulse quickened, joy racing in her veins. "Oh, Julian—"

"Lisa, I need you." He lifted his head and stared into her eyes. "God, how I need you. In every way."

She understood what he was trying to tell her and her vision blurred as she reached up to cup his cheek. "I need you, too, Julian." She paused, their gazes locked, and Lisa felt herself drowning in his shimmering gray eyes. "Julian, I love you."

He froze. His expression was stunned and joyous at once. He appeared to be very near tears.

"I love you," Lisa repeated vehemently. "I always have, I always will."

He laughed roughly, and Lisa smiled, equally moved, and then his hand fluttered over her face. "I love you, too," he said suddenly, his tone thick.

Lisa began to weep. The kiss which followed was long and deep. Time stopped for them.

Julian's mouth began an unerring descent. Lisa began to squirm as he kissed and nibbled her throat and chest. She did not protest as his hand went underneath her, unbuttoning her gown. Her heart was pounding so hard with excitement and anticipation that she felt faint. Except for the astounding torment building between her legs.

Shifting restlessly, Lisa allowed him to remove her dress between kisses, her body deeply flushed. She was vaguely aware of the impropriety of making love like this, with the room utterly alight and herself immodestly naked and a houseful of guests on the floor below. Yet she did not protest. Breathless, her eyes transfixed, she watched Julian's hands cupping and molding her firm breasts through her sheer silk chemise. Lisa's nipples were erect and when Julian lowered the edge of the chemise, prominently displayed. "You are the most beautiful woman I have ever met," he whispered.

Lisa was about to refute him, then thought the better of it, for Julian's tongue was flicking out to tease each erect tip. She gasped. And as his mouth finally claimed one nipple, his hand moved over her silk-draped thighs, roving there gently, finally brushing her pubis. She began to breathe in earnest. She could not believe the torrent of sensation coiling inside of her. *"Julian."*

Julian made a harsh, ragged sound. Before Lisa was completely aware that she was utterly naked—and that he was still fully dressed—he was nuzzling her thighs and the hot juncture between them. Lisa *was* shocked, but even more, she was fascinated, especially because he was kissing her there, kissing her as if she had a second mouth, oh God . . .

Lisa began to pant, her mind shutting down. Her hips began a fierce undulation of their own. His tongue played havoc with her swollen lips and the painfully aroused protrusion between them, while his fingers combed through her hair. He spread her wider. Lisa sagged against the pillows as he kissed her fully again and again. Suddenly she was arching up off the bed, crying his name, lights sparking inside of her head, blinding her, dazzling her . . .

"Yes, Lisa, darling," Julian whispered, and then he continued his exquisitely thorough torturing of her.

Lisa had been returning to this world, but her body tightened and tensed and her pulse picked up its beat all over again. She was shamelessly gripping Julian's head. Shamelessly moaning his name.

Julian loomed over her now, his thighs pushing hers as far apart as possible, something huge and hard and warm and wet prodding her. Lisa managed to focus just enough to realize that his eyes blazed with lust, just enough to understand what he intended. She looked down at his manhood as he rubbed languidly against her. Oh, God, she thought, because he was beautiful and magnificent and so powerfully male. "Julian, come to me," she whispered.

His eyes flared hotter and he obeyed, thrusting just enough to insert his swollen head inside of her. Lisa tensed, her eyes widening.

"Don't be afraid," he murmured. "It will hurt, but only for one brief moment."

Lisa wet her lips, staring downwards at their partially joined bodies. "I am not afraid," she managed.

He laughed—a harsh, male sound, bent and kissed her mouth, her ear, and then tongued her nipple. All the while pushing gently against her, into her. As Lisa relaxed he invaded inch by hard, vibrating inch, until he had sheathed himself inside of her as far as he could go without doing the necessary damage. Lisa wrapped her arms around his broad back and clung to him.

"Now," he told her, and he thrust deep.

The pain was brief and inconsequential, because Lisa now possessed all of him, body and heart and soul, and as he moved inside of her, his rhythm increasing, she found herself beginning that otherworldly ascent again. "Julian," she cried as their mouths mated.

"Lisa," he cried in response and then he was above her, straining, and when Lisa could stand it no more she shouted his name wildly, exploding, and he bucked in response, convulsing inside of her. And there, while inside her, he began to weep, as they found ecstasy together, and love.

Twelve

Julian lay back, his eyes closed, one arm flung outwards, towards Lisa. She was floating slowly back to reality. Her body felt delicious, soft and nearly boneless, still quivering with delicious sensations. *Julian.* Lisa's eyes opened and she turned to him, her heart bursting with joy and hope and love. And for the first time since she had met him, she saw his face devoid of tension, his expression utterly relaxed and at peace. Lisa waited for him to return to reality, too.

His eyes fluttered open and he turned his head and looked directly at her. For a single moment they stared at one another, unsmiling. Lisa was suddenly stiff with anxiety—and then Julian smiled.

It was a smile filled with warmth and tenderness and it came from the heart.

Lisa smiled back, overwhelmed with relief.

He reached out and pulled her into his arms and up against his body. Lisa snuggled against him, thinking, *thank you, God, thank you.*

"Lisa," Julian whispered, stroking her dark hair.

Lisa shifted to meet his gray eyes. She was stunned to see tears there. "Yes?"

"I am not good with words," he said ruefully. "Somehow, I want to apologize—and thank you."

Lisa laid her palm on his chest and leaned upwards to kiss his mouth lightly. "You need not apologize, Julian, not for anything. I understand completely."

"You are an angel," he murmured, his tone low and seductive, his eyes far warmer than before. His hand slid down her spine, sending hot little shivers up Lisa's back.

"Don't be silly," she retorted, although she was secretly very pleased. If he wanted to insist that she was an angel, who was she to protest? "Julian, there is no need for you to thank me, either."

His smile was tender, in stark contrast to the smoldering heat of his eyes. "My life has been miserable, Lisa. I did not really realize how unhappy I was until you entered it. Of course, then I was even more miserable, wanting to touch you, to love you, yet unable to do either." His lips feathered hers. "Thank you, Lisa, for being a *determined* angel of mercy."

Lisa laughed, filled with pleasure.

"It is one of the things I like best about you," Julian said, smiling at her.

"That I am an angel?" Lisa quipped.

"That you are determined, and strong, and brave."

Lisa's smile faded. "Oh, Julian," she whispered, unbearably moved. "That is the nicest thing you could possibly say to me."

He did not hesitate, and pulling her close, he said, "That is why I fell in love with you."

Lisa blinked back tears, and managed to say, "You mean, it wasn't my ravishing face or exquisite body or feminine ways which did you in?"

He laughed. "I admit to being enticed on other, more mundane, levels." His hand slipped over her breast.

Lisa knew she should be shocked, but she was too interested in her body's nearly magical response. "How can such a big man be so gentle?" she murmured huskily as he began to caress her. "Perhaps I shall have to explore this contradiction further."

"Explore as you will." Julian laughed, pulling her down onto the bed, claiming her lips with his.

And Lisa kissed him back fiercely, the sounds of his warm laughter lingering in her mind.

* * *

Three days later, Robert paced the dining room, brooding. Clearly Julian and Lisa were reconciled. No one had seen hide nor hair of them since the night of the ball, as they remained locked in Julian's suite. No one, that is, except for O'Hara, who had faithfully brought refreshments upstairs. And every time he had returned, he had been beaming.

Robert was thrilled, of course. But now he had a serious dilemma to face. The truth would have to come out. Julian was going to be furious, absolutely furious, when Robert told him all that he had done.

Robert sighed. Perhaps he would put off his confession just a little while longer. He was not pleased at the prospect of sporting one or two black eyes.

O'Hara paused on the threshold. "Lord Robert, sir, Lady Tarrington is here."

Robert had already spotted her standing behind the butler, her cheeks pink, no doubt from her habit of riding like the wind. He felt tension coiling within him. "How come this is no surprise?" he said rudely.

Edith had already entered the dining room, but his tone caused her to halt abruptly.

"As you can see, we are alone," Robert continued in the same harsh voice, gesturing around the room.

She was flushed. "Good morning, Robert. The ball was a success. The entire county is talking about little else."

"Come, Edith, let's forego the small talk, shall we? We both know why you are here."

Edith's small smile vanished. Her eyes were hurt, not angry. "Why must you be this way with me?"

Robert ignored the question. "Julian is upstairs, abed. In fact, he has been upstairs, abed, for the past three days. And he is not alone."

Edith turned a fiery shade of red.

He strode over to her until he towered above her, his expression furious. "He is with his bride, my dear."

Edith's hand shot out. Robert was prepared this time and he seized her wrist before she could strike him. "Once was enough," he growled. "Never try to slap me again!"

"You are disgusting," Edith hissed. But her eyes were suspiciously moist. "No gentleman would ever refer to what you have referred to in the presence of a lady."

"A true lady would not be chasing a married man, darling," Robert said with contempt.

"I am not chasing Julian," Edith cried, still trying to yank her wrist free of his grasp and failing. "What do I have to do to convince you of that?"

"Edith, all of Connaught County has known for years that you yearn for my brother."

"All of Connaught County is *wrong*," Edith snapped, her gaze openly furious.

They stared at one another coldly.

"I do not believe you," Robert finally said. His grip on her wrist had eased.

"That is because you are a fool."

"Hardly."

Edith wet her lips. "Tell me something, Robert. Tell me why you despise me so much?"

His head jerked. He did not reply immediately.

"You are gallant with all the ladies, even with your London trollops, but with me, you are cold and cruel. Why?" Edith cried.

He hesitated. "Because of Julian."

"But it is not Julian I am in love with," Edith said fiercely.

Robert's gaze turned sharp.

Edith hesitated, then did the unthinkable. She stepped forward, gripped his lapels, and, eyes closed, she planted a solid kiss on his mouth. Robert did not move.

For a moment Edith remained on her tiptoes, her mouth pressed to his, her heart pounding wildly. Robert did not respond. Choked with bitter defeat, she released him and stepped away. Edith began to tremble, appalled with her own behavior.

Robert stared at her in amazement.

Edith turned abruptly, intending to flee.

As she raced for the door, Robert overtook her with three long strides. Edith cried out as he caught her from behind, whirling her around. Their eyes met, hers frightened, his dark and wide. And then his arms went around her as he crushed her to his chest, and his mouth was on hers, hot, hard, impatient and demanding. Edith gasped.

And Robert kissed her with a decade's worth of longing, again and again.

When Lisa and Julian finally came down for a late breakfast the third day after the ball, they were holding hands and smiling. O'Hara beamed at them as they approached him in the corridor. "Good day, m'lord; good day, m'lady."

Julian smiled at his manservant. "Good morning, O'Hara. It's a beautiful day, is it not?"

Tears welled in the butler's eyes. So that His Lordship would not see, the old man turned away, blowing into a handkerchief. He had not seen the Marquis smile quite like that since the tragedy, and he was undone.

"It is a good day, isn't it, O'Hara?" Lisa sang sweetly. Her face somehow glowed. She flashed him a wide smile; she had never been lovelier.

O'Hara finally regained control just as they passed him. " 'Tis the best o' days," he murmured happily.

Lisa and Julian halted abruptly on the threshold of the dining room. "Oh, dear," Lisa said softly, as she and Julian caught Robert and Edith in a passionate embrace. "Oh, my," she added.

Julian laughed. "I cannot say that I am surprised," he said. "I have waited for this day for a very long time."

"Oh, really?" Lisa cocked her head.

At the sound of their voices Robert and Edith leapt apart, both of them flushing brightly. Edith's long, platinum hair had come loose from its coil and was streaming down her back.

"Good morning," Julian said heartily.

Robert appeared dazed. He blinked at Lisa and Julian. "Hello." He hesitated, then glanced at Edith, who was frozen with embarrassment and indecision. Their eyes held.

Robert put a comforting hand upon her waist, her eyes instantly softened. "Why don't you tidy up and join us . . . me . . . for breakfast?"

Her mouth opened, but she made no sound.

Robert smiled at her. "I shall not take no for an answer," he said softly.

"Then my answer is yes," Edith whispered, smiling.

"But you might want to wait a moment," Robert said suddenly, flushing. He coughed several times.

Julian had begun to pull out a chair for Lisa, but he paused at the sound of Robert's cough. His brow furrowed with concern.

Robert forced a smile. "I am only clearing my throat, Julian. There is something I wish to say to everyone."

Julian's relief was visible. Lisa reached for his hand and gripped it, her newfound happiness pierced with the dark shadow of dread. How could she be so happy when Robert was ill with consumption? When he would one day die? Julian had already suffered so much—Lisa wished that she could spare him yet another tragedy. But at least she would be there when the time came to comfort him.

Robert coughed again. Everyone faced him expectantly.

Robert wet his lips. "First I would like to say that my greatest dream has come true." He smiled, looking at Lisa and Julian. "And that dream was to see my brother happy and whole again." His gaze warm, he regarded Lisa. "Thank you, Lisa. I knew you were up to the task of winning my brother's heart."

Lisa beamed. "Thank you, Robert, for your advice and help."

Julian put his arm around her. "I never had a chance," he said, serious and teasing at once.

Lisa laughed.

Robert glanced at each and every one in turn. "But there is something I must confess." He was grim and pale. "Julian, promise me that you shall hold your terrible temper in check."

Julian cocked his head. "Have you done something I should be angry about?"

"I'm afraid so," Robert said uneasily. "Remember, I am your only brother and you adore me."

"I can hardly forget who you are, Robert. Out with it, then, so we may eat breakfast and enjoy the day."

Robert glanced at Edith as if she might help him with his confession, but she was openly perplexed.

"What is it?" Edith asked softly. "What could be so terrible? Julian will not be angry with you, Robert, I am certain."

"I am afraid that you are very wrong." Robert sighed, glancing heavenwards just once. "Julian, everything I did, I did for you."

Julian eyed him suspiciously.

"I knew that you had to start living again. At the very least, to manage the estate responsibly. We needed money, of course. Clearly you had to be motivated to go out and wed an heiress. I decided to provide the proper motivation."

"The proper motivation," Julian repeated. His eyes narrowed. "Go on." It was a soft command.

"But my motivations were even grander than wanting you to have the means to provide for us and manage Castleclare and our holdings. I was sure you needed a woman—a wife— to make you happy again. And I was certain you would not wed a woman you were not secretly fond of. And I was right, was I not?" Robert's face brightened hopefully.

"You were very right," Julian said, sharing a warm glance with Lisa. "What is it you are trying to tell me, Robert?"

"Well, here is the good news," Robert said as he laughed nervously. "I am not dying."

Everyone stared.

"The bad news is that I deceived you so that you would be forced to wed," he added in a rush.

"Oh, my God," Lisa whispered, shocked.

Edith stared at Robert and began to weep.

Immediately Robert reached for her. "Edith, there's no need to cry," he began.

She wept harder.

Lisa was beginning to cry, too. This was the most wonderful news possible! She reached for and clung to Julian's hand. But he did not notice.

Julian gawked at Robert. "You are not dying?" he said roughly.

Robert faced him squarely, nodding.

"You pretended to be ill?" Julian said.

Robert nodded again. "Julian, remember, you do love me!"

"I think I might kill you myself," Julian cried, rushing forward.

"Julian, no! This is wonderful," Lisa cried, trying to grab him and missing.

Robert tensed.

"The agony you have put me through!" Julian shouted, and then he embraced Robert, hugging him so hard that he lifted him off of his feet. "Damn you," Julian whispered against his brother's cheek. Then, setting him back down, he said, "Thank you, God!" He released his brother, tears spilling down his cheeks.

"You will not kill me?" Robert said in his usual roguish manner.

"I will wait until tomorrow to kill you," Julian promised hoarsely. He put his arm around Lisa. "Today I am too gloriously happy. You are well—you little bastard—and I am in love." He turned and Lisa moved into his arms. He held her there, the two of them absolutely motionless and content just to hold one another.

"I think we must forgive him, Julian," Lisa whispered, deliriously happy. "Do not forget, Robert's deception brought us together. We owe him, darling."

"Yes, we will have to forgive him, won't we?" Julian murmured, stroking her hair. "But I will forgive him only after I throttle him, hmm?"

Lisa laughed and strained upwards as Julian bent to kiss her. Their mouths touched, fused. The kiss deepened and deepened and did not appear to have any inclination to end.

Robert smiled and held out his arm as Edith moved against him. Silently, so as not to disturb the newlyweds, they left the room.

Lisa and Julian did not notice.

Epilogue

Castleclare, 1904

Lisa could not stand it.

Stealing a glance at Julian, who remained soundly asleep in their bed, she slipped to the floor, quickly donning a quilted wrapper. As she stole across their bedchamber, shivering, she peeked at him again. But he remained unmoving, breathing deeply, eyes closed. The barest of smiles graced his handsome face. Lisa could not help but marvel at the magnificent sight. She still could not believe that she was his and he was hers and that they were deliriously in love.

Lisa fled their room.

The castle was eerily silent. It was Christmas Day, 1904. And Lisa could not wait another moment to find out what Julian had given her as a present on their first real Christmas together.

She grinned as she hurried downstairs. Her gift to Julian was going to be a big and, she hoped, happy surprise.

Lisa paused in the ballroom. They had had a Christmas ball a few days ago for most of the county, and a huge Christmas tree stood in the center of the far wall, heavy with tinsel and candy canes, a pretty angel gracing its peak. The angel was symbolic and Lisa knew it.

Lisa rushed to the tree and began pawing through the many gifts. She found presents for everyone, including herself, but nothing from Julian. She checked again. Robert and Edith, who had married in the fall and were already expecting a child, had left gifts for Lisa, as had O'Hara and her maid, Betsy. But there was not a single package from Julian.

Lisa was in shock. She sat down hard on the wood floor in her nightclothes and bare feet. Had he forgotten? Was it possible?

"Is something amiss, darling?" Julian said teasingly from the threshold of the ballroom.

Lisa knew he had forgotten. She forced a smile. "No, of course not! Good morning, Julian. Merry Christmas." She stood up.

His gray eyes were twinkling mischievously. "Merry Christmas, angel."

And Lisa realized from his low, sexy tone that he was up to something. She regarded him suspiciously, perplexed.

"Merry Christmas!" shouted a group of voices in unison, and suddenly three people came barging into the room.

Lisa cried out as her father, Benjamin Ralston, reached her first. He lifted her off her feet and swung her around. "Lisa, Merry Christmas!"

"Papa!" she gasped. Over his shoulder she spied her beloved stepsister, Sofie, and Sofie's dashing husband, Edward Delanza. When Benjamin released her, Lisa flew across the room. Sofie met her halfway. Both women were crying as they embraced.

"Don't I get a turn?" Edward asked roguishly.

"Of course you do," Lisa cried, and was instantly swallowed up in his arms.

Finally the tearful greetings were over. Lisa moved to Julian's side, looking around at everyone. "I am in a state of disbelief," she confessed.

He laughed, putting his arm around her. "That is obvious."

Lisa glanced at her father and stepsister. "I have missed you so—I am so glad you are here!" Then she turned to her husband. "Julian, this is the most wonderful Christmas I have ever had."

His smile faded, his gaze intense. "This is only our very first one, angel. There will be many, many more."

Tears filled Lisa's eyes. As she moved into his embrace, the rest of the room ceased to exist; there was only Julian and herself. "How I love you," she whispered.

"You are my life," he said, and his eyes were shining and moist.

Lisa smiled shakily, then said, "I have a surprise for you, too, Julian."

His glance did not stray to the gifts beneath the tree. "Really? Last night I failed to find a present from you, darling, when I sneaked downstairs myself."

Lisa laughed, realizing that Julian had also checked the gifts beneath the tree surreptitiously. "You won't find my present gift-wrapped and in a box," Lisa said huskily.

His brow lifted. His hands were still clasped behind her back. "What will I find, then?"

"I do hope you will not be disappointed," Lisa said, then added, "five months from now."

He froze.

Lisa wet her lips. "I am having our child, Julian. In May."

His expression was transformed. Joy lit up his face. Lisa found herself in his arms, her feet no longer touching the floor, as Julian crushed her to him.

Lisa began to laugh. "I am having Julian's baby!" she shouted to the interested onlookers.

Edward and Benjamin cheered. Sofie laughed, crying, "That is wonderful, Lisa!"

Then Julian slid her to the ground, inch by interesting inch. Lisa found her thoughts quite distracted by the time her feet reached the floor. "Julian . . ."

"I have never been happier," he whispered huskily. "Nor have I ever loved anyone the way I love you. Thank you, Lisa, thank you."

"I have done nothing," she said.

"You have wrought a miracle," he replied unevenly. "And you know it."

Lisa did know it. She lifted her hand and cupped his cheek.

"Let's have our own private celebration, angel," Julian whispered.

Lisa was about to agree, but they were suddenly besieged by her family. "Forget it," Edward said jovially. "This is a family day and we have traveled the Atlantic to share it with you."

"That's right," Benjamin said, clapping Julian on the shoulder. "C'mon, son, all that hiding has given me an appetite. Lead the way to your dining room."

Sofie shared a warm look with Lisa, smiling. "I want to know *everything*," she said.

Lisa sighed happily and looked at Julian, who was being propelled across the ballroom by her father. She shrugged helplessly. "It *is* a family day," she cried.

Pausing, he gave her an intimate look and said, "Later, angel."

Her heart flipped hard. Julian smiled as Lisa decided that she could, indeed, wait. Their gazes locked soulfully.

"Merry Christmas, darling," she whispered.

"Merry Christmas, angel," he said.

Put a Little Romance in Your Life With
Fern Michaels

__Dear Emily   0-8217-5676-1 $6.99US/$8.50CAN

__Sara's Song   0-8217-5856-X $6.99US/$8.50CAN

__Wish List   0-8217-5228-6 $6.99US/$7.99CAN

__Vegas Rich   0-8217-5594-3 $6.99US/$8.50CAN

__Vegas Heat   0-8217-5758-X $6.99US/$8.50CAN

__Vegas Sunrise   1-55817-5983-3 $6.99US/$8.50CAN

__Whitefire   0-8217-5638-9 $6.99US/$8.50CAN

Call toll free **1-888-345-BOOK** to order by phone or use this coupon to order by mail.

Name_____

Address_____

City _____ State _____Zip_____

Please send me the books I have checked above.

I am enclosing $_____
Plus postage and handling* $_____
Sales tax (in New York and Tennessee) $_____
Total amount enclosed $_____

*Add $2.50 for the first book and $.50 for each additional book.

Send check or money order (no cash or CODs) to:

Kensington Publishing Corp., 850 Third Avenue, New York, NY 10022

Prices and Numbers subject to change without notice.

All orders subject to availability.

Check out our website at **www.kensingtonbooks.com**